A Ration Book Christmas

Jean Fullerton is the author of eleven historical novels. She is a qualified District and Queen's nurse who has spent most of her working life in the East End of London, first as a Sister in charge of a team, and then as a District Nurse tutor. She is also a qualified teacher and spent twelve years lecturing on community nursing studies at a London university. She now writes full-time.

Find out more at www.jeanfullerton.com

Also by Jean Fullerton

A Ration Book Christmas

JEAN FULLERTON

CORVUS

Published in paperback in Great Britain in 2018 by Corvus,
an imprint of Atlantic Books Ltd.

10 9 8 7 6 5 4 3 2 1

A CIP catalogue record for this book is available
from the British Library.

Paperback ISBN: 978 1 78 649140 4
E-book ISBN: 978 1 78 649141 1

Printed and bound by CPI Group (UK) Ltd, Croydon, CR0 4YY

Corvus
An imprint of Atlantic Books Ltd
Ormond House
26–27 Boswell Street
London
WC1N 3JZ

www.corvus-books.co.uk

To my Hero@Home,
Kelvin, who has long since accepted that
although I might be next to him physically,
my mind is quite often in another century.

Chapter One

PUTTING HER FEET on the brake and clutch, Josephine Margaret Brogan, known to everyone as Jo, stuck her right hand out of the driver's side window of the five-year-old Morris 8 delivery van, then, seeing the road was clear, turned across Melton Winchet High Street into Garfield General Store's back yard.

Bringing it to a halt by the side wall, she pulled on the handbrake and switched off the engine. Jutting out her lower lip, she blew upwards to dislodge a brunette curl resting over her left eyebrow but the lock refused to budge. She wasn't surprised.

It was the first Friday in September and with the hot early-autumn sun blasting fully through the van's windows, the inside of the vehicle was like an oven and Jo was perspiring accordingly.

It might not have been so bad if she'd been able to deliver the shop's weekend orders in the sleeveless frock and cotton underslip she'd put on that morning, but no. Mrs Garfield was having none of it. Despite the BBC forecasting that the afternoon temperatures would nudge at 70 degrees Fahrenheit, the shopkeeper had insisted that Jo wear her regular dull green rayon overall so she looked 'tidy', which was a cheek as the blooming thing fitted her like a sack and had to be turned at the cuff so the sleeves didn't cover her hands.

Jo got out of the green van and swinging the keys back and forth around her fingers she walked between the stacked crates into the storeroom that was connected to the side of the shop.

Mrs Garfield, who was flitting a duster over a card of girls' pastel-coloured hairslides hung on the wall behind the counter, looked around from her task as Jo walked in.

The owner of Melton Winchet's general store was a woman on the wrong side of forty, with hips so extensive she had difficulty turning around in the space behind the counter. She stood a little over five foot and had frizzy grey hair and an expression that would lead you to believe she sucked lemons as a hobby. As her deep-set eyes alighted on Jo, her lips pulled into a tight bud.

'Where have you been?' she asked, scrutinising Jo through the lenses of her spectacles.

'I was held up at Rider's Bridge,' Jo replied, strolling behind the counter to hook the keys on the nail in the wall. 'And Mrs Veres asked me to tell you she's got some cooking apples from her orchard; they're two shillings a crate, if you're interested.'

'Two shilling!' snapped the shopkeeper. 'They were half that last season.'

Jo smiled sweetly. 'Well, there is a war on, you know.'

Mrs Garfield gave her a sour look. 'I don't suppose you've seen that brother of yours on your travels, have you?'

'Can't say I have,' Jo replied.

The shopkeeper tutted. 'Probably in detention again.'

'Or playing football in the meadow with the other lads,' Jo countered.

'Well, I've got a shop to run so if he's not here soon he'll have to go without lunch,' said the shopkeeper. 'And he'd better not come home with mud all over his trousers either, like he did last week. I wouldn't have volunteered to take in evacuees if I'd realised I'd have to skivvy for them. And tidy your hair,' she continued, waving a couple of fat bluebottles away from the loaves on the counter. 'I know you're not used to such things in East London but out here we're very particular about cleanliness.'

The shopkeeper's gaze flickered disapprovingly over Jo again and then she disappeared through the door behind her into the small parlour.

Although it wasn't the sort of thing a seventeen-year-old young woman who'd just gained a merit on her matriculation should do, Jo stuck out her tongue at the closed door.

Tucking the offending curl back behind her ear, she stepped behind the counter to mind the shop until Mrs Garfield reappeared.

Garfield General Store was a double-fronted affair with two large windows and a central door. It sat like a well-worn and overloaded portmanteau halfway up Melton Winchet's High Street and supplied the inhabitants of the small village ten miles east of Colchester with most of their day-to-day household needs. On the left as you entered the store was a serving counter, scrubbed smooth by Mrs Garfield and her mother before her, on which the baker deposited what remained of his morning stock when he closed at midday. Alongside the bread basket was a block of cheddar on a marble slab, protected by a glass dome, and a ham draped with a muslin on a china plinth, from which Mrs Garfield carved her customers' requirements. On the floor in front of the counter were artistically stacked tins of pilchards, pease pudding and Carnation milk, along with square boxes of fig rolls, garibaldi, arrowroot biscuit and a selection of all three in the broken biscuit box at the end. On the shelves behind the counter were packets of tea, tins of custard, Ovaltine and tins of National Milk, hermetically sealed to preserve it against gas attack. In a small section tucked in the corner were tins of condensed milk for babies, nappy pins and, in discreet grey striped packets, Dr White's sanitary pads.

The household items such as carbolic soap, washing soda, candles and horse embrocation, metal polish, starch and blacking for the fire grates were stacked on the other side of the shop along with brooms, shovels and zinc buckets.

The bell above the door tinkled as Mrs Toffs, wife of the village doctor, strode in. She was a well-groomed woman with a massive bosom and an opinion of herself to match. While most women wore a frock and modest headgear to run their daily errands, Mrs Toffs had decided a navy suit with a red velvet collar and cuffs plus a wide-brimmed feather-laden hat would be more appropriate attire for a visit to the village shop.

'Can I help you?' asked Jo.

'I hardly think so,' Mrs Toffs replied, running her critical gaze over her. 'Is Mrs Garfield in?'

Before Jo could reply, the door behind the counter opened again and Mrs Garfield bustled out.

'Mrs Toffs, what a pleasure,' said Mrs Garfield, her sharp features lifting into an ingratiating smile. 'What can I do for you?'

'We're having a few friends over next Saturday,' Mrs Toffs replied. 'Nothing grand, you understand, and Footman's delicatessen department has sent most of what's needed but' – slipping her hand into her pocket she withdrew a sheet of paper – 'there are a few things Cook still requires, so if you would be so kind.'

Mrs Garfield pushed her spectacles back up her nose and looked at the proffered list.

'A dozen eggs!' A worried expression pulled the shopkeeper's heavy eyebrows together.

'I hope I can rely on you, Mrs Garfield,' Mrs Toffs cut in. 'After all, my husband does buy all the surgery's surgical and methylated spirits through you rather than the wholesalers in Colchester.'

Mrs Garfield paused for a second then folded the list and shoved it in her overall pocket. Her beady eyes shifted to Jo. 'Don't stand there eavesdropping. Get on with the rest of the deliveries.'

Biting back a retort, Jo went back into the storeroom and took the list pinned to the corkboard. She collected together the half a dozen bulging brown-paper bags, placed them in one of the spare fruit boxes stacked on the floor and carried it out to the van.

Balancing the load on one arm, she opened one of the van's back doors and slid the box onto the floor of the van. Holding the list in her right hand, she walked the fingers of her left over the twisted-topped brown-paper bags as she checked off Mrs Benboe in High Meadow Lane, Mrs Pedder, The Green, and Mrs Adams at Pucks Farm. Reaching the last name, Jo realised she'd left the Tillet sisters' order in the storeroom.

Shoving the scrap of paper in her overall pocket, Jo retraced her steps and re-entered the storeroom.

Spotting the overlooked brown-paper bag containing the spinster sisters' provisions still on the order shelf, Jo walked between the stacks of boxes and jars to get it. She'd just grasped the order when Mrs Garfield's voice drifted in from the shop.

'I tell you, Mrs Toffs,' said the shopkeeper, 'I don't care if Rev Farrow preaches on about giving succour to orphans and widows from now to doomsday, if I'd known the trouble they'd both be, I wouldn't have said yes to the placement officer.'

'My husband says it's a disgrace,' said the doctor's wife. 'All the evacuees he's had the misfortune to have in his surgery are running alive with nits.'

'Their mothers ought to be ashamed of themselves for sending their offspring in such a condition and raising children with such terrible manners,' the shopkeeper went on.

'*No* manners, don't you mean,' said Mrs Toffs.

'As you say,' agreed Mrs Garfield. 'You give them a roof over their heads and are they grateful?'

'Grateful!' echoed the doctor's wife. 'They don't know the meaning of the word. The scruffy lad Mrs Yates at Three Trees Farm got saddled with complained that he has to get up at five to help with the animals and does nothing but moan about being hungry.'

'She's fortunate she's only lumbered with one,' said Mrs Garfield. 'I've got that troublemaker Billy and his mouthy sister. And they're Catholics.'

'Still, at least the girl can earn her keep in the shop,' said Mrs Toffs.

'When she puts her mind to it,' said Mrs Garfield. 'But that's not the worst of it.'

'I suppose you have to keep an eye on the till,' said Mrs Toffs in a meaningful tone.

'And on my Norman,' said Mrs Garfield.

'No!'

'Not that my son's done anything wrong,' added the shopkeeper. 'But you know how impressionable young men can be around . . . around . . .'

'Flighty girls?'

'Exactly,' said Mrs Garfield. 'No young lad is safe with girls like that around. You want to keep an eye on her in case she takes a fancy to your Eric.'

'I will,' said Mrs Toffs. 'So what happened?'

There was a pause before Mrs Garfield answered in a hushed voice. 'Well, the other day I—'

Jo strode into the shop.

'Only me, Mrs Garfield,' she said, smiling pleasantly at the shopkeeper. 'I can't seem to find the Tillet sisters' order.'

'It's on the order shelf,' the shopkeeper replied as a mauve blush spread over her multiple chins.

Turning back into the cupboard, Jo picked up the bag she'd just put down and went back into the shop.

'Found it,' she said in a sing-song tone and giving both women a dazzling smile. 'Sorry. Did I interrupt something?'

'Not at all,' said Mrs Garfield.

'We were just chatting,' added the doctor's wife, struggling to hold Jo's gaze.

Jo savoured their discomfort for a few seconds longer then smiled again.

'I'll be on my way then, Mrs Garfield. Nice to see you, Mrs Toffs, and tell your Eric I'll see him at the harvest dance.'

Turning away from the two women, Jo's mouth pulled into a hard line as, clutching the missing order, she marched through the house to the back yard.

Yanking open the door of the van, Jo threw the bag of mixed vegetable into the box with the others then slammed the door.

Leaping into the driver's seat, Jo jammed the key in the ignition and turned the engine on. With a face like thunder

7

she slammed the gearstick into reverse and backed out of the yard. Swinging the wheel, Jo forced the van into first and roared out of the yard.

St Audrey's Church clock was showing quarter past five by the time Jo drove back down the High Street having completed Garfield's afternoon deliveries. After leaving the shop earlier that day, she'd more or less calmed down by the time she'd turned up the lane to Pucks Farm, which was three miles out of town. A freshly made glass of lemonade from Mrs Adams the motherly farmer's wife had restored her equilibrium. Having decided she'd take her own good time to return to the store, she took the long way around along the river to High Meadow Lane then a leisurely trip to the elderly Tillet sisters who lived in an old cottage with no electricity near to the railway cutting.

One of their cats had just had a litter of kittens so after accepting another very welcome offer of refreshment – elderflower cordial this time – Jo enjoyed playing with the new arrivals before she got back into the boiling van and drove the half-mile back to Melton Winchet.

As she passed Tanners the butchers, Wilf, the proprietor's spotty eighteen-year-old son, walked out of the shop balancing a freshly butchered side of lamb on his shoulder.

Seeing her, he hooked the meat on a vacant spot in amongst the other carcasses hanging outside the shop and then waved her down.

Applying the brakes, Jo stopped the car and wound down the window.

'Afternoon, Wilf,' she said, as the engine ticked over.

'Afternoon, my lovely.' Resting his arm across the roof of the car he leaned in. 'Just a word to the wise, before you go in the shop: Old Nutty's inside talking to Mrs Garfield.'

'Why? What's PC Beech doing there?' asked Jo.

'I don't know but he's just cycled down from the school,' Wilf replied. 'I thought I ought to warn you.'

'Thanks, Wilf,' said Jo, as her heart sank to the pit of her stomach.

'Perhaps I'll see you at the church dance next Friday?' he said softly.

Jo forced a smile. 'Perhaps.'

Shoving the car in gear again, Jo drove the remaining few yards before turning into the shop's back yard once more. Parking the van by the wall, she got out and, feeling as if her summer pumps were made of lead, she headed for the back door of the shop.

Jo walked into the kitchen behind the shop just as PC Beech was about to sink his unevenly spaced teeth into a generous slice of Mrs Garfield's fruitcake.

By the sag of his jowls and peppering of grey amongst his springy ginger hair, Jo guessed Cuthbert Lionel Beech must have been in his early to mid fifties. He'd served in the last war against Germany, as the faded ribbons on his chest testified, and as far as Jo could make out, he had been the village bobby for most of his twenty-year service.

He'd unbuttoned his uniform jacket, giving a brief respite to the buttons and their daily struggle to remain within their allotted buttonhole. With its antiquated houses and locals who considered the high life to be a trip to Colchester on market day, Melton Winchet wasn't exactly a hot spot for crime. Just as well, as the village's sole custodian of the law was a man who felt it vital to keep up his strength by consuming a 'bit of something' on an hourly basis.

He was sitting at Mrs Garfield's kitchen table with a steaming mug of tea and his Essex Constabulary helmet in front of him. The shopkeeper sat opposite him with her arms resting on the table, hands tightly grasped together and a look on her face as if she'd eaten a pound of lemons. Standing between them with his head bowed and cap scrunched in his hand was Jo's brother Billy. All of them turned to look at Jo as she walked in.

'I didn't do it,' said Billy. 'Honest, sis. I didn't.'

'Now, boy,' said the constable, brushing the crumbs from his overhanging moustache as he struggled to his feet. 'You just hold your tongue until I says as—'

'What happened to your face?' said Jo, striding across the room to her brother.

Taking her brother's freckled face in her hands, Jo tilted it up to inspect it and saw a red hand mark across his right cheek and temple.

Jo's mouth pulled into a hard line. 'Who did this?'

Billy didn't answer but his tear-filled eyes flickered on to PC Beech.

Jo spun around and glared at the police officer. 'Did you hit him?'

'He got a clip around the ear for contradicting an officer of the Crown and I hope it'll learn him not to do it again,' PC Beech replied, flicking a stray crumb from his shirt.

Jo put her arm protectively around her brother's shoulder.

'So what's this about?' she asked, holding him firmly to her.

'Ten shillings' been taken from the tuck shop's money box,' PC Beech replied.

'I never took it,' sobbed Billy.

'Lying won't help you out of this one, my lad,' said Mrs Garfield, giving Billy a sour look.

'Cross my heart, Jo,' said Billy, gazing up at her with wide-eyed innocence. 'It wasn't me.'

Jo studied her brother's upturned face for a moment and chewed her lip.

Mrs Garfield tutted loudly. 'Such lies! See what I have to put up with, Cuthbert.'

'Don't worry, Mabel,' said PC Beech. 'I'm trained to get the truth out of miscreants.' He turned his attention back to Jo and Billy. 'Now, son,' he said, giving them what Jo supposed was his coaxing smile, 'we all know you took the ten shillings out of the tuck box so why not be a man and admit it?'

Billy stuck out his lower lip. 'Because I didn't.'

Mrs Garfield and PC Beech exchanged an exasperated look.

'Who said Billy took it, anyway?' asked Jo.

A chair scraped across the floor as Mrs Garfield jumped to her feet. 'Miss Dixon,' she snapped. 'And you can't think the schoolmistress would lie about such a thing.'

'Did Miss Dixon actually see Billy take the money?' asked Jo.

'Not as such,' replied PC Beech. 'But she found him and a couple of others loitering outside the tuck-shop window the day before.'

'I believe thieves call it casing the joint,' said Mrs Garfield, with relish.

'Just so,' agreed PC Beech. 'The criminal underworld are known to use such colloquialisms to disguise their felonious intents.'

Resisting the urge to roll her eyes, Jo turned to her brother. 'Who else was in the playground, Billy?'

'Jim Potton, Peter Danson and Mark Smith,' Billy replied, wiping his nose on his sleeve. 'We were playing marbles.'

Jo looked back at PC Beech. 'Have you questioned them about the money?'

'No I haven't,' he replied. 'Because I can tell you straight, it weren't any of them.'

'Why not?' asked Jo.

'Because they all come from families in the village that's why,' said Mrs Garfield.

Billy started to cry.

Jo squeezed her brother's shoulders. 'It's all right, Billy.'

'A taste of the birch is what he needs,' continued Mrs Garfield, glaring across at them. Her gaze shifted onto PC Beech. 'Aren't you going to run him down to the station?'

The officer chewed his moustache but didn't reply.

Mrs Garfield looked puzzled. 'Cuthbert?'

'He can't,' said Jo, 'because he's got no evidence.'

PC Beech's jowls quivered. 'Not this time I haven't but—'

'Billy,' Jo said, turning her back on the officer and ruffling her brother's mop of red-gold hair. 'Why don't you trot upstairs and do your homework until supper?'

Rubbing his red-rimmed eyes with the heel of his hand, Billy nodded.

Twisting his cap in his hand and his head bowed in abject misery, Billy slunk from the room.

Jo regarded the two people opposite her coolly. PC Beech held her unwavering gaze for a few seconds then grasped the front of his uniform jacket.

'We'll say no more about it this time,' he said, working his way up the silver buttons. 'But let me tell you, I'll be keeping a very close eye on your brother, miss, so you make sure he keeps his nose clean in future.'

Snatching his helmet from the table, he flipped it on his head and, after another quick glance at Mrs Garfield, marched out through the shop.

The shopkeeper's mouth pulled in an ugly line and she rounded on Jo. 'I don't care what you say, I know your brother stole the money.'

'Do you now?' Jo replied. 'Well, in that case, where is it? Where's the ten shilling you're so certain Billy took.'

Mrs Garfield was taken aback. 'Well, he's spent it, of course.'

'What, ten shillings in an hour?' said Jo. 'And on what? The baker's shut so he couldn't have spent it on pies and cake. You sell sweets and comics so if he'd come in flourishing a ten-bob note you would have mentioned it before now, so where is it? I'll tell you where,' she continued before the older woman could reply. 'In the pocket of the person who took it, that's where.'

'Everyone knows crime is a way of life to you East Enders,' said Mrs Garfield. 'So who else could it have been?'

Jo shrugged. 'I don't know. Maybe the caretaker had a hot tip for the three-thirty at Kempton Park or perhaps Miss Dixon herself took it to fund a wild night of gin and dominos in the Thatcher's Arms. If PC Plod bothered to do his job properly rather than bullying a ten-year-old boy he might even find out.'

Mrs Garfield glared at her. 'I'm going to have a word with the placement officer about you both. Do you hear?'

'You do that,' shouted Jo over her shoulder as she stormed across the room towards the hallway.

Leaving Mrs Garfield fuming in the shop's back room,

Jo made her way upstairs past the snug family bedrooms on the first floor and towards the narrow door at the far end of the corridor behind which the roughly made stairway led to the old servants' quarters.

Knocking lightly on Billy's room she opened the door. Still in his school uniform, he was lying on the bed propped up against the headboard reading a copy of *Champion*, which he set aside as she walked in.

'You should be doing your homework.'

'It's boring,' he replied.

'Well, you'll never be able to join the RAF if you don't pass your school exams,' Jo replied.

Billy pulled a face. 'You sound like Mattie. She's always going on about me getting my matriculation.'

'Well, she's right,' Jo replied.

'I'll join the army instead then,' Billy replied. 'As long as I can kill some Germans.'

Shaping his two fingers into a pistol he aimed at the bare light bulb over his bed and let off an imaginary round.

Jo smiled and reaching out, tousled her brother's ginger hair.

Billy pulled a face and jerked his head away.

'Joooo?' he moaned.

'What?'

'Why can't we go home?' he asked.

'You know why,' said Jo. 'Because the Germans will be bombing us soon and it's safer for children to be out of London.'

'I hate it here,' said Billy. 'The local kids are always picking on us and saying we've got fleas.'

'I've told you to ignore them,' Jo replied.

'It's all right for you,' Billy said sullenly. 'You don't have to go to school.'

'No, I have the life of Riley working like a slave in the Garfields' poxy shop instead of being at secretarial college like I was supposed to be,' Jo replied.

'At least you get money of your own at the end of the week,' Billy replied.

The corner of Jo's lips lifted in a satisfied smile as she remembered the way Mrs Garfield's piggy eyes had bulged when Jo had refused point blank to be an unpaid shop assistant.

Billy's face suddenly lit up. 'Perhaps if Old Face-ache downstairs does speak to the placement officer like she's always saying she will, we'll get sent home.'

'I wouldn't get your hopes up,' Jo replied. 'For all her threats, Old Garfield's not going to complain because she doesn't want to lose the fifteen bob a week the government are paying her to keep us.'

The miserable expression returned to her brother's face.

'Even if it is safer here,' said Billy, 'I don't understand. When Mrs Reilly from across the street asked Mum at Christmas if she was going to evacuate us Mum told her "over my dead body". Why did she change her mind?'

Jo shrugged.

'Do you think Aunt Pearl told her to when she turned up last time?' he persisted.

'I supposed she might have,' said Jo, knowing full well it was.

Billy gave her a puzzled look. 'But what about you? Why did mum send you away too?'

'What does it matter, Billy?' said Jo, sidestepping his question. 'We're here now so we'll just have to make the best of it.' She brushed his upper arm with a pretend punch. 'Come on! Chin up.'

Billy forced a cheery smile.

'All right, sis, I'll try.' He delved into his trouser pockets and pulled out two crumpled letters. 'I picked up the late post.' He thrust them at her. 'There's one for both of us from Mum and another addressed to you.'

At last!

Jo put the letter from their mother into her pocket then, with her heart thumping uncomfortably in her chest, turned the other envelope over hoping to see Tommy Sweete's bold handwriting on the envelope but instead she recognised her sister Mattie's neat round lettering.

With her heart somewhere in her boots, Jo shoved aside the feeling of despondency in her chest and tousled her brother's hair.

'Finish your comic, Billy,' she said. 'I'll see you downstairs for supper.'

Chapter Two

WITH THE RED light of the September sunset cutting through the window, Tommy Sweete mashed the last mouthfuls of potato into what remained of the liquor then scooped it up on his fork. Popping it in his mouth he skimmed down the front page of the *Evening News* which was propped against the condiment set. A year ago he'd have turned straight to the racing results on the back page, but now he was interested in the account of yesterday's fight between the RAF and the Luftwaffe over Beachy Head and the aftermath of the bomb that had been dropped in Hackney the week before.

It was just after five on the first Friday evening of the month and he was sitting in his usual booth in The Centurion Pie & Mash shop opposite the LCC Fire Station in Roman Road. As ever, it was crowded with workmen in rough clothing like him, stopping off for something to eat on their way home from work, and mothers with children having a meal before going to Friday-evening Mass at the Catholic Church five minutes away in Victoria Park Square.

With its white and black Victorian tiles decorating the walls, wooden benches either side of the scrubbed-pine tables and the steaming vats of stewed eels behind the counter, The Centurion had been feeding East Enders since the turn of the century. Like the décor, the menu hadn't changed much since then and remained either stewed eels or a steak pie served with mashed potatoes – with the traditional lumps

– smothered in opaque liquor. This pale gravy was in fact parsley sauce made with the water used to boil the eels, which gave it a unique flavour and a green tinge.

Tommy's grandmother had brought him and his brother here each Friday and, using a few coppers from her hard-earned wages, had treated them to a bowl of stewed eels followed by an aniseed twist which they'd both slurped all the way home on the tram. Although he no longer had an aniseed twist after his plate of double pie and mash, a visit to The Centurion was still something Tommy treated himself to each Friday evening at the end of a tiring working week.

Although labouring, by definition, was always heavy physical graft, the last week had been particularly long and hard. Long because, with half the men in London called up he'd had a full week's work and hard because hammering girders into place needed muscle. Thankfully, after years of training and fighting in Arbour Amateur Boxing Club he had plenty of that and, at a shade over six foot tall and with a forty-two-inch chest, he had the height and bulk to manhandle the ten-foot-long, six-by-six timber props needed to prevent buildings from further collapse. Now, though, he was aching all over.

Skimming through the account of how the Ministry of Food was issuing new ration coupons with watermarks to frustrate black-market racketeers from forging them, Tommy picked up his mug of tea and washed down the last morsel of his supper.

'That all right for you, was it, Tommy?' called Dolly, from behind the marble counter.

Somewhere in her late fifties, Dolly was dressed as usual in a floral wrap-around apron and had her bright orange hair tied up under a mauve chiffon scarf. With an apple-round face and arms like a wrestler, Dolly Walker gutted and chopped live eels and peeled mountains of potatoes each day as her mother had before her and her mother before that.

'Nectar from heaven, Doll,' Tommy replied.

''ark at you, and your old blarney,' she replied, dimpling up like a schoolgirl. 'I suppose you'll be wanting roly-poly and custard.'

Tommy grinned. 'Do you need to ask?'

Grasping a ladle sticking out of the blackened saucepan at the back of the range, Dolly set to work and within a minute she was standing beside him holding a steaming bowl in her hand.

'There you are,' she said, as she set a dish of sponge floating in a pond of yellow custard before him. 'I've given you a bit extra to fill those long hollow legs of yours.'

Tommy smiled at her. 'What would I do without you to feed and fuss over me?'

'I wouldn't need to if you pulled your finger out and found yourself a wife,' she replied, picking up his empty plate. 'Now eat your pudding before it gets cold.'

She returned to serve the queue of customers at the counter.

It was true she always made a fuss of him but then Dolly made a fuss of everyone, and gave so many of her customers a 'bit extra' it was a wonder she earned a living.

Tommy picked up his spoon and made short work of his pudding, finishing the last mouthful with a satisfied sigh. Folding the newspaper, he stood up and shoved it in his pocket before taking his old donkey jacket from the back of his chair. He shrugged it on then, grasping the handle of his tool bag which he'd placed on the chair beside him, he went to the counter to pay for his meal.

'You seeing Ruby later?' Dolly asked.

Pocketing his change, Tommy nodded.

'Well then, you can heat this up for her,' she said, sliding a battered Oxo tin full of pie and mash across the counter then wiping her hands on her faded apron.

'Thanks, Dolly,' he said, placing it in his bag amongst his hammer and chisels. 'You're a true diamond gal.'

Dolly's already red cheeks glowed a bit brighter but she shrugged. 'Even with everything it wouldn't be Christian to let her go hungry.'

'Thanks, all the same,' said Tommy. 'And see you next week.'

Outside, the streets were full of the early-evening bustle of people making their way home. Crossing the road, Tommy started up Globe Road towards Stepney Station and spotted the postman cycling away from the letter box with a full sack in his basket.

Damn! He'd missed the evening post. Still, after four weeks what difference would it make if his letter arrived on Monday instead of tomorrow?

In truth, if he'd had the sense he'd been born with, he'd have written it sooner instead of trying to pretend he didn't care that Jo had stopped writing.

They'd exchanged letters weekly for the first couple of months but since the beginning of August she'd not written back. At first, he wasn't too perturbed and, not wanting to press her, he'd forced himself to be patient, but now after almost four weeks he was worried. Worried that, despite her telling him over and over how much she loved him, in the three months since she'd been sent away, she'd found someone else. Some well-heeled country type with a car and a brace of hounds trotting behind or some white-collar professional – a doctor or a solicitor – who could offer her a better life than someone with a dodgy reputation and very little prospects. After all, she was gorgeous enough to attract any man's attention and he was certain she had.

Dolly was right on the nail when she said he needed a wife. But not just a wife. He needed Jo.

Perhaps rather than beating about the bush he should have come straight out and asked her to marry him. It was for that reason he had spent all his lunchtime in Bishopsgate library around the corner to where he was working writing a letter telling her exactly how he felt about her and that he would be catching the early train next Saturday to see her. Because Dolly was right: he needed a wife and even if he had to wait another four years until she was twenty-one, he would shift heaven and earth to make Miss Josephine Margaret Brogan Mrs Thomas Sweete.

Three-quarters of an hour later and after a brisk walk via Stepney Green Station, St Dunstan's Church and Limehouse Basin, Tommy stepped over the slurry of rotting vegetables and horse dung congealing around the blocked drain and crossed Gravel Lane.

By rights, at seven o'clock on a warm late-summer's evening, the pubs dotted along the ancient riverside thoroughfare should have been noisy and full and the warehouses quiet and empty. However, since the country had declared war on Germany last September the reverse was now true. Instead of the dock hooter sounding the end of the day at five, the dockers and stevedores in all the London docks were now working double shifts.

In the long, summer days of 1940 the cranes fixed to the quays and jetties swung back and forth from dawn to dusk unloading vital supplies from ships that had escaped the German U-boats lurking in the Thames Estuary. Dodging between the hand carts piled high with crates and sacks, and imagining Jo running into his arms as he stepped off the early-morning train from Liverpool Street Station, Tommy turned the corner into Brewhouse Lane.

Passing the dilapidated row of once elegant terraced houses with their peeling paintwork and cracked and missing window panes, he came to the ten-foot-high double gates with 'Sweete & Co Builders' painted in an arch across it. Pushing open the door set within the left-hand gate he strolled into the yard. The area, which was perhaps fifty-foot-long by twenty wide, ran behind the row of houses and backed onto the solid brickwork of the Tilbury to Minories railway line. Parked in front of the small office with its one dirty window was Reggie's three-ton Bedford lorry.

Due to the coal and domestic fuel rations, Maguire & Sons, the coal merchants in Poplar, had been forced to sell off some of their fleet and Reggie had jumped at the chance to buy one of their trucks. He'd paid them a fiver over the asking price, thereby nabbing himself one of their new vehicles. Stacked around Reggie's new acquisition were various piles of building materials, while the pallets of bricks and the rows of picks and shovels lined up along the back wall all gave the impression of a thriving business. Anyone looking more closely, however, would soon see that the sand had become solid, and that there were weeds sprouting amongst the paving slabs, and rust on the tools. Although he took on the odd bit of navvying just to show willing, everyone knew

Reggie Sweete's main line of work had nothing to do with bricks and mortar.

As Tommy stepped through into the yard, Fred Willis and Jimmy Rudd walked out of the office.

Fred, who'd been his brother's shadow for as long as Tommy could remember, was a wiry chap with a jagged scar along his chin. In contrast, Jimmy was a low-browed, heavily built individual who even Tommy had to look up to.

As they spotted Tommy they both looked relieved.

'Fank Christ, you've arrived, Tommy boy,' said Fred, lolloping across. 'Your Reggie's in one of his tempers.'

'Yeah,' added Jimmy. 'Been biting our bleedin' heads off all bleedin' day, he has.'

'What's happened?' asked Tommy.

'God knows,' Fred replied. 'But me and Jimmy are skedaddling before he starts going off on one again.'

'See you,' said Jimmy, giving Tommy a light-handed cuff on the arm as he and Fred headed for the gate.

The two men left, closing the door behind them.

Tommy found his brother Reggie sitting behind a desk strewn with papers that had been anchored down with a bag of nails and an open bottle of Scotch. Behind him was a dusty three-shelved bookcase stacked haphazardly with files and ledgers. Nailed on the wall opposite the window was a cork board with last year's calendar pinned on it showing Miss December, in high-heels and a scant negligee, making a snowman.

Seven years his senior, Reggie was four inches shorter than Tommy and instead of his tight, athletic frame he had the physique of a prize bull.

Dressed in a wide-collared shirt, a chocolate-brown three-piece suit with a flowery tie and fob chain dangling across his middle, his brother looked as if he were going out on the town rather than working in a builder's yard.

He looked up as Tommy walked in.

'I was beginning to fink you'd got lost,' he said, the half-smoked cigarette dangling from his lips moving as he spoke.

Dropping his tool bag on the desk, Tommy dragged a paint-splattered chair over and sat astride it.

'Who's been yanking your chain, then?'

'Poxy council that's who,' said Reggie. 'Sent me this bloody summons.'

He searched out a crumpled manila envelope from amongst the paperwork and shoved it at Tommy.

As Tommy scanned the letter, Reggie took the last drag on his cigarette and flicked it on the floorboards then taking one of the stained enamel mugs from behind him, he threw the dregs on the floorboards.

Grabbing the whisky, he waved it at Tommy who shook his head. His brother poured himself a large measure.

'Bloody cheek of it,' he continued after swallowing a mouthful. 'Who said they could sign me and my chaps up as part of their Civil Defence tosh?'

'The Air Raid Precautions Act,' Tommy replied, handing the compulsion order back.

'And if that ain't enough piggin' cheek,' Reggie continued, screwing up the council letter in his fist. 'They've sewest . . . sekest . . . me lorry too.'

'Sequestered,' said Tommy.

'Bloody fancy word for a bloody liberty, however they want to dress it up,' said Reggie.

'There is a war on and you want to count your blessing, Reg,' said Tommy. 'You've been allocated to the Shadwell. Some builders have been ordered to report to command

24

centres on the other side of London not to mention you'll get paid £2 17s 6d a week.'

'I'm earning three times that now,' scoffed Reggie. 'And they'll bleedin' tax me too.'

'Probably,' said Tommy. 'But if you don't want to end up in front of the beak having to explain yourself then—'

'All right, smart arse, you've made your point,' said Reggie, knocking back the last of his Scotch and pouring another. 'But I'm listing you as one of the crew. Unless of course you want to freeze your bollocks off doing fire watch on top of the India and Imperial warehouse all winter.'

'All right, count me in,' said Tommy. 'As long as it's all above board and legit.'

Holding his little finger down with his thumb Reggie raised his right hand. 'Boy Scouts' honour.'

Tommy gave him a wry smile. 'Anything else in the post?'

Reggie grinned. 'I suppose you mean from your bit of fluff in the country.'

Tommy's mouth pulled into a hard line. 'Her name's Jo.'

'Sorry, no,' said Reggie. 'There was nothing from Jo.'

Tommy's shoulders sagged.

'Come on, cheer up.' Reggie shoved the bottle across the table at him. 'Have a drink and forget about her. Plenty more fish in the sea and haven't I always told you to follow your big brother's example and love 'em and leave 'em.'

Tommy didn't reply.

Reggie held his gaze for a second then his eyes flickered onto the tool bag on the desk. 'I did think when they released you from Borstal we'd go back to our old games, you know.' He gave Tommy an ingratiating smile. 'The Sweete brothers, quick and crafty, living by our wits.'

'By breaking in and nicking stuff, you mean?' said Tommy.

'Yeah, but didn't I teach you everything you needed to know?' said Reggie.

'True,' Tommy conceded. 'If it weren't for you I'd never have learned how to shin up a drainpipe, pick a lock or open a three-tumbler safe using a drinking glass.'

'I know it's that bi . . . that Jo who's been stuffing your bonce with all that going straight nonsense,' said Reggie. 'And it's understandable, you being swayed by her. You're young and your sap's rising, making you frisky, but you shouldn't let that get between us.'

Tommy forced a smile. 'It won't. Now, I should be off.'

There was a long pause then Reggie picked up the crumpled pack of Senior Service lying amongst the paper debris on his desk. 'I suppose you're going to see her.'

'Of course.' Tommy stood up.

'I don't know why you bother,' his brother said.

'Because I have to,' Tommy replied.

The two brothers stared at each other for a moment then Reggie looked away.

'I'll see you later at the Admiral?' he said out of the side of his mouth as he held the flame to the tip of his cigarette.

'Not tonight,' Tommy replied, picking up his tools. 'I'm freezing me bollocks off fire-watching on the India and Imperial.'

Tommy turned and headed for the door.

'Don't bother to give her my love,' Reggie called after him.

'Don't worry,' Tommy replied, without breaking his stride, 'I never do.'

•

Twenty minutes after leaving his brother's yard, Tommy turned down Limehouse Causeway carrying a full shopping bag in one hand and his tool bag in the other. He continued on until he reached the bend in the road at Milligan Street. Staring past the line of warehouses, his gaze fixed on Potter Dwellings. Despite being just a stone's throw from Limehouse Basin, the solid yellow brick tenement had survived the night's bombing, and Tommy gave a sigh of relief.

As the plaque on the wall informed those who might be curious, the three-storey council block had been opened less than forty years before in 1904 by Alderman Henry Potter who gave the building its name. Walking under the wrought-iron archway and into the central courtyard, Tommy headed for the furthest staircase then took the steps two at a time to the top floor. He strode along the balcony until he reached the door at the far end.

With two bedrooms, a kitchen with running water and one toilet for every three families, the flats were much sought after and all tenants maintained them to a high standard, as the freshly painted doors, window boxes and scrubbed stairways testified.

All, that is, except the one Tommy was standing in front of now.

He looked at the faded front door for a second or two and then, knowing it was never locked, pushed it open. Stepping over the discoloured door mat and ensuring he didn't kick the three-day-old milk bottle beside it, Tommy walked inside.

'Mum,' he shouted, as the foetid air clogged his nose. 'It's Tommy?'

Nothing.

Shutting the door behind him, Tommy walked down the narrow passage and into the main living room. With the exception of perhaps a few additional stains on the sofa and more dust on the mantelshelf, the ten-by-twelve room looked much as it had looked when he'd visited last week. The pile of newspapers remained stacked haphazardly in the corner and each surface had an item of used crockery on it. There were a couple of lazy flies buzzing around a half-eaten piece of fish and a handful of last week's dried chips nesting in a screwed-up piece of newspaper on the floor. Although he paid the rent on it each week, the thought of living there made his stomach churn. He and Reggie lived in Tarling Street instead.

There was a shuffling sound behind him and Tommy turned to see his mother leaning against the doorframe.

Ruby Sweete was just forty-five but looked at least ten years older. She was wearing the dressing gown he'd bought her in Boardman's a few Christmases ago but lack of regular washing meant the bright pink garment was now grey. The lace around the collar was mostly missing while the matching decoration on the cuffs hung in twisted threads around her bony wrists. In the photos of her as a young chorus girl at the Hackney Empire, Ruby's blonde hair was a riot of curls but now it looked like an abandoned bird's nest. The remnants of last night's make-up were still smudged around her eyes and what remained of her lipstick had sunk into the etched lines around her mouth.

She had never been what you'd describe as full figured, but in the last couple of years her slender figure had become gaunt and even the rouge on her cheeks couldn't disguise the grey tinge to her skin.

She stared uncomprehendingly at him a moment then a light flickered on in her eyes. 'Tommy.'

'Hello, Mum,' he replied. 'How you been keeping?'

'Oh, you know,' she replied. 'You?'

'I'm in the pink,' he replied. 'I thought I'd just pop down to see if you're all right. Where did you go last night?'

'Down to the Angel,' she replied. 'You get a nice crowd in there.'

'No, I meant when the air raid siren went off.'

She looked puzzled. 'Air raid—'

'Which shelter did you go to?' Tommy persisted.

'I stayed in the pub, of course,' she replied. 'I reckon if your number's up, your number's up. You got a fag?'

Reaching into the bag, Tommy took out a packet of Senior Service and handed them to her. Fumbling, she unwrapped it and took one out. Placing it between her lips she took a box of Swan Vesta from behind the motionless clock on the mantelshelf.

After a couple of attempts to strike a light, Tommy put the bag on the sideboard and walked over to his mother. Taking the matches from her, he lit one.

Her hand shook as her nicotine-stained fingers closed over his and she drew on the cigarette.

'Thanks, luv,' she said, looking up at him through bloodshot eyes. 'It's this weather. Plays havoc with me circulation.'

Moving away before the smell of her unwashed body made him gag, Tommy returned to the sideboard.

'Dolly sent you some pie and mash,' he said.

Shoving aside a half-empty bottle of Gordon's, Tommy started to unpack the shopping. 'There's a couple of tins of pilchards, some of that rice pudding you like, a tin loaf. It's off the first tray of the evening batch.'

He laid the tissue-wrapped bread that he'd bought after leaving Reggie's yard next to the collection of tins. The smell of freshly baked yeast and flour drifted up and almost masked the stale odour of the room.

His mother studied the collection unenthusiastically and blew a stream of smoke towards the discoloured ceiling.

'I know,' he said, pulling out the tin Dolly had given him from the bottom of the bag, 'why don't I find a plate for your supper?'

'Ta, luv, but,' she patted her stomach, 'I'm a bit jippy. I'll have it later. But you can make yourself a cuppa if you want. There's milk on the doorstep.'

'No, it's all right, Mum,' he said.

'Have you seen Reggie?' she asked.

He nodded. 'I dropped in at the yard earlier. He says hello.'

'That's good of him,' she replied sourly.

'He's busy, Mum,' said Tommy.

'Too busy for his mother,' she said, the cigarette dangling from her lips sprinkling ash as she spoke. 'It ain't right. Do you hear me, boy? It ain't right.'

Tommy said nothing.

'I suffered agonies for two nights bringing him into this world and this is how he treats me,' she continued, with tears of self-pity shining in her bloodshot eyes. 'My own flesh and blood. And after all I've done for him.'

Memories of him and Reggie, hunger gnawing at their innards, huddled under a dirty blanket for warmth, shot through Tommy's mind.

'He's busy, Mum,' he reiterated.

His mother mulled this over for a moment and then a maudlin expression spread across her face.

'Not like you, Tommy,' she said. 'You don't forget your old mum, do you?'

'No, Mum,' he replied in the same flat tone.

'You always were my favourite.' She smiled, showing her irregular, nicotine-stained teeth. 'You know that, don't you?'

There was a long pause punctuated only by the echo of the dripping tap in the kitchen.

'I've got to go,' said Tommy.

Walking across the sticky rug he headed for the door.

'Tommy.'

He stopped and looked back at her from the doorway.

'Can you spare me a couple of bob?' she asked.

'What happened to the half a crown I sent round on Tuesday?' he asked.

Her pale lips lifted in a self-pitying smile. 'You don't begrudge me a bit of comfort, do you, Tommy?'

Tommy studied his mother for a couple of seconds then shoved his hand in his pocket. He pulled out his change and selected a couple of florin.

Retracing his steps, he dropped them in his mother's outstretched hand.

'Thanks,' she said, her chipped, painted nails scraped the back of his hand as her fingers snapped around the coins. 'You're a good boy.'

Tommy turned, marched back across the room and left the flat.

The sun had crept around the end of the block, illuminating the grimy and smeared window behind him. Resting his hands on the rough brickwork of the balcony, Tommy took a deep breath to clear the cloying stench from his nose and mouth.

He'd been born in this flat and somehow survived there, until Reggie had offered him a bed with him and the woman he was knocking about with at the time. Family life for him and Reggie had been dirty clothes, hungry bellies and random aggression. For a while he'd gone along with Reggie's philosophy towards women and had begun to drink more than was good for him to numb the hollowness of his hand-to-mouth existence, but then he'd met Jo and everything had changed. Seeing the possibility of a different life with her had formed a steely resolve in Tommy, and he'd sworn by all that was holy that no child of his would ever have to endure the nightmares he had.

Chapter Three

'SO,' SAID LUCY Tomlinson as Jo wound the end of the crêpe bandage around her toe, 'there's still no letter from Tommy.'

'No.' Jo sighed, pulling the strip of fabric taut to mound around her friend's heel. 'Nothing – just one from my mum and my ruddy big sister.'

It was now half past eight and she and Lucy were in Melton Winchet's village hall at the end of a line of St John Ambulance cadets all intent on bandaging various bits of each other. They'd been at it for an hour and had already demonstrated putting a casualty into the recovery position, splinted both legs, arms and fingers, shown how to wash noxious substances from the eyes and how to apply a tourniquet to stop an arterial haemorrhage. Now they were on their last test.

Lucy Tomlinson was a friendly easy-going blonde with a wide smile and a snub nose splattered with freckles. She lived on the other side of the village green with her parents and four brothers. Although Lucy was a year older than Jo, the two girls had struck up a friendship immediately, mainly due to Lucy's insatiable interest in London. Having travelled no further than Chelmsford, she was forever quizzing Jo about events and places in the capital.

As the plaque on the wall proudly announced, the village hall had been built to celebrate the Old King's coronation in 1910 and opened by the local landowner's wife, Lady Williamina Tollhunt. With a stage for concerts at one end and a serving hatch through to the kitchen at the other, the wall between reflected the building's role in village life.

Above the door was a carved wooden plaque listing the local good and great who had donated generously to the building of the hall. Beside the main door was a list of the parish council and the time of the next meetings. Side by side on the wall were the Boy Scouts' and Girl Guides' cork boards displaying the respective troops' monthly activity and badges achieved. Opposite them, above the cast-iron radiator, was the Women's Institute noticeboard on which were pinned the dates of future meetings, as well as appeals for members to knit hats and gloves for seamen and donate unwanted clothing for those 'less fortunate'. In addition, there was a hand-drawn thermometer in the shape of an aeroplane with an RAF bull's-eye on each wing and sections blocked out, indicating how much the worthy ladies of Melton Winchet had raised towards purchasing a Spitfire.

Although supper with the Garfields was something Jo never looked forward to, the meal this evening had been particularly gruelling. Apart from Mrs Garfield's usual unappetising offering of boiled pig's heart, onion and lumpy mash potatoes being thrown rather than placed in front of them, they'd eaten their almost indigestible meal under the shopkeeper's hateful stare. The only mercy was that Norman, the Garfields' son and heir, had been held up so was not at the table.

Having forced the tasteless meal down, Jo had changed into her navy St John's uniform and gathered her emergency manual from under the bed. She'd set Billy to do his homework at the kitchen table before heading off for the usual St John's weekly meeting.

Except tonight it wasn't a usual meeting as Miss

Prendergast, the Area Superintendent, and her team were in attendance to examine Jo and half a dozen other recruits for their intermediate first-aid certificate.

Jo had joined St John's almost as soon as she arrived three months ago as a way of escaping Mrs Garfield's critical gaze in the evening. After just a couple of meetings, however, she was hooked. So much so that her allocated non-fiction library tickets were used each week to take out first-aid and nursing books.

'What are you going to do?' asked Lucy.

'I don't know,' said Jo, trying to hold back the feeling of despondency hovering over her.

'Perhaps he's signed up like you said he was going to and your letters are sitting on his mantelpiece,' said Lucy.

'I suppose that's possible.' Jo chewed her lower lip thoughtfully. 'But he wouldn't have left for camp without letting me know.'

'Well, maybe his letter went astray,' said Lucy.

'Maybe,' said Jo, in a tone that said the opposite. 'But everyone else's seemed to get through.' A lump formed in her throat. 'He wrote such lovely things about missing me and wanting us to be together. In his last letter, he even hinted at us walking out together seriously and him coming to meet my family.'

'So how long have you known him?' asked Lucy.

'Forever,' said Jo. 'We were at infants' school together.' She laughed. 'That is, when he turned up. He's three years older than me so he didn't even notice I existed even though I've had a crush on him since I was five.'

An image of Tommy, dressed in a ragged shirt and short trousers, standing half a head above all the other boys in the playground, flashed through her mind.

'He was handsome even then,' she continued, wrapping the crêpe strip around the back of her friend's knee, 'with his unruly black hair and a cheeky smile that got him out of trouble more than once. He was the boy that everyone wanted in their gang. Me and all the other girls in our street spent hours hanging around waiting for him and his mates to appear. He always had a different girl on his arm and they all wanted to dance with him at the Palais. In fact, I'd almost given up on him ever noticing me when I was walking home one night and the strap went on my satchel and all my school books fell out. I was just gathering them together on the pavement when he walked around the corner.'

The memory of the light of desire in Tommy's eyes as he looked down at her that late spring afternoon four months ago sent a fizz of excitement through her.

'He noticed one of my history textbooks was about the Romans,' she continued, 'and he asked me if I knew that Whitechapel Road was an old Roman road and I said I did and that it went to Colchester. He said he'd always been interested in history and I said I was too, but I like the Tudors. Then he said we had a lot in common and then he asked me if I'd like to go out for a drink and I said yes. We went out a couple of more times and really got on well and were just getting to know each other when my sister found out and she told my mum.'

'Perhaps you should open your sister's letter to see what she has to say,' said Lucy.

'I know what she's going to say,' said Jo. 'She'll say she told mum about me and Tommy for my own good because the Sweete brothers are trouble.'

'Are they?'

'Tommy's older brother Reggie certainly is,' said Jo. 'He's got a record as long as your arm for everything from burglary to GBH.'

'What's that?' asked Lucy, as Jo looped the bandage back on itself.

'Grievous bodily harm. It's what you're charged with when you bash someone with a weapon and put them in hospital,' Jo explained. 'And you can bet your bottom dollar if it's not nailed down Reggie will pinch it, but Tommy's not like that.'

Taking the open safety pin she had stuck in her uniform sleeve for safekeeping, Jo carefully passed it through the layers of bandage and clipped it together. Sitting back on her heels, she surveyed Lucy's lower leg.

'What do you think?' she asked, checking to make sure the chevron formation of the binding was evenly spaced. 'Will Miss Prendergast pass it?'

'Spot on.' Lucy sighed. 'I wish I could get mine to sit as neat as that.'

'Finish off, cadets, if you please,' said Mrs Dutton, the wife of the postmaster who had been a nurse in the previous war and now ran the village's St John's troop.

Jo rose to her feet and stood at ease with her hands behind her back beside her casualty.

After a moment or two Mrs Dutton blew the whistle.

Miss Prendergast, a hefty woman in her late fifties with steely grey hair cut in a straight line just below her ears and whiskers to rival the milkman's horse, started down the line on her inspection.

Having poked and prodded the other cadets to check the bandaging techniques, the organisation's senior officer in East Anglia reached Jo and Lucy.

37

'Who have we got here?' she asked, gazing down her clipboard at the list of candidates to be examined.

'Miss Tomlinson and Miss Brogan,' said Mrs Dutton. 'With a toe-to-knee bandaged.'

Both girls stood to attention.

'I don't think I've seen you before, Miss Brogan,' said the superintendent, peering over her half-rimmed glasses at Jo's handiwork.

Jo stood up a little straighter. 'No, Superintendent. Me and my brother were evacuated three months ago after Dunkirk.'

Miss Prendergast's considerable eyebrows rose in surprise.

'But it says here,' she jabbed the clipboard with her index finger, 'you're doing your intermediate certificate. Is that correct?'

'Yes,' said Mrs Dutton. 'Miss Brogan took her novice certificate six weeks ago with merit at the Marks Tey troop.'

Miss Prendergast sniffed and glanced over Lucy's bandaged leg. 'It looks neat enough.'

'Thank you, madam,' said Jo.

'Spacing's right,' Miss Prendergast went on, reaching out and measuring the spacing between the overlaying bandage with her thumb. 'But the heel is the tricky bit.'

Grabbing Lucy's foot, the superintendent raised it high, forcing Lucy to grasp the sides of the chair to keep herself upright.

Miss Prendergast's deep-set eyes flickered over the series of angled turns Jo had painstakingly wound to accommodate the awkward shape.

She sniffed and dropped Lucy's foot.

'Miss Brogan seems to have made a reasonable job, but the proof of the pudding is in the eating. Get up and walk to the door and back,' Miss Prendergast barked.

Lucy did as she was told.

The superintendent looked down hopefully at the bandage but it hadn't budged.

'I think it's safe to say Miss Brogan has passed, Superintendent,' said Mrs Dutton.

Miss Prendergast's mouth pulled into a tight bud and without glancing at Jo she scribbled on the clipboard. 'Fall the troop in, if you please, Staff.'

'Attention,' shouted Mrs Dutton.

Jo and the rest of the troop formed three equal lines in front of the regional officer and stood to attention.

Miss Prendergast's heavy features formed themselves into what Jo guessed was a smile.

'I'm very pleased to tell you that all of you who were tested tonight have passed your intermediate St John's certificate in First Aid.' The superintendent checked the clipboard. 'The scores are as follows . . .'

She read out the scores in ascending order.

'And finally,' she smiled benevolently over them, 'the top score goes to . . .' She paused and reread the entry: 'To Miss Brogan whose score of ninety-two out of a possible hundred means she has passed with merit.'

There was a round of applause and murmurs of congratulations and well-done, which Jo acknowledged with a smile.

Mrs Dutton dismissed the troop and while the leaders were bidding each other farewell, Jo and Lucy helped the rest of the troop clear away.

After accepting Lucy's offer of Sunday tea for Billy and herself, Jo waved her goodbye, and retrieved her coat from the pegs at the end of the hall.

The big hand of the church clock ticked right on the hour at nine o'clock as Jo walked out of the hall into the cold Essex night.

Flicking on her torch and shining the light on the pavement just in front of her feet, she started back up the High Street to the Garfields' shop. However, as she reached the village's only telephone box, she hesitated for a moment then pulled the heavy metal door open and stepped in.

The women from Melton Winchet's WI mopped out the bright red cubicle and polished its Bakelite fitments on a weekly basis so unlike those in and around London Docks this phone box smelt of Windolene and disinfectant rather than urine and cigarettes.

Rummaging around in her handbag she found her purse and pulled out a handful of coppers. Setting them on the shelf, she paused for a second then picked up the handset.

'What number please, caller?' asked the tinny voice at the other end.

'Wapping 712, please,' said Jo.

'Thank you, caller, please wait.'

The line clicked as the girl at the other end dialled the number.

There was a pause and then the receiver was picked up at the other end.

'The Admiral—'

The pips went.

Taking a threepenny bit from the pile, Jo pressed it into the slot and pressed the A button.

The coins fell into the box and the line connected.

'Is that the Admiral pub in Brewhouse Lane?' Jo asked, clutching the mouthpiece with both hands.

'I just said that, didn't I?' said the woman on the other end.

Jo's heart sank as she recognised the flat nasal tones of the Admiral's resident barmaid, Rita Tugman.

'Sorry, I couldn't hear you over the pips,' Jo replied. 'Is Tommy Sweete there?'

'What's it to you if he is?'

Jo's heart thumped in her chest. 'I'd like to speak to him, please.'

'Would you now?' Rita replied.

'Yes, I would,' Jo replied.

'And who are you, when you're at home?'

'Is he there?' Jo persisted.

Rita chuckled down the phone. 'You're the Brogan girl, aren't you?'

'For the last time, Rita, let me talk to Tommy.'

'No, cos he ain't here.'

'When will he be back?'

'Search me,' Rita replied. 'I ain't seen him. I could ask Lou when she gets in. She's our new barmaid. She and Tommy were getting on like a house on fire when him and Reggie were in last week. Perhaps she knows.'

A heavy lump settled on Jo's heart.

'Well, when you do see him, will you tell him I phoned?' she asked, as tears pressed at the back of her eyes.

'If I remember,' Rita replied.

'Thank you,' Jo croaked.

The pips went again and she put the phone down.

With tears distorting her vision, Jo pushed button B and retrieved her unused coins. Pushing the door of the telephone box door open, she stepped outside.

*

Thankfully, when Jo got back to the shop, Mr Garfield was in the upstairs parlour at his nightly task of totting up the day's accounts while through in the shop Jo could hear his wife stocking up the shop for the next day's trading.

Above her in the Garfields' best room the muffled strains of 'Ain't Misbehaving' drifted down as Norman listened to the Tommy Dorsey Orchestra on the wireless.

Going through to the scullery, Jo lit the gas under the kettle, took a cup from the dresser and spooned in two heaped helpings of Ovaltine. Having made herself a hot drink, Jo carried it upstairs to her room. Setting her mug on the bedside table she sat on the bed and took the two letters Billy had given her earlier from her pocket.

Dropping her sister's one on the faded candlewick counterpane, she opened her mother's.

In the dim light from the table lamp's 30-watt bulb Jo's gaze skimmed down the scribbly handwriting and she smiled.

Despite the daily threat of death raining down from the sky, life for the Brogans and their neighbours in Mafeking Terrace seemed to be continuing much as before.

Prince Albert, Gran's moth-eaten parrot, had escaped his cage and evaded capture for three days by roosting in the outside lavatory. Samson, the horse that pulled her father's rag and bone wagon, had shed three shoes in as many weeks. The police had taken Gran in for questioning about taking bets for Fat Tony but didn't have enough evidence to hold her, and her mother had had a set-to with Nelly Flannigan after finding her old man dead drunk on her doorstep last Saturday morning. Of course, some things had changed. Her older brother Charlie, who was one of the last to be plucked from the beach at Dunkirk, had been reassigned to a new artillery regiment and no one had seen an orange or a banana for months. The letter concluded as always with her mother urging them to eat all their greens, for Jo to look after Billy and for Billy to keep out of trouble. There was assurance that the whole family sent their love and an 'X' for each of them under her mother's signature.

Folding the pages together again, Jo rested her head back against the wall and closed her eyes.

From St Audrey's Church at the north end of the village down to the medieval cattle bridge that spanned the brook at the other, Melton Winchet's chocolate-box perfection was everything that Churchill said Britain was fighting for. But it wasn't home.

For Jo, home was streets of two-up two-down houses packed so tightly you could hear your neighbours arguing after chucking-out time on a Saturday night. Instead of the scent of summer flowers on the breeze, home was the sour smell of simmering hops from Charrington Brewery or, if the wind was blowing up the Thames, the smell of the sea. Home was where the rain glistened on the cobbled streets after a storm and each front door had a scrubbed white step denoting the diligence of the women of the house. That's where she should be. Back in Wapping, back where she belonged. At home and with Tommy.

Setting her mother's letter aside she slipped her hand under her pillow and pulled out her communion Bible. Opening it on the page marked by the rosary her gran had given her, she picked up one of the letters she'd placed there for safekeeping.

She ran her fingers lightly over her name written on the envelope in Tommy's bold script then took the three pages of Basildon Bond paper from within.

Although she knew what it said by heart, Jo reread Tommy's letter.

Skimming over the section telling her about how his probation officer had secured him work with a company reinforcing basements as air raid shelters, and the paragraphs telling her about the team of fellas with whom he did his nightly fire watch and the amateur boxing night at York Hall, Jo moved down to the last paragraph.

With a lead weight pressing on her chest Jo read:

But don't you worry none, Jo, even though Reggie is forever trying to rope me into his schemes I've kept my nose clean. That stint in Borstal made me think about the sort of life I want. And it isn't spending half my time behind bars at His Majesty's pleasure like Reggie has but it is being with someone as lovely as you.

I know we've only been walking out for a couple of months so perhaps I'm being a bit too forward but I'm starting to think that maybe one day, when you get back, you'll take me home to meet your family and we can start thinking about the future. Our future.

I miss you, Jo, and think about you all the time, and hope you are thinking about me too.

Love,

Tommy

XX

Kissing the bottom of the page, Jo carefully folded it and slid it back in the envelope.

Her gaze flickered on to the post mark: the 8th – a full month ago. She'd written him four letters since then so why hadn't he replied?

Placing Tommy's letter back between the pages of her Bible, Jo picked up her sister Mattie's letter.

Although her older sister had got her out of scrapes and trouble for as long as Jo could remember, Mattie had over-stepped herself when she told their mother about her and Tommy and got Jo evacuated with Billy.

And it wasn't as if Miss -Know-it-all was in any position to be calling Tommy a wrong 'un, not after getting herself up the duff and having to get married on the hush-hush to some chap so quickly that none of the family were invited, not even Jo.

Not that she'd have gone, of course, because she wasn't speaking to Mattie but even so . . .

Jo studied Mattie's bold handwriting for a moment then ripped the envelope in half.

Billy was right. She hated being here. But in truth, Hitler wasn't to blame for her being stuck in this rustic backwater. No, the real reason she was miles away from Tommy was because of her interfering elder sister.

With the first hint of light creeping under the threadbare curtains hanging at her bedroom window the following morning, Jo lay, as she had for the past hour or more, staring at the light bulb hanging from the ceiling.

She didn't know what time it was but guessed from the handful of birds that had started chirping a little while ago that it was close to five in the morning. A full hour before Mr Garfield got up to take delivery of the daily supply of milk, potatoes and greens from Top Acre Farm.

The church clock chiming the hour at the other end of the village confirmed her guess and Jo swung her legs out of bed and stood up.

Going to the door she opened it, poked her head out and listened. Other than Mr Garfield's faint snoring from the floor below where the family slept, the house was completely silent.

Tiptoeing across the landing she grasped the handle of Billy's door and crept in. Closing the door behind her, Jo picked her way across the room between his scattered clothes and comics and went over to his bed.

Putting her hand on his shoulder she shook him. 'Billy!'

He groaned and grabbing a handful of the candlewick counterpane and blankets dragged them over his head.

'Billy,' Jo repeated, pulling the covers back down. 'Wake up.'

Her brother opened his eyes. 'What's the time?'

'About five,' she replied. Going to the window she ripped open the curtains to let the sunlight, just peeking over the distant hills, into the room.

Billy groaned again and rolled back into the dishevelled mess of his bedclothes.

Jo stripped them back.

'Get up, Billy. We're going home.' Stretching up, she took his suitcase down from the top of the wardrobe. 'Unless of course you'd rather stay.'

'Not on your blooming nelly,' said Billy. Flinging back the sheet and blankets, he scrambled out of bed.

She plonked the half-size suitcase on the bed he'd just vacated. 'Get dressed and pack your stuff while I sort myself out.'

Billy nodded, and thumping across the bare boards, he dragged the top drawer of the dresser out so quickly it shot straight out. Lurching forward, Jo caught it just before it crashed to the floor.

'And do it quietly,' she said, giving him a meaningful look. 'We don't want to wake the house, do we?'

Leaving Billy throwing his clothes into his case, Jo returned to her own room. Without bothering to fetch warm water from below, she poured what remained of yesterday's water from the jug into her wash bowl. She washed and dressed, choosing a light-weight blue skirt, white blouse and navy cardigan. Dragging her brush through her hair she secured it in a ponytail then taking a fresh pair of ankle socks from the top drawer she put them on before lacing her shoes up tight.

Having got herself ready she reached under the bed and dragged out her tan weekend case. Dumping it on the counterpane she flipped the catch and flung the lid open. Pulling open the top drawer she scooped up her underwear and dumped it in the case then did the same with her handful of skirts, dresses and tops, then she closed the case and snapped the locks. Taking her Bible and Tommy's precious letters from under her pillow she shoved them and her purse in her handbag.

A quarter of an hour later, taking everything with her, Jo went back into Billy's room.

He'd dragged on his school uniform, including his tie, and his suitcase was set beside the bed.

'Ready?' she asked.

Billy nodded.

'Well, let's go,' said Jo.

Picking up his suitcase, Billy followed his sister as she crept down the stairs to the shop's back parlour. Without turning on the light, Jo went over to the sideboard and took the ration books from behind the tea caddy. Shuffling through them she found hers and Billy's and put the other three back.

Opening her handbag, she slipped them in. She was just about to unlock the back door when the kitchen door opened and Mrs Garfield, wearing her quilted dressing gown and with curlers in her hair, stepped into the kitchen.

She looked from Jo to Billy and back again.

'And where do you think you're going?' she asked, folding her arms tightly across her chest.

'Home,' said Jo.

'You can go, and good riddance to you,' said Mrs Garfield. 'But the boy stays. He can't be removed without the placement officer's say-so.'

'Can't he?' said Jo.

'No, he can't,' Mrs Garfield replied, giving her the smuggest of looks.

Jo held the shopkeeper's belligerent gaze for a moment then she smiled. 'Billy's coming with me, Mrs Garfield, and I'll tell you why. Because while you were at the WI meeting last week I borrowed a quarter of a pound weight from Wilf Tanner across the road for a little experiment and do you know what? When I put it on the scales with yours, Mr Tanner's four-ounce weight was much heavier,' continued Jo pleasantly. 'In fact, I had to add the one-ounce weight to yours before they would balance.'

All the colour drained from Mrs Garfield's pinched face.

'I'm sure all your customers would be interested to know that when you weigh out their weekly four ounces of bacon and marge or their two-weekly ration of tea and cheese they are, in fact, getting only three-quarters of their entitlement. I didn't have time to test your eight- or two-ounce weights but . . .' She smiled sweetly. 'You see, Mrs Garfield, one of the advantages of being brought up somewhere where "crime is a way of life" is that you can spot a fiddle a mile off.'

The shopkeeper gripped the edge of the table to steady herself as, presumably, her life as an upstanding member of the village community flashed before her eyes.

Jo took her brother's hand. 'Come on, Billy, we've got a train to catch.'

'Are we there yet?' whined Billy, as they turned left off Halt Road towards the branch line that served Chappel and Wakes Colne villages.

'Yes, look, there's the station,' she said, pointing at the square red-brick building with two staircases leading up to the entrance. 'And there's loads of people waiting so there must be a Colchester train soon. Come on.'

'Good, cos my belly thinks my throat's been cut,' said Billy.

It had been almost two hours since they left Mrs Garfield's shop and they'd walked five miles without breakfast.

'Me too,' said Jo, as they reached the foot of the brick and concrete steps. 'But look, there's a station tea room so we can get a cuppa and a sandwich while we wait.'

Changing her suitcase into the other hand to relieve her burning palm, Jo trudged up to the entrance hall with Billy on her heels just as a Sudbury train arrived on the up line.

Opening her handbag, Jo took out her purse and counted her money.

'Blast,' she said.

'What's a matter, sis?' asked Billy.

'I should have remembered it was Saturday. Mrs Garfield owes me this week's wages but I stupidly forgot to ask for them,' said Jo. 'And now I'm wondering how much the train fare will be.'

'Haven't you got enough?' her brother asked.

'Just about,' said Jo. 'But I don't know if I can run to breakfast and we'll have to walk from Liverpool Street instead of catching the bus.'

Billy studied her in the bright sunlight streaming in through the station's windows for a moment then tugged at his tie.

'What are you doing?' asked Jo.

He didn't reply. Removing the tie, he turned back the broad end and poked his fingers in. With his tongue sticking out one side of his mouth he fished about for a bit then smiled.

'There you go, sis,' he said, handing her a brown, ten-shilling note. 'And can I have a sticky bun as well as a sandwich?'

Chapter Four

'ONE CUP OF Rosie Lee, Mattie,' said Francesca, placing a mug of tea and a slice of cake in front of her.

Mattie and Francesca Fabrino had been best friends since they were sat together in Miss Gordon's class at Shadwell Mixed Infant school.

Francesca had enviably flawless olive skin, almond-shaped ebony eyes and black hair so long she could sit on it, but this afternoon it was wound up in a bun at the nape of her neck.

'Thanks, Fran,' Mattie said, giving the slab of brown on the plate a dubious look. 'That looks a bit solid.'

It was Saturday 7 September and Mattie was sitting on the window seat in Lil and Harry's pie and mash shop in Watney Street.

As usual on a Saturday the shop was filled to the gunnels with women who'd scoured the market for the freshest vegetables and a decent joint for the family's Sunday dinner and, shopping done, were now catching up on the gossip over loaded plates of pie and mash or bowls of stewed eels with an accompanying chunk of bread to soak up the juice.

Mattie had been on duty at ARP Post 7 since six that morning and, as Francesca was due on duty at Bethnal Green Fire Station at three, the girls had decided to meet for lunch at one.

Although she worked as a full-time sales assistant in Boardman's in Stratford all week, like almost everyone else,

Francesca had volunteered for war work and was now part of the Auxiliary Fire Service. She was dressed ready for duty in her navy combat jacket but instead of the standard-issue skirt, Mattie had altered a pair of men's trousers to fit Francesca's curves, which made jumping on and off fire engines much easier. Francesca also had her red helmet with AFS stencilled in white on the front and her kitbag filled, no doubt, with a sardine or fish-paste sandwich and the flask of tea Mattie's mother would have insisted she take on duty with her to 'keep body and soul together'.

Her best friend had been staying with them since her father and brother were burnt out of the fish and chip shop and interned with hundreds of other Italians in the days after Italy entered the war.

Having just polished off a beef pie and potato smothered in liquor sauce, Fran had gone to fetch them a cuppa and a slice of cake each.

'It's date and walnut,' explained Francesca. 'But without the nuts, chopped damsons instead of dates and made with powdered eggs. I know,' her friend continued, as Mattie pulled a face, 'but you're eating for two now so you can't be finicky.'

'I suppose not,' laughed Mattie.

'How did you get on at the clinic?' asked Fran, as she stirred in her sugar.

'Fine,' said Mattie. 'The midwife says I'm the right size for my dates and as it's a first baby I should book into the East London Maternity Lying-in Hospital to be on the safe side, especially as it's due over Christmas and some of the midwives at Munroe Clinic will be off.'

'Can you afford that?' asked Francesca.

Mattie nodded. 'I've got all of Daniel's army pay in the bank still.'

'Of course.' Francesca took a sip of tea. 'I keep forgetting you're an old married woman.'

'So do I!' Mattie replied, twisting a still-shiny wedding ring on her finger.

'It's hardly surprising given you were only married for eight days before he shipped out,' said Francesca.

'Ten,' said Mattie. 'Ten days and eleven nights. Still,' she said, patting her middle, 'at least he left me something to do while he's away. Anything in the post from the Home Office?'

'Just this.' Francesca pulled a rectangular manila envelope from her pocket with 'His Majesty's Service' stamped in large across the top. 'It says my father and brother's cases are being reviewed and I'll be informed by the Department for the Internment of Foreign Nationals in due course.' Pressing her lips together she fixed her eyes on the black speckled fly-paper suspended from the light fitting for a moment then her gaze returned to Mattie. 'I know Papa was born in Italy but he came here when he was three, he's even got a cockney accent, and me and Giovanni were born here so surely those in charge can't really think we're spying for Mussolini.'

Francesca had lived with her father and brother above the Empress Fish Bar until Italy had declared war on England three months ago and an angry mob had ransacked and set fire to the chip shop. Now the family-run business that had stood opposite the Troxi on Commercial Road for almost seventy years was a boarded-up charred shell and Francesca's fifty-three-year-old father and twenty-five-year-old brother were in an intern camp.

'Have you heard from your brother? Did he say where they were?'

'I had a letter from him last week, a few days after the one from the ministry arrived. He said they were driven north for about three hours so he thinks it's somewhere near Birmingham or Leicester but he's not sure,' said Francesca. 'He said that Dad's perked up a bit since the move but they still don't know when their appeal will be heard.'

'I'm sure they will both be back home soon,' said Mattie, trying to sound convincing.

'I hope it is soon as it won't do Dad's chest any good if he's living in a damp hut when the winter comes,' Francesca replied.

With the nerves of the whole country on a knife edge and everyone on the lookout for German paratroopers falling from the sky, signalling the start of the long-expected invasion, those in Whitehall's corridors of power probably had other things on their minds.

Francesca gave her a sad look. 'I'm afraid there's nothing from Jo.'

Mattie forced a smile. 'I only posted my letter the day before yesterday.'

Her friend's coal-black eyes softened. 'I'm sure she'll reply this time.'

'I really hope so,' said Mattie, 'otherwise I'll have both my sisters not speaking to me: Jo because she blames me for being evacuated and Cathy for helping put her husband in prison.'

Reaching across the table, Francesca placed her hand over Mattie's. 'Well, at least you've heard from Aunt Fanny.'

Mattie smiled. 'Thank God, yes.'

'And,' her friend fished in her pocket, 'this came from Charlie. I recognised the handwriting.'

'The scrawl, you mean,' said Mattie, taking the letter from her friend.

She opened it and scanned the single page covered by her brother's squiggly letters.

'Is he all right?' asked Francesca.

For her sins, Francesca had been hopelessly in love with Mattie's brother Charlie for years. Hopelessly, because for some unfathomable reason he couldn't see the pearl of great worth under his nose and had become engaged to Stella Miggles, the girl with the slackest knicker elastic west of Bow Bridge.

Looking up into her friend's anxious face, Mattie smiled.

'He seems to be,' she said. 'He can't tell us where he is but he says the sea air is bracing and he's seen lots of ugly grey birds flying overhead each day. He also can't say what he's doing but he says he'll be thrashing everyone at darts in the Catholic Club when he gets home.'

'Sounds like he's on the ack-ack guns somewhere on the south coast,' said Francesca. 'Anything else?'

'Not really,' said Mattie, omitting the bit about her brother's fiancée visiting camp to save her friend further heartache. 'Just that the food's awful, that his gun crew are agreed that the drill sergeant doesn't have a father and that Charlie's keeping his fingers crossed for a few days' leave over Christmas, which will please Mum no end.'

Francesca glanced at the clock on the wall behind the counter.

Popping the last piece of cake in her mouth and swallowing her last gulp of tea, she stood up. 'I'd better be off. See yar!'

'Not if I see you first,' Mattie replied.

The two friends exchanged a fond look and Francesca left.

Mattie took the postcard from her pocket and gazed at the jolly seaside image of Brighton Pier. She turned the card over and, resting her hand lightly on her swelling stomach, she reread the message.

My dearest Mattie,

Just a quick note to let you know that we are all well. We also heard from Cousin Danny yesterday. He has been busy but is in fine health and asked us to pass on his best wishes to you.

Will be in touch when we are in town so we can meet for tea.

Love

Aunt Fanny & Uncle John

Under her fingertips she felt a little flutter and Mattie smiled.

Aunt Fanny was, in fact, Brigadier Francis Lennox, who had been her husband's commanding officer during his time in Spain as part of the British Battalion of the International Brigade. He was now MI5's head of operations in Europe and the 'Cousin Danny' referred to in the chatty greeting was actually her husband, Captain Daniel McCarthy.

However, unlike the rest of the British army that was holed up in England waiting for the Germans' next move, Daniel was already doing battle with the enemy in France with the Resistance.

Tears pricked the back of her eyes. Determined not to shed them, Mattie looked up and saw, through the rivulets of condensation trickling down the window, her mother, shopping basket in the crook of her arm, talking to Breda O'Conner as they waited in a queue.

Tucking the postcard back in her pocket and feeling her back ache as she rose from the chair, Mattie took her used crockery to the counter and left the shop.

'Hey, Mum,' she called across the crowded street as the door closed behind her. 'Wait for me.'

'Only us,' shouted her mother, kneeing open the back door.

Ida Brogan was just over forty and at an inch or two over five foot could look all three of her daughters more or less in the eye. She'd been a slip of a girl with a waistband that her future husband could span with his outstretched hands but now after twenty-four years and five pregnancies she was a little more rounded.

As it was Saturday and she was likely to meet any number of acquaintances as she roamed the market, Mattie's mother had left her wrap-around hooked behind the kitchen door and was wearing the navy suit she'd had for at least a decade. Perched on top of her short brown hair was her close-fitting navy weekend hat, which was decorated with a brooch in the shape of a thistle.

Despite the Ministry of Home Defence posters and the BBC public service broadcasts urging the population to keep their gas masks with them at all times, Ida, like nearly everyone else, no longer carried the cardboard box when she left the house, something Mattie had already nagged her about twice.

It had taken Mattie and her mother just over half an hour to walk home. This was something of a record as Ida had only stopped to speak to two people on what should have been a ten-minute stroll from Watney Street to Mafeking Terrace.

Lumbering over to the kitchen table, her mother deposited her shopping bag of vegetables on the table. Mattie followed her in and, closing the door behind her, unburdened herself of her kitbag and tin helmet, hooking them and her heavy seaman's greatcoat on the back of the door over the rest of the family's outer clothing.

The door to the parlour opened and Queenie came in.

'Oh, there you are,' she said, on her way to the stove. 'I thought you'd got lost on the way home, Ida.'

'I ran into Madge Bingly,' Ida replied, 'who says she's heard that Cohen's fishmonger in Ben Johnson Road is getting some stock in tomorrow. I'll take a stroll up there when I've been to confession. What do you fancy?'

'Sure anything that swims will be grand by me,' said Queenie, lighting the gas ring under the kettle. 'It's been such an age since I've had a bit of fish I've almost forgotten what it tastes like. While you're there, Ida, will you see if you can get a bit of something for Father Mahon?' Queenie rolled her eyes. 'I don't know how Mrs Dunn has the nerve to call herself a housekeeper when she's not feeding the poor man enough to keep the spirit from fleeing his body.'

'Isn't Jerry back from the yard yet?' asked Ida, hooking her coat behind the door.

'Been in and gone out again,' said Queenie. 'The home guard's platoon has been called back on patrol cos someone spied a couple of iffy characters lurking around by the Shadwell Basin.'

The kettle whistled and Queenie reached for the tea caddy while Mattie went back out into the yard to fetch the milk from their cold keep.

The cold keep was in fact a marble butler sink, double the size of the laundry sinks at St George's Baths where the women did their weekly wash. As the lid was half of someone called Sven Kristiansen's gravestone, it was too heavy to lift so had to be slid back in order to take anything in or out. The whole thing sat against the wall of the yard that never got the sun and even in the height of summer it could keep milk fresh for two days.

Shoving the flat stone back a little, Mattie reached in, took out a pint and returned to the kitchen.

Her mother had already gone through to the back parlour while Queenie poured the tea.

'Where on earth did that come from?' said Mattie, eyeing the large rib of beef almost spilling over the dinner plate on the kitchen table.

Her gran tapped her nose with a gnarled forefinger. 'That's for me to know and you to wonder.'

'I bet Mum was pleased when she saw it,' said Mattie.

'She was,' said Queenie. 'Although it nigh broke her front teeth to say as much. But she could say no other when I only parted with hers and your father's meat coupons to fetch it. And I'll be sure you and your babby has a good thick slice or two. How's my great-granddaughter today?'

'Lively,' Mattie replied. 'But, Gran, you do know it might be a boy?'

Queenie's lined face lifted in a soft smile.

'Of course,' she said in a tone that said otherwise.

Queenie went to the dresser. 'I noticed a letter to yourself from our Charlie in the midday post, is he all right?'

As she set the mugs, spoons, sugar bowl and biscuit barrel on the tray Mattie told her gran what she'd told Francesca but this time included the section about Stella.

'Men!' said her gran when she'd finished. 'Will they never stop letting their jocks do the thinking for them?'

Mattie laughed. 'Oh, Gran!'

'Well, tis true!' said Gran. 'If your brother could see past his balls he'd see full well she's a floozy. It's a shame, too, when that lovely friend of yours would be such a better wife to him.'

Mattie looked surprised. 'But how . . .?'

Queenie chuckled. 'Sure, haven't I seen enough men and women in love in my time to know the signs? Tis as plain as the nose on your face she's in love with Charlie.'

Mattie sighed. 'Well, it's a pity he can't see it.' She reached for the tray but Queenie got there first. 'Not in your condition.' Grasping the tray at either side, she picked it up. She gave Mattie a gummy grin. 'And don't worry about your friend. Charlie will have his eyes opened soon enough.'

Her mother was already dozing by the fire by the time she and Queenie joined her in the parlour. Her worn-heeled shoes were where she'd stepped out of them and she now lounged back with her feet on the old pouffe, her lisle stockings rolled around her ankles, enjoying a well-earned five minutes to herself.

Putting her mother's cup on the table beside her, Mattie took her own and went to the domed Bush radio on the sideboard. Switching it on, she stepped out of her shoes and tucked herself into the corner of the sofa, savouring the peace of the familiar front room.

Despite having a fickle income and five children to feed, Mattie's father Jerimiah had done his best to furnish the family home to some degree of comfort. This had mainly been achieved by spotting the odd gem amongst the junk and scraps harvested from his daily rounds. The three easy chairs were a mismatch of styles, ranging from her Gran's chair with its elaborately carved wooden arms and padded seat, through to her father's button-back leather porter's chair with a wobbly arm. The mantelshelf too was cluttered with objets d'art including a Staffordshire dog with an

60

ear chipped off, a Wedgwood bowl without a lid, a pair of silver-plated candlesticks with most of the top coat rubbed away and a Punch toby jug with no handle. But in pride of place, and dominating the whole room, was a tall mahogany bookcase which contained her father's prize acquisition: a set of eleventh-edition *Encyclopaedia Britannica* that had been printed in 1913.

There was a buzz as the wireless valves warmed up.

'With only a quarter of an hour to go,' the excited football commentator shouted out of the hemp mesh at the front of the set, 'Woodgate is tearing down the wing towards Tottenham's goal and—'

'Can you find us some music, Mat,' said her mother, with a heavy sigh.

Mattie stood up.

'She ought to be resting not waiting on you hand and foot,' said Queenie.

'It's all right, Gran,' said Mattie, as she twiddled the station knob. 'Mum's been on her feet all morning whereas I spent most of the shift sitting at the Post 7 control desk doing next week's rota.'

'Thank you, my dear,' said her mother, giving her a sweet smile. 'It's nice to know someone notices what I do for this family.'

She gave her mother-in-law a caustic look and got the same in return.

The melodious strains of *Saturday Bandstand* filled the room as Mattie resumed her seat.

Cradling her mug in her hand, she rested back into the soft upholstery and closed her eyes as the orchestra played its rendition of 'Blue Moon' before seamlessly moving into 'Night and Day'.

A lump formed in Mattie's throat.

The memory of Daniel's arm encircling her and the vibrant tone of his voice singing softly in her ear as they swirled around the Lyceum's dance floor shot through her. It had been just two days before he left for France and before the handful of brave pilots flew up to meet the Luftwaffe's challenge in the skies above Sussex and Kent in the desperate battle to defend Britain. Her mind had just drifted on to when they'd returned to the hotel later that night when the back door slammed.

'If that's you, Jerry,' shouted her mother, 'there's tea in the—'

The room fell still and Mattie opened her eyes to see her sister Jo and brother Billy, who should have been in Essex, standing in the doorway. Both were carrying a suitcase and both looked utterly exhausted.

Jo stared at her mother, gran and eldest sister in silence for a moment then put her case on the floor.

'We've come home,' she said, keeping her eyes on her mother but sensing Mattie's unwavering gaze.

'Yeah, because we hated it there,' Billy added, gripping Jo's hand a little tighter.

Ida stood motionless for a few moments then flung her arms wide.

'Billy! Jo!' she cried, rushing over to them.

Billy dropped his case as their mother enveloped them in her arms.

'My luvs, my luvs,' she sobbed, planting noisy kisses on Jo and Billy in turn.

Mattie and Queenie rose to their feet as, clutching them to her soft bosom, Ida sobbed uncontrollably for a full minute before Billy wriggled out from her smothering embrace.

'You're making me all wet, Mum,' he said, wiping his cheek with the back of his hand.

'Sorry, luv,' laughed Ida, ruffling his head.

Mattie hugged him tight then returned him to Ida who fussed over him and then, despite his protests, smothered him with another round of kisses.

Jo looked across the affectionate melee at Mattie.

Her sister held her gaze for a couple of seconds then came forward.

'Hello, Jo,' said Mattie, giving her a warm smile.

Jo answered it with a cool look. 'Hello, Mattie.'

'You're looking well,' said Mattie.

Jo didn't reply.

'And ... and ... you look parched,' said Mattie. 'There's tea in the pot so I'll fetch a couple more cups.'

'Good idea,' said Ida.

Mattie went into the kitchen as their mother took Jo's and Billy's hands again.

'Let me look at you both,' said Ida, holding them at arm's length. 'You've shot up, Billy,' she said, eyeing him approvingly. 'And you!' she said, turning her attention on Jo. 'Well, you're all grown up, too. Quite the young lady.'

'I should hope so,' laughed Jo. 'I am almost eighteen.'

'Not until March, you're not,' Queenie replied. 'And you could have asked how your sister was keeping.'

Jo felt her cheeks grow warm under her gran's penetrating gaze.

'Leave her be,' said Ida, waving her mother-in-law's words aside. 'She and Mattie will have plenty of time to talk later.'

'I hope so,' said Queenie, meaningfully.

Mattie came in carrying two more cups and a plate with slices of cake stacked on it.

'I thought they might be hungry, Mum, so I've cut into Sunday's cake,' she said, putting the cups on the sideboard.

'Course,' said her mother with a fond smile at her younger two. 'Tuck in.'

Breaking free from his mother, Billy pounced on the cake, grabbing a slice and cramming it in his mouth.

'Thanks, Mat,' he said, spraying cake on the carpet.

Ida resumed her seat in her fireside chair.

'Now, Billy, come and sit with me.' She patted her lap. 'And you and Jo can tell us all about it.'

Jo perched on the upright chair by the sideboard.

'Don't be daft,' said her mother. 'There's plenty of room next to Mattie.'

Forcing a blasé smile, Jo walked across the room to the sofa and, tucking her skirt under her, sat down next to her sister.

As her mother, gran and Mattie listened, Jo, between Billy's interruptions, told her family about the tough time they'd had with the Garfields.

'And so I suppose them falsely accusing poor innocent Billy of stealing was the last straw,' said Ida.

An image of Tommy with his arms around some unknown barmaid flitted through Jo's mind.

'Among other things,' she said, again feeling the weight of her gran's eyes on her.

'It's a disgrace the way those people treated you,' continued her mother. 'They ought to be reported to the government or someone, they should.'

Wriggling on her lap, Billy turned to face his mother.

'I told all of them I hadn't taken the money, Mum,' he said, gazing up with his butter-wouldn't-melt face. 'But no one believed me.' His chin started to wobble. 'Please don't send me back.'

'Don't worry, luv.' Ida gave her son a sympathetic pat on the knee. 'In fact, if it weren't for Aunt Pearl—'

The sound of the air raid siren cut Ida short.

'Bloody hell,' shouted Ida crossly, 'don't the bosh have a day off?'

Billy hopped off his mother's knee.

'Where are you going?' said Ida.

'I didn't see one German plane while we were away,' he shouted over his shoulder as he dashed to the front door. 'So I don't want to miss them.'

'You won't now,' Ida replied. 'It's probably just another false alarm.'

'You'd better go to the shelter, though,' said Mattie, dragging herself wearily to her feet. 'I'll make the flask if you fetch dad's suitcase from under the bed, Mum.'

She went into the kitchen.

'What shall I do?' asked Jo, shouting to hear herself over the incessant two-tone wail.

'Get the pram in the yard and then load the hopping box into it,' said Ida. 'There's no rush. Most of the time the all-clear sounds before we can get halfway to the shelter.'

Jo turned and headed into the kitchen.

Mattie was standing by the sink pouring tea into their father's Thermos flask. She looked around as Jo walked through but didn't say anything.

Jo found the old pram in the lean-to with a tarpaulin covering it. Like everything else her family owned, the ancient contraption that the Brogan children had been transported in as tots had been acquired by her father on his rounds. It was a deep-bodied design and made of brown leather. Unlike the coach-built prams on sale in the baby department of Wickhams, it had no C spring to smooth the journey, just a small wheel at each corner. The wooden handle had been polished smooth by countless hands, and one of the brackets which moved the rain hood back and forth had been broken for as long as Jo could remember.

Dragging it out into the middle of the yard, Jo tipped it almost upside down and shook it to empty out any stray leaves or mouse droppings and then she pushed it through the back door into the kitchen.

'Where's the hopping box?' she asked.

'Under the table. I'll get it,' said Mattie.

The hopping box was in fact a battered workman's chest with a solid handle at each end and a heavy lid. It was the place where all their old clothes, chipped plates, and battered pans were stored for the family's annual trip to Kent to help pick the hops harvest.

Pulling the chair out of the way, Mattie reached below the table and took hold of the handle but Jo grabbed her arm. 'I'll do it.'

Mattie gave her a grateful smile.

'Thanks,' she said, putting her hands into the small of her back and stretching. 'It's getting a bit of a struggle to bend.'

Jo suppressed the urge to smile back.

Mattie might have been the big sister who'd stopped Gladys Williams picking on her at school and given her a cuddle when she awoke from a nightmare, but she'd also been the one who told on her to their mother. If she hadn't, she and Tommy would still be walking out.

Forcing a detached expression on her face, Jo shrugged.

'Don't thank me. I just don't want to have Gran on my back for weeks about letting you lift.'

Heaving it up, she placed it in the body of the pram. She waited until Mattie had deposited the flask inside then wheeled it into the parlour. Her mother had returned from upstairs carrying a small attaché case containing her father's post office savings book, all the family's birth, marriage and insurance certificates plus an album of sepia photos Gran had brought with her from the 'Old Country'. She was also carrying a large handbag which she handed to Mattie.

'Thought I'd save you a trip, luv,' she said, squeezing it into the pram.

Gripping the handle, Ida headed for the door. Mattie and Jo followed but instead of falling in behind, Queenie sat back in her easy chair.

'Gran?' said Jo. 'The Germans will be here any moment.'

'I'm sure you're right, me darling,' said Queenie, picking up her knitting, 'but I'm not fecking hiding in a hole when they do.'

'But you can't just sit there like that waiting,' Jo persisted.

Queenie chewed her gums. 'You're right.'

Setting her needles aside, Queenie stood up and scuttled into her room at the front returning almost immediately carrying a glass with her false teeth floating in it.

'I nearly forgot.' Jabbing a bony finger into the glass she hooked out her dentures and popped them in her mouth.

'I can't meet St Peter at the Pearly Gates without me gnashers, now can I?' she said, snapping her jaw up and down a couple of times to make the point.

Ida rolled her eyes.

'Right, let's go,' said Ida, shrugging on her coat. 'With a bit of luck we'll be back before *ITMA* starts at six.'

Leaving Queenie with her feet up by the fire, Jo followed her mother out into the street. Billy had already met up with several playmates who were firing at imaginary planes overhead while dodging between the upended cannons dotted along the street.

A handful of their neighbours were also pushing prams or carrying bundles of bedding and bags of food for their unplanned visit to the public shelter. However, it was also noticeable that there was a great number who weren't bothering.

'Billy,' bellowed Ida, 'get yourself over here.'

Ignoring her, Billy dashed across the street to the lamp-post, firing off an imaginary round as he ran.

'Now! William Brian Brogan,' she bellowed. 'Or I'll be putting you back on that train tomorrow.'

With his shoulders slumped and dragging his feet, Billy sloped back to join them.

'That's better,' said Ida, straightening her son's cap. 'I might have said you can stay but—'

A throbbing drone that seemed to muffle Jo's eardrums drowned out her mother's voice.

Shielding her eyes against the late-afternoon sun she looked up to see hundreds of planes flying in a V configuration high above their heads with shiny dots of something trailing in their wake.

'German bombers!' shouted Billy, hopping from one leg to the other in excitement.

The whole street swung around to follow as they swooped down the Thames. The noise stopped for a second then a second smaller formation of fighters followed after.

'There're our boys,' Mattie said. 'Spitfires, I think.'

A cheer went up from the residents of Mafeking Terrace.

'Go on, boys, shoot the lot of them,' someone shouted.

'Bloody Jerry bastards,' a second voice shouted.

A frantic fire-engine bell cut through the droning engines and an explosion shook the ground. A flume of black smoke shot up and then another.

Other fire bells started sounding and grew louder.

Mattie turned and went back in the house, emerging a few minutes later with her tin helmet with a white letter W painted at the front and her kitbag over her shoulder. She was wearing her warden's jacket too, unbuttoned to accommodate her swelling stomach.

'Where are you going?' asked Ida.

'Back to the Post,' Mattie replied.

'But you've finished your shift,' her mother protested.

'I know, but they've dropped incendiary bombs on the docks so it'll be all hands to the pump.' Mattie gave them all a weary smile. 'Hopefully, I'll be back once the all-clear sounds.'

She turned and, setting her bag more securely on her shoulder, headed off down the street.

A pang of something unsettling fluttered in Jo's chest as she watched her pregnant sister walk towards the blanket of black smoke hovering over the London Docks.

'Quick, Tommy,' Alf Smith shouted across from the other side of the roof. 'There's another one fizzing over here.'

Grasping the sand bucket in one hand and a shovel in the other, Tommy dashed between Shapiro's Fashion's glass skylights towards his fire-watch partner who was crouched behind a chimney with their stirrup pump.

Alf Smith was a veteran of the previous war and was now the nightwatchman at the Sugar Islands Distillery Warehouse in Limehouse. Reggie hadn't been pleased when Tommy made it clear he wasn't going to try to coerce the veteran of the Somme and Ypres into letting his brother and his light-fingered crew swift a couple of dozen crates of Jamaican navy rum out of the back door.

It was probably somewhere close to eight o'clock and, although the all-clear had sounded some time ago, Tommy and the other fire-watch personnel from around the Shadwell Basin were still up on the factory and warehouse roofs searching out and extinguishing incendiary bombs.

The Moaning Minnie on the top of Union Wharf had gone off just before five, heralding the first squadrons of enemy planes droning their way up the Thames. In the following two hours, wave after wave of bombers had rained down thousands of cylindrical incendiary bombs over the docks and surrounding streets, setting both sides of the river ablaze. From his vantage point high above the cluster of terraced streets, Tommy could see a cloud of thick black smoke hanging in the soft autumn breeze above North Woolwich, while to the south the timber wharfs of Surrey Docks looked like nothing short of Hell's inferno with flames leaping high into the sky.

Although the fire-watchers were instructed to stay with their allocated buildings, within half an hour of the first shower of two-foot-long magnesium-filled cylinders landing it was clear that the fire brigade was becoming overwhelmed. Tommy's crew, like all the others, lugging their equipment with them, had moved from building to building to deal with small blazes.

They'd also been called to houses to help because although instructed repeatedly in all the Civil Defence leaflets and films shown at the cinemas not to spray water on the bombs, many householders did just that, and almost sent their houses up in smoke as a consequence.

Skidding to a stop, Tommy set the sand bucket down then went and joined Alf behind the brickwork.

'Over there,' said Alf, pointing towards the small parapet wall.

Tommy followed his mate's gaze to where a cracked incendiary with its contents leaking out was trying to ignite.

'Right,' said Tommy. 'You pump and I'll spray around.'

'All right, boy,' said Alf, putting his hand in the small of his back and easing himself into an upright position. 'But you mind yourself. You won't look as pretty with no eyebrows.'

Although he was pretty sure as he towered over the elderly fire-watcher he no longer qualified as a 'boy', Tommy nodded.

Pulling his gas mask back over his face, he took the nozzle.

Once Alf had fixed the pump and hosepipe to the side of the bucket, Tommy crouched low and, on all fours, inched across the slate tiles towards the frothing bomb.

Even through the gagging odour of rubber Tommy could smell the acrid chemical reaction. He gave Alf the thumbs-up and felt the surge of water as he held the pipe. Setting it to spray, Tommy flipped the valve open with his thumb and then doused the dried leaves in the gutter and then the lead casing on the roof beams until the water pooled around the device.

He signalled to Alf who, breaking cover, slid the shovel across the damp surface towards him. Tommy caught it and, without taking his attention from the blistering canister, stood up.

Bracing his legs ready to throw himself flat should the bomb go off, Tommy crept forward until he was within a foot of the device. Through the insect-like glass eyeholes of the gas mask, Tommy cast his gaze over it again and, satisfied that the effervescing contents hadn't spread, he gently slipped the edge of the spade under it.

He waited for a second or two to be sure then, flexing his shoulders and biceps, Tommy took the strain and lifted it free from the detritus around it.

Sweat, and not just from the strain of holding a two-pound bomb at arm's length, trickled down his forehead as he trod slowly across an uneven rooftop. At last, after what seemed like an eternity, he reached the sand bucket. Resting the spade on the rim, he eased the metal tube of the device in, nose first.

A sliver of the internal compound trickled down and started to fizzle, indicating the bomb was about to shower the roof and him with white-hot magnesium.

Fighting the urge to dive for cover, Tommy carefully pressed the edge of the spade into the sand and flicked it over the escaping chemical. Stepping sideways, he did the same again and then repeated the action a third time. The body of the bomb was more or less covered but when he dug the edge of the shovel into the sand again a small fountain, not unlike a Guy Fawkes' Night sparkler, sprang out of the jagged crack in the casing.

Tommy dug deep and dragging up a full shovel of sand dumped it on top of the bomb. Then he scraped the spade across the rooftop, collecting accumulated dirt, which he also deposited in the bucket. Grabbing the hose again, Tommy sprayed it over the debris. A single curl of smoke drifted up for a couple of seconds then vanished.

Tommy held his breath for several heartbeats then ripped off his mask and dragged in a lungful of air.

'Well,' he said, running his fingers through his hair, 'that was a close—'

The air raid siren on Shadwell Police station started again and stole his voice as an explosion a quarter of a mile away on the other side of the river shook his eardrums.

Dropping the shovel, Tommy curled forward as a blast of wind sprayed him with shards of glass from the roof skylights.

Opening his eyes, Tommy stared down at the loop of the Thames that formed the Isle of Dogs but instead of seeing the shimmering river meandering round on its way to Barking Creek, both sides of the river from the Royal Dock to St Katharine's were ablaze. Moving across the cloudless night sky above him, dark against the red glow from the burning warehouses, wharfs and houses, were hundreds of enemy aircraft, flying in such tight formation that there was hardly a gap between them as they droned overhead in the second wave that night. In their wake, a line of bombs exploded in neat succession amongst the tightly packed houses in Silvertown.

All around sirens wailed and ambulance and fire-engine bells ran out. A blinding flash tore through the sky followed by an ear-shattering explosion as the gas works by the canal received a direct hit. Tommy took an involuntary step back as the force of the blast hit him.

Grinding slivers of broken glass beneath his size-ten boots, he stumbled across the warehouse roof to join Alf.

'Do you think this is it?' the old man asked. 'The invasion, I mean?'

Tommy nodded. 'They'll try bombing us into submission like they did with Franco in Spain then they'll land on the south coast.'

'They can try if they like,' shouted Alf, shaking a gnarled fist at the hundreds of aircraft high above his head. 'But we beat the bloody Hun last time and we'll bloody well do it again.'

Tommy smiled and punched his old companion lightly on the shoulder. 'Well, we'd better bloody well get on with it then, hadn't we?'

Picking up their fire-fighting equipment, Tommy turned and as he did a handful of bombs exploded somewhere in the Watney Street direction.

Thank God, he thought, as another blast went off behind him. Even if she had forgotten about him and found a new love, he was thankful at least that Jo was safe in the country.

Chapter Five

JO WAS IN the meadow behind St Audrey's Church and running barefoot across the fresh grass towards Tommy who was standing at the kissing gate by the stream. Just as she was about to run into his arms, Mrs Garfield sprang out from behind the drystone wall. Stepping in front of Tommy, the shopkeeper opened her mouth and let out a long, toneless wail.

'Praise Mary for that,' said her mother, as the all-clear siren dispelled the last threads of sleep from Jo's mind.

She rolled her shoulders to relieve the stiffness. 'What time is it?'

'Just after five, I think,' her mother replied.

It had been a long night. After the first all-clear they'd gathered up their things to go home but her mother had stopped several times on the way to chat to a couple of her cronies, so they had only just got back to Mafeking Terrace when the second alarm went off. This, however, gave them a head start, which meant they were some of the first to reach the shelter again, thereby being able to bag the driest and cleanest spot on which to unroll their blankets.

Jo, her mother and Billy had been there all night but with the ground shaking as bombs landed, children crying and people sobbing with every explosion, Jo had barely slept. Like everyone else her heart had hammered in her chest and had jumped out of her skin at every blast, and she wasn't ashamed to say that on more than one occasion she truly believed she was just seconds away from meeting her maker.

The same couldn't be said for Billy who was still in the land of Nod, tucked up in a blanket next to their mother.

People around them were now gathering themselves together and packing away their bedding ready for the trek home.

'Ah, look at him,' said Ida, smoothing a lock of red-blond hair off her son's unruffled forehead. 'Such an angel.'

Studying her brother's cherubic face with the scattering of freckles across his nose and cheeks, Jo didn't comment.

According to her mother, Billy was supposedly the 'face of' Ida's brother who had died after the sulphur used for fumigating bugs had leaked through from the house next door. However, Jo never ceased to wonder why none of the eagle-eyed gossips in the market had noticed that Billy looked nothing at all like anyone else in the family. Of course, he probably looked like his father, but as Aunt Pearl didn't know which one of her man-friends had fathered him they would never know.

He was luckier than most kids born without a father to claim them because although Aunt Pearl had left him in the workhouse without a second thought, Jo's mother's heart overflowed with motherly instincts. On hearing her sister had abandoned her new-born to the council institution and still wild with grief having just buried her own three-week-old son, James, Ida had stormed in to the foundling infant ward at the Bancroft Hospital and demanded they give her three-day-old Billy. No doubt thankful for having one less hungry baby to feed, the matron had handed him over without a quibble and, despite Pearl spasmodically pitching up to lavish presents on him, he had always called Ida 'Mum'.

'He can be when he wants something,' Jo said.

Easing her son's head off her lap, Ida scrambled to her feet and yawned. 'Well, we'd better get our bits together and head off home.'

Standing up, Jo and her mother packed away their bedding and what was left of their overnight picnic then they woke Billy.

Ida directed him outside to relieve himself and she and Jo loaded up the old pram again.

Picking their way through those still sleeping on the floor, they made their way to the entrance. As they emerged into the chilly morning, the light from the sun rising in the east was all but obliterated by the choking pall of pulverised brick dust hanging in the air. Around them people coughed and spluttered as they breathed in the acrid fumes. Jo's eyes started to stream, so taking her handkerchief from her pocket she placed it over her mouth and nose to ease her breathing.

'Sweet Jesus,' whispered Ida, crossing herself repeatedly as she surveyed the destruction in front of them. 'It's like the end of the world.'

Her mother was right.

The scene that greeted them was one of utter destruction. Across from the shelter's entrance, the five-storey warehouse had not a window left intact while the tarmac on the road itself had bubbled into uneven lumps from the fire still raging in the gutted office block further along the street.

'I hope everyone's all right,' said Jo, wondering truthfully how anyone could have survived such devastation, as an ambulance swerved up Leman Street avoiding newly formed craters.

'I can't answer for your gran,' her mother replied, 'but I expect Dad's been in the thick of it all night. Cathy'll be out of harm's way in the Anderson shelter with little Peter but it's Mattie I'm worried about!'

An image of her pregnant sister heading off the night before flashed through Jo's mind.

'She shouldn't be running around the streets in her condition,' she said, without thinking.

'I told her that but will she listen? Will she heck?' Ida said. 'Stubborn, that's what, she is like your blooming father. Still, there's no point standing here all morning, let's get home and have a cuppa. Where's Billy?'

As if he'd heard his name, Jo's brother came tearing over holding what looked like a shiny cauliflower in both arms.

'What on earth have you got there?' asked his mother.

'The tail of a bomb,' he replied, holding it aloft. 'Can I keep it, Mum?'

'I suppose so,' said Ida. 'Now let's get home.'

Grasping the pram's handle, Ida set off with Billy skipping beside her, swinging his trophy.

Yawning, Jo followed them.

As they wearily retraced their steps home along Cable Street they passed the long queue of people waiting for a cuppa and a sandwich at the Women's Voluntary Service mobile canteen outside the Town Hall. The red-brick block of Victorian flats they'd walked past on their way to the shelter eight hours before now looked as though some giant hand had reached down and scooped out the middle.

Staring at the private rooms of the residents, with carpets dangling from damaged floorboards and the contents of wardrobes fluttering from shattered brickwork and splintered rafters, Jo wondered if their owners were lying in a hospital bed or the cold slab in its mortuary.

The whole country had been making ready for over a

year for the horror of blanket bombing. The papers were full of the destruction wrought in Spain by the Luftwaffe's Blitzkrieg way of cowering the civilian population, but all the Ministry of Information's pamphlets and films in the world couldn't prepare you for the reality of being huddled underground while the world you knew and your loved one were being destroyed.

And it was oddly impersonal. The German pilots flying hundreds of feet above weren't trying to kill you or your family for some wrong they'd done them. No, they weren't out to kill you in particular; they were out to kill anyone.

Finally, after what seemed like an eternity, they were home. They trudged down the narrow side alley to the back door into the yard. Her mother opened the latch and they went in.

'What the bloody hell's all this doing here?' asked Ida, standing stock still with her fists on her hips as she surveyed the scene.

Forcing the fog in her brain aside, Jo cast her gaze around their small back yard.

Although the back windows were still intact, oddly, there seemed to be a great deal of rubble strewn across the worn flagstones.

'And what's that doing here?' asked her mother, spotting a metal sheet advertising Bluebell Metal Polish lying at an angle across a clump of bricks.

'Must have been blasted off a building,' said Jo.

'Can I keep it?' said Billy.

'No, it'll have to go to Dad's yard for salvage,' Jo replied.

'Please let me have it, Mum,' pleaded Billy, grabbing his mother's hand and shaking it. 'As a trophy.'

'Jo's right, and if the council find out we're hoarding stuff that could go to the war effort your dad could lose his scrap metal licence,' Ida replied. 'Besides, you've already got that tail whatsit.'

'But I want it,' he shouted.

Throwing aside his mother's hand, he dashed over to the sheet of tin and grasped the edge.

He yanked it upright.

An old bedspring jumped into the air and something whizzed between Jo and Ida and thumped into the shed wall.

Jo turned to see a carving knife embedded in the wood.

'Jesus, Mary and Joseph,' said Ida, staring at the blade quivering in one of the wooden end posts.

'Ha, ha,' laughed Queenie, dancing out from behind their brick-built outhouse. 'I haven't lost me old touch, that I haven't.'

Jo stared in disbelief at her gran who, while dressed in her usual wrap-around apron and old slippers, was also wearing a balaclava that Mattie had knitted for Charlie last Christmas.

'What in the fecking name of all that is holy are you doing?' Ida screamed at her mother-in-law.

'Getting ready for those Hun devils if they come,' laughed Queenie.

'But you could have killed us,' said Ida.

Queenie rolled her eyes. 'For sure, Ida, it's clear you know nothing about the matter as it would take more than that to kill a man.'

'But—'

'No,' continued Queenie, 'the aim is to get them on the ground so you can finish them off.' Clenching her fists, she put one on top of the other and twisted them in the opposite directions to illustrate her point. 'That's how we used to deal with the Black and Tans in my day.'

'Cor, Gran, will you show me how to make a booby trap?' said Billy, his eyes round with admiration for the sixty-five-year-old saboteur.

'No, she will not,' said Ida, pulling her son away from Queenie.

The back yard opened and Jo's father Jerimiah walked in.

Although just short of his fiftieth, Jerimiah Boniface Brogan stood over six foot tall and, with a fifty-inch chest, could best a man half his age. Although he would shed a tear at a sentimental song, if roused to anger, he was a terrifying sight to behold. On the rare occasions the police were called to arbitrate between him and another fella, they knew to send at least six of their number as he'd once carried Pat Horan's donkey on his shoulders the length of Cable Street for a bet. To Jo, however, he was the man who worked from dawn to dusk and in all weathers to put shoes on his children's feet and food in their mouths. To her he was always the warm embrace she could snuggle into.

Mind you, she wouldn't be hugging him at the moment as her father was covered from head to foot in brick dust and soot. His soft sea-green eyes looked unnaturally bright as they regarded his family through a layer of dirt caked on his face, and even his flamboyant red neckerchief that he insisted on wearing with his Home Guard uniform was indistinguishable from the khaki of his dust-laden battle jacket.

His gaze flickered over his family for a second and then he spoke. 'Jo, Billy, what are you doing back?'

'It was so horrible that we had to come home, Dad,' said Jo. 'And beside, we missed you all so much. Didn't we, Billy?'

'Yeah,' her brother agreed. 'They all spoke funny and called us guttersnipes.' His lower lip started to tremble. 'Please don't send us back, Dad. Please!'

'Course we won't, will we?' their mother cut in, giving her husband a firm look.

Jo's dad studied them for a moment then ruffled Billy's hair and then held out his arms.

Jo hurried into them and was enfolded into her father's all-encompassing embrace.

'Thanks, Dad,' she murmured, hugging him back.

He kissed her forehead. 'Mind you, you've picked the wrong moment,' he said, releasing her. 'It looks like Hitler's decided to make his move.'

'Never mind Hitler,' snapped Ida. 'It's your mother we've got to worry about.' Ida jabbed a finger at Queenie. 'She tried to kill us—'

'For the Love of God, Ida,' said Queenie, pulling off her headgear and leaving her hair standing on end like a feather duster, 'don't take on—'

'Take on! Take on!' screamed Jo's mother. 'What's that then when it's at home? Irish mist?'

She pointed at the knife sticking out of the wood.

Queenie gave the blade a quick glance and then looked at Jerimiah.

'Sure, she's over-seeing things as always, I was only—'

'To take someone's eye out—'

'Bejesus, will you not interrupt—'

'I shall speak when I like, Queenie, in me own hom—'

'Son, tell the women to—'

'Quiet!' roared Jerimiah.

Both women jumped.

'That's better,' he said in his normal tone. 'Now, I don't know how you idled away the time while the bloody Jerries were trying to send us all to Kingdom Come, but I've been digging people out from under their homes and fighting with

82

fire hoses trying to quell the inferno along the river.' He raked his fingers through his black curly hair, dislodging a shower of grit. 'So I'd be obliged if you'd both wait a while before telling me all the whys and wherefores.' He glanced around and scowled. 'And while you're all shouting and screaming at each other, have any of you a thought to where Mattie may be?'

The colour drained from Ida's face. 'She said she'd book off when the all-clear sounded.'

'That was an hour ago,' said Jerimiah. 'And there's a fire in the paper mills a few streets down from Post 7 fit to warm Hell itself—'

The back gate opened again and Mattie staggered through it.

With a face the colour of cold porridge and dark circles under her eyes, she looked dead on her feet. Seeing her family looking at her Mattie gave them a weary smile which was taken over by a massive yawn.

'Morning,' she said, blinking and stretching away her exhaustion. 'Glad to see you're still in one piece.'

Ida drew a deep breath. 'We wouldn't be if—'

'That we are,' cut in her father, giving his wife a meaningful look. 'And praise the saint above it's the same with you, me dear, but,' he put one of his bear-like arms around her, 'you look as if you need to sleep for a week.'

'I feel like it, too.' Mattie yawned again.

'There's porridge on the stove,' said Queenie.

'Thanks, Gran, but I had a bite at the WVS canteen while I was booking off so I think I'll just tuck myself under the blankets and pray the Luftwaffe don't come calling for a few hours.'

'Amen to that,' said Ida, crossing herself. 'Off you go, luv.'

Mattie's gaze flickered onto Jo's face for a second then she went into the house.

'She shouldn't be running around the streets in her condition,' said Ida, when her daughter was out of earshot.

'We've all got to do our bit,' said Jerimiah. He looked at Queenie. 'Will you fetch me a bucket of water, Ma, so I can clean up a bit before I go out again?'

Queenie hurried off into the kitchen.

'Where are you going?' asked Ida.

'To the yard,' her husband replied, as he stripped off his jacket. 'And you'd better say a prayer to St Philip that I don't find old Samson dead in his stall after all the fireworks of last night.'

Ida yawned. 'I suppose we'd better make ourselves respectable and get to church. Young Father McInnis was down to do it but I expect after last night Father Mahon will want to say the Mass.'

'Father McInnis?' said Jo. 'What happened to Father McCree?'

Her parents exchanged uncomfortable looks.

'Well, you see now . . .' started her mother. 'It's like this. Father McCree—'

'Joined the army,' cut in her father.

'Yes, that's right,' said Ida. 'Father McCree joined the army.'

'That's a shame,' said Jo. 'I really liked him. I hope he keeps his head and stays out of danger.'

Her parents exchanged another uneasy look then her father spoke again. 'So do we, Jo, so do we.'

*

'Right,' said Jo, pressing the lid of their old biscuit tin down firmly, 'that's two rounds of jam sandwiches and a slice of cake each.'

'Good,' said her mother, her brawny forearms cording as she screwed the lid on the Thermos flask. 'That should keep body and soul together until the all-clear.'

It was the Monday after her and Billy's return and she was in the kitchen with her mother. Her father was out on his rounds, Billy was playing football in the street with half a dozen other lads and Mattie and her friend Fran were on duty at their respective ARP depots. Gran was out doing whatever she was up to and, as her father always said, it was better not to know so you didn't have to lie if the police asked.

Although it was only two days since she had walked into the house with Billy at her side, for Jo, the past forty-eight hours had become a blur of sirens, disrupted sleep and the world shaking and crashing around her. This would have been nightmare enough in itself but the horror was amplified by being surrounded by the multitude of souls huddled around her in the shelter who sobbed and screamed with every explosion. Having survived the night, Jo had finally crawled home to collapse in her bed for six hours of dreamless sleep before the sirens went off again at sunset. To be honest, after just two nights of the damp and foul-smelling Tilbury Shelter, she was beginning to come around to her gran's way of thinking.

However, as her mother's primary aim in life was to see her family fed and watered, tonight Ida had decided to get herself organised for the night ahead by making sure they had plenty of food and drink if they were stuck in the shelter again, as it was clear that the Luftwaffe would be paying them a visit every night for the foreseeable future. If they did find themselves greeting St Peter at the Pearly Gates, the Brogans wouldn't arrive on an empty stomach.

'Put it in the box alongside the extra blankets,' said her mother, as Jo's thoughts started to drift. 'And I'll load it on the pram ready. In fact, I thought we might stroll to the shelter in a bit to see if we can get a better spot than last night, away from the toilets.'

'Well, if that's the case do you mind if I pop around to Daisy Kemp's to let her know I'm back?' said Jo.

Ida glanced at her watch. 'It's a bit late.'

'It's only just gone six,' said Jo. 'And it's still light outside.'

'I know, but for the past few nights the sirens have gone off before seven and I don't want you out roaming the streets when they do tonight,' said her mother.

'She only lives in Mercer Street,' Jo replied. 'And if the Moaning Minnies go off I'll head straight for the shelter and meet you there.'

Her mother looked unconvinced.

'After all,' Jo continued, 'aren't we supposed to keep calm and carry on; carry on with everyday things like seeing friends? Please, Mum.'

Ida bit the inside of her mouth.

'All right,' she said, after a long moment. 'But the minute that siren goes off I want you to get your skates on and get to the shelter.'

Jo let out a breath she didn't know she was holding.

'Promise,' she said, making a quick cross with her finger across her chest.

'Off you go then,' said Ida, heaving the box into the pram.

'Thanks, Mum,' said Jo, planting a kiss on her mother's soft cheek.

Snatching her handbag from the table, she hurried towards the kitchen door.

'But woe betide you, Jo, if you're not in that shelter when the first bomb hits the ground,' her mother called after her.

Throwing the door shut behind her, Jo sped out of the yard and down the side alley. Turning left she headed for the Highway but instead of crossing over to Mercer Street she carried on towards the market until the telephone box opposite the Town Hall came in to view.

Mercifully there was no one in it so Jo pulled open the door and stepped inside, carefully avoiding the suspicious pool of liquid in the corner.

Apart from the possibility of instant death beneath a German bomb, the other problem created by the Luftwaffe's determination to obliterate East London and all its dwellings was that although she'd been back a full two days she hadn't yet been out of her family's sight long enough to let Tommy know she was home.

Rummaging around in her handbag, Jo found her purse and picked up the handset.

'What number please, caller?' asked the distant voice at the other end.

'Wapping 712, please,' said Jo.

'Is this an essential call?'

'Why?' Jo replied.

'Because during an air raid all telephone lines are reserved for Civil Defence purposes only,' said the operator.

'Well, if the siren goes off I'll hang up, now would you kindly put me through?' Jo replied.

Sensing rather than hearing the operator bristle, Jo waited, then the line clicked as the girl at the other end dialled the number.

There was a pause and then the receiver was picked up at the other end and the pips went.

Jo pressed threepence into the slot and pressed the A button.

The line connected.

"'allo!' said the rasping tones of Sam, the Admiral's ancient potman.

'Is that the Admiral?' asked Jo.

'Yeah,' Sam replied. 'Wot you want?'

'Is Tommy Sweete there?'

'Who?'

'Tommy Sweete,' repeated Jo.

'Never 'eard of him.'

'Reggie Sweete's brother,' said Jo. 'You must know them?'

'Look, luv, I don't know nuffunk about nobody,' said Sam. 'And Reggie would have my guts for garters if he heard I was blabbing about him and his bruver so—'

'Who are you talking to?' asked Rita's sharp voice at the other end of the phone.

'Some chit asking for Tommy Sweete,' the potman replied.

'Give it here.'

Jo's heart sank.

'Right, who are you,' snapped Rita, 'and why are you after Tommy?'

'Because I'd like to speak to—'

'It's you again, ain't it? The bloody rag and bone man's kid, Lil or Jill or—'

'Jo!'

'Jo, I should have known,' said Rita. 'All you bog-trotters are named after some dead saint or another.'

'For your information,' said Jo, struggling to keep her voice even, 'my dad said saints are ten a penny so he named

88

me and my sisters after empresses.'

'Is that a fact?' said Rita.

'Yes, it is,' said Jo. 'Now if Tommy's there I'd like to speak to him, please.'

'Shall I tell you what else is ten a penny?' said Rita.

'If you must,' said Jo.

'Women trying to get Tommy's attention,' said Rita. 'And in my opinion you'd—'

'Actually,' snapped Jo, 'I don't want your opinion; what I want is to speak to Tommy.'

'Why?'

'That's personal,' Jo replied.

Rita sniggered down the phone. 'I bet it is.'

'Look, Rita, I—'

'No, you look here,' cut in Rita. 'I'm running a bleeding pub not a lonely hearts club for little girls so sod off and don't ring again.'

The line went dead.

Jo stared at the unresponsive receiver for a second or two then a winding wail penetrated the muted interior of the telephone box as the air raid siren on top of the Town Hall went off.

With tears gathering in her eyes, Jo pressed button B and retrieved a couple of coppers. She pushed open the door and joined the stream of people hurrying for the shelter.

Chapter Six

AS FRED STACKED a wooden crate full of rum bottles on top of the one by Reggie's feet, an explosion pulsed around the warehouse's enclosed yard.

'Bugger me, that was a bit close,' he shouted, above the bedlam taking place all around them.

After their first success at setting the docks ablaze and destroying homes, the Germans were back for another go. The sirens had gone off at a quarter to seven, forcing people to leave their supper on the table and flee to the shelters.

But not Reggie and his men. They'd already shifted some gear they'd acquired two days ago to a safe location by Hackney Marshes and delivered yet another haul of pilfered goods to the designated rendezvous in Epping Forest for collection. Now, at just after eleven, they were on their last job of the night.

Once the powers-that-be actually declared war a year ago, it had taken Reggie just a couple of weeks to suss out that having most of the population tucked away in shelters all night was a gift for those in his profession. Also, the nightly air raid warning saved him both time and trouble. Time because, by and large, business owners often left their premises unlocked when they dashed to their places of safety, and trouble because instead of shinning up walls and picking locks to gain entry, he just had to slip in through a shattered front window and let the boys in the back. In addition, as the police were busy trying to control the nightly stampede to the shelters and keep the population from mass hysteria, they had very little time to worry about loaded lorries driving about in the dark.

While searchlights criss-crossed the black London sky and waves of Dorniers, Heinkels and Junckers roared above, Reggie and his men were finishing the night behind the tall closed gates of the East London Trading Company warehouse.

He, Fred and Jimmy, along with a couple of others from his regular night-time crew, dressed in navy overalls as if they were ARP workers, had been hard at it for almost two hours and the lorry was already low on its axles.

As always, Jimmy did the heavy lifting, ferrying the boxes and crates they were acquiring out to Reggie who had been struggling to tally them up using a stubby pencil and screwed-up notepad in the dim light of his torch.

'How we doing?' asked Fred, just the whites of his eyes and teeth showing in the blackness.

'By my reckoning we've had three boxes of printers' ink, two of assorted woodworking tools, three dozen shovels, a dozen crates of rum and four of gin,' said Reggie as Jimmy appeared out of the shadows and deposited another crate onto the lorry's back board.

'I thought it was a dozen of gin and four of rum,' said Fred, peering into the black void of the vehicle's interior. 'And weren't it two dozen spades and ten garden forks?'

'Does it matter?' hollered Reggie. 'As long as we can flog it. What about the three cartons of American cigarettes?'

'They've been loaded,' shouted Fred over the roar of a blast a few streets north of them.

'Have they?' yelled Reggie. Hawking noisily, he spat the cinders and soot clogging his mouth onto the cobbles at his feet.

'Yes,' bawled Fred. 'Jimmy brought them out on his third trip—'

The booming sound of masonry falling and a fire engine screaming past on the other side of the warehouse's tall back gates cut off their conversation.

'It's a pity Tommy's not here or he'd have the whole lot listed off pat in his bonce,' said Fred.

'Well, he's not,' roared Reggie, his throat hurting with the effort to be heard. 'Anything else?'

'Just a couple of sacks of coffee beans,' Fred replied. 'Although God only knows where you'll get shot of those.'

'I got a mate in Soho says those poncy clubs in Mayfair will pay a small fortune for the real stuff,' Reggie replied. 'Is that it?'

'Just a crate of posh soap that smells like violets,' added Fred. 'I've told the fellas not to put it next to the coffee, and this little lot,' he indicated the remaining three boxes of rum at his feet, 'and then we're done.'

'Good,' Reggie replied. 'Not bad for two hours' work.'

Grasping the tailgate's chain, Fred heaved himself up into the back of the lorry as Jimmy deposited the final boxes of rum. While they secured the load for transportation, Reggie paid off the other two helpers who then slipped away through the gates.

Taking the cigarette from behind his right ear, Reggie lit it and took a puff as the nightwatchman shuffled over. Reggie peeled off ten-pound notes from the roll in his back pocket then slipped them into the warehouseman's waiting hand and he too disappeared into the darkness.

All finished, Jimmy and Fred slammed the tailgate shut and Fred climbed into the lorry's cab. Reggie flicked his half-smoked roll-up away and then he and Jimmy strode to the back gates.

'Let's go,' shouted Reggie.

Jimmy unbolted the metal gates and, holding one each, he and Reggie walked backwards until the gap was wide enough for Fred to drive the lorry through. Loaded to the gunnels with stolen crates and boxes, the Bedford growled into life as it rolled across the yard and into the silent blacked-out streets.

Slipping through to the outside they pulled the gates shut as tightly as they could for the warehouseman to secure later. Fred stopped the lorry and Reggie opened the passenger door.

Jimmy climbed in first and shuffled into the middle of the bench seat as Reggie clambered in behind.

Another explosion flashed red and yellow fire across the sky in front of them, the shockwave from it shaking the vehicle from side to side.

'That looked like it was over Shadwell Basin way,' Fred said, gripping the steering wheel tight with both hands.

Reggie looked through the windscreen across the shimmering waters of the docks before them to where the ragged-topped wharfs and spindly arms of the dock cranes stood silhouetted against the blazing skyline.

An image of Tommy, dog tired from dealing with the onslaught the previous night, and dressed in his rough clothes and a tin hat with his red scarf tied around his mouth, flashed through Reggie's mind but he pushed it aside.

Just like when they were boys, hiding from their mother's drunken rage, it could be either one of them that copped it or neither, and no amount of fretting would make a difference.

Locking his childhood memories back into the deepest recesses of his mind, Reggie turned.

'Right, boys, that's us done,' he said, grinning at the two men sitting alongside him. 'Let's pull our fingers out and get this lot tucked up smartish like and then we can have ourselves a well-earned pint or two back at the Admiral.'

An hour later, and just as an explosion somewhere close by shook the ground under his hobnail boots, Reggie strolled through the side door into the Admiral public house with Fred and Jimmy on his heels. The bar, as you'd expect in the middle of an air raid, was dark and empty. However, Lenny Walker, the publican, wasn't one to let the Luftwaffe interfere with business and so he'd made contingency plans.

Sliding in behind the counter, Reggie pushed open the door to the right of the bar and descended the stone steps.

The cellar below, with its crude stone pillars and roughly plastered walls, showed the Admiral had a history going back centuries. There was even a rumour of a secret passage leading from the public house to the river that the Thames pirates had used for smuggling; but if it existed, it had never been found.

Now, though, the low-ceilinged vault was packed with drinkers who had decided that if they had to spend all night below ground they might as well do it somewhere with booze and company. Last orders at ten thirty had been hours ago but with bombs dropping all around them, the police had more to worry about than the licensing laws. Lenny had set up an improvised bar made out of an old door balanced on a couple of barrels behind which he and Rita, the Admiral's long-serving barmaid, were standing. Rita, a slim blonde in her late thirties, wearing a tight skirt and red striped blouse and down-trodden high heels, looked up from wiping the counter with a rag that looked suspiciously like a pair of dirty underpants.

"Ello, Reggie,' she said, adjusting her neckline to give him the benefit of her disproportionately large breasts. 'What can I get you?'

'A pint each for me and the boys and I'll have double Scotch as a chaser.'

Rita nodded and took a glass from the apple crate behind her.

'I see Lou stayed?' said Reggie, nodding at the Admiral's newest employee who was washing up glasses in an enamel bowl and stacking them on a tea towel on the earthen floor to drain.

'Yes, she's a good kid,' said Rita, holding the first glass under the tap hammered into the side of a keg. 'Although, I think it was because she's hoping your Tommy would be in. She's a bit sweet on him, in case you hadn't noticed.'

Reggie hadn't but then Lou wouldn't be the first pretty thing to cast her eye in Tommy's direction. He studied the new girl a little more closely.

Probably a year or so younger than Tommy, with a pretty heart-shaped face, a warm smile and blonde curls, Lou was the sort of woman a man wanted to see pulling his pint at the end of a long working day.

'He could do a lot worse,' he replied, as Rita put the last of the three pints in front of him. Fred and Jimmy took their drinks and moved off to try to find seats.

'I'll tell you who else seems to have taken a bit of a shine to your little brother, Reggie,' Rita went on, reaching up for a bottle of Black & White.

'Who?'

'That Brogan girl whose old man is the rag and bone man down Chapman Street arches,' Rita replied, as she poured him his Scotch. 'Saucy madam. You should have heard how she spoke to me.'

'Jo's been here?' he asked, panic starting in his chest.

'No,' She placed the whisky in front of him. 'She phoned a few days back and again today, just before the siren went off.'

An uneasy feeling niggled behind Reggie's breastbone. He took a long swallow of beer to steady the vein pulsing in his temple.

'Did you mention it to Tommy?' Reggie asked.

She shook her head. 'It slipped my mind the first time and I haven't seen him today.'

Reggie relaxed.

All this nonsense about 'making something of himself' and 'not wasting his life' that Tommy kept carping on about had only begun when he'd started knocking about with that Paddy girl, so when she'd been evacuated Reggie had counted it a top-score result. He'd hoped that would be the end of it and that, after a week or two of mooning about, Tommy would be back to his old useful self, but then the silly little girl had started sending Tommy soppy letters. Still, he'd soon put paid to that by slipping their postie ten bob to give the letters to him instead of Tommy.

'Did she say what she wanted?' he asked.

A smirk slid across Rita's face. 'I think it was personal.'

Reggie took another mouthful of his drink. 'Will you do me a favour, Rita?'

'Anything,' she said, popping the cork back on the bottle.

'Don't mention her to Tommy,' said Reggie. 'He's a bit

easily led and I wouldn't want to see him get himself tangled up with a bit of pikey skirt so . . .'

'My lips are sealed,' said Rita, placing a friendly hand on his arm. 'If I had a brother I wouldn't want to see him get mixed up with those Paddies. Bunch of bloody thieves they are, the lot of them.' Reggie put his hand in his pocket to pay for his drinks but Rita raised her hand. 'Keep your money, Reggie. On the house.'

'You're a good 'un, you are, Rita,' said Reggie. 'I'll fetch you down a couple of pairs of stockings when I next come by.' He winked. 'On the house.'

Someone called her at the other end of the bar and she wiggled off to serve them. Reggie took another mouthful of drink and then he noticed the new girl Lou hovering around.

'Oi, sweetheart,' he beckoned.

She hurried over, grabbing at a crate of brown ale to steady herself as the ground vibrated again with the impact of a high-explosive bomb.

'Get us another Scotch, luv?' Reggie said, shoving his glass across at her. 'Make it a double.'

'Of course, Mr Sweete,' Lou said, picking up the bottle from the shelf. 'Tommy not with you?'

'No,' said Reggie as she refilled his glass. 'He's freezing his nuts off on the top of the India and Imperial.'

She looked puzzled. 'Do what?'

'He's on fire watch duty,' Reggie explained.

Another high-impact explosion boomed somewhere, making the hurricane lamps swing and grit fall from the ceiling.

'He's so brave,' she said, her eyes shining with admiration.

'He's a pillock, you mean.' Reggie grinned. 'After all, what sort of man prefers to be stuck on top of a warehouse when he could be down here with a drink in his hand and gazing into your pretty little face?'

She dimpled pleasantly. 'I know the customer is supposed to always be right but I still think your Tommy is very brave. And I shall tell him so when I see him.'

Reggie laughed and took another large mouthful of Scotch.

A bomb burst somewhere close by, setting the bottles rattling on the shelf behind Lou.

'So how are you liking it at the Admiral?' Reggie asked when the noise subsided.

'It's very nice,' Lou replied. 'Much better than where I was before.'

'Well, you certainly brighten the place up,' Reggie said. 'And I'm not the only one who thinks so. Tommy's noticed it, and that you've got class, too.'

A hungry look spread across her pretty face. 'Did he say that?'

'Not in so many words but I know my brother.' Watching her over the rim of his glass, Reggie swallowed a mouthful of spirit.

'I didn't think he'd even noticed me,' Lou said.

'Course he has,' said Reggie. 'But he's a gentleman, is my Tommy, and not one to press his attentions until he's certain they'll be welcomed.'

Lou picked up a tea towel and started polishing a glass. 'Rita says he was knocking around with some Irish girl.'

'He was,' said Reggie. 'And half a dozen others. After all, with his good looks he's had women throwing themselves at him since he started wearing long trousers, lucky bugger. But you know what?' Resting his arms on the bar, Reggie leaned forward. 'For all that, I'm hoping one day, my brother'll find himself someone a bit special.' He took another mouthful of drink. 'Someone with a bit class like—'

Lou's gaze shifted past him and her mouth dropped open.

Reggie looked around to see Tommy, his face and clothes smeared with mud and grime, standing at the bottom of the stairs.

'Well, talk of the devil,' said Reggie, 'and he will appear!'

Feeling as if he'd rubbed his face into a cinder pan and with legs made of lead, Tommy trudged across the beaten-earth cellar to the improvised bar.

'Look at the state of you,' said Reggie, as he reached him. 'Where you been?'

'Helping the Auxiliary Fire Service,' Tommy replied, putting his tin hat on the bar. 'The cardboard factory on Stepney Causeway is ablaze and we had to evacuate the boys' home next door.'

'I hope none of them were hurt,' said a voice to his left.

Tommy turned to see the new barmaid gazing at him.

'No, most of them have been evacuated so it was just the matron and a couple of the older boys,' he said, trying to remember her name.

'I think you're very brave,' she said, gazing admiringly up at him.

Tommy gave her a vague smile and turned back to his brother.

'I was hoping to find you here, Reg. One landed at the railway end of Bow Common Lane.'

Alarm flashed across his brother's face. 'Did it hit the lock-up?'

Tommy shook his head, dislodging a quantity of grit in the process. 'But some of the yard fences are down so I thought you might want to know.'

Reggie knocked back his drink in one.

'Fred! Jimmy!' he barked.

The two men ambled over. Reggie gave them their instructions and they left.

The ack–ack guns on King Edward Memorial Park just south of them popped off rapid rounds, sending the glasses jiggling again. Reggie signalled to Lou who glided over.

'Gi' us another,' said Reggie, placing his empty glass in front of her. 'Do you want one, Tommy, or are you going back out?'

'No, the fire brigade chief has stood the fire watch down for the night,' Tommy replied, 'so a bitter would go down a treat.'

'A pint for the hero,' said Reggie. 'Have one yourself, Lou.'

Lou went off to get their order.

An explosion shook the ground under their feet and sent the hurricane lamps' beams flashing chaotically around the space as glasses and a couple of bottles of spirit shattered on the floor.

Tommy whistled through his front teeth. 'That was a bit close.'

Reggie shrugged. 'If your number's up, your number's up.'

A smile spread across Tommy's face. 'That's just what Mum said.'

Reggie shot him a hard look. 'I don't know why you bother with her.'

'Because however bad she was she's still our mother,' said Tommy.

'Some mother she was,' said Reggie. 'Or have you forgotten?'

'I haven't forgotten,' said Tommy, as the terrors of his childhood clawed at him. 'But you have to look after your flesh and blood.'

'Well, you can if you like but not me,' said Reggie. 'If I had my way I'd leave her for the Sally Army to deal with like they do all the other meths drinkers in Whitechapel.'

Tommy gave his brother a sad look and Lou returned with the drinks.

Taking his, Tommy swallowed a large mouthful, feeling the cool liquid wash the dust from his throat. Reggie paid for the drinks and they drank in silence for a moment or two then Lou's giggly laugh cut between them.

'Our new barmaid's a pretty little thing, ain't she?' said Reggie.

Taking the glass from his lips, Tommy glanced across at her. 'Not bad.'

She was sweet enough, with her fluffy blonde hair, but he'd recently developed a preference for curvy brunettes with deep brown eyes.

His letter to Jo would arrive in tomorrow's morning post and please God he'd have one from her by return telling him she'd be waiting at the station for him when he arrived on Saturday.

Reggie knocked back his drink and signalled at Lou and she came over.

'Same again?' she asked.

'Not for me, luv.' Tommy swallowed the last mouthful. 'I'm heading home to get some shut-eye.'

'Funny,' said Lou, 'I was just thinking about doing the same.'

'Well then, my brother can walk you,' said Reggie. 'Can't you, Tommy?'

'Would you, Tommy?' Lou asked, gazing wide-eyed up at him.

Although every bone in his body was screaming for sleep, Tommy smiled. 'Of course, where do you live?'

'Creasey Buildings in Hannibal Road,' she replied, refilling Reggie's glass and recorking the bottle. 'It's not far.'

It wasn't but it was in the opposite direction to their place in Tarling Street.

He forced a weary smile. 'Get your things.'

She hurried off to return in a few moments later wearing her coat and hat with her handbag over her arm.

'Ready when you are, Tommy,' she said as she joined them.

He picked up his tin hat. 'See you later.'

'I shouldn't think so,' said Reggie. 'Me and Jimmy are going to stroll down the Limehouse and try our luck at Charlie Chang's tables after I'm done here so I probably won't be home tonight.' He winked. 'So you'll have the place to yourself.'

Having joined Lou at the top of the cellar steps, Tommy pushed open the public house's side door so she could step through. Although the enemy aircraft still droned overhead and the red glow from the burning wharf a few streets south of them lit the night sky, Brewhouse Lane was remarkably peaceful.

'Probably best to cut up to Sutton Street and through to Stepney Green that way,' said Tommy, turning his collar up against the night chill. 'And you'd best take my arm so you don't miss your footing in the blackout.'

She slipped her arm through his and they headed for the Highway but within minutes found their path blocked by a fire engine frantically pumping water into a blazing shop while a heavy rescue crew hammered a brace beam against the neighbouring building to shore it up.

'Oi, you,' shouted an ARP warden, clambering over the rubble towards them. 'Where you going?'

'Stepney Green,' shouted Tommy, as an ambulance screeched around the corner.

'Well, not up Sutton Street you're not,' said the warden. 'There's a UXB at the back of Newton's timber yard that could go up any moment. And if you want my advice, I'd get your girlfriend off the streets. We've got enough walking wounded to deal with without adding you to the list. There's a street shelter in Maroon Street or you can head back to the Tilbury.'

Tommy looked at the woman clinging onto his arm. 'Where do you want to go?'

'Your place,' she replied. 'It's only around the corner, isn't it?'

'Well, yes,' Tommy agreed. 'But we haven't got an Anderson shelter or a cellar so if there's a direct —'

'Please, Tommy,' she said, the flames from the burning building around them dancing in her eyes and giving her face a warm glow. 'I'll feel safe there, with you.'

Tommy opened his mouth to speak but a long creak cut off his words. There was a peculiar moment of absolute quiet then the blazing building at the end of the street crumpled to rubble, shooting flames into the black night sky.

Lou jumped and her fingers dug into his arm.

'All right,' said Tommy, feeling it would be ungallant to argue further. 'But keep close.'

He took her hand. Shining his dimmed torch on the pavement before him, Tommy led her though the dark streets until they reached his front door. Retrieving the key from his pocket, he let them in.

Walking into the front room he flicked the light switch. Nothing!

'Power's down.' Crossing to the window, Tommy pulled back the blackout curtains. The light from the blazing docks a few streets away bathed the room in a red glow. 'Let's hope the gas isn't so we can have a cuppa.'

He turned.

Lou had discarded her coat and was perched on the arm of the sofa with her legs crossed and her figure-hugging dress hitched up over her knees.

'I'd rather have something stronger,' she replied, giving him a wide-eyed smile.

He went to the sideboard and picked up a bottle of Gordon's.

'Perfect,' she said as he held it aloft.

Unclipping her handbag, Lou took out a packet of Benson & Hedges and offered him one.

Tommy shook his head. 'I don't.'

She looked surprised as she lit her cigarette.

'I used to swap my fags for extra grub in Borstal and got out of the habit,' he explained, handing her the glass.

She took it and her fingers slid over his. 'You not having a drink yourself?'

'No, I've had enough,' Tommy said. 'I've been up since six so I'm ready for my bed.'

Her smile widened as she gazed up at him. 'So am I.'

A tingle of interest crept up Tommy's spine.

'You make yourself comfortable,' he said, moving away from her. 'I'll sort things out.'

Leaving her sipping her drink, Tommy raced upstairs.

Knowing Reggie had entertained at least three of his women friends in the past couple of weeks without changing the sheets and that his *Continental* girly magazines were scattered over the floor, Tommy went straight into his own room.

Overlooking the back yard, his was the smaller of the two upstairs rooms and was situated above the kitchen. Although the furniture only just fitted in the space, the room was tidy and clean. The brass bedstead had the counterpane smoothed over it, his clothes hung in the wardrobe, his underwear and socks were in the drawers and, other than the one on his bedside table, his books were on the alcove shelves. Even the mantelshelf over the cast-iron fireplace had only his cufflinks and loose change on it.

Opening the ottoman at the foot of his bed, Tommy grabbed a blanket but as he stood up, he came face to face with Lou standing behind him.

'All done. You have my room and,' he held the blanket aloft, 'I'll kip down on the sof—'

'You know, Tommy,' she stepped closer and a mixture of flowery perfume and beer drifted up, 'I think you're ever so handsome.'

Tommy took a step back.

'Do you?' he said, feeling the bedframe pressing against him.

'I do.' She placed her hands flat on his chest. 'You're the sort of man that makes a girl forget everything her mother told her not to do,' she continued, smoothing her fingers upwards.

Tommy swallowed.

Although he'd been barely able to keep his eyes open when he'd walked through the front door twenty minutes before, all of him was wide awake now.

Gazing up, Lou gave him a crotch-tightening smile.

'And,' her hands finished their exploration of his chest and snaked around his neck, 'you don't have to sleep on the sofa.'

The ack-ack guns rattled off a round somewhere to the south of them as another blast shook the house and rattled the windows.

Moulding herself into him, Lou stretched up and pressed her mouth onto his. Excitement pulsed through him and his arms wound around her. Without her lips leaving his, Lou's fingers walked down his arm then slipped between them. Delving down, her hand closed around his rigid penis.

'Oh, Tommy,' she murmured breathlessly.

The ground rumbled again as another bomb found its target nearby. Tommy's arm tightened around her and her mouth opened under his.

Suddenly a memory of brown flashing eyes, a throaty laugh and another kiss, less practised and charmingly hesitant, flashed through his mind.

Although every part of his body urged him on, Tommy tore his lips from the woman in his arms.

'I'm sorry,' he said, taking her hand from his throbbing crotch. 'I can't.'

Her eyes heavy with latent desire, Lou looked puzzled. 'Why not?'

'Because there's someone else,' he replied, moving out from her embrace.

'But we could be dead under the next bomb, Tommy.' An explosion sent a flash of red and gold across the bedroom.

'So why not? At least we'd arrive at the Pearly Gates with smiles on our faces.'

She reached out to grasp him again but Tommy caught her.

Hesitation hovered around him but he forced it and her hand aside. 'I'm sorry, Lou.'

Holding the blanket in front of him like a shield, Tommy forced his legs to move and walked out of the room before his crotch got the upper hand.

The house trembled again as Tommy hurled himself down the stairs and into the lounge, shutting the door firmly behind him.

Then he crossed to the sofa and flung himself on it.

As another explosion shook the foundations he shoved a cushion under his head and wrapped himself in the blanket and tried not to imagine the willing woman between his sheets above. Tommy stared up at the fringed lampshade swaying overhead and took several long deep breaths.

Of course, when he stepped off the train in Essex only to discover that Jo had found someone else, then Tommy knew he'd be cursing himself for being a love-sick fool by turning down such a tempting offer. However, with the memory of Jo Brogan's sweet lips responding to his kisses, and the feel of her shapely body in his arms never far from his mind, Tommy knew he would curse himself more if he betrayed her.

Chapter Seven

BENDING DOWN TO check her hair in her dressing-table mirror, Jo picked up her Cherry Frost lipstick and applied another coat.

'For the Love of Mary, Jo, get a move on,' bellowed her mother up the stairs.

'Coming,' she called back.

'So's Christmas,' Ida shouted. 'And I was 'oping to get to Cathy's before then.'

It was about ten o'clock the following morning. The all-clear had sounded at 5 a.m. and although her mother had gone straight to her cleaning job and her father to harness the horse, she and Billy had spent four blissful hours asleep. All the better, as far as Jo was concerned, because Mattie had gone straight to Post 7 from the shelter. Not that it mattered that she wasn't speaking to her sister: since Jo's return she'd hardly seen Mattie for more than a minute or two.

She had been woken by the council workmen drilling at the end of the road as they attempted to reconnect the street's water supply, which had been damaged in the night's bombing.

It was also the day after her run-in with Rita on the phone. As it was clear none of her messages would be passed on to Tommy, Jo had decided she'd have to go and seek him out. It was for that reason she'd tried on and discarded three outfits before settling on her three-quarter-length-sleeved apple-green dress with the white scalloped collar and matching cuffs.

Taking the bottle of Cote d'Amour, Jo dabbed a splash behind each ear. She then grabbed her handbag from the candlewick counterpane, hooked it over her arm and hurried downstairs.

'About time too,' said her mother, as she walked into the front room.

'Sorry,' Jo said, slipping on her coat which she'd lifted from the hall stand as she whizzed past.

Rolling her eyes, Ida headed off towards the kitchen and Jo followed. Gran was standing by the sink scraping potatoes for dinner; she looked up as they walked in.

'We're popping around to Cathy's for a cuppa,' said Ida, as she picked up her handbag from the table. 'We won't be long.'

Queenie nodded and then her gaze shifted to Jo. 'You're a bit dolled up for a trip to your sister's, aren't you?'

'Oh, you know, Gran,' said Jo, smiling light-heartedly at her Gran. 'Just trying to keep my chin up.'

Amusement twinkled in her gran's eyes and Jo's cheeks grew warm.

'Come on then if you're coming,' Ida called from the yard.

Telling herself that it was a scientific fact that even Irish grannies who believed in the little people couldn't read minds, Jo followed her mother down the side alley and out into Mafeking Terrace.

After her mother had stopped half a dozen times to catch up with gossip and news of the latest casualties they finally turned into Dorset Street and found their path completely blocked.

What had been a neat row of terraced houses at the end of the street was now little more than a pile of rubble. In amongst the shattered brick work and timber, the residents of the houses scrambled over the wreckage of their homes, salvaging what they could. Alongside, welfare officers took the names of those who were missing as a stout matron dressed in the green uniform of the WVS comforted a bewildered mother with two small children clinging to her skirts.

'The bloody Germans,' muttered her mother.

Letting an ambulance go by, they crossed the road but as they reached the other side, a police officer with gold embossing on his peaked cap marched around the corner, closely followed by another four policemen with a sergeant at their head and an inspector alongside.

'Right, line everyone up,' barked the senior officer. 'And look sharp about it; they're only around the corner.'

The officer rushed over and herded Jo and her mother along with the handful of residents and the odd member of the rescue service not actually digging people out of the wreckage into some semblance of order then stood to attention behind the little gathering.

Her mother looked at her and Jo shrugged.

She turned to one of the other officers standing next to her. 'What's happening?'

He didn't answer but his eyes darted meaningfully past her.

'Oh Gawd, luvva duck,' whispered her mother. 'It's ... it's ...'

Jo's head snapped around just as the King and Queen walked around the corner.

They were flanked by the mayor, wearing his corporation chain, and H Division's police commander, while behind the royal couple was a group of well-heeled individuals.

The King, dressed in a naval uniform complete with gold encrusted cap and five or six rows of medal ribbons on his chest, started chatting to the rescue workers standing to attention next to the shovels. While her husband was otherwise engaged, the Queen, wearing a lilac dress with a matching coat and a cockade hat with a diamond brooch pinned to the upturned brim, offered a gloved hand to the woman holding a baby standing at the end of the line.

'What shall I say?' hissed Ida.

'Well, it sort of depends what she says to you,' Jo replied in the same hushed tone.

The Queen moved on to the next woman in line.

'Should I curtsy?' Ida asked.

'I suppose so,' Jo replied. 'But don't fall over, whatever you do, Mum.'

'I wish I'd put my best hat on,' Ida replied, as the Queen shifted on to the next in line.

'Just be thankful you aren't wearing your overall,' Jo whispered.

Smiling and bidding the woman she was talking to farewell, the Queen took a couple of steps and stopped in front of Jo and her mother.

Ida started to curtsy but lurched to the side so Jo caught her elbow and pulled her up.

'Good morning,' the Queen said, in clipped tones, smiling coolly at them. 'Do you live around here?'

'N . . . no . . . Yo . . . Your . . .'

'Majesty,' hissed the police inspector to them.

'No, Your Majesty,' said Ida, a crimson flush spreading up her throat. 'We live across the road.'

'And were you bombed out like these poor unfortunate people?' the Queen asked.

A photographer stepped forward and a flashlight popped.

'No, we were lucky,' said Ida, as white specks danced in Jo's vision. 'But I 'eard the palace was struck last night.'

'Yes,' said the Queen. 'It was frightful. Tell me, do you and your family go to the shelter?'

'Me, Billy and Jo do but me husband is out with the Home Guard and our Mattie's an ARP Warden,' Ida replied.

'Marvellous,' said the Queen. 'Our civil defences are doing a simply splendid job, don't you think?'

Jo and Ida nodded.

'So where are you off to now?'

'To see to my daughter around the corner,' Ida replied.

'How delightful,' said the Queen, patting the half-dozen rows of pearls around her neck into place.

'I have three,' said Ida. 'This is Jo.' Grabbing Jo's arm she pulled her forward. 'She's my youngest.'

The Queen's attention shifted to Jo and she gave her stiff-upper-lip smile. 'And what do you do?'

'Nothing at the moment,' said Jo.

The Queen's smile slipped a little.

'She was evacuated, Your Majesty, and 'as only just come home,' said Ida quickly.

'Well, I hope you sign up for war work,' said the Queen. 'The country needs everyone to do their bit to defeat the Nazis.'

'She will,' said Ida, scowling at Jo as if her inaction was jeopardising the whole country's freedom. 'My boy Charlie's in the army.'

'You have a son, too,' said the Queen.

'I have two,' Ida replied. She stole a quick look at those around her. 'That's to say,' she continued in a hushed tone, 'Charlie's mine but Billy's my sister's. No one knew she was having him until she went into labour in the bog at Liverpool Street Station. She didn't want him so she left him in the workhouse, well, it was called the children's home by then but . . . well . . . anyways, when I heard wot she'd done I went and fetched him so now 'e's mine.'

The Queen's heavy eyebrows rose and there was a long pause before she adjusted the silk embroidered clutch bag under her arm.

'Jolly good show,' she said, as her polite, brittle expression reformed. 'So nice to have met you both.'

She moved on to the next person in the line-up.

Ida gazed after her as the monarchs and their entourage made their way down the street.

'What on earth did you have to go on about Billy like that?' asked Jo as soon as the Queen was out of earshot.

'We were just chatting, that's all,' said her mother defensively, as the group around them started to disperse. 'And fancy them coming all this way to see the likes of us.'

'Well, it's only about five miles to the palace and I don't think they caught the bus,' said Jo.

Her mother shot her an exasperated look and slipped her basket into the crook of her arm.

'Say what you like, Josephine Margaret Brogan, but I think it's good of them to put themselves out and,' a smirk spread across her mother's face, 'I can't wait to see the look on Breda O'Conner's stuck-up face when I tell her I've met the King and Queen.'

'I still can't believe that you actually met the Queen, Mum,' said Jo's sister Cathy.

Ida puffed out her bosom and a satisfied smile spread across her face. 'Well, I did and they'll be a photograph in tomorrow's *Daily Sketch* to prove it.'

It was some thirty minutes since their encounter with royalty and Jo and her mother were now sitting in Cathy's lounge drinking tea.

Cathy's jaw nearly scraped the floor when Jo walked in beside her mother but having given her the biggest hug she and Cathy had been chatting away as if it was three days not three months since they'd last seen each other.

Her sister lived in an Edwardian terraced house in Senrab Street, which was situated on the other side of the Commercial Road and a twenty-minute walk from Mafeking Terrace. It was Cathy's mother-in-law's house and she and her husband Stan had moved in with Mrs Wheeler after they'd got married, but now Stan was away Cathy and the baby lived there with Stan's widowed mother.

With its leather three-piece suite, just a few years old, matching sideboard and occasional tables and tastefully arranged china figurines on the mantelshelf, the room was comfortable and spotlessly clean.

Unlike Mattie, Charlie and Jo who all had dark complexions and hair, Cathy, with her blonde curls, smoky-blue eyes and freckles dotted across her nose, favoured their mother's side of the family. However, her sister's angular hips and modest bust-line had rounded off since Jo had last seen her, mainly due to three-month-old Peter who was having his mid-morning nap in his pram in the back garden.

Cathy had had her baby while Jo and Billy had been stuck in the back of beyond in Melton Winchet, so this was the first time Jo'd actually seen her new nephew. She had oohed and aahed over him when she arrived, but as Cathy said it had taken her thirty minutes to get him to sleep, Jo resisted the urge to scoop him out of his pram for a cuddle.

'Was there much up this way last night?' asked Jo, setting her plate aside.

Cathy nodded, dislodging a bright curl from behind her ear. 'I was surprised to see anything left standing when I came out after the all-clear.'

'Buckingham Palace was hit last night,' said Ida.

'Yes, I heard it on the nine o'clock news this morning,' said Cathy.

'The Queen said it was frightful,' said Ida.

Cathy and Jo exchanged amused glances.

She and her mother had only been at Cathy's for fifteen minutes and Ida must have mentioned the Queen at least as many times since.

'How's young Peter taken to spending his nights in the Anderson shelter?' asked Jo.

'He doesn't seem to notice,' said Cathy. 'Although even he felt the one that landed next to the coal yard in Prescott Street the night before last. It took me a full hour to get him back to sleep.'

'Poor little lamb.' Ida sighed. 'I wonder if the bombing keeps the two princesses awake?'

'I wouldn't have thought so; I doubt the royal family are squashed into a damp Anderson shelter in the back garden like Cathy is.'

Her mother gave Jo a tight-lipped look but didn't reply.

'How's your mother-in-law with the bombing?' asked Jo.

'She lies on the bunk all night with her eyes tight shut and crosses herself every time there's an explosion,' said Cathy.

'Is she upstairs?' asked Ida.

Cathy shook her head. 'There's a jumble sale at St Philip's this afternoon so she's giving a hand with the sorting this morning.'

'Did you hear that school in Canning Town that the council were using as a rest centre had a direct hit?' said her mother.

'I did,' said Cathy. 'Someone said the coaches that were supposed to fetch them got lost. It's all the Government's fault for not organising things properly and now they're trying to stop people sheltering in the underground.'

'Well, at least you've got your own shelter,' said Jo. 'Not like us being wedged in with a load of sweaty cattle in the Tilbury.'

'I heard it was bad,' said Cathy.

'It's not bad, it's appalling,' said Jo. 'After just two days stuck in with a load of drunks and crying babies, I can understand why Gran's happy to take her chances up top. There was even a couple of prostitutes from Wellclose Square touting for business under the arches at the back last night. As shelter warden, Mattie's supposed to be down there to keep order but—'

'Don't mention her name to me,' cut in Cathy. 'She and that husband of hers are the reason my Stan's not allowed to see his son—'

'I thought Stan was in the army,' said Jo, giving her sister a puzzled look.

'That's enough, Cathy!' said their mother, giving her middle daughter a fierce look.

Cathy gave her mother a baleful look and buried her nose in her teacup.

The second hand on the carved ebony clock on the mantelshelf ticked off a minute and then Cathy looked at Jo.

'So, Jo,' she said, with a heavy sigh, 'what are you going to do now you're back?'

'I'm not too sure,' Jo replied.

'The Queen said you should sign up for war work,' said her mother. ''Cos the country needs everyone to do their bit to fight the Nazis.' She crossed her arms and adjusted her bosom. 'And apart from it being your patriotic duty, with Charlie gone and the government fixing the price of scrap metal and with the prices rocketing, you'll have to start bringing something in to the house.'

'There are posters on every wall asking people to sign up for war work,' said Cathy. 'So I'm sure they'll snap you up, especially now you've passed your school certificate. What do you fancy?'

'I don't know,' Jo replied, truthfully.

'You could sign on as a full-time ARP warden like Mattie,' said her mother. 'She earns good money.'

'What, stuck in a shelter all night with a bunch of screaming kids and trying to stop people fighting over the best billets?' Jo scoffed. 'Not likely.'

'What about joining the ATS or WRNS?' said Cathy. 'Or even the WAAF—'

'She ain't joining the army,' cut in their mother. 'I'm grey enough worrying over Charlie without having your sister in the army too.'

'All right, the Land Army, then,' said Cathy.

Jo gave her sister a wry look. 'I've just come home from the ruddy country, why would I volunteer to go back?'

'A pity you can't drive, as the ambulance service is crying out for drivers so—'

'I can drive,' cut in Jo.

Cathy looked surprised. 'Can you?'

Jo nodded. 'I got my provisional licence while I was away so I could use the shop's van for deliveries. In fact, I don't know why I didn't think about the ambulance service myself. I'll go along to the Town Hall first thing tomorrow and enquire.'

Cathy drained her cup. 'Shall I top up the pot?'

'Not for me,' said Ida, placing her empty cup in the saucer. 'Your dad'll be in the Catholic Club having his lunchtime pint and I want to catch him before he sets off for the afternoon.'

Ada rose to her feet and so did Jo. They all went through to the kitchen. Jo and her mother unhooked their coats from the back of the door and put them on.

'Nice to have you home,' said Cathy, hugging her sister briefly once she was all buttoned up.

'It's nice to be home,' Jo replied. 'I'll pop by again in a few days, and give that little sweetie a kiss from his Auntie Jo when he wakes up. I'm looking forward to giving my new nephew a cuddle next time I come.'

'Stay in the warm,' said Ida, shoving aside the blackout curtains and opening the door.

There was a bit of a nip in the air so, tucking their collars up, Jo and her mother stopped only briefly to admire the youngest addition to the Brogan family as he slumbered in the fresh air before heading through the back gate and down the side alley to the street.

As they started off towards home, Jo surreptitiously glanced at her watch.

'Mum, can I pop around to see Daisy Kemp?' she asked as they reached Commercial Road. 'She said that she's signed on for war work so I could find out a bit more about it from her.'

'You can, but like I said before,' said Ida, 'if the sirens go off, you go straight to the shelter, do you hear?'

'Thanks, Mum.' Jo gave her a quick peck on the cheek.

Leaving her mother heading off down Sutton Street towards the Catholic Club at the back of St Bridget's and St Brendan's, Jo turned and headed off in the opposite direction.

Chapter Eight

SCRAPING THE RAZOR down his jaw, Tommy flicked the suds in the kitchen sink and turned his head so he could see the other side of his face in the mirror on the window sill.

In the other room, Billy Cotton's Band were playing their signature tune, signalling the start of their midday music programme.

He'd laid awake for at least an hour after he'd rebuffed Lou's advances but despite the regular boom of bombs landing and the artillery batteries along the Thames firing, he must have dropped off to sleep sometime around three, only to be woken again an hour or so later by the all-clear sounding. Since then he'd been dead to the world and only woke up when the postman shoved the mid-morning delivery through the letterbox.

Knowing Jo must have got his letter telling her how much he loved her and that he planned to visit on Saturday, he'd rushed out, hoping there might be one from her telling him the same, but when he'd sifted through the government pamphlets and bills his battered heart had sunk even further. Of course, there might be something in the afternoon post but . . .

He'd had a strip wash and had put yesterday's vest and shirt into the bucket under the sink to soak and was now standing in his trousers with his braces dangling from his waistband and the cold tiles chilling his bare feet.

Raising his chin, Tommy scraped the razor up either

side of his windpipe then rinsed it in the enamel bowl in the sink. Twisting this way and that, and satisfied no stubble remained, he dropped the razor into the handleless jug. He picked up his bottle of Clubman Spice just as the front door banged shut.

'Oi, oi!' shouted Reggie.

'In here,' Tommy called back.

Emptying aftershave into the palm of his hand, Tommy splashed it over his face, feeling it tingle on his freshly shorn skin.

Reggie strolled in. He was dressed in the new chalk-striped brown suit he'd picked up from Maxi Cohen's the week before, his lucky green tie and a fresh shirt.

'I see you found somewhere to kip last night,' Tommy said, recorking the bottle and putting it back on the window sill.

'I did, although I didn't get much sleep.' Reggie winked. 'What about you?'

'An hour or so after the all-clear,' Tommy replied.

'And what about Lou?' asked Reggie.

Picking up the towel, Tommy shrugged. 'You'll have to ask her when she gets up.'

Reggie gave him a pitying look. 'Sorry, Tommy boy, I thought she'd have been all over you.'

'She was,' said Tommy, dabbing his face, 'but I've got other things on my mind.'

His brother rolled his eyes. 'Bugger me. Not that bloody Paddy . . .'

Tommy shot him a hard look.

'All right, all right.' Reggie raised his hands in surrender. 'I'm saying nuffink more except if you're starting to turn down a bit of 'ow's your father with crackling like Lou you'd better trot along and ask one of those head-quacks to take a look at yours because you ain't thinking right.'

Tommy threw the towel over the clothes dryer suspended from the ceiling above the cooker. 'You're a bit spruced up for a swift half in the Admiral, aren't you?'

'I thought I might go and see what's happening up west later,' Reggie replied, dusting an imaginary speck of dirt from his sleeve. 'Want to come?'

Tommy shook his head. 'I'm on fire watch later. I'm going to show the bloke who's replacing me the ropes. Have you got the crew together yet?'

'More or less,' Reggie replied.

'Who you got?'

'Apart from you and me, there's Fred and Jimmy plus I've asked Sunny Merton, Lofty "the cat" Innis and Ugly Ore,' said Reggie, reeling off the names of his most trusted henchmen. 'Plus Squeaky McClean.'

'Squeaky?' asked Tommy. 'He couldn't dig his way through a bowl of semolina let alone a half hundred weight of rubble.'

'But he can lay his hands on some quality picks and shovels and save us sweating our balls off using council rubbish,' Reggie replied. 'So, I said I'd cut him in as the driver.'

'"Cut him in"?' Tommy's eyes narrowed. 'I hope you're not—'

'I mean be part of the crew,' said Reggie, giving him a sheepish grin. 'Sorry, force of habit.'

'It had better be,' said Tommy. 'Because I'll tell you straight, Reggie, I'll shop you myself if I find you or anyone else on the crew pinching stuff.'

His brother looked hurt. 'Honestly, Tommy, what *do* you think I am?'

Raising one eyebrow, Tommy gave him a wry smile.

'All right, all right, but on my life, Tommy, I promise.' Reggie put his hand dramatically on his chest. 'Me and the fellas will play it straight.'

'I hope so, for your sake,' said Tommy. 'And it will be your life because they're hanging looters now.'

He went to walk past his brother and into the lounge.

'Ain't you forgetting something?' asked Reggie. 'Like your bleeding vest and shirt.'

'They're in my wardrobe. I was hoping Lou might have got up by now,' said Tommy. 'But as she hasn't, I'll have to go up and fetch them.'

'Well, you walk in on her half naked like that,' said Reggie, 'and she might try and get you to change your mind so I'll get what I came for and head off to the Admiral.'

Giving his brother two fingers, Tommy left the kitchen and, while Reggie delved into his money stash hidden under a floor slate in the larder, he made his away upstairs to his bedroom.

Half an hour after leaving her mother, Jo stood under the awning of Wenger's tobacconist and gazed down the row of Victorian workmen's cottages in Tarling Street.

She chewed the inside of her mouth.

Perhaps she could just wait until Tommy came out and then pretend to be strolling past. It would look as if she was there by chance and they just happened to meet. It would be the best way, of course, but she was already getting funny looks from customers going in and out of the corner shop and she didn't even know if Tommy was actually at home.

She waited for a second and then, fixing a nonchalant expression on her face, she pinched her cheeks to give them a bit of colour and strolled slowly down the street towards Tommy's house.

Usually, on a bright autumn day such as today, the street would have been full of women gossiping while toddlers ran up and down under the watchful eyes of their mothers. However, as the whole neighbourhood had spent the last few nights under constant bombardment from the Luftwaffe, the street was uncharacteristically quiet as people caught up on some sleep.

As she reached Tommy's front door, Jo glanced through the front window, trying to see if there was any movement inside. Nothing!

She walked on and around the corner then stopped and looked at her watch.

Twelve thirty.

The Admiral would be open so perhaps . . . Jo dismissed the idea.

Her mother would hear that Jo had gone to see Tommy in a pub and would not only skin her alive but probably put her on the next train back to Essex for good measure.

Jo glanced down the street again.

Just one more quick look, she told herself as she strolled back the way she'd just come, and if she still couldn't see anything she'd come back later.

She was two strides from Tommy's front door when it opened.

Excitement shot through Jo as her heart thumped painfully in her chest.

Feeling a little light-headed she smiled, expecting to see

Tommy's much-dreamed-off face appear. Instead, Reggie Sweete stepped out.

He was dressed as always in a flashy chalk-striped brown suit with wide lapels and turn-ups, which stretched to accommodate his bulky frame. His apple-green tie with small playing cards printed on it was tied at his throat with a massive Windsor knot, a gold pin anchoring it to his shirt.

Puzzled, he looked her over for a second then a smile spread across his face. 'It's Jo, isn't it? Jo Brogan.'

Jo was taken aback that he recognised her. 'Well, yes, it is but I'm surprised you remember me.'

'Course I remember you, Jo.' He chuckled. 'You're Tommy's girl.'

'I am?' Jo's heart took flight. 'I mean, yes. Yes, I am.'

'He was talking about you only a minute ago,' continued Reggie.

A little glow started in Jo's chest. 'He was?'

'Yeah,' said Reggie. 'He was telling me what a lovely girl you were but he said you'd gone away.'

'I was evacuated with my brother but I came home on Saturday,' said Jo.

'I suppose you're down here to see Tommy,' said Reggie.

'No,' Jo replied, feeling her cheeks grow warm. 'I . . . I was just passing.'

The corners of Reggie's fleshy lips twitched for a second.

'Well, he's in if you've got time to say hello. I'm sure he'd be happy to see you, Jo.' Smiling, he placed a pudgy hand on the door and pushed it open. 'Go on. Surprise him.'

Jo's heart thumped again and, unable to speak, she walked in.

Standing in the square-shaped hall, Jo glanced up the stairs to the two bedrooms above.

'Hello!'

No one answered.

Taking hold of the curved Bakelite handle she walked into the Sweete brothers' main living room.

Like the rest of the houses in the street the one downstairs room ran from the front to the back of the house. However, unlike the other homes in the street, which usually had one family living upstairs and another downstairs, Tommy and his brother were the sole occupants. Well, except for whichever woman Reggie was currently shacked up with.

The front room itself was just fifteen by twenty, with one window overlooking the street and a door leading to the minute scullery. The stairwell cut across the room, creating an alcove in which stood a squat sideboard with a crate of beer on it.

Apart from being a bit dusty the room was clean enough but it lacked a woman's touch: there were no ornaments on the shelves, no photos over the mantelpiece or antimacassars on the back of the four easy chairs. Instead, there was an over-spilling ashtray, a copy of the *Racing Times* tucked in the side of the chair and one of Reggie's boxing periodicals on the box-shaped radiogram under the back window. Although there was a decent set of curtains at the front window, the window overlooking the rear of the property was bare.

The door to the kitchen area was ajar so Jo walked over.

'Anyone there,' she said, pushing it back and stepping through.

Like the lounge, the kitchen was devoid of all the home comforts you would expect to see and it was clear that Reggie was between women as the pots on the stove were encrusted with dried food and there were the burnt remains of fish and chips in a greasy newspaper on the kitchen table.

Casting her gaze past the pile of dirty crockery clogging the sink to the shaving mirror on the window sill, she noticed the safety-razor with a stick of soap and a bottle of Clubman Spice next to it.

Trailing her fingers along the edge of the table, Jo walked over to the sink and picked up the aftershave. Uncorking the top, she held it closer and breathed in.

Images of Tommy's smile, Tommy's twinkling eyes and Tommy's hard mouth pressing on hers flooded Jo's mind, sending a bolt of disturbing yet enjoyable emotion through her.

Shutting her eyes, she heaved a deep sigh.

'Jo?'

She spun around to find Tommy standing in the doorway behind her.

He was dressed – or rather undressed – in just his trousers, which fitted snuggly and rather too low on his hips as the unfastened waistband revealed a line of hair tracking down. Of course, it took her eyes a minute to shift down there as they seemed glued to his chest covered with dark chest curls that stretched upward to his collar bones and tracked down the middle of his muscular stomach. His arms too, although relaxed, were textured with veins and corded sinews under a generous dusting of hair. The unsettling emotion that should have sent her straight to the confessional settled in the pit of her stomach as her gaze ran slowly over him and came to rest on his blunt chin, angular face and finally his dark eyes.

Jo gave him a dazzling smile. 'Hello, Tommy.'

His jaw dropped. 'Jo!'

'I hope you don't mind, Reggie let me in,' she said, recorking the bottle and putting it back where she found it. 'Pleased to see me?'

'Well yes, of course,' he replied, looking baffled. 'But I thought you were still in the country—'

'Who is it, Tommy?' called a woman's voice from the lounge.

Before he could answer a slender young woman wearing only a nylon underslip and with her hair piled up in an untidy blonde bird's nest slinked into the room.

Her mascara-smudged eyes gave Jo the once-over and then she wound her arm possessively around Tommy's.

Pain gripped Jo's chest and she only just stopped herself from letting out a gasp.

She stared wordlessly at Tommy for several heartbeats and then, with tears distorting her vision, she dashed past him and out of the kitchen.

'Wait, Jo,' Tommy called after her.

But Jo didn't. She just fled the house.

Somehow, once his brain had caught up with his eyes, Tommy managed to have his shoes on and tied within two minutes of Jo dashing past him but even so, when he tore out of the front door, struggling into his shirt, she was already at the bottom of the street.

'Jo! Wait!' he shouted, but she didn't look back as she disappeared around the corner.

Heedless of the amused stares of his neighbours, and with his open shirt streaming behind him, Tommy raced after her. With hooters honking, wheels screeching and drivers cursing him through their open windows, Tommy dodged between the vehicles and pelted after her.

She veered left to take the short cut down King David Walk, clearly heading towards the Catholic Club at the back of St Bridget's and St Brendan's. He had to catch her before she got there.

She was halfway down the passageway when he entered the cool dampness of the alley.

'Jo! Stop, please!' he shouted, his voice echoing after her.

She didn't.

Cursing, Tommy stretched his legs and ran after her. As he emerged from the other end of the alley, he saw that Jo had dropped her handbag. She turned to retrieve it, and saw him close on her heels. Snatching it up, she bolted towards her destination on the other side of the road but the delay put Tommy only a few paces behind her so, within a few yards of the Catholic Club's front door, Tommy caught up with her and blocked her path.

'Jo, wait,' he said, breathing hard.

'Get out of my way,' she screamed, her lovely brown eyes swimming with tears.

'Let me explain—'

'You're there half-dressed and so was she, so I don't need it explaining,' she spat out, the hurt in her voice cutting him to the core.

'Sweetheart.' He took her arm but she snatched it back.

'Don't you *sweetheart* me, Tommy Sweete. I'm not a bloody fool so don't treat me like one.'

'All right.' He raised his hands in surrender. 'I know what it looked like but honestly, I—'

'Honest!' She gave a hard laugh. 'That's a bloody joke coming from a Sweete. You don't know the meaning of the word.'

Tommy frowned. 'I know you're upset but—'

'Upset. I'm not upset, I'm bloody furious. Furious with myself for ever believing you.' Her mouth pulled into an ugly shape. 'My sister Mattie told me what you were like but I wouldn't listen.'

'If you'd just let me get a word in sideways—'

'"I love you, Jo, I miss you, Jo, I can't wait to see you again, Jo,"' she mimicked in a falsetto voice. 'That's what you wrote and all the while you were carrying on with someone else.'

Taking a long breath to hold back his rising anger, Tommy looked down at her.

'So you won't hear me out, then?' he asked, in as controlled a tone as he could muster.

'I know what I saw,' she replied.

They stared at each other for several heartbeats then Tommy grabbed the front of his flapping shirt.

'Well, then,' he said, fastening the bottom button, 'there's nothing more to say, is there?'

Gazing up at him with those lovely brown eyes of hers, Jo folded her arms tightly across her by way of reply.

'In that case,' he continued, hastily tucking his shirt in his waist band, 'I'd better get back to Lou.'

Pain shot across Jo's pretty face but she held his gaze. 'Yes, you had, Tommy.'

They glared at each other for a heartbeat them Tommy turned and strode away, wondering just how Jo managed to look so furiously angry and yet so furiously beautiful at the same time.

Chapter Nine

REGGIE HAD JUST sunk his second pint when the Admiral's main door crashed back and Tommy strode into the public house. The handful of men lounging against the bar or perched on stools looked over and, seeing the look of thunder on the younger brother's face, knew their quiet lunchtime drink was over.

With his mouth pulled into a hard line, Tommy strode across the floor to where Reggie was sitting surrounded by a handful of his usual crew.

'I suppose you thought that was funny, did you, Reggie?' he bellowed.

'Come on, Tommy, it was only a bit of a laugh.'

'Well, I'm not bloody laughing, am I?' Tommy yelled, smashing his fist onto the table and making the glasses rattle.

Out of the corner of his eye, Reggie spotted drinkers hastily downing their pints and sloping out of the bar.

Mindful his men were within earshot, Reggie rose to his feet and grabbed his brother's upper arm.

'Let me buy you a drink,' he said, dragging Tommy to the bar.

'What do you want?' asked Reggie.

'Half a bitter shandy,' said Tommy.

Resisting the urge to mock him about having a poof's drink, Reggie beckoned the elderly potman.

'Same again for me, Sam,' said Reggie, flourishing a ten-bob note. 'And half a bitter shandy for Casanova.'

Tommy's eyes narrowed and he loomed over Reggie.

'I tell you, Reggie, I'm this close,' he pinched his thumb and index finger together and shoved it in his face, 'this close, to landing you one, so you crack one more bloody joke and I swear I'll deck you.'

His brother's fury hit Reggie like a right hook to the jaw and he only just stopped himself from stepping back.

The bar fell silent as the two brothers, their noses inches apart, squared up to each other.

Although Reggie and Tommy had fought like dogs in a pit ever since they were small, in a funny sort of way it had solidified their relationship and seen them through their terrible childhood. Tommy had often left Reggie with a bloody nose or a black eye but, being seven years his brother's senior, Reggie had always been the victor. However, Tommy wasn't a stick-thin lad any more, he was all muscle and bone.

Standing toe to toe, Tommy's eyes bore down into him and for the first time in a very long time Reggie felt himself panic.

He held his brother's angry gaze for as long as he could then lowered his eyes.

'Come on, Tommy, don't take on,' he said, putting a brotherly arm around his brother's broad shoulders. 'Don't get all Doris and Ruby on me, and it's only natural for a lad to sow his wild oats but, do yourself a favour, if you don't want to feel the weight of Jerry Brogan's fist in your moosh, I wouldn't try to have it away with his daughter.'

Tommy cut in as Sam returned with their drinks. 'I'm not trying to "have it away" with Jo. Firstly, because she's not that sort of girl and secondly, because I'm hoping to marry her.'

'For Gawd's sake, Tommy,' said Reggie, 'that silly bugger

132

Stan Wheeler got involved with the Brogans by marrying their middle girl and now he's behind bars.'

'He didn't get arrested because he married Cathy Brogan, Reggie,' Tommy said, giving his brother an exasperated look. 'He was arrested for trying to smuggle German spies into London.'

'I know, I know.' Reggie slurped the froth off his pint. 'But having a bunch of Micks as relatives wouldn't have done him any favours with the magistrate, would it? Especially as Jerry Brogan's batty old mother is a bookie's runner for Fat Tony and must spend more time in Arbour Square police station than the desk sergeant.'

'Well, it doesn't matter now, does it?' snapped Tommy. 'Not after your bloody prank.'

A despondent expression turned the corners of Tommy's mouth down. 'I tried to explain to Jo but she wouldn't even listen.'

He took a mouthful of drink.

Thank Gawd for that, thought Reggie as an image of the dozen or so letters the postman had slipped him flashed through his mind.

'Look, Tommy,' said Reggie, forcing a sympathetic expression onto his face, 'I know you're heartbroken and all that but if you ask me I think you've got this all arse about face.'

Tommy raised an eyebrow. 'How do you make that out?'

'Well, you and her were getting serious, like you say,' Reggie said. 'You've got to ask yourself why did she stop writing?'

Tommy frowned. 'I don't know.'

'Well, did you ever think perhaps she stopped writing because she'd taken up with some yokel?'

Tommy's shoulders sagged. 'It did cross my mind.'

'Perhaps she came by to give you the heave-ho,' said Reggie.

Tommy shook his head. 'That makes no sense because if that were the case why would she run crying out of the house when Lou appeared and then give me a full roasting about being a liar when I caught up with her?'

'For Gawd's sake, Tommy, a bird's brain is a jumble of odd ideas at the best of times so who knows what they think and why,' said Reggie.

Tommy gave a heavy sigh and stared into his glass.

'I hate to see you like this, Tommy, especially when there are plenty of pretty little fish swimming around in the sea. There's Lou, for a start,' Reggie continued, hoping to remind him that only a complete tosser turns down a bit of free 'ow's your father. 'She'll take your mind off this Jo girl and ease your balls at the same time.' He grinned. 'I bet you wish you hadn't spent the night on the sofa now, Tommy boy.'

Tommy looked up in horror.

'No, I'm bloody glad I did,' his brother said. 'At least if I do get Jo to listen to me eventually I'll be able to tell her truthfully that I didn't two-time her with Lou.' He glanced up at the Guinness clock behind the bar. 'I'd better go.'

'Go where?'

Tommy shrugged. 'I don't know. Somewhere. Somewhere so I can figure out what to do.'

Downing his drink in one, Tommy put his glass on the bar. With his head hung low and his broad shoulders hunched, he retraced his steps to the door.

Watching his brother as he walked across the bar, Reggie felt an odd mix of relief and frustration. Relief because, although he only knew Jo by sight, it was a fact that all Micks had a fiery temper so she was unlikely to give Tommy the time of day and he would never find out about her missing letters.

He didn't like to see Tommy boy so down in the mouth, though, and if truth be told, he did have a rarely felt niggle of guilt about the whole thing but he'd only stepped in because he wanted to see Tommy get back to being his old roguish self. Truth be told, Sweete Independent Trading, as Reggie liked to think of his little side-lines and schemes, wasn't running as well as it should have been because Tommy wasn't there totting up the orders and payments.

And besides, even though he was a bit lovelorn now, Tommy would get over her, if not with Lou then between some other willing pair of legs, but what really broke Reggie's heart was that after everything he'd taught Tommy about the way of the world, his brother still clung to the stupid notion that being honest was a good thing to be.

Pressing her wet handkerchief to her eyes, Jo waited a moment then took it away and looked back at her red-eyed reflection in the toilet mirror.

Sweet Mary, her eyes still looked like a pair of marshmallows.

It was ten minutes since her argument with Tommy outside the Catholic Club and she was now in the ladies' toilets trying to restore her complexion.

She surveyed her blotchy face again. She dunked the handkerchief under the cold tap and repeated the process once more then opened her handbag.

Taking out her compact she dabbed a bit of powder under her eyes and applied fresh lipstick before returning them and the damp handkerchief to her bag.

Taking a deep breath and hoping the dim light cast by the newly installed regulation 40-watt bulbs would help to disguise her blotchy face, Jo left the toilet and headed for the club's main bar.

Pausing briefly at the door she took another deep breath then, pushing it open, walked in.

From family weddings to the Shamrock League's children's Christmas party, Jo had been in and out of the Catholic Club for as long as she could remember.

Situated around the corner from the church, it had been built fifty years ago and was a square, functional building typical of the Victorian period. Its high windows let in light despite the fine mesh that had been fitted over them to protect the glass from the threat of stray footballs and poorly aimed catapults. Of course, now the windows had the extra protection of gummed tape criss-crossing them to stop shards of broken glass littering the room in the event of an explosion. The faded photos of past club presidents and other notable members that had lined the walls had been put away for safekeeping and in their stead were government posters warning people to carry their gas masks and urging them to dig for victory.

The main hall below the bar was used to host everything from the Brownies, Guides, Cubs and Scouts to Irish dancing classes. The nurses at Munroe House also used the hall to run a baby clinic on Tuesdays. The clinic still ran but, with most of the local children evacuated, many of the children's clubs had disbanded and now the large hall was lined with trestle beds as it had been taken over by the WVS for a relief centre for those bombed out of their houses. Thankfully, even though the flock wallpaper was getting a little tatty and most of the furniture had seen better days, the bar, where Jo was now standing, was much as it had ever been. It was packed, as it was most lunchtimes, with fellow communicants of St Bridget's and St Brendan's who were determined not to let the Luftwaffe interfere with their lunchtime Guinness. However, in addition to the rough-trousered dockers and labourers in donkey jackets, there were also a number of people dressed in various Civil Defence uniforms.

Casting her aching eyes around the room, she spotted her mother sitting in her usual booth to the right of the small stage at the other end from the bar. Unfortunately, Mattie was sitting next to her.

Anger surged up in Jo, setting her head pounding again. If it hadn't been for her bloody sister interfering, Tommy wouldn't have taken up with that trollop.

'Hello, luv,' said a familiar voice behind her.

Blinking away the tears forming in her eyes, Jo turned and smiled up at her father.

Although he'd been out on the wagon that morning collecting shrapnel, shell cases and busted bomb metal from the streets, he was now wearing his khaki Local Defence battle jacket, with his field service cap tucked in the epaulette, ready to go on duty after he'd finished his day's work.

'Hello, Dad,' said Jo.

His soft eyes flickered over her face. 'You all right?'

Resisting the urge to throw herself into his arms and sob, Jo nodded. 'Tired, that's all.'

He gave a hard laugh. 'Aren't we all? Bloody Jerry. What do you want? A lemonade or ginger beer?'

'Gin and tonic?' said Jo.

'When you're twenty-one you can have one but until then, as I'll not be wanting Pete to lose his licence, it'll be a ginger beer or lemonade, miss,' he said.

'Lemonade, please,' she replied.

'That's better.' He winked. 'Now you go over and join your ma, and I'll fetch it to you.'

Jo nodded and wished she hadn't as the pounding headache intensified. Weaving through those standing around the bar, Jo made her way across the room. As she reached her mother's table, Ida looked up.

'There you are,' she said. 'I was just saying to Mattie I wondered what was keeping you.'

'Sorry, Mum, I lost track of the time,' said Jo, feeling her sister's eyes on her.

'Hello, Jo,' said Mattie.

Jo ignored her and sat down.

'There you go,' said her father, placing the tumbler in front of her.

'Thanks,' said Jo, taking her drink to her lips and burying her nose in it.

'Can I get you another one, Mattie?' her father asked.

She put her hand over her glass. 'Not for me, thanks, Dad. I'm going to finish this one and then get a bit of shut-eye before I go back to post.'

'Brandy and orange,' Ida replied, thrusting her empty glass at her husband. 'And make it a double to save yourself a second trip.'

Jerimiah picked up the glass and sauntered back to the bar.

'How was Daisy?' her mother said.

'Daisy?' asked Jo.

'Your friend you popped in to see,' said her mother. 'And did you ask her about war work?'

'Oh, yes, Daisy,' said Jo, the image of Tommy and his floozy replaying again in her mind. 'Yes, she said I should go to the Town Hall and enquire.'

'Oh,' said Ida, looking over Jo's head towards the bar. 'There's Breda O'Conner. I can't wait to see her face when I tell her about the Queen.' She stood up. 'I won't be long.'

She and Mattie sat in silence for a long moment then Jo lowered her gaze and took another sip of her drink.

'Your friend Daisy,' said Mattie.

Jo looked up. 'What about her?'

'Is she the one who lives in Patterson Street?'

'Yes, she is,' said Jo. 'Number twelve, if you must know. Why?'

Mattie raised an eyebrow. 'Oh, no reason except perhaps that a ten-tonner flattened the paint factory at the top end of Patterson Street last night and all the families were evacuated to the rest centre in Red Coat School.'

The pain behind Jo's eyes stabbed like needles as she held her sister's searching gaze. Feeling tears gathering in the corners of her eyes, Jo buried her nose in her glass again.

'Are you all right, Jo?' asked Mattie softly.

'Of course I'm all right,' snapped Jo, lifting her head and gazing defiantly across at her sister.

'It's just that you look a bit red-eyed,' said Mattie.

'There was a lot of dust floating about where the council's clearing the road,' said Jo. 'And I got grit in my eyes, that's all.'

'Where was that? In Patterson Street?' asked Mattie.

Narrowing her eyes, Jo glared at her sister and Mattie glared back.

'I suppose you just tore up the letters I sent you,' she said.

Jo didn't deny it.

'That's a pity,' said Mattie. 'If you'd bothered to read them you'd know why you were evacuated—'

'I know why,' Jo cut in. 'You saw me and Tommy Sweete together so you went running to Mum and told her. Two days later I'm shipped off to some godforsaken dump in Essex and now Tommy's got someone else.'

Mattie gave her a pitying look. 'So it was Tommy not Daisy you went to see and you found him with another woman.'

Again, Jo didn't reply.

'I'm sorry you had to find out that way, Jo.' Mattie sighed. 'But at least now you know the truth and you're not the first woman who's ended up crying into your pillows because of Tommy Swe—'

'I wouldn't be if you hadn't snitched to Mum,' said Jo as tears distorted her vision. 'I trusted you, Mattie, but after what you've done I'll never speak to you again.'

Leaping to her feet, Jo grabbed her handbag and with pain tearing through her like a wide-toothed saw she dashed blindly for the bar door and straight into the rough fabric of a khaki greatcoat.

Jo looked up into a pair of brown eyes so very like her own, and recognised her brother Charlie.

In full battledress, with his field service cap set at an impossibly rakish angle on his clipped black curls, her older brother was a good two inches taller than his father's five-foot-ten but he shared with Jerimiah his square jaw and ready smile.

'Hello, Squirt,' he said in a deep voice, grinning down at her.

She opened her mouth to reply but the words got stuck on the lump in her throat and as his strong arms closed around her, Jo burst into tears.

*

'I still can't believe you're actually here,' said Mattie, as her brother Charlie scraped the last of his fried bread from the plate.

He grinned. 'Me neiver.'

She was sitting at the kitchen table with her feet up on the chair opposite and a cup of tea in her hand while he, with his tie off and shirt unbuttoned, finished off the plate of scrambled egg their mother had insisted he have before doing anything else.

The four o'clock pips had just sounded from the wireless in the next room where the rest of the family were gathered to hear the early-evening news.

It was now three hours after he'd walked into the bar in the Catholic Club and Charlie and the rest of the family were finally home. Mattie's hope of getting a few hours' kip before going on duty at seven had gone but she didn't care. It was good to have her brother home, if only for their mother's sake. It had taken Ida a full twenty minutes before Charlie was able to convince her that he was whole and hearty and that although he missed her home cooking he had, in fact, put on rather than lost weight in the six months since she'd last seen him. Mattie wasn't surprised.

Working on the wagon alongside their father since he was just fourteen had developed Charlie's strength but after six months being part of a six-man gun crew he had added muscle too.

'You're looking well, sis,' he said, his eyes flickering to her swollen stomach and back to her face. 'How far gone are you now?'

'Five months,' she replied.

He raised his eyebrows. 'And you're still running around as an ARP warden.'

'I might as well,' said Mattie. 'I'd be stuck down in the shelter each night anyway so I might as well get two quid a week for it.'

'Surely you don't need the money, not with your husband's pay?' he said, placing his knife and fork together on the empty plate. 'In fact, given that his captain's pay is twice what a poor old gunner like me gets, I'm surprised you're working at all. And why are you still squashed into the front bedroom with Jo instead of living in a nice house in Leyton or Woodford?'

'Because I want my family close by when my time comes,' said Mattie. 'And as far as working goes, I'll have to live on Daniel's money after I have the baby but until then I'll stand on my own two feet, thank you very much.'

Charlie pulled a face. 'You're so like Dad.'

Mattie smiled. 'I'll take that as a compliment.'

'Any news on Daniel?' he asked, picking up his mug of tea.

'I got a postcard from his colonel last week,' said Mattie. 'So at least I know he's still alive.'

Charlie gave her a sympathetic look. 'I'm sure he'll be home soon.'

Mattie forced a smile. 'From your lips to God's ears, as they say around here.'

The door opened and her mother stormed in to the kitchen closely followed by Jo. Ida was wearing her rough hopping clothes under her oldest coat and had her hair tucked under a scarf turban. Jo was also wearing her old clothes but, in her case, it was a pair of serge trousers and a chunky jumper under last year's coat topped with a red beret. Both were carrying rolls of bedding. Ida also carried the battered briefcase with the family's bank books, photo albums and certificates while Jo had a novel and a couple of magazines tucked under her arm.

'You off to the shelter already?' said Mattie.

'We are,' her mother replied. 'I want to make sure that bloody Mrs Hennessey and her snotty kids don't nick our pitch like they did last night,' Ida said. 'You want me to save you a spot, Charlie?'

Charlie shook his head. 'I'll take my chances here with Gran.'

'You'll be as safe as 'ouses then, boy,' said Ida, throwing a sour look over her shoulder. 'Only the good die young.'

Mattie and Charlie exchanged amused looks.

'Right, Jo, get the sandwiches and flask,' said Ida, 'while I load up the pram.'

Their mother strode out of the back door and Jo went into the pantry. She lifted out the scruffy hopping box. Leaning back to balance the weight, she headed after her mother.

'See you later, Jo,' Mattie said.

Jo gave her a narrow-eyed look and left.

Charlie shrugged on his shirt. 'I can understand why you and Cathy are at odds after all that business with Stan and the Nazis, but what's with you and Jo?'

'It's a long story,' she replied.

'I'm sure,' he said, fastening the first button. 'And I'm betting there's a bloke involved.'

Mattie smiled. 'I wouldn't get involved if I were you.'

'I blooming well won't,' he replied. 'I learned to stay out of your, Cathy and Jo's fights years ago, but I hope you sort it out soon.'

'So do I, Charlie,' said Mattie.

The back door opened and Francesca walked in dressed in her navy WAFS uniform. After finishing work at Boardman's at three thirty, when the blackout had come into force, she had gone to the Town Hall for extra fire training.

Her jaw dropped as she saw Charlie.

'Hello, Fran,' he said, grinning at her as he rebuttoned the collar of his shirt tie.

'Charlie,' she said, breathlessly devouring him with her eyes. 'What are you doing here?'

He stood up.

'Is that any way to greet a returning hero?' He stretched his arms wide. 'Come on, give us a hug.'

Gazing up at him, Francesca walked into Charlie's embrace and his arms closed round her. Resting her head on his upper arm and with a look of pure joy on her face, Francesca closed her eyes.

They held each other for a moment then Charlie released her.

'So,' she said, making a play of patting her hair into place, 'what are you doing here?'

'I came up from the south coast with the ack-ack guns,' he replied. 'We were stationed up by Beachy Head outside Eastbourne but now our boys in blue have given the Luftwaffe a pasting and they've turned their attention to the capital, we've been posted to Hackney Marshes. We arrived two weeks ago but what with setting up the guns and all the action each night, I've only just managed to wangle a pass. The top brass has taken over a school as their headquarters and we've been billeted all over Hackney, so it should be easy enough for me to pop down and see you all when I'm not on duty.'

Francesca's eyes shone.

'That will be so nice,' she said, a flush spreading across her cheeks. 'For . . . for your mum, I mean. How long are you home for now?'

'I've got a forty-eight-hour pass,' he replied, tightening

the Windsor knot at his throat. 'But don't worry, Fran, I'll bed down on the sofa so you don't have to shift. I have to say, now Jo and Billy are back the old house is almost splitting at the seams so goodness only knows what you're going to do when Mattie's baby arrives.'

'I'm hoping Dad and Giovanni might be home by then so I'll be moved out once I've found somewhere to rent,' she replied.

'Any news?'

'I had another letter last week from the officer in charge of the appeal panel saying there should be a decision before Christmas,' she replied.

'Bloody hell,' said Charlie, looking at her. 'That's three months off.'

Francesca's shoulders slumped and she hung her head. 'I know.'

'Now, now,' he said. 'Chin up. No one in their right mind would think your dad and Giovanni are spies, even if he's stupid enough to support Arsenal.'

Francesca smiled.

'That's better,' he said. 'Can't have that pretty face of yours looking glum.'

Francesca gazed up at him adoringly and Mattie's heart ached for her.

'Perhaps, Charlie, we should send Mum down to sort it out,' said Mattie.

'Or you, Mat,' he replied with a broad grin. 'You'd put the bejesus up those blooming pen-pushers in the ministry, and no mistake.'

'Oi, watch it,' said Mattie, scowling at him in mock annoyance.

He laughed and Mattie and Francesca joined in.

Charlie lifted his battle jacket from the back of the chair and put it on.

'Where're you off to then?' asked Francesca.

'Round to Stella's,' Charlie replied.

Francesca's happy smile vanished in an instant as pain cut across her face.

'Does she know you're back?' asked Mattie.

Charlie shook his head. 'I'm going to surprise her.' He shrugged on his jacket. 'Have you seen her around?'

Mattie and Francesca exchanged looks.

'Not much,' said Mattie.

'Have you heard from her lately?' asked Francesca, with a desolate look in her lovely brown eyes.

'I've had a couple of letters,' Charlie replied, working his way up the buttons. 'But what with working double shifts in the tyre factory, I bet that fiancée of mine is asleep before her head hits the pillow.'

Her brother was right. After drinking and dancing up West with every Tom, Dick and Harry all night, Stella probably did fall exhausted into her bed each night or, more accurately, each morning.

Mattie looked across at her best friend who was gazing adoringly at Charlie.

'All right, then,' he said, spreading his arms wide, oblivious of Francesca's feelings for him. 'What do you think?'

Francesca smiled at him with love and longing in her eyes.

'Very handsome,' she said, with a tremor in her voice. 'I'm sure Stella will fall faint at your feet when she sees you.'

He grinned, and then taking his field cap from his epaulette, Charlie set it at an angle on his black curls.

He marched to the door but as he grasped the handle he turned back and looked at her.

'By the way, Fran,' he said, smiling at her, 'you look a right treat in that WAFS uniform.'

Chapter Ten

'RIGHT,' SAID REGGIE, yanking on the Bedford's handbrake. 'Wake up, you horrible lot, we're here.'

It was just after dawn on the third Monday in September and he'd just pulled into Shadwell School, which he and Tommy had attended spasmodically as boys.

The place of learning for riverside youngsters was a nondescript late-Victorian building. Like many other schools of that era, it was comprised of three floors with staircases in each corner of the building, and a half-tiled hall on each floor with classrooms running off it. In addition, surrounding the school, there was a high brick wall with wrought-iron spikes running along the top to keep pupils in, strangers out and the lead on the roof.

However, when the pupils had been evacuated a year ago the Local Authority had commandeered the building and turned it into ARP Post 7, the Wapping and Shadwell sub-division of the Stepney Civil Defence.

Jumping down from the cab, Reggie strode around to the back of the vehicle and knocked the bolts from the tailgate.

'Come on, you buggers,' he said, pulling it down. 'I ain't got all day.'

Jimmy jumped down from the back. He was followed by Fred and then Lofty, the best cat burglar this side of the City, who could pick any lock known to man, and Ugly Smith, with a face so long it looked as if it were about to slip off.

After Fred and Jimmy, Ugly was Reggie's first choice for any job.

Dusting themselves down after their half-mile drive from the yard, they passed each other cigarettes.

Tommy, who had sat in the passenger seat for the entire journey without speaking a word, came around to the back of the van, wearing the same miserable expression that he'd had glued to his face for the past week.

'Come on, lover boy, cheer up,' said Reggie, raising his voice to include the rest of the crew in the conversation.

The men milling about waiting laughed.

Tommy gave his brother another blistering look but didn't rise to the bait.

Taking a packet of Senior Service from his pocket, Reggie lit one.

'So,' he said, striking the match, 'what do you think of The Sweete Brigade?'

'Where did you get the boiler suits and boots from?' asked Tommy, casting a disinterested eye over the assembled men.

'Some bloke up Watford way,' Reggie replied, shaking the match out and blowing smoke skywards. 'They're military quality so good schmutter. I don't know why you didn't want one.'

Tommy raised an eyebrow.

'I got Olive to cut out all the labels so they can't be traced,' continued Reggie.

'Reggie,' said Tommy, giving him that don't-be-a-fucking-idiot look of his, 'the ARP-issue rescue uniform is grey. They're Air Force blue!'

'No one will notice,' said Reggie. 'And you'd look a bloody sight smarter in new overalls than you do in that washed-out bit of rag you're wearing.'

Tommy regarded him coolly. 'We should report in.'

Turning, he started to walk towards the school's main door but Reggie caught his arm.

'How long you going to carry on moping after this Brogan girl?' Reggie asked as his brother turned back.

'Until I figure out a way of getting her back,' Tommy replied.

'Bugger me, Tommy, why don't you just forget about her?' said Reggie. 'After all, you've got Lou still as hot as mustard for you and, with your bloody looks, when you've done with her you can pull a dozen more.'

'How to deal with women the Reginald Sweete way.' Tommy gave a hard laugh. 'Thanks for the brotherly advice but I'm big enough to make my own decision as far as Jo's concerned. Now you and your bloody pretty boys can stay out here all morning if you like but I'm going in.'

Pulling away, he continued towards the school.

'You should take my advice, Tommy boy,' Reggie shouted after him. ''Cos I ain't the one who has to hold me own prick at night.'

Fighting the urge to argue with his brother, Tommy continued towards the infants' doorway, which was Post 7's main entrance. The asphalt playground where he'd once kicked a football around was now a car park filled with a hotchpotch of lorries, vans and private vehicles marked with the ARP designation. Along with the various larger vehicles there were also half a dozen messengers' bicycles in the rack, and parked next to them was an old GPO van and a 1930 Ford Model Y. Both had red crosses daubed on their sides to indicate that they were Post 7's ambulances, while their mismatched wheels had been painted white to aid visibility in the blackout.

At the far end of the yard were two decrepit-looking lorries: one a Scammell Mechanical Horse and the other a Morris 2 farm truck. Both were loaded with picks, shovels and brace beams, indicating that the lorries belonged to Post 7's two heavy recovery teams.

Walking through the brown-and-cream-tile-clad corridor into the hall, Tommy barely recognised the space he'd known as a youngster.

The educational posters, with their images of British trees and flowers, and the colourful maps of the Empire had vanished and in their place were instructions on what to do in a gas attack, a print of enemy aircraft silhouettes and reminders to check the blackout and not to waste water. On the stage, where Tommy had once received his prize for being top of the class, was a massive desk with black, green and red telephones sitting on it. Behind the desk were half a dozen blackboards with the telephone numbers of all the local hospitals, fire stations and undertakers chalked on them. In addition, there was a waxed map of Wapping and Stepney pinned on the wall, with specific areas marked out by heavy black lines.

In front of the stage, the teachers' desks had been dragged out of the classrooms and now various members of the Civil Defence service were sitting around them. The air raid wardens were gathered around the large desk beneath the window, while a little way along from them the ambulance crew were checking through the first-aid boxes that had been laid out on a refectory table.

Clustered around the school's blackened pot-bellied boiler were an assortment of armchairs. There were a couple of coffee tables too with a variety of magazines and used coffee mugs on them. This area was occupied by men from the gas and electric companies. Dressed in their buff-coloured overalls and with their hobnail boots resting on a convenient coffee table, they were enjoying a quiet smoke before the next call-out. Dotted amongst them were a handful of spotty boys who were playing a noisy game of cards.

As Tommy took in the hive of activity, Reggie and his crew came in behind him. The room fell silent as everyone looked their way.

Muscling past him, Reggie marched in to the middle of the room.

'All right, playmates,' he said, looking around. 'Who's in charge here?'

'I am,' replied a high-pitched voice from amongst the blackboards.

Tommy looked up to see his old Scout leader Cyril Potter, resplendent in black ARP battle dress and a polished tin helmet, standing at the front of the stage.

Cyril, who was probably in his late fifties, had short arms, greying ginger hair and a face like a cherub blowing up a balloon. In addition, he had deep-set eyes, which looked unnaturally enormous as he stared out at the world through the strong magnification of his spectacle lenses.

He studied Reggie for a moment then, tucking his officer's stick under his arm, marched down the stage steps and across to them.

He stopped just in front of Reggie.

'I'm the appointed senior Civil Defence warden in charge of this post,' he said, drawing himself up to his full height of five foot six. 'And I'm guessing you're the new heavy rescue squad.'

'Reggie Sweete and his merry men reporting for duty, Admiral,' said Reggie, snapping to attention and giving the senior ARP warden an exaggerated salute.

The men behind Tommy sniggered and a flush coloured Potter's cheeks. 'We're not part of the military so Mr Potter will suffice.' His gaze flickered over Reggie's men. 'There's supposed to be ten in a crew.'

'There is,' said Reggie. 'But Squeaky's not all the ticket this morning.'

'He's unwell?' said Potter.

'He went a bit heavy on the sauce last night but he'll be in later,' Reggie explained.

'Well, I hope he won't make a habit of it,' said Potter.

'Don't worry he won't, Colonel,' said Reggie. 'He only drinks when there's a y in the day.'

There was another titter of laughter from behind Tommy and the muscle under Potter's right eye started to twitch.

'What do you want us to do, Mr Potter?' asked Tommy.

'Firstly, you and your crew need to familiarise yourselves with the area,' said Cyril.

'Well, seeing as how we all live hereabouts that won't take long, will it, lads?' said Reggie.

The men muttered their agreement.

'However,' continued Cyril, 'as you're one of the HR crews who've been drafted in urgently you'll have to learn on the job but if you have a chat with my second in command, Mrs McCarthy, she'll be able to fill you in on the basics of our little operation here.'

'Right you are, Field Marshal,' said Reggie, giving him another comic salute. 'But mind if we have a cuppa first?'

Cyril blinked rapidly and the flush on his cheeks returned. 'Well, I really think—'

'Oi, sweethearts,' Reggie called to a group of women ARP wardens queueing in front of the school kitchen hatch, 'it's your lucky day; the cavalry have arrived so be a darling and pour me and the lads a cup of Rosie Lee.'

The women nudged each other and giggled.

With his crew following in his wake, Reggie sauntered passed Cyril and over to the WVS refreshment station.

The muscle under Cyril's eyes started twitching again.

'Don't worry about them, Mr Potter, I'll sort them out,' said Tommy. 'Now, where can I find Mrs McCarthy?'

Reggie's laughter filled the hall as he and his crew joked with the handful of women getting their breakfast.

'On the stage.' Taking off his glasses, Cyril rubbed the lenses vigorously. 'She's chalking up tonight's patrol rota.'

Leaving Reggie and the rest of the team chatting up the bevy of women at the other end of the hall, Tommy took the half-dozen steps to the top of the stage two at a time and made his way past the side curtains to where a woman in a black ARP warden's uniform was crouched down as she wrote on the central blackboards fixed to the back wall.

'Excuse me, Mrs McCarthy,' he said. 'I'm part of the new HR crew assigned here and . . .' Resting her hands on the chair beside her, the woman started to ease herself up. Tommy stepped forward. 'Let me help you.'

He offered her a hand and she took it.

For a split second Tommy had the impression it was Jo on the floor in front of him until the woman turned and he found himself face to face with her very pregnant older sister Mattie.

'Thanks,' she said, putting her hands in the small of her back as she straightened up. 'It's a long way down in my condition.'

He'd not seen her for some time and he'd forgotten how much Jo looked like her, even down to the sprinkling of freckles across her nose.

As she recognised him her eyes narrowed.

'Hello, Mattie,' he said flatly.

'Tommy Sweete,' she said, looking more than a little unsettled. 'What are you doing here?'

'As I said, I'm part of the new heavy rescue squad allocated here,' he replied.

'Are you?' she asked.

'Yes, I am, along with my brother and the men he employs at the yard,' he said. 'Mr Potter said you'd be able to give me a rundown of how things are run around here.'

She glanced past him to where his brother and his men were now lounging in armchairs by the boiler.

'They seem to have made themselves comfortable,' she said.

'Don't worry about them,' said Tommy. 'I'll make sure they do what's expected of them.'

She looked less than convinced but she beckoned him forward. 'Follow me.'

She headed over to the large map fixed to the side wall of the stage and Tommy followed.

'Post 7 covers all of Wapping, Stepney and Shadwell. We have three dozen air raid wardens who are responsible for getting people to their allocated shelters during an air raid. The wardens are also in charge of keeping order in the shelters. There are also three gas decontamination parties, four auxiliary fire teams, who tackle a blaze until the fire engine arrives, and four light rescue teams to patch up the walking wounded and get them to rest centres. Finally, we have six heavy rescue teams, of which you are one,' she said.

They moved to the main blackboard fixed at the back of the stage. It had a grid marked on it with dates along the top and the ARP teams down the side.

'There are three heavy rescue squads on duty at any one time. You're Blue Squad and your duties will be chalked up here.' She pointed to where the team's name was written on the left-hand side of the board. 'As you can see, for the next three days you're on early-day duty – that's eight a.m. to eight p.m.; then three days on late-day duty, which is two p.m. to two a.m.; then you have a day off then two days of early duty followed by seven days on nights, which is eight p.m. to eight a.m.. Although to be honest, in the past three weeks, all the crews have stayed on until all civilians have been accounted for.'

Tommy nodded.

'And that's more or less it,' she concluded. 'If there's anything you're not sure of just ask me or Mr Potter.'

'Thanks,' said Tommy. 'And for taking the time.'

He gave her a friendly smile, which she didn't return.

'I heard you were going to volunteer for the army,' she said. 'But I suppose that was just another lie you told Jo.'

'I am,' Tommy replied. 'But I've got some things to sort out first.'

'Well, if one of those things is getting back with my sister,' Mattie replied, 'forget it, after the way you've betrayed her.'

Tommy frowned. 'Well, firstly, Mattie, for your information, I didn't betray Jo and secondly, perhaps if you hadn't had her packed off to the country none of this would have happened.'

'I had nothing to do with Jo's evacuation,' snapped Mattie. 'And although it pains me to see my little sister so heartbroken at least she's found out the truth about you,

Tommy Sweete.' Picking up her warden's bag, she slung it across her. 'Now,' she said, giving him a tight icy smile, 'in case you haven't noticed, there's a war on so if you'd excuse me, I've got things to do.'

Tommy stepped aside and Mattie swept past him.

'And I'd be grateful if you could give Jo my love when you see her,' he called after her as she waddled to the steps at the side of the stage.

Chapter Eleven

PULLING DOWN THE hem of her skirt, Jo recrossed her legs and glanced up at the clock above the door where the last volunteer had entered some fifteen minutes ago.

'Taking their blooming time, aren't they?' said the young woman with bouncy blonde hair sitting next to her.

It was ten o'clock on the last Thursday in September and she was sitting in the LCC Eastern Division's ambulance headquarters in Homerton, just around the corner from the Fever Hospital. It had been just two weeks since she'd presented herself at Stepney Town Hall and filled in the form to join the ambulance service. The invitation for her to attend an interview had arrived in the afternoon post on Tuesday so she'd damp-sponged her best suit, unrolled her only pair of stockings from the tissue paper and spent an hour taming her wayward curls into something approximating tidy before getting a tram to Stratford Broadway. She'd walked the two miles across Hackney Marshes to reach the Victorian double-storey ambulance station where she was now waiting.

'I suppose they have to be thorough,' said Jo.

'Gillian West,' said the young woman, offering Jo her hand.

'Jo Brogan,' Jo replied, taking it. 'Where you from?'

'Bow Common, you?'

'Wapping.' Jo yawned.

'I didn't get a wink of sleep last night either,' said Gillian. 'It was bad, weren't it?'

158

Truthfully, with German planes raining high-explosive bombs and incendiaries down on them from dusk to dawn, it had been bad for the past nineteen nights. However, Jo, like everyone else huddled in shelters across London, was learning to survive on the odd half an hour's sleep between the waves of bombers. To be honest, it wasn't the Luftwaffe robbing her of sleep but that bloody two-timing Tommy Sweete. And it was just so unfair. After the way he'd behaved she would never forgive him but annoyingly, even with the image of him with that half-dressed tart fixed in her mind, somehow the memory of his arms around her and his mouth pressing onto hers still sent excitement coiling in the pit of her stomach.

The door opened and the previous applicant came out, clutching a large, manila envelope. She hurried off. There was a pause then the door opened again. This time a middle-aged woman, wearing an expensive navy suit, polished brogues, and a close-fitting hat, stepped out.

Glancing over her half-rimmed spectacles she scanned down the clipboard she was holding.

'Miss Brogan,' she said, looking up.

Jo stood up.

'Follow me.'

She was led into a room containing a long table behind which sat a man and a woman.

The woman who'd ushered her in indicated that Jo should take the vacant chair placed centrally in front of the interview panel, so Jo sat down while the woman joined her companions on the other side of the desk. Tucking her knees together and placing her handbag on the floor, Jo studied the three people in front of her.

The man on the panel was probably her father's age. He had a long thin face and was completely bald except for a couple of tufts of steel-grey hair over his ears. He was dressed in a black uniform with a white sash that went diagonally from his right shoulder to his left hip, his jacket had white chevrons on his right sleeve and sewn on each shoulder was a metal badge with the St John Ambulance symbol on it. Sitting on his left was a scrubbed-faced woman wearing a matron's navy uniform with a starched white cap pinned to her short, mouse-brown hair.

'Good morning, Miss Brogan,' said the man sitting opposite her. 'I'm Captain Brinton, senior training officer for the London St John Ambulance, and this,' he gestured towards the woman who'd called her in, 'is Mrs Willis, coordinator of voluntary and full-time ambulance personnel for the eastern district.' He then turned to his other side and said, 'This is Sister Smith, the senior nursing officer for ARP emergency services in East London.'

'Good morning,' said Jo, smiling at them.

'Now, Miss Brogan,' Captain Brinton continued, glancing down at the pile of papers in front of him, 'I can see from your application form that you went to Coburn Grammar School for Girls and left in June having successfully gained your school matriculation certificate.'

'Yes,' said Jo. 'I was going to secretarial college but after Dunkirk I was evacuated out of London with my younger brother.'

'It also says you passed the St John's Intermediate certificate with merit,' said Sister Smith.

'Yes,' said Jo.

'And,' said Mrs Willis, consulting her notepad, 'you've been working in a general store in Essex over the summer and driving their delivery van.'

'Yes,' said Jo. 'Mr Garfield, the owner of the store, showed me how to work the gears and brake and sat with me for a couple of days but then let me go out on my own.'

Captain Brinton's straggly eyebrows rose. 'This shopkeeper allowed you to drive his shop van around the countryside on a provisional licence?'

Jo nodded. 'I would have taken my test but they've been suspended for the duration of the war so he had a word with the local police constable so they knew I had his permission.'

'And did you ever hit anything?' asked Miss Smith.

'No,' laughed Jo. 'Although I did scatter the odd pigeon or two and occasionally trimmed some of the hedgerows.'

'Which is why, presumably,' said Captain Brinton, 'you applied to be a driver rather than ambulance crew.'

'Yes,' said Jo. 'I know I haven't got as much experience as some but I'm very keen.'

Captain Brinton's small mouth pulled into a tight bud. 'I'm sure you are, Miss Brogan, but—'

'Please, give me a chance,' cut in Jo, edging forward on her seat. 'I know the emergency rescue services are stretched to the limit and I want to do my bit like everyone else.'

The two women on the panel exchanged looks and then Sister Smith leaned in and whispered something to the man between them. He looked dubious and turned to Mrs Willis. There was some more whispering as Mrs Willis jabbed her finger at Jo's application and both women nodded.

Mr Brinton paused for a moment as if considering their words then he placed his hand flat in front of him and looked across at Jo.

'The ambulance service is, as you rightly say, Miss Brogan, stretched to the limits and because of that we are happy to accept your application into the ambulance service but as an ambulance assistant to work alongside an experienced driver,' he said. 'However, because you have a recognised first-aid certificate we can allocate you immediately and you can undertake further training as you go along. The pay is £2 3s a week, the same as the other emergency ARP services, and if you'd like to take up the post then—'

'Yes. Yes, I would,' said Jo. 'And I could start tomorrow.'

The severe lines of Sister Smith's face lifted a little. 'Monday will do, Miss Brogan.'

'There'll be a confirmation put in the post to you tonight, formally offering you a post,' continued Captain Brinton. 'And you can bring your acceptance letter with you when you report for duty at the St Katherine's Ambulance Station on Monday. All the details regarding what time and who you're to report to will be sent with our acceptance letter.'

'Also because of the problems some ambulance crew are having finding their way around unfamiliar streets, we have decided to allocate you to the Ancillary Ambulance Station in St Katherine's School, Stepney.' Mrs Willis smiled. 'Have you any questions?'

Jo stared at them for a moment and then gathered her handbag from the floor.

'No,' she said, rising to her feet. 'None at all. And thank you. Thank you very much.'

Hooking her handbag over her arm, Jo turned and headed for the door, happy in the knowledge that if she had to spend the night awake, after Monday it would be for a much better reason than Tommy-bloody-Sweete.

'Only me,' called Jo as she walked through her sister Cathy's back door.

'I'm just changing Peter's nappy,' Cathy called from the front room. 'Put the kettle on and I'll be with you in two shakes.'

Closing the door, Jo took off her coat and hooked it on the back of the door. After fetching the kettle from the stove, she carried it to the sink. Holding it under the tap, she gazed through the window at the Anderson sitting squarely in the middle of her sister's small back garden. Having filled the kettle, she set it back on the hob and lit the gas under it before sitting at the table and flicking her way through the copy of *Woman's Realm* that had been left lying on the breadbin. She'd just got to an article explaining how you could make a stylish skirt from a pair of men's trousers, when her sister came in carrying baby Peter.

Cathy was wearing an old dress covered by a wrap-around apron, and her golden hair was captured in a scarf with a knot at the front. Although it was the collective uniform of every housewife who spent their days sweeping and scrubbing the house, on Cathy the tied apron emphasised her narrow waist, which, as far as Jo could judge, was almost back to its pre-baby size, even if the rest of her was still a little more curvy.

'Who's this then, Peter, come to see you?' she asked her four-month-old son. 'It's Auntie Jo,' she continued, answering her own question.

'Hello, young man,' said Jo, making a happy face at her bemused-looking nephew. 'And look at you, getting bigger every time I see you.'

She tickled his tummy with her finger but young Peter's solemn expression remained.

Cathy planted a kiss on her infant son's downy head. 'Isn't he just like his dad?'

'The image of him,' said Jo.

He certainly was. Stan never understood a joke either.

'Can I have cuddle?' she asked.

'Be my guest,' said Cathy, handing him to Jo. 'Do you want a cuppa, Mrs Wheeler?' she called to her mother-in-law who was sitting in her chair by the fire in the front room.

'If you're making one,' came the reply.

The whistle started to rattle and splutter so Cathy lifted the kettle off the heat and filled the teapot.

Jo tucked Peter on to her hip and cuddled him to her. He sat there staring at her for a moment then his chin began to wobble. He twisted in Jo's arms to look at his mother who was making the tea and then started grizzling.

'Now, now, Master Wheeler, we can't have that, can we?' said Jo, rocking back and forth.

'He's tired,' said Cathy, popping the lid on the teapot to brew. 'Give him here and if you pour the tea and bring it through I'll go and tuck him in his pram.'

She took Peter back. Finding his thumb, he rested his head on his mother's shoulder.

'There's some biscuits in the tin if you want a couple,' Cathy called over her shoulder as she carried her son through to the front room.

Jo quickly set out the crockery and the tin with flowers painted on the lid on a tray then after giving the pot a quick stir she carried the whole lot through to the front lounge where the sounds of the BBC band playing 'Pennies from Heaven' filled the room.

Mrs Wheeler was sitting huddled in several shawls by the fire with her slippered feet up on a low stool and her knitting on her lap.

Violet Wheeler was probably a decade older than Jo's mother, and favoured the sombre colours and corseted shape of the pre-Great War fashions. Today was no exception as she was wearing an ankle-length brown dress with a high collar and tight cuffs.

'Good morning, Mrs Wheeler,' said Jo as she set the tray on the coffee table in front of the fire. 'How are you?'

'Never without pain, but I mustn't grumble,' Stan's mother replied. 'I was just telling her,' she glanced over at Cathy leaning over the pram in the corner, 'that she ought to put him out in the yard so he can get some air in his lungs.'

'Fog don't you mean,' Cathy replied. 'It's almost a pea-souper out there and it's damp.'

Mrs Wheeler tutted and was about to speak but Jo stepped in.

'Sugar, Mrs Wheeler?' she asked, standing poised with a spoon.

'Two, if I may,' the old woman replied.

'None for me,' said Cathy, rocking the pram. 'I'm saving my sugar rations for Christmas.'

Mrs Wheeler tutted again. 'How many times must I tell you? All this stupid rationing will be over once the Germans get here.'

Cathy gave her mother-in-law a sharp look, which the older woman completely ignored.

'And then,' she continued, jabbing a crooked finger at Cathy, 'it'll be your sister and that Jew-loving husband of hers who will be in jail and not my Stan—'

She was cut off mid-sentence by her grandson's scream.

'For goodness' sake,' shouted Mrs Wheeler, 'can't you keep that child quiet, girl? All he does day and night is cry.'

'He's a baby!' said Cathy, picking Peter up again and rocking him in her arms. 'I'm sure your precious son cried just as much when he was this age.'

'I can assure you he never.'

Grasping the arms of her chair, Mrs Wheeler heaved herself to her feet and, taking her walking stick from its resting place in the hearth, hobbled to the door.

She paused and glared across the room at Cathy as she opened it. 'Because I was a much better mother!'

With her stick tapping on the hall lino she swept out, slamming the door behind her.

Peter, who had just started to drift off in his mother's arms, jumped and started crying again. Tears welled up in Cathy's eyes.

'Right, give him to me, Cath,' said Jo, walking over to her sister. 'I'll get him settled while you drink your tea.'

Cathy handed her son over and taking her mug from the tray slumped in the sofa under the window.

Popping Peter back in his pram, Jo tucked his blue crochet blanket tightly around him. She grasped the pram's handlebar and rolled it back and forth. The baby found his thumb almost immediately and, within a few rocks, his delicate eyelids fluttered down.

Jo sat down on the opposite end of the sofa from her sister and blew across the top of her cup.

'Now that the old bag's gone,' said Cathy, 'let's talk about something else. How did you get on?'

Putting on a mockingly superior expression, Jo dusted her shoulders with her fingertips. 'You are looking at the London Ambulance's latest recruit.'

'Well done,' said Cathy. 'Although I knew they'd take you, what with your grammar school certificate and everything.'

'They won't let me drive yet but . . .'

As they drank their tea, Jo told her sister about her interview.

'Oh, I do envy you,' said Cathy when she'd done. 'I wish I was out there doing something for the war effort night after night rather than stuck in that smelly hole out the back with old misery guts wailing in the bunk above me.'

'Well, you can,' said Jo. 'There are dozens of adverts for volunteers needed in the WVS canteens and rest centres. Mum's just joined.'

'Mum?' said Cathy, unable to hide her surprise.

'Yes,' said Jo. 'I think she took the Queen's words about everyone doing their bit as a royal command and has signed for the housewife service. She is now Mafeking Terrace's official WVS person. She's even got a badge and an armband and is talking about getting a uniform too.'

'What does she have to do?' asked Cathy.

'Make tea and look after people after an air raid,' Jo replied. 'And generally, keep an eye on what's going on in the street.'

Cathy laughed. 'So what she does anyway.'

'Pretty much,' agreed Jo.

Her sister pulled a face. 'I'd rather do something that would get me away from Stan's mother.'

'Well, the WVS have free nursery places where you could leave Peter for a few hours while you give a hand,' Jo suggested.

Cathy glanced at the pram. 'Stan's mother would probably have something to say about me leaving him.'

'To be honest, Cathy,' said Jo, 'from what I can tell, she's going to have something to say whatever you do or don't do, so you might as well do what you please.'

Her sister's sad expression lifted a little. 'You're right, Jo. Peter will be well over seven months after Christmas so I'll pop down and see if there's something I could do for a couple of hours to help out.' She laughed. 'Who knows, we might even end up working together.'

167

Jo pulled a face. 'As long as we don't get posted with old bossy boots, Mattie. It's bad enough having to put up with her at home without having to see her at work, too.'

'It won't matter if we are,' said Cathy. 'She's town hall ARP while you're LCC ambulance so she can't tell you what to do and, with a bit of luck, what with her marshalling the crowds down in the shelters and you dashing around the streets picking up casualties, I doubt you'll run into each other very often. And don't forget she's five months' gone so will have to stop work in a month anyhow.'

'You're right,' said Jo. 'I bet I don't even notice she's there.'

Cathy took a sip of tea. 'Jo, I didn't like to ask in front of Mum, but what have you fallen out with her for, anyway?'

'It was her fault Mum sent me off to live with the yokels in Essex,' said Jo.

'Was it?'

'Yes,' said Jo. 'She caught me and Tommy Sweete in Glasshouse Street shelter an—'

'You were knocking about with Tommy Sweete!' gasped Cathy, her eyes wide with horror.

'Yes,' she squeaked. 'I'm surprised Mum didn't tell you.'

'I'm not,' said Cathy. 'Having your daughter become one of the Sweete brothers' conquests isn't something you want to talk about even to your family.'

Jo felt her cheeks grow warm.

'She caught us having a kiss and a cuddle, Cathy, not having it off,' said Jo. 'But even so, she shouldn't have dobbed me in it with Mum. You wouldn't have, would you?'

'Er, no,' said Cathy. 'No, course I wouldn't have, Jo, I would never do such a thing, and Mattie shouldn't have done either. I don't blame you for not speaking to her but even so . . .'

The look of horror returned to her sister's face. 'You're not still—'

'No, I'm not,' cut in Jo, hoping Cathy wouldn't ask about the details.

'Thank goodness,' sighed Cathy, placing her hand on her chest in relief. 'Those Sweete brothers are nothing but bad news.'

'So everyone says,' said Jo, trying to sound as though she agreed.

'That Reggie's been in and out of prison more times than you've had hot dinners,' her sister continued. 'And no one would be surprised if Tommy followed in his footsteps.'

Lowering her gaze, Jo took a mouthful of tea.

'So, Cathy,' she said, putting her cup back precisely in the middle of its saucer, 'your turn now. Where is Stan if he's not in the army?'

Cathy took a deep breath. 'In prison—'

'Prison!'

'Yes,' said her sister. 'For treason. But it's all Mattie's fault. It's her fault my poor Stan hasn't even seen his son yet and I had to spend my first wedding anniversary all alone.'

'No,' gasped Jo. 'I knew Stan had been in some sort of trouble, Cath,' said Jo, 'but I didn't realise . . .'

'Well, you wouldn't have, would you, as you and Billy were away when it all blew up, but it all happened the same weekend I got taken in to have young Peter,' Cathy replied. 'And having your other half marched away in handcuffs isn't something you broadcast. Thankfully, the judge saw that Stan didn't really understand what he was getting into so let him off but, as Stan was technically guilty of treason, the court couldn't very well just let him go. Instead, the judge gave him the option of being sent to prison for three years or serving his sentence in the services, so he chose the army. He won't be allowed leave but I can visit twice a year. I'm hoping to take Peter with me for a Christmas visit. If it wasn't for Mattie's ruddy husband my poor Stan wouldn't be—'

She stopped and pressed her lips together.

'What's this husband of Mattie's got to do with it all?' asked Jo.

'I can't say,' her sister replied.

'At least tell me who he is,' said Jo.

'I can't,' said Cathy, taking a sip of tea. 'Because Gran dragged me down to St Bridget's and St Brendan's and made me swear on the cross I wouldn't breathe a word about what happened to anyone.'

Jo pulled a face. 'It all sounds very mysterious, but I have to say, Cathy, when I got Mum's letter telling me Mattie'd married some chap called McCarthy and she was in the family way, you could have knocked me down with a feather. Especially as the last bloke she was walking out with was that nice Christopher who worked in the bank.'

'Nice! Christopher! I—' Cathy clamped her mouth shut and pressed her lips together.

'What?'

'I'm sorry, Jo,' said Cathy. 'Although I'll never forgive Mattie for what she's done, I wouldn't want the murder of innocent people on my conscience. You know: "Careless Talk Costs Lives".'

Chapter Twelve

SLINGING HIS CANVAS kitbag across him, Tommy picked up his keys and the loose change from his mantelshelf and, closing his bedroom door behind him, trotted down the stairs and out of the front door.

It was just after 3 p.m. on Friday and he was heading off for his end-of-week pie and mash, but before then he had another errand to run.

Turning towards the river, Tommy stretched his legs and within a few minutes found himself in Commercial Road. Dodging between the lorries, he continued down Cannon Street Road until he reached Cable Street. Turning East, Tommy headed for the double-fronted Town Hall.

The building housing Stepney's municipal government was a square, Victorian four-storey structure with a grand staircase leading up to a pair of solid front doors. However, now a year after war had been declared, its imperial grandeur was tempered by the criss-crossed tapes on its long stately windows and the sandbags stacked against the basement window, where the area Civil Defence headquarters were housed. In addition, to save it from the attention of the Luftwaffe, it had silver barrage balloons anchored by tensile cables floating overhead. However, it wasn't the nerve centre of the public services that Tommy was heading for but the more unassuming building next to it, St George's public library.

Taking the steps two at a time, Tommy pushed open the door and strolled into the echoing hall. Striding past the reference room to his left, where half a dozen roughly dressed men pored over the late editions of the national newspapers, he headed straight up the grey mottled staircase to the floor above. Through the open door to the children's library, Friday-evening story time was in full swing, with Miss Green perched on a chair amidst a sea of enraptured young faces. Tommy smiled, remembering himself, bare-foot and dressed in rags sitting at the feet of the children's old librarian, Miss Farthing, when he was seven.

He'd discovered Friday-evening story time when, as a small lad, he'd ducked into the library as a way of evading the police who were after him for swiping a hot bagel from Mosher's market stall and he'd been a regular visitor to St George's ever since.

Now, placing his palm on the brass plate worn smooth by countless hands, he pushed open the half-glazed door to the main collection and walked in. There were a handful of people browsing the shelves and a couple glanced over briefly as the door swung closed behind him but then their attention returned to their reading matter.

As you'd expect, the main area of Stepney's central library was lined with tall wooden cases stacked with books. The multitude of closely packed paper and cardboard housed in orderly, alphabetical rows absorbed sound and gave the room a muted tone. The calm atmosphere was further enhanced by the shades being pulled down over the top sections of the criss-crossed taped window to stop the sunlight fading the colours of the dust jackets.

Two clerks stood on either side of the polished mahogany U-shaped desk in the middle of the room, one checking books in and the other stamping them out. Ranged behind them were four light-wood cabinets with rows of small drawers that housed the index cards of the library books, which were sorted by author and subject.

Tommy scanned the room until he spotted the person he wanted to see in the far corner.

Opening his bag, Tommy delved in and pulled out the three books he'd taken out the month before and put them on the counter. The assistant, a pretty-looking young girl with dark hair, red lips and a pair of spectacles perched on the end of her nose, opened the front cover and found its corresponding buff marker.

'They're a week overdue,' she said, handing him his tickets.

'What's the damage?' he asked.

'Threepence,' she replied.

Tommy dropped the coins in the box on the counter then slipping his tickets in his trouser pocket, strolled over to where St George's senior librarian was stacking books into their allotted places on the shelves.

'Afternoon,' he said, stopping just behind him.

Tapping a book into place, Mr Grossman turned around.

Slightly built with hunched shoulders and thinning colourless hair, and dressed as always in a single-breasted grey suit with leather elbow patches, David Grossman didn't look any different from the first time Tommy had seen him a little over twelve years ago.

Then, he and his wife were newly arrived from Austria, both with accents so thick that the locals struggled to understand. This didn't stop the elderly couple from setting to work. Mrs Grossman was now the local coordinator placing newly arrived Jewish children in families while Mr Grossman was a senior librarian and also the local councillor for the East Smithfield ward.

Some said he was a professor from Vienna while others swore he was a scientist from Munich, but whoever he was, having secured the post of librarian, David Grossman then set up a number of evening clubs in the library for the local children. These included nature, science and reading clubs and pretty soon the junior library was filled each evening with boys and girls of all ages. Hard-pressed parents, who up until then had to leave children to fend for themselves after school closed, loved the clubs as it stopped their offspring from getting into mischief and coming to the attention of the police. But it was four years ago, when Mr Grossman stopped one of Mosley's thugs from throwing a young Jewish girl through a shop window during the Battle of Cable Street, that the locals really took him to their hearts.

Now, although his accent had mellowed, his all-encompassing passion for his fellow man had not, and his latest initiative was making a selection of library books available in the public air raid shelters.

'Tommy,' he said, his long face lighting up with pleasure. 'I was hoping you'd stop by. I've been saving something for you. Come.'

Putting the books he was holding in his arms on the shelf, the elderly librarian shuffled off towards his office at the far end of the room.

Tommy followed and soon found himself in the ten-by-ten room containing a small desk and two decrepit chairs, all three of which were surrounded by books stacked to waist-height and topped off with newspapers.

'Sit, sit,' Mr Grossman said, waving towards the nearest chair.

Dropping his kitbag on the floor, Tommy lowered his frame into the old seat, which creaked worryingly.

'I'm sure I have it here somewhere,' Mr Grossman said, rummaging around amongst the papers strewn across his desk. 'Ah, here it is.' He flourished a newspaper cutting. 'It was in the *Telegraph*. It's a crossword and mathematical competition set by some lord or another to boost morale and I thought of you straight away. It's open to anyone and—'

'To be honest,' Tommy replied, 'after spending the past week shifting rubble, I'm having trouble remembering my own name let alone working out some toff's puzzle.'

Mr Grossman rolled his eyes. 'Oy vey! I haven't seen you since you started; but tell me, how are you getting on in the heavy rescue squad?'

Tommy gave a hard laugh. 'Every bone in my body is screaming and I feel like I could sleep for a month but,' he raked his fingers through his hair, 'I'm no better or worse than anyone else.'

'One of my regular Mills and Boon ladies who works in the WVS canteen at the Cubit Town depot said it's been bad,' said Mr Grossman.

Tommy gave him a wry smile. 'That's one way to describe it, but "sheer hell" would be more accurate. Our first job on Monday was in Rope Walk Terrace. A high-explosive bomb had collapsed all the houses on one side of the street and we spent hours hand-searching through the rubble looking for survivors.'

'Were there any?' asked the librarian.

Tommy shook his head. 'We located the ten residents but we were too late. Two of them were just kids.' His shoulders sagged. 'Even Reggie stopped larking about when we carried them poor little mites out.'

'*Baruch dayan ha'emet*,' the librarian muttered, shaking his head.

'It was the same in the houses opposite the paper factory in Duckwood Road. Those old houses went over like a row of kids' building bricks, crushing everyone inside. The only bright spot in the whole night was when we found a family and their pet dog alive in their Anderson under three ton of rubble,' said Tommy. 'Then when we got back to the post at six, almost asleep on our feet and with our hands raw and bleeding, the Canning Town sirens sounded and the Luftwaffe dropped by for their evening visit so we were sent out again.'

'What did Reggie say to that?' asked the librarian.

'I couldn't repeat it,' Tommy replied. 'But we spent the next twelve hours digging out casualties and shoring up houses. I could barely keep my eyes open when the all-clear sounded at five but as we got back, a full twenty-four hours after we clocked on, the control room at the Town Hall rang through, telling us that Bow Common Post needed help as there were people trapped in the basement of a factory so us and White team were sent over.'

'My goodness, when did you get home?'

'Just after lunch,' Tommy replied. 'After a few hours lying dead to the world in bed I went back on duty at eight. It's been the same all week. I've got a day off at the end of my nights but the way I feel at the moment, I doubt I'd wake even if the siren went off next to my head.'

'My poor boy,' said the librarian, his eyes soft with sympathy.

'Don't worry about me,' said Tommy. 'I'll survive, but it's the old 'uns who've been bombed out of their homes and lost everything I feel for.' He clenched his fist. 'Makes me even angrier that I'm not free to volunteer.'

Mr Grossman gave him a sympathetic look. 'Perhaps if you ask Reggie again—'

'There's no point,' Tommy cut in. 'As far as he's concerned he hasn't got a mother and I can't say as how I blame him for that, but if I don't look after her now I'd be no better than she was.' He gave a rueful smile. 'And when all's said and done, she's flesh and blood.'

'You're a good son,' the librarian said with a sigh. 'So may God reward you for it.'

Tommy gave a mirthless laugh. 'Well, if he does he can start by helping me put things right between me and Jo.'

He told the librarian about her unexpected arrival the week before.

When he'd finished the librarian pulled a sour face. 'What a *tsures*.'

Tommy raised an eyebrow. 'Don't you mean a *schmuck*?'

'That, too,' agreed the older man. 'But don't tell me you haven't tried to tell her the truth?'

Tommy nodded. 'I found out she was helping at the junior Irish dancing class at the Catholic Club on Wednesday afternoon, so after getting home as the milkman was on his rounds, I snatched a couple of hours' sleep. Then I dragged myself out of bed, but as I walked down the side of the church, the siren went off and so I only managed to catch a glimpse of her as she herded the children off in the opposite direction towards the shelter,' said Tommy.

'Oy-yo-yo,' said Mr Grossman, throwing his hand up.

'I know, but to be honest, although I know Jo finding me with Lou like that looked bad—'

'Bad?' cut in Mr Grossman. 'She walked in on you and a scantily dressed woman. And you call it bad.'

Tommy frowned.

'All right, bloody terrible,' he conceded, as the scene in the kitchen flashed through his mind again. 'But you think she'd know me better than to think I'd two-time her. And she's the one who hasn't sent me a letter in weeks.'

He raked his fingers through his hair again as misery pressed down on him.

An indulgent look spread across the elderly librarian's long face. 'Can I give you a bit of advice, my boy?'

Amusement tugged at Tommy's lips. 'Is this one of your old Yiddish sayings about goats or fig trees?'

'No, this is an old married man's one about women,' Mr Grossman replied. 'A wise man who wants a happy life with a full belly and a warm bed admits immediately, no matter what the argument is about, that he's the one at fault, preferably with a bunch of flowers in one hand and a box of chocolates in the other. Although in your case, son, as you're up to your neck in *dreck*, you might want to consider swapping the flowers for diamonds.'

Tommy raised an eyebrow. 'And those are your pearls of wisdom, are they?'

'How else do you think I've managed to stay married for thirty years?' Mr Grossman replied.

Tommy regarded the old librarian sitting across the desk from him for a long moment then grabbing his bag from the floor beside him he stood up.

'Perhaps I'll give it a go,' he said, forcing a smile. 'Although Jo'll have to make do with flowers as I can't run to buying diamonds just at the moment.'

'You might if you enter this.' Mr Grossman offered him the newspaper clipping about the competition again. 'There's a hundred-pound prize for the winner.'

This time Tommy took it, scanning down it quickly.

'It looks straightforward enough,' he said, folding it carefully and slipping it into his inside pocket. 'I might give it a whirl if I get a spare minute or two. I don't suppose you know if the book I reserved about Caesar's Teutonic campaign is in?'

'It arrived yesterday and it's under the main desk,' Mr Grossman replied.

'Thanks,' said Tommy, adjusting his bag strap. 'I'll pick it up on the way out. See you next week.'

'If Jehovah wills it,' the librarian replied.

Tommy turned but as he reached for the handle, his old friend spoke again.

'Tommy.'

He looked round.

'My boy, the truth about dealing with women is showing them in everything you do and say that you love them,' said the older man.

Tommy smiled. 'I know, and if I can persuade Jo to give me a second chance that's exactly what I'm going to do.'

Trotting down the library steps some twenty minutes later Tommy turned right to head off to Dolly's pie shop but as he entered Watney Street someone called his name.

'Oi! Sweete!'

Squaring his shoulders, Tommy turned.

Standing some hundred feet behind him with their hands in their pockets and their fedoras pulled down over their foreheads, looking like extras from a gangster movie, were a couple of very familiar faces.

'Inspector Tovey,' said Tommy with a broad smile. 'And Sergeant Flowers. Fancy meeting you here!'

'It's Detective Sergeant to the likes of you, boy,' sneered Tovey.

'Or sir, Sweete,' added Flowers, earning an approving look from his superior officer.

Leonard Tovey, Arbour Square's longest-serving detective, was a thick-set individual with a ruddy face, virtually no neck and stumpy fingers. As a beat officer, he'd given Tommy many a clip around the ear for various misdemeanours, real or imagined.

The pride of Arbour Square's CID was dressed at his usual level of sartorial elegance in a baggy-kneed grey suit, with a crumpled shirt beneath. A stain on the collar indicated that either his wife or his girlfriend favoured an orange shade of lipstick.

Detective Sergeant Eric Flowers, in contrast, was seven inches taller than his boss's five foot eight and so lean that he'd be hard pushed to get wet in a passing shower.

'Where you off to, then?' asked Tovey, sidling up to Tommy.

'For a bite to eat after a day at work,' Tommy replied.

'Work!' snorted Flowers. 'When did a Sweete ever do a day's work?'

'How's Reggie?' asked Tovey.

'Well enough,' said Tommy.

'Not hurt himself yet, then, catching stuff falling off the back of lorries?'

Tommy said nothing.

'Stuff like three dozen crates of cigarettes that were taken from Taylor and Sons' van while it was parked up in the company's yard last week,' continued Tovey. 'Heard anything about it, have you, Tommy?'

'Perhaps he don't need to have *heard* about it, Sir, cause he was there, unloading the gear,' said Flowers.

Tommy regarded both officers with a cool, unwavering gaze but again said nothing.

The two policemen matched his stare for a moment then the sergeant's piggy eyes alighted on Tommy's canvas bag. He snatched the bag from Tommy's hands and opened it.

'What's this, then?' he asked, grabbing the weighty volume that the librarian had stamped out on loan not ten minutes before.

'It's a book,' said Tommy.

'Why have you got it?' asked the constable.

'To read.' Tommy gave him a wry look. 'You should try it. You might learn something.'

Flowers glared at him and Tommy smiled.

'Give him the once-over,' said Tovey.

Flowers dropped the bag. 'Come on, Sweete, you know the drill.'

Tommy turned out his trouser pockets and spread his arms. Keeping hold of his rising temper, he forced himself to regard Inspector Tovey impassively as Flowers patted him down. Shoving his hand in Tommy's jacket pocket he pulled out his handkerchief and discarded it then investigated his inside breast pocket and dragged out Tommy's ARP wage packet.

'Whose is this?' Flowers asked, waving it in front of Tommy's face.

'Mine,' he replied. He took it from the officer and returned it to where it had come from. 'You can check at the Town Hall if you like.'

The Sergeant looked at his superior.

Tovey gave a quick jerk of his head and Flowers stepped back.

'All right, you can be on your way, Sweete,' said the sergeant, his stale breath wafting in Tommy's face as he spoke. 'But watch it.' He jabbed Tommy in the chest with a chubby index finger. 'Cause I've got you and that low-life brother of yours in my sights.'

Tommy smiled coolly.

Tovey eyeballed him for a moment then he and his sidekick retraced their steps back to Wapping High Street.

Scooping up his scattered tools, Tommy put them back in his canvas bag then turned and carried on down Brewhouse Lane.

Chapter Thirteen

'HAVE ANOTHER SANDWICH, Charlie,' said Ida, holding a plate of pilchard sandwiches under his nose.

'Not for me, Mum.' Jo's brother tapped his stomach. 'I'm full.'

It was just after two on Saturday afternoon and Jo and her family were sitting in the back lounge. Jo's letter of acceptance had arrived and she was looking forward to reporting for duty with the ambulance service on Monday morning.

As Queenie was having a lunchtime drink at the Catholic Club, Mattie was taking advantage of her absence by sitting in her gran's chair with her feet up on the leather pouffe.

'You sure?' persisted their mother.

Charlie shook his head. 'No, honestly, Mum. I couldn't eat another thing.' He turned to the young woman sitting beside him on the sofa. 'What about you, Stella luv?'

Stella Miggles was a curvy blonde an inch or two shorter than Jo. She'd been in the same class as Cathy at school so at twenty was four years younger than Charlie. However, Stella had always been older than her years and by the second year of secondary school she was participating in extra-curriculum activities behind the bike sheds with the fourth-year boys. With a 36D bust that was forever spilling out of her blouse or dress and a skirt so tight she couldn't sit without flashing her stocking tops, it was little wonder she'd caught Charlie's eye. Although why he'd let himself become engaged to her was a complete mystery as Stella lavished her favours on anything in trousers.

Stella shook her head.

'No ta, Mrs B.' She snuggled up to Charlie, pressing her breasts into his upper arm. 'I've got to watch my figure to stop my Charlie looking elsewhere.'

Basking in his fiancée's extravagant adoration, a smug smile spread across Charlie's face.

Men, thought Jo, the image of Tommy flashing through her head. As Gran says, they all think with their cods.

'So,' said Stella, turning her attention to Jo. 'You're starting on the ambulances on Monday.'

'Yes, I'm all set,' Jo replied.

'Well, I think you're very brave,' said Stella. 'Driving around with all those bombs exploding around you.'

'No more than anyone else,' said Jo.

'As Her Majesty the Queen said when we were chatting,' said Ida, as if she and the sovereign had met in the queue outside Sainsbury's, 'everyone has to do their bit. Just like my Jo in the ambulance, my Mattie as a warden and me,' she turned so Stella could see the grey band around her arm with WVS stamped more clearly, 'as the street's WVS organiser.'

Stella glanced at the insignia then turned her attention to Mattie.

'Are you still managing all right?' she asked, giving Mattie a syrupy smile. 'I mean, now you're getting bigger.'

'I'm doing fine,' said Mattie. 'Once I'm down in the shelter I'm in the same boat as everyone else and just have to wait until I hear the all-clear.'

'Have you heard from your husband?' asked Stella.

A tight emotion flitted across Mattie's face for a second and she forced a smile. 'Yes, I have.'

'It's a pity he hasn't been to see if you're all right, like Charlie did,' said Stella innocently.

'Yes, isn't it?' said Mattie flatly.

Jo assumed that, for all her supposed cleverness, her sister Mattie had done what thousands of women had done before her and fallen for some flash fella who, after being forced to do the right thing, was now enjoying the single life again in the army.

Although Jo kept telling herself that after the way she'd behaved it served Mattie right if her husband had forgotten about her, something in her sister's tone caught in Jo's chest.

The sound of the back door opening cut through her pondering and Francesca walked in, slightly red-faced and breathless.

'You're early, luv,' said Ida, rising from her chair. 'The pot's still hot. Do you want a cuppa?'

'Yes, please, Mrs Brogan,' Francesca replied. 'I managed to get away on time and catch the earlier bus.'

Casting a look around the room, she smiled at everyone until her gaze alighted on Jo's brother.

'Oh, hello, Charlie,' she said, her brown eyes softening as they rested on him. 'I wondered if you'd still be here.'

'My train doesn't go from London Bridge until four so we've got half an hour yet before me and Stella have to leave,' Charlie replied.

Francesca looked at the woman clinging onto Charlie's left arm.

'How are you, Stella?' she asked, forcing a smile.

'All the better for having Charlie home,' Stella replied, giving Charlie a wrinkled-nosed smile and pressing her breasts against his arm again.

Pain flitted across Francesca's face as Ida returned from the kitchen. She handed Francesca her tea and then resumed her seat.

'Park yourself here,' said Mattie, swinging her feet off the footstool.

Francesca sat down and cupping her drink in her hand took a sip.

'I'm surprised you're wearing your new dress to work?' said Ida.

A blush coloured Francesca's cheeks.

'Well, I change into my overall when I get there, Mrs Brogan,' she said, straightening the front pleats of the powder-blue dress over her knees.

'Even so,' said Ida, 'what with the price of clothes being so dear, I'm a bit surprised you chanced ruining it jumping on and off the bus.'

'Perhaps Francesca just wanted to cheer herself up, Mum,' said Mattie, earning a grateful look from her friend.

'And that would do it too,' said Charlie, 'because that colour suits you.'

Francesca's face lit up.

'Do you think so?' she asked, gazing adoringly at him.

'I do,' he replied. 'In fact, I'd go as far as to say blue is your colo—'

'Perhaps we should be making a move, Charlie,' Stella cut in. 'In case there's a hold-up on the underground.'

Ida looked aghast. 'You've got bags of time yet—'

'I know, Mrs B,' Stella continued, 'but you wouldn't want Charlie to be up on a charge for reporting late or AWOL because we girls were chatting about dresses, would you?'

'Well, no,' said Ida.

'And haven't you told me often enough it's better to be early than late?' Stella concluded.

'I suppose so but—'

'So.' Stella wiggled to her feet and held out her hand. 'We'd better be off.'

Charlie took her hand and rose to his feet. 'She's right, Mum, I don't want to blot my copybook by missing the troop train.'

'I know,' said Ida, dashing away her gathering tears.

Charlie retrieved his fiancée's coat from the hall stand and held it while she slipped it on. Hugging it around her, Stella took out her cigarettes and stood there gazing out of the window while Charlie dried his mother's tears and hugged Jo and Mattie.

Finally, he turned to Francesca.

She gazed up at him but just as he was about to move towards her, Stella caught his arm.

'Bye for now,' she called over her shoulder as she dragged him to the door.

The front door banged shut and he was gone.

'Give us a hand, Jo,' said her mother as she gathered up the used crockery.

Jo stooped down to pick up Charlie and Stella's cups but as she stood up she saw tears shimmering in Francesca's eyes as she stared after Charlie.

Pain shot through Jo's chest. She must have had that self-same stricken look on her face when she found Tommy with that blonde.

*

Taking a sip from his pint, Tommy replaced the glass on the table in front of him and turned the page of his newspaper.

It was just after midday on Sunday and two days since his heart-to-heart with David Grossman at the library. Although Sam had only just taken the shutters off the Admiral's windows, West Ham were kicking off at three so the main bar was already awash with claret and blue.

Reggie had still been snoring like a bear in a cave when Tommy woke an hour ago, so leaving his brother to fester in his pit, he'd trotted down to St George's public baths for a soak. Well, not so much a soak as a paddle as the bathing superintendent strictly enforced the five inches of water rule. Still, even though it had taken him a bit of shifting about, and using the enamel jug provided to wash his hair, Tommy felt free of grit and soot for the first time in a week. He'd finished off his ablutions with a visit to the Jewish barber in Hessle Street. As the only gentile in the minute shop, he'd had a couple of funny looks but they were worth it to rid his chin of three days' worth of itchy bristles.

Having changed into a fresh set of clothes and feeling if not a new man then at least a restored one, Tommy had strolled along to the seaman's café and polished off three slices of fried bread, bacon and tomatoes. He'd have liked to have had an egg too, but since the start of rationing they had become like the dodo: extinct.

Tommy turned back to his paper but as he scanned down the report about the RAF's bombing raid on Berlin, a shadow fell across the page.

'Hello, Tommy,' said a familiar voice.

He looked up. 'Hello, Lou, how you doing?'

She was dressed in a navy, figure-hugging polka-dot dress with a scooped neckline and white collar. Her hair was swept up as usual but with one long tendril snaking down over her shoulder.

'All the better for seeing you, Tommy,' she replied, her blood-red lips lifting in an inviting smile. 'I thought perhaps you'd forgotten the way to the Admiral.'

He smiled politely. 'I've been busy.'

'So I heard from Ronnie,' she replied. 'He said you and him were right in the thick of it.'

'The same as the rest,' Tommy told her.

'Don't you be so modest, Tommy,' she said, giving him a smouldering look.

Bending forward to give him the benefit of her cleavage, she arched her neck to look at the newspaper he was holding.

'That's a queer-looking paper,' she said, a puzzled look creasing her powdered brow.

'It's the *Telegraph*,' he replied.

'Oh, you're so brainy.' She gave him another smouldering look that caught his interest in an instant. 'I always did have a terrible weakness for brainy men like you.' Stepping closer she pressed her leg against his thigh. 'And I can show you how much if you like, Tommy.'

With his crotch urging him on, Tommy's gaze ran slowly over her.

Credit where credit's due, Lou was a good three steps up from most of the barmaids in the area. She was classy but with a dollop of sensuality that promised a man a very saucy encounter. He only had to reach out his hand and run it up her leg and, to be honest, as it had been a while and Jo had already judged him guilty of sleeping with Lou, why not?

'Thanks, luv,' he said, moving his leg aside. 'That's kind of you to offer.' He drained the last of his beer and handed her the glass. 'I will have another.'

Chapter Fourteen

'AS TIME IS pressing on, I'll just give you a quick rundown of how the station works then I'll take you out to meet your teams,' said Captain Fletcher, the controller of St Katherine's Ancillary Ambulance Station, his handlebar moustache twitching back and forth as he spoke.

'About time,' whispered Gillian West, the girl Jo had met at the ambulance crew interview and who was standing beside her. 'We've been stood here for over an hour already.'

It was just before two thirty in the afternoon on Monday and she, Gillian and half a dozen new recruits were squashed into the controller's small office.

She'd reported for duty as instructed at ten o'clock that morning at area headquarters in Homerton, where she'd been interviewed. She and the new trainees were then subjected to a long lecture by London's senior officer who'd impressed upon them the vital job they were doing. After a quick mid-morning cuppa in the canteen they'd had another long lecture from the Civil Defence coordinator about the ARP structure and then they'd finally been taken to collect their uniform, which consisted of a buff-coloured overcoat, a tin hat and a rubberised mac. They were then bused to their respective ambulance stations, which is where Jo was standing now.

The station controller was a portly gentleman and, although he must have been close to sixty, still had a remarkably full head of steely grey hair. He'd introduced himself as a veteran of the last war with Germany, although he was a bit vague as to where and in what capacity he'd served.

'Now, firstly,' he continued, fixing the half a dozen raw recruits with a hard stare, 'these are desperate times and in desperate times we have to adopt desperate measures. Ideally before you start as ambulance crew you would have completed and passed your St John certificate. However, the-powers-that-be have decided that, as all of you have had some first-aid training, you are safe to be sent out as drivers' assistants and are fit to undertake such emergency first aid as deemed necessary to ensure that your casualty arrives at the hospital still alive.'

There were titters from a couple of young lads standing behind in the ranks. Captain Fletcher fixed the miscreants with a furious stare and the merriment subsided.

'Now, lastly, as you're no doubt aware,' continued Captain Fletcher, 'unlike the air raid wardens and heavy rescue crews who are under the control of the Civil Defence wallahs at the Town Hall, we in the London Ambulance Service answer only to our superior officers in the LCC. Remember, while I expect you to work *with* the ARP services, if any of those jobsworths in tin hats start bossing you about, you come straight to me or my deputy Mr Biggins, and believe me, we'll soon put them in their place. Now, if you follow me, I'll introduce you to your ambulance drivers.'

Picking up the clipboard he'd signed them in with, Captain Fletcher marched out of the office. Jo and those around her trooped out after him and into the tarmacked school playground where a line of assorted vehicles painted white with red crosses on the side stood. Although they were clearly ready to speed off to tend to the injured, the most amazing thing about the St Katherine's fleet of ambulances was that none of them was actually an ambulance. However, the most bizarre vehicles parked in the yard were the two horseboxes with their wooden sides also painted white with a red cross.

Walking past the empty alcoves where sculptures of a boy and a girl dressed in old-fashioned school uniform used to be, they entered the single-storey red-brick school where the crews of the vehicles were lounging about in old armchairs, smoking and playing cards or, in the case of the female members of the team, knitting and flicking through magazines. They looked around as their new colleagues walked in.

The controller stepped forward and cleared his throat. 'Oh Gawd, not another speech,' whispered Gillian under her breath.

'Let's hope not,' said Jo. 'Or the war will be over before we get into an ambulance.'

'Right, pay attention, everyone, while I tell you who is going where.' Taking a pair of pince-nez from his top pocket he jammed them on his nose then peered at the clipboard. 'Adams!'

A young chap with the shadow of his first moustache on his upper lip stepped forward.

Captain Fletcher ran through the list of names and each new recruit went off to join their new team.

'West,' barked Captain Fletcher.

Gillian stepped forward smartly. 'All present and correct!' she said, saluting.

'Charlie's team will look after you,' the captain said, indicating the group relaxing in the armchairs.

'Now then, that leaves just you two,' he said, peering through the lenses on the end of his nose. 'Which of you is Brogan?'

Feeling like a five-year-old, Jo raised her hand.

'Well, because you and Naylor here,' he pointed at the slim young man standing next to her, 'have passed your St John's Intermediate certificates you've been allocated to our two mobile dressing stations. You, Naylor, are with A MDS and you, Brogan, are attached to B MDS. Your driver's over there, Naylor.' He indicated a middle-aged man in a tweed suit, smoking a pipe and sitting under the window reading. 'But your driver, Brogan, doesn't appear to be here. I expect you'll find her in the ambulance. It's got a sign in the front window so you can't miss it.'

Leaving her standing in the middle of the recreation area, the ambulance station controller marched off towards the tea trolley.

Jo looked around for a moment then, looping her gas mask more securely on her shoulder, she retraced her steps and headed back out to the yard. The wind had picked up and the fog that had hung around last night was beginning to disperse. It was obvious that the only vehicles that could be used as mobile dressing stations were the horseboxes, so with the gravel crunching under her leather soles, Jo marched across the playground and found the one with a sign reading 'B MDS' propped up on the dashboard.

As there was no one sitting in the front cab, Jo went around to the back and, as one of the doors was ajar, poked her head in.

Inside, the vehicle had been adapted to treat casualties so now one of the stalls had been fitted out with stainless-steel cupboards, which Jo presumed was where the dressings were stored. The far end, the area where the second horse would have been secured, was hidden by a floor-to-ceiling curtain. In front of this section was an examination couch, which had been welded to the floor, with a stainless-steel dressing trolley next to it.

'Hello,' called Jo. 'Is there anyone there?'

The curtain rustled and then the sound of metal hitting metal pinged around the interior space.

'Drat and botheration!' barked a woman's voice, as an enamel kidney bowl flew out under the curtain. It skidded across the floor and Jo stooped and caught it just before it shot through the door.

She stood up as a woman with a scrubbed, ruddy-pink face and pale eyes emerged from behind the curtain.

She was about Ida's age but that was the only thing her mother and the woman standing in front of her had in common. Jo's mother's girth may have spread over the years but the woman standing before her was roughly the shape of a whipping top. She had such an abundance of wild grey hair that even though it was pinned in a massive bun on the top of her head, it still surrounded her face like a foggy halo. She was dressed in a tweed hacking jacket, with worn velvet collar and cuffs, and a dark cream blouse beneath. A pair of buff-coloured jodhpurs encased her massive hips and rear while knee-length riding boots completed the tally-ho look.

'You must be Josephine,' she said, rocking the vehicle's chassis as she bounced towards her.

'Yes, but call me Jo. Everyone does.'

'Eddie Frobisher.' The woman thrust out a beefy hand. 'I drive this old boneshaker.'

'Nice to meet you,' said Jo, as her fingers were crushed in the driver's grip. 'Although, I've never met a woman called Eddie before.'

'It's short for Edwina,' Eddie replied. 'Actually, it's Edwina Christobelle Diana Wake-Frobisher if you want the whole bally mouthful but, if I might paraphrase the blessed St Matthew, as the German sendeth the bombs on the rich and the poor alike we've all got to pull together, don't you agree?'

'I certainly do,' said Jo.

'Right then,' said Eddie, rubbing her hands together. 'Store your gear and follow me through.'

Jo stowed her coat and bag in the locker tucked alongside one of the cupboards and then followed Eddie through into the front cab.

Eddie was already sitting behind the wheel and Jo slipped into the passenger's seat.

Pumping the clutch, Eddie turned the key and the engine rumbled into life.

'Don't we have to wait for a call from HQ?' asked Jo, as the woman beside her fought with the gearstick to find a gear.

'The ordinary ambulances do,' said Edwina. 'But us mobiles are attached to an ARP depot so we're on the spot when needed.'

'Oh,' said Jo. 'Which one are we heading off to, then?'

'Post 7.' Releasing the handbrake, Eddie grasped the steering wheel. 'It's in Shadwell School, I don't know if you know it at all.'

Jo forced a smile. 'I do. My sister Mattie is an ARP warden there.'

'You want in, Tommy?' asked Reggie, holding up the reshuffled pack of cards.

Without taking his eyes from the newspaper clipping resting on the book he had balanced on his knee, Tommy shook his head.

It was Monday afternoon and he and the rest of Blue Squad were on duty at Post 7 and had been since midday. The afternoon session of *Music While You Work* was blaring out from the radio, which meant it must be just after half past three.

'Fank God for that,' said Willy Arkwright, a member of Red Squad, as he flicked ash in the overloaded ashtray at his elbow. 'I never bloody win when 'e plays.'

'Me neiver,' added Brian Kelly, the ARP warden for Limehouse. 'But I ain't figured out 'ow.'

'I'll tell you how,' said Reggie, as he dealt out the card. 'Cos my little brother's a bloody genius, that's how. In fact, he's such a brainbox that he could be a professor at one of those poncy universities 'ad he a mind to.'

'Yeah,' grinned Fred, who was the other player, 'if he'd ever turned up at school.'

'He didn't need to,' laughed Reggie, spreading out his hand of cards and setting it face down. 'Cos I taught him everything he needed to know. Ain't I right, Tommy?'

Tommy looked up and smiled across at his brother. 'Course you are.'

Reggie threw in a couple of pennies and the other three gathered around the upturned fruit box that was serving as a card table did the same.

'What's that you're doing then, Tommy?' asked Fred, re-sorting his cards.

'It's this quiz from the *Telegraph*,' Tommy replied.

'Whooo hoo!' sang out the four card players in unison.

'The *Telegraph*, don't you know,' Brian said, in a sing-song falsetto voice.

'What, what, old bean,' said Fred, in the same tone.

'Tell the butler to saddle the carriage,' said Reggie.

'You saddle the horses not the carriage, you silly bugger,' said Tommy, giving his brother a pitying look. 'And you'll all be laughing on the other side of your faces when I win the hundred-nicker prize money.' They looked impressed. 'Now, you get back to your cards and let me concentrate, and if I win, I might stand you all a drink in the Admiral.'

Reggie gave him two fingers then threw in another couple of pennies from the pile in front of him.

Tommy returned to his task. The competition Mr Grossman had saved from the up-market newspaper was in two parts and on the face of it looked straightforward enough. He'd polished off the word puzzle over breakfast that morning in the Post's WVS canteen but the arithmetic section, while looking simple at first glance, was actually quite difficult. It had to be, of course, otherwise this lord what's-his-name would have to give away thousands of pounds. Although he'd had to resort to pencil and paper, after a couple of false starts, Tommy had worked out the first three sequences of numbers. Now he just had to figure out the last two blocks of numbers.

Actually, making sense of the jumble of numbers was easy in comparison to the other task he'd set himself: winning Jo back. But as the future he was striving to build for himself, with a comfortable home and a handful of children, would not be complete if it didn't have Jo at its centre, he had no choice. He didn't know why she hadn't written or tried to get a message to him that she was coming home but that didn't matter. All that mattered was that she was home and he wouldn't rest until she was in his arms again.

That's why, even if he had to camp outside her house for a week, he wouldn't budge until she heard him out.

'My game I think, gentlemen,' said Reggie, cutting across

Tommy's thoughts as he slapped the queen of hearts on the table.

Muttering obscenities and their doubts about Reggie's paternity, the other players threw in their cards. Lighting a fresh cigarette from his spent one, Reggie flicked the butt on the floor and then scooped up the coppers on the box.

'Double or quits?'

The other players nodded and Tommy returned to his task.

Twiddling the pencil back and forth in his fingers, he mentally ran through the groups of four numbers again, searching for the correct configurations.

'You do know gambling is prohibited in this ARP post, Sweete,' said a voice to Tommy's left.

He looked up to see Cyril Potter, in his black ARP uniform, standing at his brother's shoulder.

'Is that a fact, Sergeant Major?' said Reggie, dealing out the cards.

'You know it is,' Cyril replied, the muscle under his right eye working overtime. 'Because there's a written order on the noticeboard stating clearly that no "games of chance where a money wager is placed on the outcome are allowed on ARP premises".'

'Ah well, that's all right then, Admiral,' said Reggie, dealing out the next hand. 'Cos this ain't no game of chance as these poor buggers never beat me.'

The men laughed and Cyril's face went as red as the warden badge on his chest.

He stood there glaring at Reggie for a moment and then as the first round of cards landed on the box he lunged at them.

Reggie's brawny hand shot out and he grabbed the wrist

of the Post's senior warden. 'I wouldn't do that, chum.'

'But you're not permit—'

Reggie tightened his grip and Cyril winced.

The chair scraped back as Reggie rose to his feet. The men around the table averted their eyes and fiddled with their cards.

Setting aside the newspaper clipping, Tommy stood up too.

'Leave him be,' he said softly.

'But he's mucked up our game,' said Reggie, like a five-year-old who'd had his sandcastle trod on.

'Reggie,' said Tommy.

No one moved.

Then Reggie released the chief warden so abruptly that he staggered back. 'All right, have it your way.'

Cyril shot him an angry look but sensibly beat a retreat to the far side of the control centre, rubbing his wrist as he went.

'Bloody tin-pot general,' muttered Reggie as he watched Cyril talking to a couple of his fellow wardens.

'Perhaps,' said Tommy, 'but he's in charge of this depot and if you want to carry on getting the extra heavy rescue petrol rations you'd better stop riling him.'

Reggie chewed the inside of his mouth for a second or two then he threw himself back into his chair and picked up his cards.

'All right, lads, by order of Colonel Blimp over there,' he jerked his head towards Cyril, who was now making sure the stirrup pumps were standing to attention, 'no money is to change hands.' Taking a matchbox from his pocket he tipped the contents on the table. 'So penny a stick and you can settle up with me later.'

The men surrounding him laughed and picked up their cards.

Thinking while he was up he might as well get himself a cuppa, Tommy slipped his unfinished competition entry into his book and, leaving it on the seat, strolled over to the serving hatch.

He'd just got himself a mug of strong tea from the elderly WVS woman behind the counter when the jolly, bouncy woman with the wild hair who drove one of Post 7's mobile dressing stations strode in. When he saw Jo walking in beside her, Tommy nearly dropped the cup.

Her wild chestnut hair was now confined in a thick plait and secured at the nape of her neck. The square-shoulder navy jacket she was wearing had a very masculine cut but this only highlighted her femininity, as did the trousers, which hugged her hips and long slim legs.

Even though she was dressed like the fireman on the footplate of the *Flying Scotsman*, Jo looked absolutely gorgeous.

Cradling his cup in his hand, Tommy stepped aside so the next person could be served. While he leaned against the wall and drank his tea, Tommy allowed himself the pleasure of watching Jo talking and smiling as she was introduced to her new team. Her eyes, sparkly with laughter at something someone said, changed to thoughtful as she was asked a serious question. He studied the tilt of her head and the curve of neck and the way her hips moved as she shifted her weight from one leg to the other.

Perhaps God had heard his plea and decided to give him a chance to put things right. Well, at least working alongside her every day beat taking up residence on the pavement in Mafeking Terrace.

Swallowing the last mouthful of tea, Tommy returned the mug to the hatch then strolled across the room.

He stopped just to one side of Jo, and the people she'd been talking to looked at him. Jo stopped talking and turned.

Tommy smiled. 'Hello, Jo.'

For a split second, surprise and joy flashed across her face but then a stony stare replaced her look of pleasure.

'Hello.' She cast her frosty gaze over him and started to turn back.

He smiled. 'Fancy meeting you here.'

'Yes, fancy,' she said, glancing over her shoulder at him.

She turned her attention back to her new colleagues.

'So,' he said, forcing a jolly laugh, 'you're the new recruit to the mobile dressing station, Jo.'

Slowly she turned back to face him again and raised a mocking eyebrow.

'Obviously.'

Tommy rolled his eyes. 'Stupid question or what?'

She regarded him coolly.

Tommy rubbed the back of his neck with his hand. 'How are your family? Are they—'

'I'm sorry, Tommy,' Jo cut in, giving him a glacial smile, 'but we're a bit busy, so if you don't mind . . .'

'Of course,' said Tommy, acutely aware of the amused expressions of the people standing around them.

He smiled again, inviting her to do the same.

She didn't. Instead, she cast her lovely brown eyes over him again then turned away.

'Well, it was nice to see you, Jo,' he said, addressing the back of her head. 'And we'll chat another time.'

She didn't reply.

He stood with his arms hanging at his side for a moment then he turned on his heels and marched back to his seat.

Snatching the book from the seat, Tommy threw himself into the saggy armchair. Taking out the newspaper cutting, he retrieved his pencil from between the cushion and the arm. As he forced his mind to concentrate on the first sequence of numbers, Jo's throaty laugh drifted over and suddenly solving a puzzle was the very last thing on Tommy's mind.

'Our main function, Jo,' said Eddie, as they stood beside the stretcher rack in the back of the ambulance, 'is to patch people up enough so they are safe to travel by ambulance to hospital.'

It was now close to five in the afternoon and she was standing in the back of the converted horsebox, with Eddie and her two new colleagues. As the blackout had come into force an hour ago they had shut the door and had lit the ambulance's hurricane lamp. Huddled in the half-light, Jo was getting a rundown of how the team operated and she was beginning to worry that her head would explode with all the new things she was expected to cram in it.

As well as the tedious morning trying to master the complex hierarchy of the Civil Defence and the London Ambulance Brigade structure, she'd had a full twenty minutes on the drive to the post getting the rundown on Eddie's somewhat eccentric upbringing.

Born in China of missionary parents, she'd been smuggled out of the European quarter in Peking as a baby by a faithful family servant during the Boxer Uprising. Her parents perished along with a hundred of their Chinese parishioners as the rebellion swept the country, but after a journey around Russia and most of Europe, Eddie had finally arrived in England. Despite her assertion that she'd never been to school, she must have learned something along the way because she'd been an undergraduate at Girton College before travelling, mostly alone, to all four corners of the Empire, but when Hitler had annexed the *Sudetenland* and, sensing 'the Old Country was heading into choppy water', Eddie had returned to do her bit. All this Jo had learned as they drove to Post 7. Shadwell School was only three miles from St Katherine's but as rubber was imported and worth its weight in gold, it was a mortal sin to damage your vehicle tyres, so Eddie drove the short journey no faster than the regulation speed of fifteen miles an hour, which gave her ample time to explain her complicated family history.

'We don't bother with superficial cuts and grazes; the nurses can sort them out,' said Percy Fisher. He had served in the last war as a medical orderly in France and the two stripes on his shoulder signified he was the senior first-aider. He was of middling height, and had carefully smoothed the remnants of his sandy hair across his head in narrow strips to try to give the impression that he still possessed a full head of hair. He lived behind Shadwell School in Crawford Walk, which meant he could pop home to keep his prize-winning budgies company when they were parked up in the depot.

'And as long as it's not pumping blood we treat deeper lacerations by slapping on a gauze dressing, binding it with a bandage and then sending them off to the hospital in an ambulance,' added Joan Green, the final member of their four-person crew.

Joan was a pretty blonde, a year or two older than Jo. She had wanted to join the Queen Alexandra nurses but her mother had objected so she'd joined the ambulance service instead.

'What about fractures?' asked Jo.

'If it's legs, bind them ankle and knee in the usual way. Same with arms.' Joan tapped the white enamel cupboard behind her. 'The straps are in here.'

'The aim is to keep the limb stable,' added Jim.

'When the bombing started, people died on the way to the hospitals from internal bleeding and lost limbs because fractures were made worse by being jigged about in the back of the ambulance without being stabilised first,' explained Eddie. 'Our job is to assess people on the spot and make them safe to transport.'

'Of course, some poor souls are too seriously injured to be moved,' said Joan.

'Which is where this comes in.' Eddie tapped the stainless-steel bench bolted to the ambulance floor. 'If needs be, it can be used as an operating table.'

'Thankfully, we haven't had to use it yet,' said Joan. 'But all the instruments are stored in the cupboard next to it if ever one of our doctors needs them.'

Jo swallowed hard.

'Don't worry,' said Jim, seeing her alarmed expression. 'You'll soon get the hang of it.'

'I hope so,' said Jo, trying to imagine herself assisting in an operation as bombs dropped around her.

'I'm sure you'll be better than I was when I first started,' laughed Joan.

'I know it's been a bit of a gallop through,' said Eddie, 'but I think I've more or less told you enough to get you started.'

'And if you can't find something just give us a shout,' said Joan.

Jo smiled. 'Don't worry, I will.'

'And on that note,' said Jim, rubbing his hands together, 'I think it's time for a cuppa.'

'Capital idea,' said Eddie, lifting the glass of the lamp and snuffing out the wick.

As the interior of the van was plunged into darkness, Jim opened one of the back doors, letting in the last rays of the setting sun and the cool evening breeze.

The other three climbed out and Jo followed.

Closing the door behind her, Jo started across the playground towards the school but as she got halfway across the space a figure emerged from the shadows. Despite her telling it not to, Jo's heart did a little double step of happiness.

As she and Eddie had bumped along towards Post 7, Jo had resolved that, despite her grievance with her sister, when she came face to face with Mattie, she wouldn't let their differences interfere with the vital work they were both doing.

As her sister was out on blackout patrol when she'd arrived, Jo hadn't needed to put this to the test. However, when she'd turned to see Tommy standing behind her, having to work cheek by jowl with her sister was the least of her problems.

In fact, staying upright was her first concern as she'd nearly dropped in a dead faint at his feet. Thankfully, she hadn't, but it had taken a full half-hour for her pulse to return to anything resembling normal.

Squaring her shoulders, Jo now continued towards the main doorway.

'Hello again, Jo,' Tommy said softly, as she drew level with him. 'How are you finding your first day?'

Jo forced a polite smile. 'Fine.'

She went to walk past but Tommy caught her hand.

Jo's heart beat faster and she looked up into Tommy's eyes, warmed by the dying rays of the setting sun.

Standing just inches from him, her body remembered the pleasure of being held in his arms. For several heartbeats Jo fought the almost overwhelming desire to throw herself into Tommy's embrace.

He stepped forward. 'Jo, I—'

The air raid siren screeched between them, cutting off Tommy's words. He took a step towards her and for an instant she thought, hoped, he would take her in his arms but then the door flew open as Post 7's air raid wardens, fire and ambulance personnel burst out and raced to their vehicles.

It was close to nine thirty by the time Jo finally made it back to Mafeking Terrace the following morning. Finally, because when the all-clear had sounded at seven she and the mobile dressing station had been almost five miles away in City Road. Defiance and rebellion had long been characteristics of the citizens of London, so it was hardly surprising that, after three days of constant bombardment, they had had enough. Ignoring police and Civil Defence mandarins' orders barring them from sheltering in underground stations, many had headed for their nearest tube station when the alarm went off. The reason officials had banned civilians from sheltering below ground was the fear that if there was a direct hit on an underground station, thousands could be killed or trapped. This was precisely what had happened that morning. Mercifully, for the two thousand plus people sheltering below Old Street Station, the bomb didn't go off but London's central control didn't know that when they dispatched Jo's MDS to Islington's ARP depot to help.

Having driven at the regulation fifteen miles an hour they'd arrived an hour after the bomb landed and were stood down immediately. The all-clear sounded soon after but it had taken an hour of navigating their way around collapsed buildings and shattered water mains to get back to Post 7.

It was just as well it had taken so long because Jo wanted to have a word with Mattie and it was probably better not to have it in front of four dozen people.

Crossing the yard, she pushed open the back door to find Gran doing what she did every morning: making the family breakfast. She turned around as Jo stormed in.

'So what's screwed your temper up so early in the day then?' said Queenie.

'Nothing,' said Jo, in what she hoped was a nonchalant voice. 'Is Mattie in?'

'She is and she's in bed, which is where she should have been three hours ago,' Gran replied, fixing Jo with an accusing stare. 'So you better not be thinking of bothering her.'

'Of course not,' said Jo, dropping her bag on the nearest chair. 'I just want to ask her a question.'

Leaving her gran turning the toast under the grill, Jo rushed through the house and upstairs.

Pushing open the door to their bedroom, she found Mattie sitting up in bed reading one of those postcards from her husband's Aunt Fanny.

'I thought you might have told me Tommy Sweete was working at Post 7,' said Jo.

'And good morning to you too, Jo,' said Mattie, slipping the card under her pillow.

'Yes, good morning,' said Jo testily. 'But why didn't you?'

'Well, for a start, Jo,' said Mattie, matching Jo's angry glare, 'every time I try to speak to you I get a dirty look and a curt answer so why should I bother to tell you anything? And secondly, I didn't think you cared about Tommy any more.'

'I don't,' said Jo. 'It was just a shock, that's all.'

'Well, I was shocked too,' said Mattie. 'Shocked that you believed I told Mum about catching you and Tommy smooching. Because I never, I wouldn't—'

Furious hammering on the front door cut off her words.

Crossing to the window, Jo looked down and recognised the sleek-looking car sitting outside their house.

'Sounds like the devil himself trying to get in?' asked Mattie.

'Not quite,' said Jo, dashing across the room. 'It's Aunt Pearl.'

Tearing open the bedroom door, she dashed downstairs just as Gran came out of the back-parlour room.

'It's Pearl,' said Jo, catching her arm.

Alarm flashed across Queenie's face and she disappeared back into the parlour, slamming the door behind her.

Jo waited until the knocker rapped on the stud half a dozen times more then, taking a deep breath, she opened the front door.

Standing on the step was her mother's younger sister Pearl.

Although she was only three years younger than Ida, thanks to weekly trips to the hairdressers, there was not a grey hair amongst her honey-blonde curls. Unlike Jo's mother's matronly figure, Pearl's waist had only expanded once to accommodate a child and was still flat and tight.

With carefully powdered cheeks, precisely drawn eyebrows and vibrantly applied lipstick, Pearl was what was referred to locally as 'well preserved'.

She was wearing a tailored suit, a hat with a pheasant feather attached to one side and a fox fur – complete with legs and head – draped around her shoulders. She looked as if she should have been gliding up the steps of the Savoy rather than standing outside a terraced cottage by London Dock.

'Hello, Aunt Pearl,' said Jo with a friendly smile. 'What a nice surpri—'

'Don't give me all that codswallop,' snapped Pearl. 'Where's my Billy?'

'My brother Billy,' said Jo, giving her aunt a hard look, 'is in Essex.'

'I don't believe you.' Pearl shoved her aside and strode in. 'I told your mother I wanted him safe in the country.'

'And that's where he is,' said Jo.

'That's not what I heard,' countered Pearl.

Pushing past Jo, she stormed up the stairs.

'Mum won't like you barging in like this,' said Jo, as she hurried up behind her aunt.

When she reached the half-turn in the staircase, Pearl stopped. She grabbed the handle of Charlie's room, which Francesca was now using, and marched in. Seeing only a dress draped over the back of a chair, a couple of pairs of women's shoes and a make-up bag on the cast-iron mantelshelf alongside a picture of Francesca's family, Pearl marched back out and continued up towards Jo's room and her mother's bedroom.

She turned right and opened Jo's and Mattie's bedroom door, then stormed in.

Mattie was sitting up in bed with the bedcovers pulled down, showing her swollen stomach. She was hunched over their old china gazunder, which was resting on her knees.

She looked up as Pearl and Jo walked in.

'Hello, Aunt Pearl . . .' She retched and with her head hung over the pot she gave them a wan smile. 'Sorry. Morning sickness.'

She dry-retched again.

Pearl put her hand over her mouth and, spinning on her heels, left the room with Jo right behind her.

Pressing herself into the wall, Jo pushed past Pearl and planted herself squarely in front of her parents' bedroom.

'Get out of my way,' snarled Pearl.

'No,' said Jo. 'It's private.'

Pearl glared at her for a moment then with surprising strength for someone who idled away their days on a bar stool with a drink in their hand, her aunt grabbed her and dragged her out of the way and burst in.

Jo closed her eyes and waited for her to see the made-up bed on the floor and Billy's clothes hanging on the wardrobe door and his toys in the box but after a few moments of ferreting around in the room, Pearl re-emerged and stomped back downstairs.

She stopped at Queenie's door. Her hand hovered over the handle for a second then, taking a deep breath, she turned it and walked in.

A tangy smell of stale chamber pot wafted out as Pearl entered and Prince Albert, Queenie's elderly grey parrot who lived in a cage by the old woman's bed, squawked its protest.

Pearl came out a few moments later looking shaken. Adjusting the fur on her shoulder, she strode past Jo into the back parlour. Her eyes narrowed as they flitted over Jo's family's mismatched furniture but as it was clear no boy Billy's size could be hiding anywhere in the room, she walked on through to the kitchen.

The room was empty and although there was a breakfast bowl and cup still on the table, Billy's satchel was missing from the back of the chair.

Pearl poked her nose in the pantry before turning to glare at her niece.

'See, I told you,' said Jo. 'Billy's not here.'

Pearl gave her a caustic glance and then, ripping open the back door, she strode out into the yard.

Marching across to the privy, Pearl banged on the door.

'Feck off,' Queenie shouted back. 'I'm having a shite.'

'I'm looking for Billy,' Pearl bawled through the outhouse door. 'I know he's—'

A rip-roaring fart cut across her words.

'For the love of mercy,' hollered Queenie from inside the toilet, 'will you not leave me in peace to grapple with the squits?'

'Is he in there?' Pearl demanded, thumping her manicured fist on the rough wood.

There was a pause and then the door creaked open to reveal Queenie, sitting on the scrubbed wooden toilet board with her skirts rucked up, and her washed-out grey bloomers gathered around her ankles.

'So,' said Queenie, resting her hands on her knobbly knees, 'perhaps now you'll be satisfied that 'tis only myself in this here bog. Or would you be after searching the bowl beneath me arse as well?'

Aunt Pearl glared at the old woman for a moment then she spun around to face Jo.

'Tell your mother, if I find out Billy is here,' she jabbed her finger at her, 'I'll get my Lenny to drive me straight back—'

'Back?' said Jo.

Pearl made a play of adjusting the angle of her hat. 'This damp has given Lenny a bit of a cough so we're going to spend a few months by the coast, in Seaton.'

'Away from all the bombing, then,' said Jo, giving her aunt a scornful look.

Pearl didn't reply.

'And is he taking his real wife as well?' called Queenie from her back-yard throne. 'Or is she staying in Southend?'

Pearl's lipsticked mouth pulled into a tight line.

'So you can tell your mother,' she said, hooking her handbag firmly over her arm, 'if I find out that my sweet boy is in danger, I'll come and take him from you.'

Pearl gave Jo and Queenie another withering look before striding out of the back gate, her heels clip-clopping as she hurried down the side alley back to the street.

No one moved until they heard a car revving away and then Jo looked at her grandmother.

'What have you done with him?' she asked.

Pulling up her knickers, Queenie smiled and raised her eyes upwards as a pair of small hands gripped the edge of the roof tiles and Billy's bewildered face appeared between them.

Half an hour later, after a breakfast of fried bread dipped in egg and a mug of hot, sweet tea, Jo finally dragged herself upstairs to bed.

Opening the door to her old bedroom at the front of the house, she crept in to find that Billy's clothes, having been retrieved from wherever her sister had hidden them, were now folded in a neat pile on the dressing table. Mattie herself was lying on her back, with her arms out of the covers and fast asleep.

Closing the door quietly, Jo kicked off her shoes and quickly got undressed. Pulling her suitcase from under the bed where she'd stored it earlier, she took out a clean nightdress and slipped it on. In the distance, fire-engine bells, no doubt from other areas, arrived to lend a hand.

Careful not to disturb her sister, Jo slipped under the covers, setting the springs creaking as they took her weight. She settled into the familiar moulds of the mattress. Mattie sighed and unconsciously she smoothed her fingers over the patchwork counterpane covering her swelling stomach.

As she gazed at her sister's hands resting protectively over her unborn child, a lump formed itself in Jo's throat.

Chapter Fifteen

WITH THE ACK-ACK guns sending an arc of light towards the Royal Docks, Tommy spread his feet and braced his back against the splintered beam.

'OK, easy does it,' he said, feeling the sweat start to trickle down his spine with the effort. 'Just a bit more and she'll be free.'

Ducking their heads to get under the obstruction, two members of A team light rescue inched forward, carrying the stretcher with a dust-covered woman on it.

It was the first Saturday in November and, as there had been six waves of German bombers overhead since the air raid siren sounded at six thirty, Tommy guessed it must be somewhere close to one o'clock in the morning. This elderly woman was the thirteenth person he'd pulled from the rubble so far, but judging by the distant high-pitched drone coming up the Thames, she wouldn't be the last. Mercifully, she was a casualty not a corpse, which made her unique for the night's work so far.

She'd taken refuge in the basement under her house but then the side wall of the house had collapsed, taking the stairs with it and blocking off the exit from the cellar. It had taken Tommy and the rest of the team an hour to dig down to her and make the building above safe. The crew had been called to another collapsed building a few streets over in Bow Common Lane. They had gone but Tommy had stayed behind in case any further muscle was required to get the old lady out.

Over six weeks had passed since he and Reggie had arrived at Post 7 and he'd now lost count of the number of dead men, women and, heartbreakingly, children he'd dug from the wreckage of their homes. For a few weeks, he had tried to remember their faces but as night after night brought a new crop of bodies, already they were merging into one. A few stood out, like the two young girls, sisters probably, still in pigtails, who'd died in each other's arms with their dolls tucked in beside them. Or the old man still sitting in the fireside chair when his home had collapsed around him; his pipe had still been alight when they'd dug him out. There had been a baby, too, blown from a second-floor window but Tommy tried not to let his mind wander back to that terrible scene.

A flash of red lit the sky and the woman on the stretcher screamed.

'It's all right, Ma,' said Tommy, as the Mudchute ack-ack guns started again. 'We'll soon have you out.'

As the stretcher bearer at the back staggered up the last couple of stairs and cleared the building, Tommy heaved the joist he was shouldering backwards, where it landed amongst the shattered bricks and mortar it had once held upright.

Collecting his crowbar from what remained of the house's upstairs, Tommy jumped down from the rubble to where the first-aid party had laid their patient.

Now they were clear of the building, he could see in the red glow of the burning building opposite that the woman's leg was lying at an odd angle.

Tommy hunkered down beside the elderly patient and her hand shot out and gripped his arm.

'Can you take me home?' she asked in a faltering voice as her bony fingers dug into his flesh.

'I think we're going to have to get our first-aid chaps to take a look at you first, my love,' Tommy replied.

Disentangling himself from the terrified woman, he straightened up. 'Have you seen any other first-aid parties?'

'No, but mobile B is parked in Gunner Street,' said the rear stretcher bearer. 'We could ferry her around there and let them sort her out.'

'Good idea,' said Tommy. 'I'll lead the way.'

He didn't need his muted torch to find the way as the fire from the blazing houses around him was so bright you could have read a newspaper by the light. Stepping over smashed brickwork and skirting around potholes, Tommy led them down to the end of the street and across Three Colts Lane. As he turned the corner, he saw the converted horsebox parked in front of the baker's shop.

As always, knowing that Jo was somewhere close, Tommy's eyes searched for a glimpse of her. His heart soared when they found her tying a sling on a patient in front of the van's open back doors.

Although she'd been one of the mobile dressing station's crew for just over a month, they had barely exchanged more than a few words and then always in the company of others. It was hardly surprising, given all anyone in Post 7 had done for eight weeks of nightly air raids was eat and sleep, often on the school's floor with their tin helmets over their eyes. With the familiar urges of regret and hope tangled in his chest, Tommy led the small party forward.

As he got within a few feet of her, Jo looked up.

Her hat was tilted back slightly on her head so the burning sky lit her face in a mellow glow. Despite the chill of the evening air, damp curls stuck to her forehead and there was dirt streaked across her left cheek. There was a light layer of brick dust on her jacket and wet patches on her trousers where she'd been kneeling on the ground. In truth, she looked like she'd been dragged through a hedge backwards, but to Tommy's mind he'd never seen her looking more beautiful, although he seemed to think that every time he saw her.

As her gaze rested on him, the soft expression in her lovely eyes vanished. Several heartbeats passed as they stared at each other and then a voice cut between them.

'We've another one for you, luv,' said the lead stretcher bearer.

Jo's attention shifted onto the two men behind him.

'I'm afraid you'll have to put her on the ground,' she said. 'We've already got four people inside.'

The light rescue pair lowered the metal frame onto the floor and then strolled off to have a quick fag while they waited.

The old woman lay with her eyes closed and even in the red glow all around them her face looked ashen.

'Pelvis?' Tommy asked Jo as she studied her patient.

She nodded. 'And femur, I shouldn't wonder. Poor thing. Will you send a runner back to Post so they can ring for an ambulance?'

Leaving Jo to tend to her patient, Tommy went over to the mobile first-aid station. After sending one of the boys pedalling back to Shadwell School, he returned to Jo.

Heedless of the hard cobbles, she was kneeling beside the old woman and although he should have been heading off to join Reggie and the rest of Blue Squad, Tommy crouched down, too.

Taking the old woman's wrist, Jo held it gently and studied her watch for a moment then put her hand on her patient's shoulder.

'What's your name, sweetheart?' she asked softly.

The ack-ack guns sent a trace of fire arching into the sky and the old woman's eyes darted back and forth as her gnarled hand plucked at her torn and dirt-caked clothes.

Tommy took one of her hands in his. 'Tell the young lady your name, luv.'

'Vera West,' she replied, the bones of her hand cracking as she gripped his.

'Well, Vera, I'm going to have to ship you off to the hospital,' said Jo. 'So they can fix you up properly.' She looked up at Tommy. 'Could you fetch me six straps from the van? Joan will show you where they are.'

Letting go of Vera's hand, Tommy stood up and climbed into the back of the van just as another explosion sent instruments crashing to the floor as the vehicle shook back and forth. Dirt-covered and blood-spattered, Jo's fellow first-aiders were dealing with a man with blood pumping from his arm, a young boy with a head injury and a man lying on one of the fixed stretchers who was white and motionless with both eyes bandaged. Joan nodded towards one of the stainless-steel cabinets and, having retrieved what he came in for, Tommy left them to it.

Jo had finished her examination and was now standing up looking down at her patient.

'Is she all right?' asked Tommy as he handed Jo the webbing.

'She's passed out,' she replied. 'Which will make putting these on a lot easier. Her pulse is thready and rapid so she's probably got internal bleeding.' She glanced down the road and bit her lower lip. 'I hope that ambulance gets here soon. Do you think you could give me a hand?'

Tommy nodded. 'What do you want me to do?'

'Take her ankles and gently pull the broken one straight,' Jo replied.

Tommy started to do as she bid but just then a blast a few streets away roared overhead. Instinctively, he caught Jo to him and tucked her into his chest to shield her from the shower of shards of glass, splinters and brick residue that rained down on them.

The ack-ack guns started again.

As the last of the grit pitter-pattered at their feet, Jo stepped out of his embrace and Tommy reluctantly let her go.

'That was a bit close for comfort,' he said, grinning at her.

She gave him an awkward smile. 'Yes, it was.'

Looking away, she continued to organise the straps.

Tommy took up his place at Vera's feet and, when Jo gave him the nod, slowly applied traction as she braced her patient's injured leg against the good by buckling the webbing across the old woman's hips, thighs, knees and ankles.

As she secured the final buckle in place, the ambulance, in this case an old Wolseley with the back seats missing, drove around the corner with its bell ringing.

Coming to a halt beside them, the ambulance men jumped out. Jo quickly handed over her patient and Tommy and the other two men eased the old woman into the back of the car, strapping the stretcher in place for the three-quarters-of-a-mile drive to the London Hospital.

Having finished their roll-ups, the light rescue chaps came back to retrieve their iron-mesh stretcher and headed off to where they were next needed.

'Oi! We have injured,' someone cried from the other end of the street.

'Coming,' Jo shouted.

She reached for her first-aid haversack but Tommy picked it up and slung it over his shoulder.

'I've got to go that way to join Blue Squad in Shadwell Walk so I'll come with you,' he said.

Jo gave him a guarded look but didn't argue, just fell in step beside him as they skirted around the mounds of pulverised rubble and mangled household items scattered across their path.

They walked down the street but when they turned the corner they found an eight-foot garden wall had collapsed across their path.

'It's all right, we can climb over,' said Tommy, leaping up onto the rubble.

He held out his hand but as Jo took it an explosion a few streets away sent a streak of white light across the sky. The blast reverberated in their ears and shook the ground beneath their feet.

Gripping her tightly, Tommy guided her over the jagged fragments of the demolished wall. Once safely on the other side, she pulled her hand away from his.

Picking his way over dislodged cobbles and shattered concrete, Tommy led them through the blazing streets until they reached the Temperance Memorial Hall halfway up Lucas Street, but then something whistled overhead.

There was a split second of unearthly silence then the row of houses directly in front of them shuddered before a burst of blinding light shattered all the windows, spewing glass onto the street. The explosion sucked Tommy's breath away and tugged at his clothes before propelling him onto the floor as gravel, glass and scraps of paper flew past him.

He shook his head, blinked the grit from his eyes and looked around.

Jo was lying face down on the pavement a few yards behind him. Scrambling to his feet, Tommy hurried over to her.

'Jo!' he shouted through the hurricane of wind whipping at his hair and face.

She didn't move.

Trying to hold the tide of panic rising in his chest, Tommy turned her over.

Despite her hair being dishevelled and the dirt streaked across her face, Jo looked otherwise uninjured. Of course, that's exactly how victims who'd had their lungs blown by a blast looked when you dug them out.

'Jo,' he shouted again, trying not to imagine the emptiness of his life without her.

Her eyelids fluttered up. 'Tommy?'

'Thank God,' he said, smoothing her hair out of her eyes.

She frowned up at him and he withdrew his hand.

'Are you in pain?' he asked.

Jo flexed her hands and shifted her feet. 'No, I don't think so. What happened?'

'We got caught in that lot,' he replied, nodding towards the crumpled row of houses a hundred yards in front of them. 'And we were just blown over by the blast.'

Jo sat up and started to get to her feet.

'Let me help,' he said, taking hold of her elbow.

'I can do it,' she replied, pulling away from him and dusting herself down. But just as she stood up another explosion deafened them as the builder's yard on the corner of the street crashed to the ground in a whoosh of sparks and flame.

As the shockwave powered towards them, Tommy gathered Jo to him and dived into the shelter of the Temperance Hall's doorway a split second before it pulsed by. As it did, Jo's knees buckled but before she reached the floor, Tommy had her in his arms.

'It's all right, my darling,' he said, feeling her hair against his cheek. 'I've got you.'

Pushing against his chest, Jo raised her head.

'And I'd prefer it if you didn't,' she snapped. 'So, if you don't mind, Tommy Sweete, I'd thank you to put me down.'

She glared at him in the amber glow of the burning buildings for a moment then Tommy set her back on her feet.

'Thank you,' she said, snatching her haversack from the rubble and hooking it across her. 'Now, I have casualties to attend to.'

'Shouldn't you go back to the wagon and get checked out,' he said, thinking she still looked a little pale for his liking.

'Look, I was a bit shaken, that's all,' she replied, in a tone you might use on a five-year-old.

She started to move away but Tommy blocked her path. 'What are you doing?' he said.

'Going back to work.'

'But you can't.'

Jo looked baffled. 'Can't I?'

'No, you can't. I mean,' Tommy raked his fingers through his hair, 'you could be injured and not know. You could collapse and no one would know where to find you. Perhaps you should go home and rest.'

An explosion burst behind them and instinctively they ducked as plumes of smoke and fire flew skyward.

Picking up her first-aid bag, Jo stood up again.

A fire-engine bell clanged a few streets over from them and Jo raised her eyes.

They were standing just a few inches apart and all Tommy had to do was reach out and she would be in his arms.

Her eyes roamed slowly over his face, sending a fizzle of excitement through him.

'Tommy . . .' she said softly, her eyes glowing large and dark in the light of the burning buildings.

'Yes, Jo,' he said, imagining the softness of her lips under his.

'I'm sure Reggie is wondering what's keeping you,' she said, giving him the sweetest smile. 'So perhaps you ought to go and rejoin your squad.'

Gripping his shovel in his left hand, Reggie grasped what was left of the banister in number 3 Shadwell Walk and heaved himself over the pile of masonry and onto the stairs.

Although the high-explosive bomb had completely obliterated the three houses at the southern end of the street, the remaining six in the terrace were still standing, albeit without a sheet of glass or a roof tile on them. He and the rest of the crew were now checking them for any casualties and to work out what internal or external timber props would be needed to make them safe.

As always, brick dust hung in the air as did the smell of freshly splintered wood and the acidy aroma of burnt explosive released by the armaments that had wrought the devastation around him.

He'd sent the rest of the crew to search through the worst affected houses while he, Fred and Jimmy took the dwelling that was only lightly damaged. He could already hear his two men searching the upstairs rooms so, keeping hold of the moulded handrail in case the staircase collapsed under his weight, Reggie trudged upstairs.

Flicking on his torch, Reggie crunched over a picture lying face down on the landing and went into the first room.

It had been a bedroom but now the small space looked like a junkyard that someone had tipped half a hundredweight of dust over. The china dressing set lay in pieces on the floor and what had once been a brightly coloured patchwork counterpane was now a uniform grey hue.

Fred was on the other side of the room, rummaging through the single wardrobe.

'All right, Fred,' he said, strolling over.

'Not bad,' Fred replied. 'I've found a nice watch in one of the suit pockets and a pair of gold cufflinks in the top drawer of the tall boy.'

'Is that all?' said Reggie.

'Well, there was a bit of loose change in the pockets,' said Fred. 'But it looks like whoever lived here grabbed their stuff as they left. These suits are nearly new.' He dragged a hanger from the wardrobe with a double-breasted suit on it.

'Sod off!' said Reggie. 'Who do you think we are, the bleeding WVS picking up rags?'

Fred's thick face took on an offended expression. 'I only asked.'

'I know, and ordinarily I might consider them as that Polish Jew boy in Hessle Street will always give me a good price for a decent bit of schmutter,' said Reggie. 'But it's too bulky to load on the wagon and with old Potter poking his nose in, we daren't chance it. Course, if you find any furs, that's a different matter.'

Taking a packet of Rothmans from his jacket pocket he offered one to Fred and then took one himself.

'I wonder what's happened to your Tommy,' said Fred as he held a match to the end of Reggie's cigarette.

'I'm buggered if I know what he's up to these days,' said Reggie, blowing a stream of smoke towards the open rafters. 'But to be honest, it's easier with him not here, ain't it?'

'Well, I know he's your brother and all, but me and the boys have said the same for a while,' Fred agreed. 'Although I thought you would have made him see sense by now.'

'So did I, but he don't listen to me any more,' said Reggie. 'Spent weeks figuring out some poxy newspaper puzzle but when I asked him if he'd sit behind me at Bald Ollie's poker game next week he refused, saying he wouldn't help me cheat. Well, I frigging wouldn't have to, would I, if he behaved like a brother should by doing that numbers trick of his and giving me the nod.'

'Do you think it's because that Brogan girl's back?' asked Fred.

Reggie shook his head. 'No, from what I see, she don't give him the time of day.'

Fred laughed. 'I'm not surprised after catching him with his trousers down with Lou.'

Reggie grinned. 'Yeah, I couldn't have planned that better if I'd tried. Still, until Tommy gets his head screwed back on the right way we'll just have to do what the Sally Army do and live in hope.' He took another long drag of his cigarette. 'Anyway, Fred, keep looking and take the boards up if you have to but see what else you can find.'

Fred nodded and yanked out one of the dressing-table drawers, scattering the contents in the dust and grit at his feet.

Pinching out his fag, Reggie stowed it behind his ear and trudged out of the room. In the back bedroom he found an expensive-looking double brass bed with a bedspread that matched the tattered curtains at the window. There was also a three-door walnut-veneer wardrobe with a matching dresser and a kidney-shaped dressing table complete with a velvet-upholstered stool.

After scanning the room quickly for anything of value that he could slip in his pocket, Reggie stomped over to the wardrobe and opened the door. The dresses and jackets smelt of mothballs and although of good quality there was nothing worth taking. He pulled open the second door and found much the same with the addition of a few winter coats. The third door only revealed a set of internal shelves with some folded jumpers and a couple of handbags. Reggie crossed to the dresser and yanked out the bottom drawer. He tipped the contents onto the carpet. An array of underwear and a few rolled-up pairs of stockings tumbled out onto the floor. He pulled out the second drawer and found more of the same, plus a few cardigans and scarfs. The two drawers above it yielded nothing of any interest either. Leaving the drawers dangling, Reggie pocketed a posh-looking bottle of scent to give to Rita and then rummaged around in the trinkets on the china tray. Stowing a pair of earrings alongside the perfume, he looked around. His gaze rested on the neatly made bed for a moment then he dropped to his knees to check underneath. There was the usual dust and flowery china gazunder beneath it but Reggie ignored them, running his eyes over the mesh base of the bed until he spotted what he was searching for.

He grinned and stretching his hand took hold of the leather wallet wedged in the springs, but as he reached it a pair of familiar size-ten boots hoved into view on the other side.

Scrambling out, he stood up.

'Cor blimey, Tommy, I was beginning to think you'd been taken away by the gypsies,' he said, grinning at his brother.

Tommy's face took on a stony expression. 'What are you doing?'

'Checking for casualties,' snapped Reggie. 'What the bloody hell do you think I'm doing?'

Tommy's gaze flickered to the wallet in his brother's hand and then back to Reggie's face.

'It's just pickings and ain't we entitled to the odd perk or two?' said Reggie, feeling like a kid caught with his hand in the sweet jar.

'Put it back,' said Tommy.

Reggie glared at his brother but Tommy's challenging gaze didn't waver. Reggie held his brother's stare for a long moment then flung the wallet on the bed.

All right,' he said, 'have it your own way. Now perhaps we can—'

'And the rest.'

Reggie turfed out his pockets and dropped the half a dozen items next to the wallet.

Tommy glanced at the small pile he'd just discarded and then back at Reggie. 'You should be ashamed of yourself.'

Reggie opened his mouth to argue but saw the loathing in his brother's eyes and thought better of it.

'There's an oil bomb landed by the water works,' said Tommy in a flat voice. 'It's blown half the street away. Control needs all hands on site or no one this side of Whitechapel Station will have any water in the morning. So let's go.'

He turned to leave but Reggie caught his arm and Tommy turned.

'You're becoming a right poxy Boy Scout,' said Reggie.

'And you're becoming a bloody irritating brainless idiot,' Tommy replied. 'But for all that, I don't want the last time I ever see your ugly mug to be through a set of prison bars so grab your shovel and let's go.'

Chapter Sixteen

SETTING THE CUP of tea she'd just made herself on the table to cool, Queenie took the green block of carbolic soap from the draining board and then grabbed the next piece of clothing from the bucket at her feet.

'This has seen better days,' she said, holding up her son's shirt so her companion could see.

Prince Albert was perched on the back of a chair. He lifted a claw and scratched behind his ear by way of reply.

It was mid-morning on the first Tuesday in November, Guy Fawkes Day in fact, although after the last few nights of having the fires of hell dropped on them no one wanted any more fireworks. Not that kids could get them if they did because fireworks, like unshielded car lights and workmen's braziers, had been banned to prevent enemy bombers finding their targets.

'Fecking Hun,' muttered Queenie.

Prince Albert whistled and side shuffled along his improvised perch.

Of course, after the unfortunate occurrence when he'd decided to decorate the cake Ida had left to cool for Sunday tea in his own particular way, Ida had banned him from the kitchen. But she was at work so Queenie figured what her daughter-in-law didn't know wouldn't hurt her and, after all, she liked a bit of company when she was doing the washing.

Turning back to her task, Queenie plunged the soap into the warm water, ran it over the faded shirt and then rubbed the garment over the ridges of the washboard.

She repeated the process twice more before throwing the scrubbed shirt into the sink with the other clothes waiting to be rinsed. She was just about to take another one of her son's shirts from the bucket when there was a knock at the door.

She gave the parrot a querying look. 'Well now, who the devil can that be?'

Prince Albert stretched his neck and whistled again.

'It can't be the rent man cos we paid him this week,' she went on, taking the tea towel from the nail at the end of the draining board. 'And Cathy would have come around the back.'

Wiping her hands as she went, Queenie walked through the house to the front door and opened it.

Standing on the step, dressed in a donkey jacket over a reasonably clean navy boiler suit and with a cap set at a roguish angle on his curly brown hair, was a very tall young man.

'Good afternoon,' he said, smiling at her. 'Mrs Brogan, isn't it?'

Queenie looked him up and down. 'That it is.'

'Well, I'm Tommy Sw—'

'I know who you are, boy,' Queenie cut in. 'Sure, haven't I given you a clip around the ear for cheek?'

'On more than one occasion,' he replied.

Her eyes strayed to the top of his head. 'Although, I'd need the wings of St Gabriel to reach you now.'

His eyes twinkled in a way that must have sent the lassies' hearts beating.

'If you're after my son,' said Queenie, 'you'll find him at the yard.'

'No, I've come to see Jo,' Tommy said.

'And what, may I ask, Tommy Sweete, would you be wanting with my granddaughter?' asked Queenie.

'To make sure she's all right,' Tommy answered.

'And why wouldn't she be?'

'She's not been at work for a few days,' said Tommy, 'and I was concerned—'

The door to number 3 on the other side of the road opened and Peggy Pollock stepped out, thus ensuring that the whole neighbourhood would know by sunset that Tommy Sweete had been on the Brogans' front step.

'Well, I can tell you now she's grand. Thank you for asking.' Queenie went to close the door.

'I was worried about her,' said Tommy.

Something in his tone stayed Queenie's hand. 'Have you time to spare for a cuppa, Tommy?'

'Well . . .' He glanced at his watch. 'I suppose so.'

Taking his cap off and shoving it in his pocket, Tommy stepped inside. Queenie shut the door behind him then led him through the house.

'Such a lot of books,' he said, glancing at the crammed bookcase that dominated the back parlour.

'My son's a one for the learning,' said Queenie.

'That's where Jo must get it then,' said Tommy, his eyes softening as they passed the photo of Jo and Mattie as bridesmaids at Cathy's wedding, which was in pride of place on the mantelshelf.

'Oh, a parrot,' he laughed as they entered the kitchen. 'Jo said . . .' He shot Queenie a self-conscious look.

'Sugar?' Queenie asked, taking a mug from the dresser.

'Two, but only if you have enough,' he said.

'You can have some of Ida's ration,' Queenie called over her shoulder as she went to the stove to pour his tea.

As she turned back to face him, Tommy was just reaching out to Prince Albert, his hand dangerously close to the parrot's sharp beak.

'I'd have a care for your fingers, me lad—' Queenie's mouth dropped open as, unbelievably, instead of taking a nip out of the flesh on offer, Prince Albert began to rub his head against Tommy's knuckles.

Queenie put his tea on the table and shooed her pet away. He gave an indignant squawk and flew off to find another perch.

Tommy sat down.

'So,' she said, taking the seat opposite, 'why is it you're fretting over Jo?'

He looked puzzled. 'Didn't she tell you about being blown off her feet the other night?'

'I can't recall her mentioning it,' said Queenie.

'I told her she ought to go home but she wouldn't hear of it.' He raked his fingers through his hair. 'She wouldn't even go back to get checked over at her first-aid station, just stormed off to her next call. She insisted she was all right. I wasn't too worried on Sunday because I knew she wasn't on duty but then she didn't turn up on Monday or Tuesday so I thought perhaps she was taken ill or something.'

Queenie studied him for a couple of seconds over the rim of her cup. 'You could have asked Mattie.'

Although his eyes remained on her face, Tommy's gaze shifted ever so slightly.

'To be honest,' he said, in a matter-of-fact tone, 'I haven't really seen Mattie and as I was coming this way I thought it would be just as easy to knock.'

'Well, I'm pleased I can relieve you of your concern because Jo is as fine and dandy as ever she was,' said Queenie.

'And the reason you've seen neither hide nor hair of her, my boy, is because she's been at the Town Hall doing her advance first-aid certificate.'

Utter relief swept across his face. 'Thank goodness.'

Throwing back the last of his tea, Tommy stood up. 'Well, thanks for the cuppa, Mrs Brogan, but I shouldn't take up any more of your time. And don't worry about seeing me out, I'll go through the yard.'

Crossing the small kitchen, Tommy opened the back door but as he did, Prince Albert let out a series of loud whistles.

Tommy smiled.

'My nan had a budgie,' he said, gazing across at Prince Albert who had taken up residence on the clothes dryer suspended over the stove. 'My father bought it down Club Row for her so she called it Harry after him.' His gaze moved from the bird back to her. 'Will you tell Jo I called?'

Queenie studied Tommy's young face and her heart softened.

Although it was decades since she herself had felt the soaring heights or unplundered depths of it, she knew what love looked like and she was certainly looking at it now.

'For sure I will,' Queenie replied.

He gave her a grateful smile and left.

Queenie finished her drink, put her cup on the table and stood up. Picking up her son's shirt again she leaned back over the zinc tub.

She raked it back and forth a couple of times but as she dropped it in the rising bucket the back door opened and her son strolled in.

'I hope there's tea in that pot, Ma,' he said, closing the door behind him.

'There is,' said Queenie, wiping her hands on her apron.

'You just take the weight off your feet and I'll fetch you a cup.'

While she poured her son's tea, Jerimiah shrugged off his coat and settled into his chair at the head of the table.

'Strong and sweet, just like you,' she said, setting his drink before him. 'Good morning?'

'Fair,' he replied, picking up his cup and cradling it in his massive hands. He blew across the top. 'Was that Tommy Sweete I saw leaving our house just now?'

'It was,' said Queenie.

Her son raised his eyes and smiled.

'Coming up before the magistrate for taking bets for Fat Tony is one thing, Ma,' he said in a soft tone, 'but getting yourself tangled up with those Sweete brothers is not something I'd recommend.'

'Well then, you put your mind at ease about that,' said Queenie, ruffling her son's hair that was so like Patrick Mahon's used to be. 'He was here enquiring after Jo. Apparently, she was knocked over the other day and he was just checking that she's fine and dandy.'

Although his expression remained pleasant, her son's eyes took on a sharp glint.

'That's mighty civil of him,' he said in the same easy tone.

Jerimiah took a mouthful of tea.

'Ah,' he said, closing his eyes. 'Second only to a nip of poteen to warm to a man's bones.'

'Well, you sit and take your leisure with it while I finish off these few bits.' Back at the sink, Queenie picked up the next shirt and plunged it into the soapy water.

'I'm wondering has Tommy Sweete been here before, Ma?' Jerimiah said.

'Not to my knowledge, son,' Queenie answered, rubbing

one of Mattie's underslips over the bevelled surface of the washboard.

The moments ticked by and then the clock in the parlour chimed the half past and Jerimiah stood up.

'Well, Ma, no rest for the wicked.' He drained his cup, set it on the table and walked across the room. 'Tell Ida I'll be in at the usual time.'

Queenie nodded.

Jerimiah shrugged on his coat but as he opened the door he turned back and looked at her.

'I'd be grateful, Ma, if you'd let me know if the Sweete lad comes asking after me darling Jo again.'

Resting her hands on the edge of the sink, Queenie smiled. 'That I will and you have a good afternoon.'

He left.

Queenie dropped the garment she was holding into the pail at her feet. Perhaps, for everyone's sake, she wouldn't mention to Jo that Tommy had dropped by.

'How's your pie?' asked Gillian, pointing at Jo's plate with her fork.

'Not bad,' Jo replied. 'What about your stew?'

It was now just after one thirty and they were celebrating passing their first-aid test by treating themselves to a full dinner in the Town Hall restaurant instead of making do with a sandwich as they usually did when they were on duty at Post 7.

The canteen at the back of the Town Hall was a rather grand affair, with a large serving hatch at one end and a couple of dozen six-seater tables arranged in two rows.

The walls were tiled to shoulder height with glossy green squares and the walls above were painted in cream emulsion. Not that you could see much of the walls as all available space had been covered with information posters. Some told you to 'Save Coal' or 'Dig for Victory', others had instructions on what to do during a gas attack.

The eating area was bursting at the seams because, in addition to the Town Hall workers it had been designed to accommodate, it now had to serve the ARP headquarters personnel who had taken up residence in the basement. Jo and Gillian were perched on the very end of one of the middle tables. They had been very fortunate to secure a space because even though extra chairs had been provided, all around them people were eating standing up, balancing trays on window sills and atop of radiators.

'It tastes right enough,' Gillian replied, 'but it's a bit like hunt the meat.'

'I reckon it'll be the same with the pudding,' said Jo, indicating the bowls sitting between them. 'It's supposed to be spotted dick but I can't see any currants.'

'Me neither, but at least there's plenty of custard,' said Gillian.

Jo nodded. 'As my Gran's always saying, "be thankful for small mercies".' She speared a potato and wiped it around in the gravy. 'How's Martin?'

'Worn out like the rest of us but well enough,' Gillian replied. 'Although he had a lucky escape two nights ago when a big one landed on the North London Line.'

Martin Hopgood, Gillian's long-standing boyfriend, was an engineer on the Great Eastern Railway based at Stratford.

'Oh my goodness,' said Jo. 'Is he all right?'

'A few scratches from flying debris but a gear wheel missed his head by inches,' said Gillian. 'He said, "So much for reserved occupations being a cushy number; I'd be safer in the army."'

'Do you think he will volunteer?' asked Jo.

Gillian nodded. 'He won't admit it but I think he feels he's not doing his bit.'

'That's daft,' said Jo. 'If it wasn't for the railways the war effort would grind to a halt.'

'I know that and you know that.' Gillian pulled an exasperated face. 'But you know what blooming numbskulls men can be. Plus, I think he's envious of all his mates in khaki who seem to be having a whale of a time.'

'I'm sure they are,' said Jo. 'My brother's certainly enjoying himself in the army; he seems to spend all his time either in the privates' mess or in the local pub.'

'Anyway, forget about my idiot boyfriend; how's your love life going?' asked Gillian. Scraping the bottom of her bowl, she popped the last drop of stew in her mouth.

Jo rolled her eyes. 'What love life?'

'I thought you said you were going to the flicks with some Auxiliary Fire Service fella,' said Gillian.

'I did,' said Jo, shoving her plate aside and sliding the dessert bowl into its place.

Moving her crockery around too, Gillian picked up her spoon. 'Well?'

Jo swallowed a mouthful of suet pudding and custard. 'Well, what?'

'Is he handsome?' her friend asked.

'Not bad,' said Jo.

'Did you have to fight him off in the dark?' asked Gillian.

'No, Larry was a perfect gentleman,' Jo replied.

'So are you going out with him again?' Gillian asked as she finished her pudding.

'I don't think so,' said Jo.

'Why? What's wrong with him?' asked Gillian.

Jo shrugged. Lowering her eyes she made a play of scraping the last of her dessert onto her spoon.

'Right, enough of this shilly-shallying! You, my girl,' said Gillian, jabbing her spoon at her, 'need a bit of fun that only a big strong man can give you.'

Despite the cloud of unhappiness hovering over her, the corners of Jo's mouth lifted. 'Do I?'

'Yes, you do,' her friend replied. 'So I'm going to fix you up. And don't give me any of that old "Good Catholic Girl" rubbish neither. My brother went out with a convent school girl and she was no nun, I can tell you. Now what about him?' She indicated a dark-haired auxiliary police officer sitting on the table opposite.

Jo laughed. 'He's not bad, I suppose.'

'All right,' said Gillian. 'What about him in the dungarees on the second table?'

Jo turned. 'Which one? They're all dressed the same.'

Gillian pulled a face. 'Well, not the three granddads, obviously, the chap at the far end with the brown hair who looks a bit like Clark Gable.'

Jo glanced across the central aisle at the young man who, to her way of thinking, had only a thin moustache in common with the Hollywood heart-throb.

'I've seen better,' she said.

Gillian rolled her eyes again. 'You know your trouble? You're too fussy by halves that . . .' She tailed off as something at the other end of the room caught her attention. 'Well hello, handsome,' she said, an appreciative glint sparking in her grey eyes.

Jo turned.

Tommy was standing just inside the door and gazing around. He was dressed in a navy boiler suit with his donkey jacket hanging from his broad shoulders and his cap set at its usual jaunty angle on his dark curls.

'Don't tell me you wouldn't be interested in him?' said Gillian.

Jo didn't answer.

She couldn't because her attention was entirely fixed on the strong planes of Tommy's face and it robbed her of all other thoughts.

'And I tell you what,' continued her friend, as Jo's heart thumped painfully in her chest, 'Martin or no Martin, I wouldn't mind having a bit of fun with that one myself. I wonder who he's looking for?'

Jo held her breath as Tommy's dark eyes ran over the heaving refectory until he saw her. Her heart did a happy little double step before galloping off again.

Time seemed to slow to a crawl as Tommy walked between the tables towards her but when he got to within a couple of feet of them, Gillian's fork shot off the table and skidded along the floor.

Tommy stopped it with his foot and then, in one fluid movement, stooped to pick it up. He placed it on the table in front of Gillian.

'Thank you,' she said, dimpling up and fluttering her eyelashes at him.

He gave her an absentminded half-smile and then turned to face Jo.

'Hello.'

'Hello,' Jo replied, feeling a little light-headed at his nearness. 'What are you doing here?'

'Er, me? I'm . . . I'm picking something up. From stores,' he said.

'I'm doing first-aid training,' said Jo, suddenly remembering the feel of his mouth pressed onto hers.

'I know,' said Tommy.

'Do you?'

'Yes,' he said. 'I dropped by your house to see if you were all right after what happened on Saturday and your granny told me.'

'Oh, yes, I'm fine,' said Jo, wondering what her gran would make of having Tommy Sweete standing on her doorstep.

'Good.'

Tommy shifted his weight onto the other foot.

'Well, I'd better go and fetch . . . the thing from stores,' he said, making no move to do so.

He smiled.

A warm glow spread through Jo and she smiled back.

'Well, I'll see you on duty tomorrow night,' said Tommy.

Mastering the urge to throw herself into his arms and kiss every inch of his face, Jo smiled back. 'Yes, see you tomorrow.'

Something Jo couldn't quite understand passed between them, then Tommy turned to go.

'I think you'll find the store is the other way,' said Gillian, giving him an expressive look.

Tommy turned around and, giving Jo another smile as he passed, headed off in the opposite direction.

Jo's eyes stayed with him until he went through the door then she shifted her attention back to her friend sitting opposite.

'So,' said Gillian, giving her a curious look, 'what happened on Saturday?'

Jo told her about them being caught in the blast.

'I was a bit shaken, obviously,' concluded Jo. 'But I'm fine now.'

'I'm pleased to hear it,' said Gillian. 'One of the depot drivers got caught by one last week and had both his eardrums blown out. Fancy another cuppa before we go back?'

'Why not?'

Picking up both their mugs, Gillian stood up and walked to join the back of the tea queue.

Resting her right elbow on the table and her chin in her hand, Jo studied the door Tommy had just left by and sighed.

The truth of the matter was that what was wrong with Larry – wrong with any man, in fact – was that he wasn't Tommy.

Putting her expansive shopping bag on the floor and unhooking the kneeler from the pew in front of her, Queenie Brogan dropped it on St Bridget's and St Brendan's flagstones and knelt down.

She took her mother's rosary from her pocket and, pressing it between her hands, looked up at the tortured figure of Christ nailed to his cross.

'*Ave Maria, gratia plena, Dominus tecum,*' she muttered, as she wondered in passing how many times she'd said the same in her sixty-three years.

In truth, she didn't say them any longer, they said themselves, leaving her mind to ponder more important matters.

It was just before three and she was in her regular place for Thursday afternoon confession, halfway back on the left-hand side of her parish church. The church had been built a century before and the Victorian architect's love of all things Gothic showed in every line and shard of stained glass. The wide central nave was flanked by the Virgin and the church's patron saints. Each had its own chapel and separate elevated altar with gold embroidered table vestments, crucifixes and candles which stood against a decorated back screen.

The church was the heir of the Virginia Street Mission that had served the swathes of her fellow countrymen who had flooded to this part of London from the old country a century before. Queenie had first walked into the holy place as a bride of three months carrying six-week-old Jerimiah in her arms and had been part of the congregation ever since.

When she'd arrived half an hour before there had been a handful of elderly women like herself in the church, who'd come to cleanse themselves of their sin before fish day tomorrow. Although, looking around at the shrivelled widows with lace squares draped over their bowed heads, she couldn't think for the love of all that was holy what sort of mortal sin they still had the strength to commit. As she did each time she went to confess to Father Mahon, Queenie held back until she was alone in the church.

The confessional door opened and the last penitent, Mrs Timpson, stepped out.

Kissing her worn crucifix, Queenie crossed herself, replaced her kneeler and, retrieving her bag, stood up. Adjusting her own net and lace scarf, she sidestepped out of the pew and walked towards the confessional. Opening the door, she stepped in and sat down.

Leaning her head against the fretted grille, she smiled.

'So, Father Mahon,' she said in a hushed tone, 'how are you this fine day?'

'My child, you're supposed to say, "Forgive me, Father, for I have sinned",' came the equally hushed response.

'Ah, don't you think I know that after all these years?' Queenie said. 'But I worry about you and that chest of yours. You were coughing fit to burst your lungs all through Mass last week.'

'My chest is fine,' he replied.

'I'm pleased to hear it,' said Queenie. 'But be sure, I'd advise you to get a good spread of mustard on a towel and fix it under your vest the next time. I remember your poor mother. She was just the same. At the first hint of damp from the river she was coughing for a week.'

There was a sigh from behind the screen. 'The priest taking the confession is not supposed to know who they are speaking, too.'

'Now, Patrick, you know full well who I am,' said Queenie, 'so don't pretend otherwise. And that it was Mary Timpson before me. I hope she told you about that so-called lodger of hers who never creases the sheets in his own bed.'

The lattice barrier slid back and Father Mahon's face appeared.

Patrick Mahon was only a few years older than Queenie but his sparse white hair cropped close to his head made him look completely bald and a decade older. The etched lines in his face spoke of a life dealing with the trouble and strife of humanity while his love of all and everyone showed in his compassionate gaze.

'How are you, Bridget?' he asked.

Queenie frowned. 'Well enough, but you look pale. Is that so-called housekeeper of yours giving you your full rations?'

'Mrs Dunn puts a full plate in front of me three times a day,' Father Mahon replied, 'and is most kind in her care. Now, Bridget, have you something you'd like to be confessing?'

She shrugged. 'Just the usual.'

'You've been goading your daughter-in-law again?' he asked.

'I have but riled so I was,' said Queenie, 'after her telling me not to put my teeth to soak in her pudding basin.'

The corner of Father Mahon's lips twitched.

'Anything else?'

'A bit of gossiping when I shouldn't,' said Queenie. 'But sure doesn't everyone to pass the time?'

'What about taking bets for Fat Tony?' he asked.

She nodded.

'You know you're breaking the law?' he said.

'I do, Father, I do,' she replied. 'But if it wasn't me it would be someone else.'

'What about the other thing?' he said.

'You mean the tea leaves?'

'And the muttering of heathen spells.'

Queenie nodded. 'I confess I have read Charlie and the girls' cups but only because I love them and want to know they'll be fair and fine.'

Father Mahon gave her a disapproving look and she hung her head. 'Forgive me, Father.'

Queenie studied the dark wooden panel between herself and the priest.

'Bridget Brogan,' he said after a pause, 'you're to say three Hail Marys and recite your rosary twice each morning until your next confession.' There was a rustle of cloth as Father Mahon raised his hand. '*Deus, Pater misericordiarum, qui per mortem et resurrectionem Filii sui mundum . . .*'

As Father Mahon repeated the familiar blessing, memories of lying in soft Irish meadows next to icy mountain streams flashed through Queenie's mind.

'. . . *in nomine Patris, et Filii, et Spiritus Sancti,*' he concluded.

Queenie crossed herself and so did Father Mahon, who then slid the screen back.

She opened the door but as she stepped back into the quiet church the priest's door opened and Father Mahon emerged. Taking off his stole he kissed the embroidered cross at the back.

'So, Bridget,' he said, folding it into his cassock pocket, 'how are things with you and yours? I heard Charlie was back.'

'He was and looking grand but he's gone back now,' said Queenie. 'And Mattie and Cathy are still fighting like pixies in a cage.'

'That's hardly surprising, now, is it?'

'I suppose not, given all and everything that's between them,' Queenie agreed. 'But now Jo and Mattie are at odds about something too.' She sighed. 'Well, I suppose that's the way of it with a houseful of girls, Father.'

'You speak the very truth there, Queenie, you do,' he said. 'I can't remember a time as a boy when one of my five sisters hadn't fallen out with one of the others.'

He paused then asked, 'Has Mattie heard from Daniel?'

'Not since she had a postcard last month from his commander,' said Queenie.

'Praise the saints,' said the old priest. 'He's in my every prayer. What about that son of yours?'

A warm glow spread through Queenie. 'Sure, he's the joy of old years and so like his father it makes my heart swell each time my eyes rest on him.'

Father Mahon chuckled. 'You know, it must be a wife's eyes because, try as I might, I can see nothing of your Fergus in him.'

Queenie said nothing.

The clock in the tower above them chimed.

'Three thirty,' said Father Mahon. 'Mrs Dunn will be serving tea. It's seedy cake this afternoon, I believe.'

'Well, you be sure and eat it,' said Queenie.

He smiled at her, then turned and headed for the vestry.

As she watched the hem of his cassock skimming over the tiles of the nave a fond smile lifted Queenie's lips. She'd first laid eyes on him when sitting at her mother's side in St John the Baptist's in Kinsale. She was no more than four years old and he was one of the altar boys serving in the sanctuary.

He'd grown into a lanky youth with a full head of springy black hair, just like Jerimiah's, and a good head taller than her, but time had taken its toll so now she only had to raise her head a notch to look into Patrick's eyes. His lovely coal-black eyes that warmed her heart even now.

Chapter Seventeen

JABBING FORWARD, TOMMY'S right-hand fist landed squarely in the middle of the punchbag then dancing back he did the same with his left, sending the leather cylinder rocking on its anchor ropes.

'Cor, I'm glad that ain't my jaw,' said a voice behind him.

Relaxing his stance, Tommy grabbed the punchbag in his gloved hands to stop its motion and grinned at Ruben 'Vitch' Marcovitch, standing behind it.

It was late afternoon on the Monday after he'd called at Jo's house and then dashed to the canteen to see her. The blackout had been in force since three o'clock but this didn't bother those running Arbour Amateur Boxing Club as they'd boarded up the windows at the outbreak of war.

No doubt the Luftwaffe would be dropping by soon to pay their nightly call but until the sirens went off, members of the boxing club were whiling away the time by jabbing at punchbags or improving their footwork by skipping in front of long mirrors. In the central ring, a couple of spindly lads sparred together while Spud Murphy, the club's youth coach, hung over the ropes and bellowed instructions.

Behind him, in pride of place on the wall, was the glass-fronted cabinet displaying the various cups and title belts won by the Arbour Boys. There were a couple of Tommy's trophies in amongst them from his time in the boys' team.

Reggie had brought him here some ten years before to 'toughen him up' and the deco, if that's what you could call the mud-coloured walls and peeling paint, was much the same as it had been when he'd first stepped into the central ring.

Barely reaching Tommy's shoulder, with arms and legs like twisted pipe cleaners and a nose so broken it had practically merged with his cheekbones, Vitch had been a fixture in the boxing club for as long as Tommy could remember. He had a flat above a baker's in Middlesex Street but he clearly only slept there because he could be found at the boxing club from dawn to dusk seven days a week.

Vitch waddled away and, thumping his gloves together, Tommy tucked his head in and flexed his arms. Focusing on the band around the cylindrical punchbag, situated roughly where an opponent's head would be, he smacked his right fist into the centre. Enjoying the blow as it reverberated down his arm, Tommy clouted it with a left hook and followed up with a sidecut, sending the horsehair-padded leather tube bouncing back and forth.

He had said that he'd drop by the Admiral before going on duty, but Reggie's lover boy jokes were beginning to wear a bit thin plus he suspected his brother was encouraging Lou as she didn't seem to want to take no for an answer.

'By the way you lay into that bag I'd say you're right riled at some poor soul.'

Tommy looked up to see Jerimiah Brogan standing behind him.

Although he was wearing his Home Guard uniform, instead of a standard service cap, Jo's father had a leather cap set backwards on his head. Round his throat was a red Kingman neckerchief and instead of the army-issue belt his trousers were held up by a black leather two-inch strap secured by an ornate polished buckle and looped back on itself. With a mass of curly black hair and weather-beaten unshaved complexion, he looked more like a partisan bandit come down from the hills than a man who gathered household cast-offs for a living.

Tommy knew Jo's father by sight but he had never had occasion to speak to him. However, like everyone else in the area, he knew the big-boned Irishman's reputation.

'Mr Brogan,' said Tommy, having to raise his head to look him in the eye.

'You've got quite a punch on you there, boy, and your foot work's good.' He gave Tommy a sneering look. 'I expect it stood you in good stead when you were in borstal.'

'Once or twice,' said Tommy.

Strolling over, Jerimiah caught the swinging punchbag. 'I used to be one for the boxing myself in my younger years,' he said, gazing fondly up at the battered punchbag between his ape-like hands.

'Were you?'

Jo's father pressed his oft-broken nose to one side. 'Sure, doesn't me twisted snout testify to it?'

Tommy didn't reply.

Patting the tatty leather cylinder, Jerimiah shifted his attention to Tommy.

'Father Gillespie who was at St B and B when I was a lad had been the County Mayo junior champion before he was called to the priesthood.' The big Irishman brought his fists up. 'Taught me the old one-two, he did.'

He jabbed his fists but Tommy didn't flinch as the air from the move brushed past his face.

'I tell you, boy,' continued Jerimiah, 'there wasn't one of us lads who didn't have a bloody nose after sparring with that old bugger but it taught me to keep my guard up.'

'I've learned much the same,' said Tommy.

Jerimiah regarded him thoughtfully for a long moment then spoke again. 'Me ma tells me you popped by home a few days back, enquiring after my Jo.'

'Yes, I did,' said Tommy, holding the other man's gaze. 'She was blown off her feet the Saturday before last and as I hadn't seen her I was afraid she might have taken a turn for the worse.'

The big Irishman gave him an ingenuous smile. 'That's very kind of you, boy, but me darling girl's fine as she ever was.'

'I know,' said Tommy. 'She told me as much when we spoke in the Town Hall canteen later that day.'

Jerimiah's jovial expression slipped a little. 'Talk to her a lot, do you?'

'In passing at Post 7.'

'Oh, yes,' said Jerimiah. 'I heard the Sweete brothers were doing their bit for the war effort.'

'Just helping out.'

'Helping themselves to things that don't belong to them, don't you mean?' Jerimiah replied.

Tommy's mouth pulled into a hard line. 'That is a lie.'

'Don't try and play the innocent,' said Jerimiah, all trace of civility gone from his face. 'Everyone knows what the Sweete boys are.'

'And what would that be, then?' snapped Tommy, holding tight to his rising temper.

'Thieves.' Taking a step forward, Jo's father thrust his face into Tommy's. 'In fact, by all accounts, you and your brother are worse than thieves: you're looters. So I'm giving you fair warning, boy.' He jabbed his index finger in Tommy's face. 'Stay away from Jo or I'll break every fecking bone in your body.'

They stood eyeball to eyeball, nose to nose for a moment then, with a lightning move, Jerimiah punched past Tommy's right ear and set the bag behind him crashing into the wall.

He poked his finger at Tommy again. 'Every fecking bone.'

Leaving the scruffy leather cylinder bouncing on its chain, Jo's father turned and marched out of the hall.

Tommy watched the man he hoped one day would be his father-in-law storm out between opened-mouthed club members. A feeling of hopelessness started to wash over him but he pushed it away. Shoving his hands back in his gloves and using his teeth to tighten the laces, he turned back to the punchbag Jerimiah had sent reeling and, with fury raging in his chest, smacked his fist into it.

'There you are, Mum, tea and cake,' said Jo, setting it in front of her mother who was wearing her newly acquired green WVS coat and felt beret.

'Thanks, luv, I'm gasping,' Ida said as Jo squeezed herself into the chair opposite. Kate's Café, which sat in the middle of a line of shops just down from St George's Church in the Highway, was packed.

It was Saturday and she had been on duty until five when a thick fog rolled up the Thames and cut short the Luftwaffe's visit.

If the clock behind the counter was to be believed, it was a quarter past three and the blackout curtains on the windows and front door were already drawn. What with that and the low-power light bulbs, the café's interior had an Olde Worlde feel about it.

A year ago, the ancient eating house that had fed dock labourers and the local population for over a century would have closed at midday, as it always had, after the rush of morning shoppers. However, since the introduction of rationing, it took the best part of the day just to find your basic necessities. One greengrocer might have potatoes but no carrots, so you'd have to go to another shop for those and possibly another for a cabbage. Having tracked down whatever it was you were after, you then had to queue with your fingers crossed they wouldn't all sell out before you got to the front.

The result of all this searching and queueing was that the weekly family shop that used to be finished by late morning could take well into the afternoon and so Kate's Café stayed open longer so that weary shoppers could still have their cup of tea and slice of cake before heading home.

'Are we done?' asked Jo, taking her slice of cake from the plate.

'I think so, but I was up and down this market three times this morning before I got everything on me list.' Ida took a slurp of her tea. 'Queue for this and queue for that, it's a bloody disgrace, that's what it is. I spent half an hour lining up for a measly bar of carbolic then spent another forty minutes in Sainsbury's but when I got to be served they'd run out of bacon so I had to take spam instead. God only knows what your father will say when I dish that up with his fried bread for breakfast tomorrow.'

'Did you speak to the butcher about Christmas?' Jo asked, cupping her hands around her drink and enjoying the warmth.

'I did,' her mother replied. 'He said he couldn't promise but if there was a bullock's heart going he'd put it by for me. I managed to get a shin of beef while I was there for tomorrow's dinner. Hopefully, there'll be a bit of fat on it. That leg of lamb last week was all string and bone even though it cost a blooming fortune. I reckon the Ministry of Food's sending all the best cuts up West for the nobs to nosh on and leaving the leftovers for our butchers.'

Jo winked. 'Perhaps Gran will "find" something for Christmas dinner.'

'Well, if she does, let's hope it's big enough to feed ten of us because Stella's joining us this year and Cathy's bringing that miserable mother-in-law of hers,' said Ida. 'It's lucky we had a blow-out last Christmas as the way things are going there's going to be very little in the shops by way of treats. Even with saving everyone's sugar rations there'll be no icing on the cake and no mince pies if I don't get hold of some dried fruit soon. Still, never mind, as long as we're all fit and well.' Her mother sighed and took a bite of her cake. 'It was good of you to come and find me in the market to give me a hand home. What time did you get up?'

'Just after one,' said Jo.

'Did Mattie get up with you?'

Jo shook her head. 'She was still fast asleep when I left.'

Her mother tutted. 'It's not right her running about the street in her condition.' She gave Jo a sharp look. 'And I wish you and her would sort out whatever it is you're at odds about.'

Jo didn't reply.

The woman behind her got up and Ida shifted her chair forward to let her get out.

'I wonder if her husband will get leave to join us for Christmas?' Jo said, taking a sip of her drink.

'I shouldn't think so,' her mother replied.

'Not even with the baby—'

'Will you just check the butter isn't too close to the soap, luv,' Ida cut in. 'I don't want to taste carbolic on me toast all week.'

Jo bent down and delved into her mother's shopping bag.

She'd been dying to ask Mattie about her husband but as no one in the family talked about him, not even Mattie, something had held her back. Thank goodness she had, with her in the family way. After all a shock could bring on the baby and as much as she would never speak to Mattie ever again she wouldn't want to do anything to damage her baby. She'd had her suspicion after what Cathy said or more precisely didn't say. Gran clammed up like a miser's fist around a coin every time the subject of Mattie's husband came up and Mum, who you could usually wheedle a secret out of eventually, was saying nothing. However, Jo could put two and two together and it was as plain as the nose on your face that this McCarthy chap who had got Mattie in the family way was one of the fascists Cathy's other half had got mixed up with. Either he was serving his sentence in the army like Stan or he was one of the ringleaders and had been hanged, which would explain why his aunt was the one keeping in touch with Mattie.

No wonder no one mentioned him for fear of upsetting Mattie and bringing the baby on too early.

As she straightened up something caught her mother's eye and she tutted. 'Disgraceful.'

Jo followed her mother's gaze and saw a woman leaning unsteadily against the wall outside the Three Feathers on the other side of the road. Her checked box-shoulder jacket hung off one shoulder revealing a grubby blouse beneath and although she was wearing a brown hat it sat precariously on the side of her head. The woman was about her mother's age but whereas Ida had a rosy, matronly appearance, this woman, wobbling about on her downtrodden kitten heels, looked sallow and gaunt.

'Who is it?' asked Jo.

'Ruby Sweete,' Ida replied.

Jo looked across the busy road at Tommy's mother as Ruby took out her compact and attempted to powder her nose.

'I don't think I've ever seen her before,' said Jo.

'It's hardly surprising,' said Ida sourly. 'She's propping up the bar in the Angel most of the time. It's no surprise either that those boys of hers turned out as they did with her for a mother. It was only because Mary Wright, their gran, took Ruby and the boys to live with her when her old man hopped it that they didn't end up in Barnardo's. Although perhaps they'd have been better off. She was a good 'un was Mary Wright, fed and clothed them. Grafter too. It must have broken her 'eart to see how her daughter turned out. She died Christmas twenty-eight, leaving the two boys to more or less fend for themselves,' her mother continued as Ruby's handbag slid off her arm. 'No one round here would see a kid go hungry so mothers gave the boys a hot meal each day but most families were already squashed in one or two rooms so couldn't take them in. Reggie had left school by then anyway so he brought a bit of money home but it wasn't long before both boys were up in front of the magistrate for pinching stuff.'

'Is it any wonder?' said Jo.

Her mother gave her a sharp look. 'Right is right and wrong is wrong and both of them know better now.'

The bell above the shop door tinkled as another customer came in.

'Oh, oh, Ida!'

Jo's mother looked around. "'Ello, Lil, your May had her baby yet?'

'Yes, last night,' Lil called back. 'Six-pound-three.'

Her mother got up. 'Watch the bags, luv, I won't be a minute.'

Leaving Jo drinking the last of her tea, and with the shopping stacked on the floor around her, Ida hurried over to hear all about her friend's new grandchild.

Resting her elbows on the table and cradling her cup in both hands, Jo looked back through the window at Ruby Sweete, who had dropped her handbag on the pavement.

Although she'd never met his mother, from the way Tommy talked about her, Jo knew that he did his best to care for her, which judging by her inebriated and dishevelled state was a thankless task. Tommy never said much about his upbringing but it was noticeable that all his happy childhood memories were with his nan. Although he never said, Jo knew just by the look in his eye when he spoke of his time at home that after his grandmother died, Tommy's life became very bleak indeed until Reggie took him in.

Watching Tommy's mother's clumsy efforts to pick up the spilled contents of her handbag scattered around her feet, Jo's heart ached with sympathy. Well, truthfully, not just with sympathy, but with something she had to give up pretending wasn't there any more. Love.

As the band struck up for the next artist, Reggie took a sip of whisky. Under the lacquered cocktail table he uncrossed and recrossed his legs then smoothed a wrinkle out of the sharply pressed trouser of his new suit.

When Isaac Stanislav, Maxi Cohen's chief tailor, had urged him to choose the square-shouldered, American-style suit, he hadn't been sure. Even when he handed over the seven guineas to the Aldgate tailor last week, he still wasn't convinced he'd made the right choice, but now he had to agree with old Jew-boy. He looked the dog's naggers.

Swirling the amber liquid around in his glass appreciatively, Reggie took another sip. It was good stuff and under other circumstances he would have knocked it back and ordered another but not tonight. The reason for his moderation was because, instead of enjoying a Scotch in the familiar surroundings of the Admiral, he was in the potentially dangerous territory of Vic 'The Blade' Bostock, or Mr Bostock Esquire, as he preferred to be known these days.

It was just before midnight on the third Saturday in November and he was sitting at one of the front tables in the Two Queens social club. This damp and dimly lit joint was situated in a basement just off Dean Street in Soho and was accessible only by a narrow passageway.

He wasn't there by choice, no man in his right mind would be. One of Vic's heavies had left a message with Rita the day before saying the undisputed boss of Soho's underworld wanted to have a word, and Reggie wasn't going to argue. To ignore an invitation from Vic Bostock would earn you a trip to the casualty department to have your face stitched back in place. That was another reason why he was measuring his drinks because whatever Vic wanted to discuss with him, he'd need to keep his wits about him.

The trumpeter in the small orchestra at the side of the stage blared out a fanfare and the fringed red velvet curtains jerked back. The spotlight flashed on, illuminating a young woman standing in the middle of the small space.

She was wearing a golden shimmering cocktail dress, elbow-length white gloves and impossibly high heels. Her red hair was swept up on top of her head and secured with an ostrich feather. She was heavily made-up with black eyeliner and crimson lips to compensate for the glare of the stage lights.

The opening bars of the tune blared out and the young woman wriggled around the stage once before stopping to face the audience. She then gripped the gloved tips of her fingers between her teeth and tugged off first one then the other glove, swinging them in turn before flinging them aside.

Gyrating to the pounding music, the young woman then unhooked the front fastening of her dress. Peeling it off, she dropped it behind her to reveal her scanty red-satin underwear.

Promenading slowly around the minute stage, she returned to the front then, with a teasing smile on her face, the young woman threaded her arms out of her straps. Holding the front of her brassiere in place with one hand she twisted behind with the other to reach the clasp.

With his eyes fixed on the young woman's lithe body, Reggie raised the glass slowly to his lips.

'Mr Sweete,' said a gruff voice behind him.

The young woman spun around to face the back of the stage, dropping the garment at her feet.

'Er . . .' said Reggie, as she kicked it away.

'Mr Bostock will see you now,' said the voice.

The stripper flung her arms wide and paused.

'And he doesn't take kindly to being kept waiting.'

Dragging his eyes from the stage, Reggie looked around to see Black George, Vic's six-and-a-half-foot-tall half-caste enforcer.

Built like a champion dray horse and with hands the size of dinner plates, George Munday had been born south of the river in the same year the unsinkable *Titanic* went down. Like any kid with a touch of the tar brush about him, George had had a tough time of it but he'd fought his way up through the bare-knuckle circuit to be recognised champion of London, maintaining his crown for an astounding five years. After dislodging dozens of teeth, breaking umpteen jaws and putting three of his opponents in the graveyard, he'd retired a few years back to work for Vic.

Having actually seen the man looming above him punch someone's eye out of its socket, Reggie stood up and gave him his full attention.

'This way,' said Black George, ushering Reggie towards a door at the back of the club.

Knocking quietly, Black George waited a moment then went in, leaving Reggie outside.

Standing with his hands in front of him like a boy waiting to see the headmaster, Reggie shifted from one foot to the other and, despite the whistling and cat-calling around him, kept his eyes firmly fixed on the door in front of him.

After what seemed like an eternity, Black George stepped back out and pushed the door open fully.

Pulling down the front of his jacket, Reggie walked in.

If you were to imagine that the criminal underworld was populated by ruffians who resembled Jimmy Cagney, Edward G. Robinson and George Raft, you'd be quite wrong. If Vic Bostock had dressed in a frock coat and gaiters, stuck a dog-collar on and hung a cross around his neck he'd have passed convincingly as a dotty country parson rather than a calculating killer who'd ruled his empire of gambling clubs and prostitution with a combination of brutality and malevolence for the past twenty years.

With rubbery features and a slack mouth, you could be forgiven for thinking he was a tad slow-witted, that was until the razor-sharp glint in his eyes rested on you and then you were in danger of pissing down your leg.

Raised in a slum overlooking Berwick Street Market, Vic had worked his way up through the ranks of criminality from street urchin picking pockets in Park Lane to king of London's underworld, controlling every trick, racket and pimp in Soho.

Tonight, he was wearing a smartly cut dinner jacket with a blood-red silk cravat anchored to his shirt by a diamond-studded pin, which matched the jewelled cufflinks at his wrists. His thinning sandy-coloured hair was plastered to his head with Grecian oil, and there was a bottle of single malt whisky at his elbow.

He was sitting behind the central table with a heavily made-up blonde curled into his right side and a matching brunette on his left. He had a fruit knife in one hand and something Reggie had almost forgotten existed in his other: a fresh peach.

Vic put down the knife and clicked his fingers.

The girls stood up and after planting a kiss on his cheeks, flounced and wriggled out of the room, their stilettos clicking on the grubby lino as they crossed the floor.

As the door closed, Vic popped a chunk of fruit in his mouth and smiled. 'Reggie. Nice to see you.'

'And you, Mr Bostock,' said Reggie. 'I hope you're well.'

'Can't complain,' said Vic. 'You?'

'Oh, you know,' said Reggie. 'Scraping by like everyone else.'

'Don't give me that, Reggie old mate,' chuckled Vic, his pliant features lifting in a benevolent expression. 'You know as well as I do business is booming.'

'Well, I didn't like to boast, Mr Bostock, but I have to admit I'm shifting stuff hand over fist,' conceded Reggie. 'In fact, I'm almost half-inching to order.'

'It's called supply and demand,' said Vic. 'The punters demand it and we supply it.'

'At a price,' said Reggie, basking in Vic's comradely tones.

Vic laughed. 'Too true, chum. Too true.'

'Well, you know yourself, Mr Bostock,' said Reggie, forcing a light laugh, 'you have to sink or swim in this world.'

Vic bit the fruit as his unwavering gaze held Reggie's for what seemed like an eternity and then he smiled.

'Ain't it the truth, but,' he picked up the knife and waggled the blade back and forth, 'I've heard as how you've been paddling in places where you oughtn't. Like in Jack Spot's manor.'

Sweat prickled out from between Reggie's shoulder blades.

'But he's inside,' he stammered, 'and—'

'Naturally, if you're stepping into his shoes you'll be needing a business partner,' interrupted Vic.

'Do I?'

With his eyes fixed on Reggie, Vic silently carved another slice of peach.

'I do,' corrected Reggie. 'Course I do.'

'I reckon twenty per cent top cut—'

'That's a bit steep, ain't it, Mr Bostock?' gasped Reggie, before he could stop himself.

'Call it a wartime premium.' Vic smiled benevolently. 'Plus a pony a month for my protection of you and your crew. Agreed?'

'Agreed,' Reggie replied, knowing the alternative was a dunk in the river with a metal bar tied to his ankles.

'Good,' said Vic. 'Now as your new partner I want you to do me a small favour.'

The space between Reggie's shoulder blades prickled again.

'Favour?' he asked in as even a tone as he could muster.

'Yes, nothing much.' Discarding the peach, Vic drew a spotless handkerchief from his top pocket and delicately dabbed his mouth with it before tucking it back. 'Just relocating a safe from Upington and Sons Engineering Company in East Smithfield to my boys waiting in Epping Forest. I want it hit next Thursday, the twenty-eighth, because the safe will have both the weekly and the monthly wage packets in it. Your cut is a ton and you can divvy it up anyway you please,' Vic went on.

'Thank you, Mr Bostock,' said Reggie, only just stopping himself from screaming 'a hundred quid!'. 'And you know me, anything to oblige.'

'What about your Tommy? Is he happy to oblige, too?' asked Vic, a calculating look creeping into his eyes.

'Course,' said Reggie, forcing a jolly laugh.

'Good,' said Vic. 'I hope so, because I heard he's been kicking up recently.'

Reggie feigned confusion. 'We've had a couple of barneys but that's just a bit of argy-bargy between bruvers, you know how it is,' he said, then wished he hadn't as Vic's brother had disappeared under mysterious circumstances some years back.

Vic regarded him coolly for a second longer and then dismissed him with a flick of his manicured hand.

Reggie stood up and, with a feeling of release spreading through him, headed for the door.

'Reggie,' said Vic.

Reggie turned. 'Yes, Mr Bostock?'

'There'll be a lot of dosh in that safe riding on this,' said Vic. 'Understand?'

Swallowing hard, Reggie nodded, thanking Lady Luck for shifting Tommy onto the Green heavy crew as it saved him the trouble of dropping a Mickey Finn in his brother's cocoa.

'Don't worry,' said Reggie, pulling down the front of his new jacket. 'I'll get it done, Mr Bostock.'

In the dim light of the strip joint's back room, Vic's eyes narrowed into malevolent slits. 'For your sake, I hope you do.'

Chapter Eighteen

JO WOUND THE last length of bandage over the old man's right eye then took the safety pin she was holding between her lips to secure the end. An explosion somewhere to the east of them shook the mobile dressing station, setting the bottle of iodine jingling on the dressing trolley beside her.

It was the third Tuesday in November and somewhere close to three o'clock in the morning. This was her tenth night on duty without a break but she wasn't complaining. Some of Post 7's ARP personnel, notably the fire and rescue teams, hadn't had a day off for double that time. Many were sleeping on the rubber lilos under the tables between shifts.

It was also the seventy-third night of unremitting bombing, despite the annual fogs that shrouded the area from mid-October to March. Although no one in London had had a full night's sleep in almost three months, after the initial shock of having their neighbourhood systematically obliterated around them, the close-knit dockland communities in East London had summoned up their natural don't-let-the-buggers-grind-you-down spirit and adapted so that life had taken on a new sort of normal.

Milkmen still left milk on the doorstep each morning even if the door itself had been blown off, and despite every window pane of the house lying shattered on the pavement, housewives still scrubbed white circles around the front door. Everyone was exhausted and, after almost a year of food rationing, some were at least half a stone lighter too.

Complaining was regarded as cowardice and unpatriotic so no one did. As always, the people of East London did what they always did in times of trouble: they took the mickey out of those in authority, the enemy and each other, and then they made the best of it.

'That should do it for now,' said Jo, sliding the pin carefully through several layers of crêpe. 'I've cleaned all the grit from the wound but it was a deep cut so it still might fester. If you spot any pus go to St Andrew's and let the emergency doctors look at it.'

'Ta, Gal.' The elderly man, who'd been dug out of what was left of his house, touched his bandage and winced. 'It bloody stings, it do, but I mustn't grumble, it could have been worse.'

Jo smiled.

It certainly could have. Two inches lower and he'd have lost his eye. Eight inches and the flying glass would have severed his carotid artery.

'Let me help you,' said Jo, as her patient struggled to his feet. She offered her hand and he took it.

'Now you toddle off to the rest centre and get yourself a nice cup of tea while the WVS sort you out,' said Jo as she helped him down from the back of the horsebox. 'I'm right off my usual patch, though, so you'll have to ask the warden at the information desk where it is.'

The driver of Post 7's other MDS had committed the heinous sin of destroying all four of the vehicle's tyres three nights before by driving though an oil fire. As the truck was out of commission until the replacement tyres arrived, Jo's team were now covering the whole area, which was why her MDS was parked up opposite Poplar High Street library in the recreation ground.

'Thanks, sweetheart,' he said, taking his cap from his pocket and plopping it on over his bandage.

The low droning of planes overhead lessened as they flew off westwards, leaving a series of explosions around the Royal Docks in their wake.

'How many more?' called Eddie, from inside the van.

She and Joan were splinting a woman's broken leg under the pale light from the hurricane lamp suspended overhead. The woman, who was about Jo's age, had superficial cuts on her cheeks and was covered from head to foot with brick dust.

Jo popped her head out of the wagon's door. Outside, sitting on the pavement, were a collection of walking wounded who had been labelled green or orange by the rescue parties who'd found them. Casualties were classified as red, orange or green. Those labelled red were transported straight to hospital. Orange casualties, like the patient Jo had just treated, didn't have life-threatening injuries but needed urgent treatment. Green bomb victims were those who could be safely left until the others had been dealt with. Of course, Rescue sometimes got it wrong, like the chap who'd nearly died because of an overlooked internal bleed, so Jo and her colleagues always gave new casualties a quick once-over.

There was one further category of bomb injury but those poor souls were taken straight to the mortuary.

'About a dozen,' Jo called back. 'Mostly green.'

'Thank God,' said Joan, wiping her forehead with the back of her hand. 'We're almost out of dressings.'

Jo started to climb back into the van but as she put her foot on the running plate one of the Boy Scouts, who'd been drafted into the war effort as a messenger, shot around the corner.

'There's a row of houses gone down behind the school and there are people trapped,' he shouted, skidding to a halt in front of her.

Jo looked at the team leader, Jim, who was dabbing iodine on a woman's arm at the other end of the van.

'We can manage so you go,' he said. 'Take care, though. Jerry's been busy tonight and I don't want you ending up on the red list.'

'Aye, aye, Captain,' said Jo, giving him a cock-eyed salute.

Jumping into the van, she swiped the emergency rucksack from its hook and stepped back into the street.

'Right,' she said to the fresh-faced messenger as she hooked her arms through the bag's straps, 'lead the way.'

'Hurry up, Mick, I'm not bloody Atlas, you know,' shouted Tommy, feeling the edge of the beam braced on his shoulders cutting into his flesh.

'Nearly done,' said Mick Riley, the guvnor of Green heavy squad, as he jammed the metal jack under the beam. He grinned, showing a set of lopsided teeth. 'And stop bellyaching. Anyone would think that ceiling joist was 'eavy.'

Tommy and the rest of Green team were in what was left of the end house in a Victorian terrace that backed onto Kersey Street School.

He and Blewitt from White Squad had volunteered to transfer to Green as three of their team had been caught under a collapsing wall the night before and were still in hospital.

To be honest, he was more than glad to join Mick's team as, although he hadn't caught him at it again, Tommy knew

Reggie and his two sidekicks were still nicking anything they could lay their hands on. It was wrong and he wanted no part of it.

'That's the fella-me-lad in place,' said Mick, kicking the bottom of the metal rod so it was placed vertically under the beam.

Green Squad's leader was a wiry man in his mid-forties whose head barely reached Tommy's chin. He was so slight that he looked as if a strong wind could carry him away. However, looks could be deceiving: Tommy had seen him move fragments of buildings men double his size couldn't shift.

Tommy eased himself out from under the rafter and straightened up.

Unlike most homes in the area, these century-old dwellings had been built for the more affluent members of the Riverside community and, as such, had basements beneath the houses. This meant that instead of having to trudge to the public shelters when the air raid went off, the residents could just go down a few stairs.

When they'd arrived at the scene just ten minutes before, they'd found that most inhabitants had managed to scramble out of their basements with just minor scrapes and bruises, which the wardens at the end of the road were now dealing with. Unfortunately, though, the family in the end terrace was trapped in the basement under the wreckage so while the rest of Green Squad checked through the other dozen or so houses, Tommy and Mick were making a start at shifting the debris.

Rolling his shoulders, Tommy studied the pile of rubble in front of them.

'How do you want to do it, Mick?' he asked.

'Now we've got the wall propped up right it shouldn't take us more than a few moments to dig out the rubble over there,' he said, indicating the narrow area at the front of the house that was below street level. 'And we can bring the family out through the basement window.'

Above their heads, German planes with empty bomb bays droned eastwards as they headed back to their bases in France.

'And we'd be wise to do it before the next wave of their Kraut mates arrive,' Mick added.

'Have you sent for a first-aid team?' asked Tommy.

Mick nodded and took the half-smoked roll-up from behind his ear and stuck it in his mouth.

'And as luck would have it, the street warden told me there's a mobile unit parked in the recreation grounds so I've sent one of the lads around to see if they can spare someone.'

He'd driven off before she'd arrived on duty that evening but the image of Jo walking into Post 7 the day before flashed through Tommy's mind. He shoved it aside and focused on the task at hand.

'I hope you don't mind me saying, Mick,' said Tommy, taking his leather gloves from his rear pocket and tugging them on, 'as the gas company blokes haven't checked the mains yet, do you think you should be lighting up?'

Mick sniffed the air.

'I can't smell no gas so it should be safe enough,' he replied, shaking the flame out.

Grabbing the pick that probably weighed more than his arm, Mick took a drag and then, with his fag dangling from his lower lips, headed towards the rubble clogging the access to the basement. Taking his pick from where he'd left it, Tommy followed him.

Grasping the handle firmly, Tommy swung at the front wall of the house, breaking it into several pieces. Usually, they didn't use picks when digging for survivors as it wasn't considered a good thing to smash a hole in your victim's head as you were rescuing them, but as it was clear that there wasn't anyone under the rubble in the narrow passageway, he and Mick went at it with gusto. It took them just a few moments of backbreaking work to reduce what had been unmovable blocks of masonry to hand-size fragments of brick.

'All right, Mick,' said Tommy, leaping up onto the pavement. 'You bowl and I'll bat.'

Mick nodded and discarding his spent butt amongst the wreckage he grasped the nearest jumble of brick and threw it up to Tommy who caught it and tossed it behind him.

As they emptied the passageway of building fragments the faint booming further down the river told them that the planes that had just flown overhead were getting rid of their remaining munitions over Ilford and Barking.

Once the top of the window was visible, Tommy jumped down into the space.

'Mind out, short arse,' he said, pretending to barge Mick out of the way.

Giving him a good-natured two-fingered gesture, Mick stepped aside.

Careful to avoid the shards of glass jutting from the frame, Tommy took his torch out and shone it into the basement.

'Over here,' screamed a woman.

'Get us out, for pity's sake,' sobbed another woman. 'We've got kids down here wiv us.'

Tommy swung the torch towards the voices.

Huddled together under a fallen beam on the far side of the basement was a handful of women and at least a dozen children clutching teddies or sucking their thumbs as they clung to their mothers.

'Right, well, you keep your chin up,' said Tommy. 'The medics are on their way and we'll soon have you all out.'

'Any sight of a first-aider?' he asked in a softer tone to the man standing next to him.

'You're in luck, Tommy boy, one's just arrived,' said Mick. 'It's that girl on that posh woman's wagon.'

With anticipation rising in his chest, Tommy climbed out of the basement access to see Jo coming towards him.

She was wearing her usual navy trousers and jacket and a seaman's duffel coat at least two sizes too big for her. Her rucksack was slung on her back and her wonderful chestnut hair was bound tightly and tucked under her white tin helmet with the red cross painted on the front. As always, the sight of her expanded his chest with love and so much more.

Watching her step as she picked her way through the rubble to the space he and Mick had just shovelled out, it was only when she was an arm's reach from him that Jo looked up.

An expression he couldn't interpret but that quickened his pulse nonetheless shot across her face.

Jo held his gaze for a second or two and then lowered her eyes.

'All right,' she said, adjusting the rucksack straps, 'what do we have?'

'A handful of women with their children,' said Tommy, trying to concentrate on what he was saying rather than the shape of Jo's mouth.

Jo nodded. 'I'll climb in and pass the children out then see to the adults.'

'Good idea,' said Tommy.

Taking the pickaxe resting against the side of the house, he carefully knocked out the remaining fragments of glass and splintered wood.

Grabbing a rug that had been thrown out onto the pavement by the blast, Tommy laid it over the window sill then using a block of brick as a step he started to climb through the window.

Jo's small hand caught his arm.

'What are you doing?' she asked as he straddled the window sill.

Tommy turned and raised an eyebrow. 'You don't seriously think I'm going to let you go in alone, do you, Jo?'

Of course, she should tell him she was quite capable of climbing through a broken window to deal with a casualty. After all, that's what she'd been trained to do, but somehow, when he gave her that quirky smile of his, she couldn't. Well, not so much couldn't as didn't want to.

She'd been on early shift the day before so hadn't heard about the men injured on the heavy rescue teams until she'd reported for duty earlier. Therefore, when Reggie and his crew had swaggered in minus Tommy a little later, Jo had started to imagine Tommy lying in hospital with his leg in plaster. Over the subsequent hours, her imagination had reached fever pitch until finally she'd worked herself up into imagining the worst: Tommy lying under a sheet on a mortuary slab. Telling herself not to be so stupid, she'd tried to get on with the rest of her day, but when she looked up to see him standing just a few feet from her, hale and hearty, utter relief had flooded through her.

Finding herself suddenly gazing up into the face that haunted her nights and her every waking hour almost overwhelmed her. Thankfully, she hadn't given in to the impulse to throw her arms around him, but only just.

Pressing her lips together, Jo watched as Tommy rolled over the sill and dropped down into the room. Adjusting her first-aid bag across her, she stepped onto the block of bricks and put her hands carefully on the protective carpet.

'If you move your leg forward there's a washstand; you can get your balance on that,' Tommy called from below her, shining his torch so she could see. 'But be careful. It's a bit of a drop.'

Jo searched with her toe until she found the surface. Planting her foot firmly on the marble top, she climbed through the window.

'Here,' Tommy offered her his hand, 'let me help you.'

He'd pulled his neckerchief up and over his mouth and nose, highwayman style, so only his eyes were showing and they were warm as they gazed up at her. A pleasant little coil of excitement started in the pit of her stomach but she cut it off.

'I can manage just fine, thank you,' she replied, throwing him her kitbag. 'You're not the only one who knows how to climb through windows, you know.'

She jumped into the small space that he'd illuminated with his torch but as she landed an explosion close by rocked the floor and Jo lurched sideward. Tommy's arms shot out and caught her and instinctively she gripped his upper arms to steady herself. Still holding onto him, Jo raised her eyes to find him gazing down at her.

'I said be careful, didn't I?' he said, his deep tone resonating through her.

A couple of heartbeats passed and then, ignoring the pounding in her chest, Jo disentangled herself from his embrace. Straightening her helmet, she went to walk across the room but Tommy caught her arm.

'Don't become a casualty, remember,' he said, reiterating the first rule of rescue that was drummed into them.

He picked up his torch from the floor and Jo took hers from her kitbag.

'What's it looking like?' Mick called through the window behind them.

'Dodgy,' said Tommy, looking at the pale beam supporting the ceiling before checking out the rest of the room. 'One of the support walls has been damaged so the rafters are sagging in the middle and the back wall looks like it could buckle any moment. Pass us through a couple of jacks and we'll need some of the lads if they're free plus the WVS women. We've got kids here.'

Mick nodded, but as his head disappeared from the window, the boom of bombs being dropped on the docks half a mile south of them reverberated around the space.

The screams of terrified children filled the basement as another bomb found its target. There was a moment of complete calm then a small creak. Jo started forward again but as she did, the beam in front of her crashed down, choking the atmosphere with grit and dust. With it came the wall above it, blocking the path to the trapped women and children.

'You two all right?' asked Mick, peering down at them through the window.

'Yes, we are, but a ground-floor wall has just collapsed so I need those jacks,' Tommy replied.

'No sooner said than done, mate,' said a ruddy-faced

individual, appearing next to Mick and helping him feed one of the ten-foot metal poles through the window.

Shouldering the massive metal pole with ease, Tommy swung it upright. Finding a support joist in the ceiling, he shoved it upwards and then kicked the base into place. Another one was handed through and Tommy did the same as before a bit further along the joist.

'That should hold it,' he said, wiping the sweat from his forehead.

Jo grabbed his forearm. 'There are children trapped down there and we have to get them out.'

'I know,' he said. 'But we'll never get through that lot.' He ran the torch beam over the ton of collapsed wall in front of them. 'Stay between these supports and don't move, while I get a couple of the lads to help shift it.'

Covering the distance in three strides, Tommy leapt onto the washstand then heaved himself up and through the window.

Jo studied the wreckage of stone wood and mortar in front of her for a moment then she shone her torch over it.

'Are you still there?' called a woman's voice from the other side of the debris.

'Yes, I'm here,' said Jo. 'And we'll have you out as soon as heavy can dig you out. They're on their way now.'

A blast shook the ground again, sprinkling them all with grit and brick dust and setting the children sobbing again.

Shining her torch through a gap, Jo peered in. The pale beam illuminated a huddle of women and young children sitting in the dirt. Two of the women had small babes in arms and there was an elderly couple at the back.

'Where's that bloody heavy rescue?' screamed a woman, with dry blood on her cheek and a toddler clinging to her.

'Yeah, where are they?' yelled another, trying to soothe a sobbing child in her arms.

'Too bloody busy riffling through our knick-knacks, I shouldn't wonder,' said another mother.

'They're getting more men to clear the rubble and dig you out,' said Jo. 'How many of you are there?'

'There's me and my two kids, my sister Betty and her three and the baby, plus Sylvia and her two toddlers, Mr and Mrs Myers from next door and their daughter with her new-born. Winnie Cooper from number six is down here too with her two boys and the twins.'

'Is anyone hurt?' shouted Jo.

'I think Mrs Myers has broken her leg and my sister's got a nasty cut on her head. One of Winnie's boys bashed his head and has a lump the size of an egg but other than that I think we'll all live to fight another day.'

Another explosion shook the ground, dislodging a shower of grit onto Jo's head. The children's screams rose to an ear-splitting pitch as they went from terrified to hysterical and the women joined in.

'For pity's sake! Can't you get the kids out at least?' bellowed a woman as brick dust settled on Jo's face.

'All right, I'll see if there's a gap,' Jo replied, as one of the babies started whimpering.

Coughing, she scanned the wall of rubble in front of her with her torch. As she ran the shaft of light along the floor she noticed one of the rafters had landed at an angle on a fragment of wall creating a space. Dropping onto all fours, she shone her torch into the gap.

A blast close by bounced the grit and dust up from the ground and shook the foundations again. Jo pressed her face onto the sleeve of her jacket to protect her eyes and waited until the tremor subsided.

'I think I can squeeze through and get the children,' said Jo, taking off her hat and first-aid bag and setting them to one side.

As another bomb exploded and set the floor shaking again, Jo pressed herself flat on the floor and started to wriggle through but just as she ducked her head into the hole something grabbed her hips and pulled her backwards.

Kicking out, Jo rolled over and found Tommy looming over her with undiluted fury contorting his handsome features.

Reaching down, he grabbed her upper arms and hauled her to her feet.

'What in God's name do you think you're doing?' he bellowed at her as he set her on her feet.

'My job,' she spat back, matching his furious stare. 'The same as you—'

'I told you to stay put,' he yelled, his fingers biting into her upper arm. 'Are you trying to get yourself killed?'

'No,' she snapped back, glaring angrily up at him. 'I'm trying to get the women and children trapped behind that lot—'

An ear-popping explosion rocked the cellar, sending a surge of air through the space, which took Jo's words and lashed her face with grit.

She staggered back and collided with Tommy who caught her. With his arms around her, Jo clamped her eyes and mouth shut while brick dust swirled around them.

Jo tore herself from his grip and started forward but as she took the first step the upright beam to her right whisked past her and hit the floor.

Black spots popped at the corner of Jo's vision as her eyes fixed on the massive timber lying just inches from her toes.

There was a faint squeak, like an un-oiled door hinge, above her. Puzzled, Jo looked up then blinked as dirt pitter-pattered on her cheeks and nose.

Suddenly, Tommy's arm looped around her waist and Jo found herself flying backwards. As she crashed into the hard muscle of his chest, a ten-by-ten ceiling joist fell from above, crashing on to the floor and throwing up a plume of earth and soil in its wake.

Jo's heart beat once possibly twice before the bricks and mortar of the damaged house above crashed into the cellar.

Hugging her into him, Tommy shielded her from flying debris with his body as screams pulsing with terror and death filled Jo's ear.

After what seemed like an eternity of roaring noise and terrified shrieks, the cellar fell silent.

Raising her head, Jo stared in utter disbelief at the mountain of bricks, mortar and broken beams for a moment before burying her face in Tommy's chest and sobbing.

Chapter Nineteen

THE OLD MAN at the front of the queue handed over his pennies to the stout woman dressed in the forest-green uniform of the Women's Royal Voluntary Service. Picking up his two mugs of soup, he moved away from the counter.

It was about five thirty in the morning and Tommy was in the Wesley Chapel in Bower Street, which had been the hub of WVS activity in Limehouse for the past year. The upper gallery where the congregation had once sat, was now given over to the sorting and redistribution of clothing to hand to those who had been left with just the clothes on their backs after a night's bombing. The vestry had been turned into an information centre where lists of the dead and injured lined the walls. In the main part of the chapel, two lines of trestle tables and chairs had replaced the box pews. Beside the solid central pulpit, the resolute members of the WVS had installed a camp kitchen which offered hot meals and sandwiches plus what every doctor prescribed for shock: a nice cup of tea.

The German bombers were still overhead but there were fewer now and the booms from the bombs were quieter, indicating that the planes were discharging what was left of their munitions over Tilbury and Rainham on their way back to their bases. Although the all-clear had yet to sound, knowing that the worst of the night's raid was over, many people were already making their way back to their homes to grab whatever sleep they could before heading off to work in a few hours' time. Other than a handful of fire patrol personnel and a couple of aircraft spotters having a cuppa before going off duty, the place was empty.

The two people in front of Tommy shuffled along and he did the same. As the volunteer behind the counter took the next person's order, Tommy gazed across the room at Jo. She was sitting at the table on the far side of the room with her hands clasped together, arms resting on the surface.

Cup of tea! Double Scotch would be better to calm his still raging emotions.

Although it was now almost an hour and a half since they'd climbed out of the collapsed basement, the almost overpowering fear that had gripped him when he'd found Jo about to crawl under a dozen tons of unstable rubble had yet to subside. But when the roof had collapsed above, instinct had taken over.

Mercifully, he'd grabbed her in time and thank God he had because a world without Jo was a world he didn't want to be living in.

The queue moved forward again and the jolly-looking woman behind the counter looked at him through bloodshot eyes.

'Two teas,' he said, rummaging in his pocket for some change.

She poured two cups and Tommy handed over tuppence. Picking them up, he strolled between the tables towards Jo.

As he got within a few feet of her, she looked up. There were black splodges on her cheeks where her mascara had run and the cherry-red lipstick she'd been wearing had long since vanished. Her tin hat was somewhere under the rubble and her plait had half fallen out and hung in uneven coils around her shoulders. Even the dim glow from the regulation 40-watt light bulbs couldn't disguise the fact that her eyes were red and puffy from weeping.

If she could see herself she'd say she looked a complete mess, and truthfully, she did, but to Tommy she'd never looked more beautiful.

'Two cups of Rosie Lee,' he said, pushing the overflowing ashtray to one side and placing their drinks on the table.

'Thanks,' she replied, her eyes large and dark as they held his.

'Sugar?'

'Two please.'

Spooning a couple in her drink and adding one to his own, Tommy pushed her cup towards her and took the seat opposite.

Cupping her hands around her drink, Jo blew across the top. 'Do you think they've recovered them yet?'

Tommy shook his head. 'It'll take hours.'

Jo bit the inside of her lower lip. 'Perhaps we ought to drink this and get back. I feel a bit guilty sitting here slurping tea while the rest of the team are still working.'

'I'm sure they can manage without us just this once,' said Tommy. 'You've had a shock, remember. And didn't Eddie herself say you were to get a cup of hot sweet tea.'

'I know but—'

'But nothing,' Tommy cut in. 'You've done more than your fair share tonight.'

She sighed.

'I wish I could have done more.' She forced a brave little smile which tore at his heart. 'But then I say that every night.'

'Don't we all?' said Tommy.

Tears welled up in Jo's lovely eyes but she blinked them away and buried her nose in her drink.

Raising his cup, Tommy took a mouthful of tea and watched her over the rim of his mug.

Tears still shimmered on her lower eyelashes but the tight pinched look across her nose told him she was holding them at bay. Still cradling it in both hands, Jo placed the cup on the table and studied the coil of steam drifting upwards.

'How are you feeling, Jo?' he asked, after a moment or two.

Lifting her head, she opened her mouth to speak.

'And don't say all right,' he added. 'Because I can tell you're not.'

'Like someone reached in and scooped my innards out.' She gave a mirthless laugh. 'It's stupid, really. I mean, it's not as if in the past two months I haven't seen people killed and maimed every day. For goodness' sake, I've even taken the body parts found by the rescue teams to Billingsgate for the coroner to identify, but tonight . . .'

Her chin started to tremble and she looked away.

The clock above the door ticked off a dozen seconds. Tommy's gaze ran slowly down Jo's profile, and he pondered again at just how much he loved her.

'It's odd, you know,' she said, turning back once she'd regained her composure, 'but somehow, speaking to the women in the cellar and hearing their names has made their deaths more real – more part of me. And what I can't stop thinking about is the two babies. My sister Cathy's boy is just five months and it could have been them trapped in a cellar.' She wiped under her eyes with the base of her thumbs and sighed. 'People tell me you get used to it – to death, but—'

'I don't believe them,' said Tommy.

'Me neither.' Her mouth pulled into a firm line. 'And I never want to get used to seeing men, women, children and babies' bodies mangled in the ruins of their homes.'

A vice-like grip tightened around Tommy's chest as an image of Jo's lifeless body lying crushed beneath a hundred tons of rubble flashed through his mind.

'And something like this,' Tommy said, in a low voice and looking deep into her eyes, 'makes you realise what's really important in life.'

Her eyes widened for a second as an emotion he couldn't interpret flashed across them then she looked down.

On the table, Tommy's left hand was only inches from her right one. Jo's gaze rested on their hands for a second or two then she placed hers back on her mug.

'Yes, it does make you appreciate your family and friends,' she said, studying the tip of her finger as she ran it around the rim.

'And others,' he replied.

Still playing with her cup, Jo said nothing

Several heartbeats passed and then Tommy spoke again.

'Why did you stop writing, Jo?' he asked softly as her finger started its third circuit.

She looked up.

'I didn't,' she said, looking puzzled at the question. 'It was you who stopped writing to me.'

'Only because you stopped writing to me,' he said. 'The last letter I had from you was on the thirty-first of July, a week before the Bank Holiday Monday, and even then I sent you at least three more letters.'

'Four,' said Jo. 'You wrote four and I have them. In fact, I sent you a letter every other day when I was away.'

'Did you?' asked Tommy, trying to make sense of what she was saying.

'Yes, I did,' said Jo. 'And I phoned the Admiral, too, and spoke to Rita. I even rang the night before I left Melton

Winchet to let you know I was coming home.'

Tommy frowned. 'She never mentioned it.'

'I'm not surprised,' said Jo. 'She told me to sling my hook.'

Tommy raked his fingers through his hair. 'I don't understa—'

'It doesn't matter, Tommy,' she cut in. 'As far as I'm concerned, it's all water under the bridge now anyway.'

She swallowed the last mouthful of her tea. 'We ought to get back—'

The wail of the all-clear siren cut across Jo's words.

'Well,' she said, placing her empty mug down and rising to her feet, 'that's it for another night. I'd better go and clock off with Eddie.'

Tommy stood up. 'I'll walk back with you.'

Jo gave him a brittle smile. 'There's no need but thanks for the tea.'

Unhooking her kitbag from the back of the chair, Jo slung it over her shoulder and turned to leave.

'Honest, Jo,' Tommy said, as she started to leave, 'I didn't get a single letter from you in August.'

Jo looked around and raised an eyebrow.

'Well,' she said, her cool expression hitting him like a blast of arctic air, 'they couldn't all have been lost in the post, could they?'

Turning, she left.

With his arms hanging at his side, Tommy watched helplessly as she walked away from him but as the rest-centre door slammed shut behind her, he clenched his fist. She was right, of course. Even with a war on, a dozen-plus letters couldn't all have been lost in the post.

*

Stifling a yawn, Reggie threw back the tarpaulin covering the pickaxes and scaffolding in the back of the lorry and slipped the corner of his shovel between the metal floor plates. Twisting it to the right, he flicked off one of the floor plates to reveal the hidden compartment he'd built underneath.

'A tidy night's work, eh, boss,' said Fred, who was standing by the backboard.

Reggie and the rest of Blue Squad had clocked off at seven and, after a swift half, had made it back to the yard about half an hour ago. The rest of the crew had wandered off with their pickings soon after that, leaving him, Fred and Jimmy to tidy the lorry and stash away the goods. The sun was now just peeking over the top of the yard gates so Reggie reckoned it must be close to eight thirty.

'I ain't complaining,' said Reggie.

'How much you reckon so far?' asked Jimmy who, having finished stowing the three bottles of brandy in the space above the office ceiling, now strolled over to join them.

The spirits, along with a gross of Senior Service, had come from an off-licence in Poplar that they'd been sent to after the shop had had its front blown off.

'I'd say, with the two bottles of malted whisky from the doctor's gaff in Whitehorse Lane, the dozen pitchforks, hoes, rakes and shovels from the hardware store in Ben Johnson Road, along with all the odds and sods we've picked up, we're at least a cock and hen up.'

Fred whistled between his teeth. 'Ten quid.'

'As long as Blue Nose Benny gives us a fair price for the lot,' said Fred.

'Don't worry, I'll make sure he does,' said Reggie, threading his fingers together and cracking his knuckles. 'Of course, it would have been double that if old Potter hadn't called the rozzers over when we were digging out that jeweller's in Whitechapel.'

'Do you think he's rumbled us?' asked Fred.

'He might have,' said Reggie. 'But it don't matter cos 'e ain't got no proof. And if he knows what's good for him, he'll keep his bloody nose out of my business.'

'Still, even with Potter sticking his oar in, we've got a tidy haul,' said Jimmy.

'Helped by the fact that your Tommy's been shifted to Green team,' added Fred.

Irritation niggled in Reggie's chest.

Fred was right, of course. Without Tommy hovering over them, they'd netted more in the past four days than they'd netted in an entire month, but Reggie didn't like it. For one, Tommy was getting a bit of a reputation amongst the Civil Defence wallahs in Post 7 as a solid, upfront sort of fella, and him offering to shift over to another heavy team meant people at the depot were now starting to give Reggie and his crew a sideward look. Secondly, knowing Tommy had moved over because of Blue Squad's little sideline made Reggie feel as if his own flesh and blood was sitting in judgement over him. Stupid, of course, because Reggie was no worse than hundreds of other who were doing the same each night but it irked him nonetheless.

However, if the truth were told, the main reason he was irked by Tommy working with another crew was because, having looked out for his brother since he was a scabby-kneed ten-year-old, it was downright ungrateful and bang out of order.

Jimmy grinned. 'Yeah, good old Tommy.'

'Good old Tommy what?' Tommy said, stepping out from in front of the lorry.

'Tommy,' said Reggie, using the toe of his hobnail boot to shift the lid back over the stash of loot. 'We were just talking about you.'

His brother's gaze flickered onto the metal plate under Reggie's foot then he looked at the two men standing beside the back of the lorry.

'I'm sure you're both ready for your beds, aren't you?' he said, in a light conversational tone.

Jimmy and Fred exchanged wary looks.

Reggie jerked his head towards the double gates and his men hurried off.

'So,' said Reggie, stepping on the compartment lid to secure it as he jumped down, 'what's yanking your chain then, Tommy boy?'

Tommy took a pace forward and loomed over his brother.

'What,' he said in a voice that could slice steel, 'did you do with Jo's letters?'

Tommy clenched his fists tight and fought the urge to smash them into his brother's lying face.

Reggie's heavy features formed themselves into a puzzled expression. 'Letters? I don't know nuffink about—'

'Don't you dare deny it, Reggie,' Tommy cut in, taking another half-step towards him.

His brother flinched and moved back.

'All right, Tommy, I won't,' said Reggie, matching Tommy's bald stare. 'I got fed up to the back teeth seeing you mooning about like a bleeding love-sick ponce after she got shipped out. And it weren't doing you nor no one no good so I thought, "Reggie, my son, old Tommy boy needs

287

your help so you've got to do what you always do and look after him."'

Tommy's mouth pulled into a hard line. 'Did you now?'

'Yes, I did,' said Reggie, thrusting his chin forward. 'After all, that's what I've been doing all your life and it pained me to see you so down in the dumps.'

Tommy raised an eyebrow.

'Well, pardon me for trying to help my little brother,' said Reggie, with a huff.

'So you did it for me, did you?'

'Course.' Reggie's big-hearted-geezer expression spread across his face. 'I just wanted to see you happy again. What do you want me to say?'

Tommy gave a mirthless laugh. 'Sorry would be a start.'

Reggie's head snapped up and his aggressive expression returned. 'Well, you can whistle for that because I was just doing what I've always done: looking out for you.'

'And I suppose you were looking out for me when you let Jo into the house knowing I was there with Lou?' snapped Tommy.

'Don't try and lay that one on me, boy,' Reggie replied, jabbing a chubby finger at him. 'I didn't force you to let her spend the night at our gaff.'

Tommy's stance lost some of its tension.

He stared down at his brother for a long moment then weariness swept over him.

'I'm too tired to argue with you, Reggie,' he said, suppressing a yawn and running his hands over his face. 'But I'm going.'

'Good idea,' said Reggie. 'You get your head down for a couple of hours and we'll have a pint or two in the Admiral later.'

'No, Reggie,' said Tommy, looking his brother in the eye. 'I mean, I'm leaving.'

'Leaving!' Reggie frowned. 'What do you mean leaving?'

'Packing up,' said Tommy. 'Moving out. Going to live somewhere else.'

'Where?'

'I don't know,' Tommy replied truthfully. 'But anywhere I don't have to turn a blind eye to you nicking stuff from people you're supposed to be rescuing. I might even kip at Mum's for a few days until I've sorted myself—'

'You're going to live in that shit hole?' sneered Reggie.

The image of decaying food in the pantry and the pool of vomit he'd found in the middle of the kitchen floor when he'd visited the week before flashed through Tommy's mind.

'I'll clean it,' he said, feeling his throat heave at the thought. 'I'm paying the bloody rent so I might as well.'

With his eyes bulging and a mottled purple hue spreading over his cheeks, Reggie stared at Tommy a moment longer then stomped forward.

'You know what you are?' he said, jabbing his index finger within an inch of Tommy's face.

'No, what?'

'Ungrateful,' Reggie bellowed, spit flecking from his lips as he spoke. 'You're all muscle and balls now, Tommy boy, but I remember what you looked like when I came and found you huddled up with hunger and alone in the dark while she was out drinking herself into a stupor somewhere. You were covered in bloody flea bites and I had to shave your head because you were running alive with nits. But I don't suppose you remember that?'

'I remember,' said Tommy, as the images that still occasionally crept into his dreams turned over in his mind.

'You're my brother, Reggie, and I'll never forget what you did for me, but you shouldn't have taken Jo's letters.' Reaching down he picked up his kitbag. 'And if you really want to see me happy you better hope to God that one day I can persuade her to give me another chance.'

Slinging his bag over his shoulder, Tommy turned, leaving Reggie standing in the middle of the yard. Without looking back, he walked out through the double gates.

Chapter Twenty

CLOSING THE TOP drawer of his dresser, Tommy glanced in the mirror on the wall above it and, satisfied that his hair was in place, left his bedroom. Closing the door behind him he strolled down the hall to the lounge.

His mother, who was sitting in the fireside chair with a half-smoked cigarette between her fingers, staring at the wall, looked around as he walked in.

She was wearing a wine-coloured dress, with a stain down the front, which hung on her gaunt frame.

'You going somewhere?' she asked, flicking the ash without regard to where it fell.

It was the last Wednesday in November and although it was only just after five the blackout curtains he'd installed had been drawn for three hours.

It was also a week since he'd confronted Reggie about Jo's letters. Although he'd dreaded returning to the house that held so many painful memories, he'd had no choice so he'd resolved to make the best of it.

When he'd walked in that morning, with his suitcase in one hand and his linen in a sack in the other, he'd found his mother in the fireside chair, sleeping off whatever she'd put away the night before. The flat was in the usual state of squalor.

He'd been so tired after the night that, despite the decrepit state of the mattress on his old bed, Tommy had curled up in his clothes and slept the day through. When he'd walked into the lounge some seven hours later his mother was still sitting in the same chair and showed only mild surprise that her son, who'd left ten years before, had moved back in.

Despite telling Reggie he'd clean the flat himself, Tommy had given two women from the floor below half a crown each to do the job. Money well spent considering they had to burn two carpets because of the vermin nesting in them. Between shifts he had given the walls and floors a coating with some chemical the gas contamination squad at the depot had given him that smelt like geraniums. Although he'd had to burn most of the furniture he'd only had time to replace the bed and mattress and other bits of furniture would have to wait. He'd arranged for one of the women below to clean the flat and do the laundry once a week for half a crown so at least the flat was fairly tidy when he came home.

'I'm on duty, remember,' he said, picking up the envelope with his competition entry from the sideboard.

It had taken him a good few weeks but he'd finished the series of number and word puzzles. He reckoned his chances of winning were slim as there were probably thousands of others who'd completed the task too, but as it would only cost a couple of coppers to send it Tommy thought he might as well.

'Oh, yeah,' she said.

Actually, Shadwell School was only a ten-minute stroll away but as the ambulance crews, including those on the mobile dressing stations, changed over at six and as Jo was on the day shift, he wanted to get there early.

As well as it being just over a week since his showdown with Reggie, it was also the same amount of time since he and Jo had spoken in the WVS canteen.

Since then it had been nothing short of hell, with bombardments starting as early as five o'clock some nights. At one point last week he and at least three-quarters of the ARP staff hadn't been home for over seventy-two hours and only then to have a quick scrub before hurrying back. He'd seen Jo in passing, usually when she arrived to tend to those he and the Green Squad had just dug out from under a ton of rubble. Although they'd exchanged a few words as he handed over casualties, it wasn't enough. She might still give him the cold shoulder, of course, but perhaps now she'd had a chance to chew things over, he might be able to explain.

Rolling over in his head what he might actually say to Jo, Tommy glanced at his mother's untouched plate of pie and mash sitting on the table.

'You want to eat your supper before it gets cold,' he said.

'Leave it there.' She indicated the coffee table next to her. 'I'll have it when I'm ready.'

Tommy placed it where she'd indicated.

'You know you ought to eat more, that dress is hanging off you,' he said, taking his jacket from the back of the chair and shrugging it on.

'I ain't never been a big eater,' she replied.

Taking a fresh cigarette from the crumpled pack resting on the arm of the chair, she lit it with the butt of the spent one in her mouth.

'I'll be off then,' he said, taking his keys and loose change from the mantelshelf.

'Can you leave us a couple of bob, son?' she asked, giving him a coy smile.

Tommy counted out two sixpences and a couple of coppers.

'The bombing was bad last night, Mum, perhaps you

should head for the shelter in Flood Street when the siren goes off rather than the Angel,' he said.

She gave him a vague smile and then returned to her contemplation of the wall.

'I'll see you later then,' Tommy said.

His mother flicked the ash off the end of her cigarette and then took another drag by way of an answer.

Tommy studied her averted face for a few seconds then, turning his collar up against the damp November evening, he strode out of the house.

Placing the artery forceps she'd just dried on the stainless-steel tray ready for the next time they were needed, Jo picked up a pair of dressing scissors and wiped them over with the tea towel.

She was in the back of Dobbin tidying away after an uneventful Wednesday patching up people who had injured themselves whilst scouring what was left of their home for anything salvageable.

Jo's day shift had actually finished twenty minutes ago at six, but while the next mobile dressing station crew was grabbing a quick cuppa before the sirens sounded and tonight's shenanigans started, she was just finishing off.

The horsebox was parked by the school wall and although the blackout was in force, Jo had left the back door open and was working by a hurricane lamp behind the screen.

She'd told Jim it was so she didn't come over dizzy when decanting the surgical spirit from the storage bottle into the smaller flasks but really it was so she could keep an eye on Shadwell School's main entrance.

Placing the scissors next to the forceps, Jo had just picked up the long tweezers when she spotted Tommy strolling through the gates. Quickly drying the instrument, she placed it with the others and turned the lamp out. She waited until Tommy was halfway across the playground and then, picking up her first-aid bag, climbed down from the back of the van.

'Jo,' he called, as he spotted her.

She turned and tried to look surprised as he hurried towards her, his long legs covering the distance in half a dozen strides.

'Goodness, is it seven already?' she asked as he came to a halt in front of her.

'No, I'm early,' Tommy replied, his eyes dark in the dim moonlight. 'It's only just after half past.'

'I wondered why the sirens hadn't gone off yet,' she said.

'Don't worry,' Tommy replied, gazing up at the twinkling stars. 'There's not a cloud in the sky and it's almost a full moon, so I'm sure Göring will be sending his boys for a visit.'

Tracing the angular shape of his raised jaw with her eyes, Jo didn't reply.

With only the hum of the breeze passing through the wires anchoring the barrage balloon above them breaking the silence, Jo's heart ached to touch him.

'Look, Jo,' he said, raking his fingers through his hair, 'I know it won't make any difference now, but the reason I thought you'd stopped writing was that Reggie had been taking your letters.'

'But why?'

'Because,' Tommy gave her that wry smile of his, 'he thinks you're a bad influence on me.'

'What!' Jo laughed.

He joined in, his deep chuckle rolling over her.

'I know it's a bit rich coming from him, but he's got this cock-eyed idea that you're the reason I won't go along with his little schemes any more. It's not true because I'd already decided.' His eyes softened, turning Jo's innards to jelly. 'Anyway, I thought I'd tell you. And that I was stupid. Stupid not to find out the reason why you'd stopped writing instead of assuming you'd met someone better. And about Lou—'

'It doesn't matter, Tommy,' said Jo, taking half a step towards him.

'But—'

'Hey, Jo,' someone shouted, 'ain't you got no home to go to?'

Jo turned to see the MDS night team emerging from the Infant Boys door.

'Just going,' she called, stepping back to let them pass.

Tommy did the same as the four-man crew strolled between them and climbed into the old horsebox.

The driver turned the engine a couple of times then the old vehicle spluttered into life, sending a cloud of exhaust into the air.

Jo stepped forward to avoid the choking fumes and her eyes met Tommy's.

Rising on the balls of her feet she was just about to cross the space between them when Mick Riley and half a dozen members of the Green Squad ambled into the playground.

'Oi, Tommy, I'm glad you're here early cos it's your turn to get the tea in,' Mick called across.

'I'm right on it,' he called back, raising his hand in acknowledgement.

Although all she wanted to do was throw her arms around his neck and kiss every bit of Tommy's face, Jo forced a casual smile.

'I'd better leave you to it, then,' she said, not moving her feet an inch.

He nodded. 'See you tomorrow then.'

'Yes,' Jo replied. 'Hope you have good night.'

'You too.'

She smiled and he smiled.

The space between them shrank for a second or two then, as another group of the night-shift ARP personnel wandered through the gate, Tommy turned and walked towards the door.

Clutching the crucifix through her uniform shirt, Jo watched as his tall, broad-shouldered silhouette disappeared into the gloom.

Keep him safe. Please, Holy Mother, keep Tommy safe.

Chapter Twenty-One

'DO YOU WANT some jam?'

Jo looked up to see her gran staring anxiously down at her.

'No thanks. I'm fine with just butter,' she said.

It was just before seven thirty on the following morning and, despite the bombs dropping on the streets either side of Mafeking Terrace, she'd slept the full night through, waking half an hour ago. She was now sitting at the square table in the scullery with the warm fug of toast, fried eggs and sugary tea around her.

Her mother had protested when Jo had announced very soon after she started on MDSB that she was no longer going to go to the shelter when the alarm went. But Jo had been adamant, pointing out that being tucked up in bed was no more dangerous than dodging bombs, which she did the rest of the time.

Jo had just finished washing when Mattie had arrived home and slipped into the warm bed Jo had vacated. Gran, as ever, was already making breakfast when Jo got downstairs.

'What about some more tea?' Queenie persisted, picking up the pot.

'No, I'm fine, really,' Jo replied.

She wasn't, of course, and wouldn't be until she clocked on at two and saw for herself that Tommy had survived the night.

When she'd woken, after six hours of dreamless sleep, her first thought was Tommy . . . Tommy and how close she'd come to kissing him the night before. Half of her wished she had, while the other half was pleased she hadn't. Either way, since the night he'd saved her from certain death and she'd realised the reason he'd stopped writing was because none of her letters had reached him, something deep within her had changed. Well, perhaps not really changed because, if she was honest, she'd never stopped loving him. There was the issue of that barmaid, of course, but after almost three months of wondering if either of them would see the dawn, even him having a fling with Lou couldn't stem her feelings for him.

The click of the back-door latch cut across her troubled thoughts.

Jo stopped stirring her tea and looked up from her cup as her mother walked into the kitchen.

'What are you doing home, Mum?' asked Jo.

'Yes, Ida, shouldn't you be cleaning at the bank by now?' asked Queenie, pouring hot water into the washbowl.

'I would be,' Ida replied, 'if there was a bank and not a bloody big crater. Pour us a cuppa, luv.'

'The Town and Country's gone?' asked Jo, as she poured milk into a fresh cup and picked up the teapot.

Her mother nodded. 'Direct hit. The hardware shop and the tobacconist next to it destroyed, too, plus the blast brought the back of the Angel pub down.'

Ida flopped in the chair opposite and Jo passed her mother her hot drink.

'Were there many caught inside?' asked Queenie.

'About three dozen,' said Ida. 'Those in the main bar were caught by the flying glass and have been carted off to hospital. One of the heavy rescue team had a lump of masonry fall on him and he was carted off too.'

'Do you know which team it was?' asked Jo, hoping only she could hear the tremor in her voice.

'One from the Poplar crew, I think.' Her mother took a mouthful of tea. 'But those poor souls sitting in the snug at the back weren't so lucky. They were bringing the bodies out as I arrived. About a dozen, and you'll never guess what: Ruby Sweete was one of them.'

Jo's heart started pounding.

'You know, Queenie, that crook Reggie Sweete's drunk of a mother. Funny that, cos me and Jo only saw her a week or so back staggering about along the Highway as drunk as a skunk as usual.'

'Ah, well,' sighed Queenie, stacking a plate on the drainer, 'didn't I always say the drink would kill her.'

Swallowing the last of her tea, Jo stood up.

'I just remembered,' she said, hastily stepping out from behind the table, 'I promised to help Gillian with ... with her ...' She grabbed her coat from the hook and opened the back door.

'Will you be back for lunch?' her mother called after her as Jo hurried through it, shrugging on her coat.

'Yes,' shouted Jo, running across the frosty yard. 'Possibly ... Maybe.' She wrenched the side gate open. 'I don't know.'

An ARP warden's whistle, signalling it was half an hour until blackout, cut through the icy November air as Jo climbed the last few steps to the top landing of Potter Dwellings. Passing blacked-out windows and empty bottles left out for the milkman, she headed for the door at the end of the landing. Stopping outside, she hesitated a second or two then reached for the knocker, but before she could bring it down, Ruby Sweete's door creaked open slightly.

'Tommy,' she called.

There was no answer.

Remembering the last time she'd arrived at Tommy's unannounced, Jo cautiously pushed open the door and walked in.

Drawing the blackout curtain across behind her, she continued down the passageway and into the lounge.

The parlour was tidy, with a decent-sized fire glowing in the grate. One side of the drop-leaf table was extended and on it were three battered biscuit tins. One was open and Jo could see papers and sepia photos inside.

Tommy was standing at the other end of the room, his broad frame silhouetted in the dying rays of the winter sun as he stared out of the window. He was jacketless with the cuffs of his pale blue shirt undone and folded back.

'Tommy,' she whispered.

He turned. The top two buttons of his shirt were unfastened and Jo's eyes flicked onto the triangle of flesh sprinkled with hair and then back to his face.

'I only heard this morning and I've been dashing around looking for you ever since,' she said. 'I'm so sorry.'

The corner of his mouth lifted a fraction.

'So's everyone. From the boy from Poplar heavy crew who dug her out right through to the almoner at the London Hospital who gave me her belongings.' He indicated a plain gold ring, a pair of earrings and the handbag Jo had seen Ruby carrying in the street the day she and Ida had seen her. 'You know, they're so inundated with bomb victims in the hospital they've set up a temporary morgue in St Mary's crypt in Whitechapel.'

Jo shook her head.

'The funeral directors are in the same boat,' continued Tommy. 'So she'll have to stay in the church until the day before the funeral. One of Tadman's funeral chaps happened to be there when I arrived to identify her so I had a word with him. As there'll only be me attending he said he'll try to get me a slot at the City of London crematorium for early next week. I said I'd pop by tomorrow with the death certificate and marriage licence but . . .' He gave a hard laugh. 'Bloody stupid, isn't it, that I should get all choked up sifting through her old letters and photos.'

'Of course not, Tommy, you're grieving,' said Jo. 'Does Reggie know yet?'

Tommy shrugged. 'He might, but as far as he's concerned she's been dead to him for years. That's why I looked after her.' A bitter expression flitted across his angular face. 'Although God only knows why.'

'Because she was your mum,' said Jo.

He gave another mirthless laugh. 'That's what I tell myself when I scrub her sick from the floor and wash her soiled clothes or buy her food that she leaves to rot because she prefers to swallow gin. Do you know something, Jo?' he said, his eyes brittle with pain. 'I can't remember her ever actually cooking us a hot meal or tucking us into bed. Can you imagine that?'

'No, I can't,' Jo replied truthfully, as a myriad joyful childhood memories crowded her mind.

'To be honest, if it weren't for my nan moving in when my father skipped off, I doubt I'd have made it to my first birthday.' He pressed his lips together and turned away but not quick enough to stop Jo seeing the pain in his eyes.

Aching to hold him to her, Jo watched silently as Tommy strove to master his emotions.

The clock ticked away half a minute and then his attention returned to her. 'You're right, Jo, I am grieving.' The brittleness returned to his eyes. 'Not for the woman who died as she lived, propping up a bar, but for the two children she discarded like stale dregs in the bottom of a glass.'

His gaze held hers for several heartbeats. Jo's brain scrabbled around in search of the right words to comfort him and then she found them.

'Tommy,' she said softly. 'I love you.'

As Jo's words cut through all the emotions churning inside him, he was suddenly still. The long-buried feelings of abandonment and rejection were still there, along with the memories of lice-ridden hair and gnawing hunger, but their hold on him diminished with Jo uttering those few small words.

He wanted to reply but couldn't. He was struck dumb by the need to look at her. Look at that upturned nose of hers with the freckles across the bridge. Look at that rich chestnut hair that he wanted to see cascade across his chest as her head lay on his shoulder. Look at those full lips that he wanted to feel kiss every part of him. He wanted to look into those beautiful dark eyes until he was lost in their depth but, most of all, he wanted to sear the memory of her so deep in his mind that, until his dying breath, he would remember what she looked like at the moment she made his life complete.

'In fact,' she continued, 'I've never stopped loving you even when . . .' Hurt flashed across her eyes for a second but then she fixed her gaze on his face. 'And I always will.'

There was a moment of utter quiet as they stood staring across at each other before a very different emotion rose up in his chest. Crossing the space between them in two strides, he slid his arm around Jo's waist and drew her to him.

She placed her hand lightly on his chest and he felt it as if it were on his bare flesh. Savouring the feel of her in his arms, Tommy studied Jo's beautiful face for a second or two then kissed her lightly on the lips. She ran her hands up his arms, her fingertips setting off a pulsing need in the pit of his stomach.

Tommy's grip tightened as his hand slid down into the small of her back to anchor her against his hips while his other hand ran up her spine and cupped the back of her head. Their eyes met for an instant then he lowered his lips on hers again. The kiss was as light as the first then his mouth pressed onto hers and her lips opened in response.

After a moment, he lifted his head and planted light kisses over her eyes, cheeks and nose before returning to her mouth. He kissed her deep and hard and she returned the same.

After a long, pulse-thumping kiss, Jo broke free from his lips. 'Take me to bed, Tommy.'

His body urged him to do just that but he held it in check. 'But Jo—'

'Don't you want to?' she asked, slipping her hand underneath the open front of his shirt and clawing lightly through the hair on his chest.

'Of course I want to, Jo,' he replied. 'But I don't want you to do something you might regret tomorr—'

The sound of the air raid siren cut across his words and Jo tilted her hips and pressed against his rigid penis. 'The only thing I'll regret tomorrow, Tommy Sweete, is if you don't.'

'For God's sake, Reggie,' grunted Jimmy, as Reggie studied the silver trophies on the glass shelf as he tried to decide which one of them he liked best. 'Give us a hand with this bloody bugger.'

'Yeah,' added Fred, the veins on his forehead bulging as he and Jimmy inched the company's safe across the polished parquet flooring of the chairman's office.

It was the last Thursday in November and the night Vic Bostock had designated as the night Upington & Sons' safe was to be nicked. He, Jimmy and Fred, dressed in their heavy rescue boiler suits and wearing their tin hats, were on the second floor of the engineering works.

The air raid siren had gone off at six so Reggie and the rest of Blue Squad had loaded up and set off as usual in their lorry to the first call. Having left the rest of the ten-man team digging out casualties from a collapsed tenement block, Reggie and his two most trusted men had then slipped away into the blackout.

With searchlights criss-crossing the sky above and fire bells ringing below, Reggie had driven them between blazing warehouses to the brick-built factory in East Smithfield. They'd arrived at the premises just after the nightwatchman had completed his eleven-thirty rounds. Waiting until he'd tucked himself back into his sandbag bunker under the boiler house, it had taken Jimmy just a couple of turns of his skeleton keys to open the double gates. Reggie drove the lorry, still laden with their heavy rescue gear, into the yard.

'Come on, Reggie,' coughed Jimmy, resting his massive hands on his thighs as he caught his breath. 'Or we'll still be here when they clock on in the morning.'

Leaving his contemplation of the tall glass-fronted cabinet, Reggie strolled over.

'There's some decent bits of silver in that case,' he said, stopping next to his two red-faced, sweating men.

'Is there?' grunted Jimmy, shifting the huge lump of metal forward a few more inches, peeling the floor wax into a small curl in the process.

'Yeah,' Reggie replied, looking at the three-foot-wide memorial plate in the centre that dominated the display. 'I'd say at least seventy nickers' worth, perhaps even a score more.'

'I'm surprised they ain't got it locked in a vault somewhere,' said Jimmy, following Reggie's gaze.

'So am I,' said Reggie. 'But don't look a gift horse in the mouth, eh?'

'Perhaps we should get this loaded before we start worrying about poxy silver,' Fred ground out as he and Jimmy shoved the squat green lump of metal another foot or so.

'That's the trouble with you lot,' said Reggie, gazing back at the display of trophies and commemorative plates. 'You don't see the possibilities right under your nose.'

A bomb whizzed overhead and found a target somewhere to the west of them, shaking the building again.

'The only possibility I can see at the moment is the possibility of me getting a double hernia after shifting this bugger,' said Fred, wiping the sweat from his forehead with the back of his hand.

Reggie pulled a face. 'You two must be getting old cos I've seen you shift twice that weight before.'

'And we'd be doing it now if Tommy were here,' said Fred.

An emotion he couldn't identify flared in Reggie's chest.

When Tommy had turned up at the house that afternoon, Reggie had been unexpectedly glad to see him. So glad, in fact, that he'd almost gone all pansy and hugged him. Thankfully, he hadn't, especially when he found out that the reason for his brother's visit wasn't because he wanted to throw his lot back in with his big brother but instead to tell him that the old drunk who'd birthed them was lying in the morgue. He'd even asked if he wanted to go with him to the bloody funeral. Stupid sod.

He glared at the two men in front of him.

'Well, he ain't,' he barked. 'And you want to be thankful he ain't or else we'd be splitting Mr Bostock's ton four ways instead of three. Now come on, you ungrateful buggers.' Spitting into his palms, Reggie rubbed them together. 'Stop acting like a couple of old biddies and let's get this thing to the loading hoist.'

Upington & Sons was housed in an old four-storey wharf and still used the original cast-iron winch-and-pulley manual crane that was fixed above the loading hatches. After ten minutes of swearing at the safe and at each other, Reggie and his two oppos finally shoved and heaved their load out of the office, past the workshop benches and finally to the second-floor loading hatch.

Kicking open the pair of half-size doors, Fred caught the chain and grappling hooks usually used to lower mechanical parts and machinery into the waiting lorries. Pulling them towards him, he began fastening them to the safe. Reggie left Fred and Jimmy securing the safe on the pulley and retraced his steps back through the offices, casting a covetous glance at the cabinet loaded with silver as he passed.

Taking the stairs two at a time, Reggie left the building through the side door and crossed the loading area to the lorry. Jumping in the back, he tore back a sheet of tarpaulin then gave a two-tone whistle. It was answered by another from above.

Shining his torch upwards to guide them, Reggie watched as Fred and Jimmy manoeuvred the safe out through the hatch and slowly lowered it down. Another blast lit up the sky and illuminated the safe as Reggie guided it the last few feet so it sat squarely between the back axle. Then, as darts of light from the ack-ack guns on Tower Hill traced across the sky, Reggie drew back the tarpaulin and shifted their shovels and pickaxes over it to anchor it down.

Jumping down from the back of the lorry, he took out a packet of cigarettes and lit one. Resting back on the door of the cab, he drew in a long breath, enjoying the tingle as the nicotine reached his lungs. Gazing up at the second floor for a second then snatching an empty sandbag and a crowbar from the back of the lorry, he hurried back in to the building, meeting Fred and Jimmy as they got to the bottom of the stairs.

'Where you off to?' asked Jimmy, grabbing his arm.

'I forgot something,' Reggie replied.

He tried to shake him off but Jimmy held firm.

'Leave it, Reggie, we ain't got time, ' said Jimmy, his massive frame all but blocking the light from the blazing building nearby. 'Not with Bostock's boys waiting for us.'

Reggie snatched back his arm.

'Just get in the lorry,' he shouted over his shoulder as he dashed up the stairs.

He burst into the manager's room minutes later and, without breaking his stride, he swung the crowbar at the cabinet, shattering the glass doors into slivers with one blow. Gouging a line diagonally across the polished surface, Reggie threw the iron tool on the desk. Flipping open the sandbag, he scooped the ornate silver items on the shelves into the sack, shoving in as much as he could fit. Then, crunching across the glass, he hurried back down the stairs.

Fred and Jimmy were already in the lorry's cab when he reached the door but, as he stepped out into the yard, one of the double doors creaked open showing a stout man wearing a Civil Defence tin helmet silhouetted by the blazing building beyond.

'Who's there?' he asked, as a weak beam of light illuminated the open space.

Stepping into the shadow of the doorway, Reggie didn't reply.

The light flashed past him and shone into the lorry's cab. Thankfully, Jimmy and Fred had had the sense to duck beneath the window so it looked empty. The torch beam ran over the side of the lorry, lingering on the Sweete & Co lettering for a second before going around to the tailgate. Carefully placing the sack on the floor so its content didn't jingle, Reggie stepped out of the shadows and crept along the other side of the vehicle. By the time he'd reached the back of the vehicle the man had lifted the tarpaulin, revealing the squat green safe beneath. The man stood motionless for a second then, after scrabbling around under his ARP jacket, he pulled out a whistle.

Reggie sprang forward and struck the warden across the back of his head, sending the helmet he was wearing spinning across the cobbled courtyard. The man collapsed like a sack of potatoes at Reggie's feet.

Bending down, Reggie grabbed his shoulders and turned him over as the lorry door opened and Jimmy and Fred jumped down from the cab.

A flash of light from a shell exploding above their heads lit up the yard and the face of the man lying still at Reggie's feet.

'Gawd, it's old Potter,' said Jimmy, as he stopped next to Reggie.

'What did you hit him for?' asked Fred.

'To stop him seeing us,' Reggie replied. 'After all, we don't want him running to the police now, do we?'

Fred turned on his torch and shone it on Cyril's face then, hunkering down beside the motionless warden, he took off his glove and placed his fingers against Cyril's neck.

'Well, he's not going to be running to the police or anywhere else from now on cos he's dead,' he said.

'Don't be daft,' said Reggie, forcing a laugh. 'I only gave Colonel Blimp a tap on the bonce.'

'Maybe,' said Fred, standing up. 'But he's as dead as a dodo now.'

Something akin to ice water trickled through his veins as Reggie stared at the chief warden's lifeless face.

'Oh God,' moaned Fred, ashen faced even in the red glow of the blazing buildings. 'We'll be up for murder when the police find out.'

'They've got to prove it was us who did it first,' said Reggie.

'So what are we going to do?' asked Jimmy, still looking in horror at the body at his feet.

'Yeah,' Fred chipped in. 'What are we going to do? It's

all right for you, you ain't got a wife and kids to worry a—'

'For fuck's sake, will you two shut up and let me think?' snapped Reggie.

Fred and Jimmy clamped their mouths shut.

Reggie chewed the inside of his mouth for a moment then, slinging the bag of silver into the back of the lorry, he bent down and grabbed the dead man under the arms. Cyril's head lolled forward and his thick-lensed glasses slipped off his nose and onto the floor.

'What are you doing?' asked Fred, looking like a rabbit caught in a trap.

'Getting him in the back,' Reggie replied, heaving the limp body upright.

'But he's dead,' said Jim, crunching the spectacles under his size tens as he moved forward.

'So are hundreds of other poor buggers,' said Reggie, scraping Cyril's heels over the cobbles as he dragged him towards the tailgate. 'Who's to say he weren't caught in a blast like the rest? Now stop yakking and give us a hand. And pick those bleedin' goggles up, we don't want to set the coppers off wondering about them now, do we?'

With one arm behind his head and the other lightly cradling the woman he loved, Tommy listened to the distant boom of the last bombs being dropped to the east. Fire-engine bells still cut through the night as they dashed to calls but the smog that had been just a few wisps the evening before had thickened to a pea-souper, causing the waves of German bombers to head back to their bases early. It was still dark, of course, as there were a good four hours before the sun rose at eight thirty but there was enough light from the burning warehouses in Limehouse Basin just half a mile away for him to see the curve of Jo's hips and legs under the bedcovers as she lay snuggled into him. Using the dip between his neck and shoulder as a pillow and with her small hand resting on his chest, she lay sleeping, her unbound hair cloaking his right arm as it held her close. Their clothes lay scattered on his bedroom floor pretty much where they'd stripped them off each other. Knowing her inexperience, he'd tried to hold back but, driven wild by her hands, Tommy had given in. By the red glow of the burning dockland he'd touched and kissed every dip and curve of Jo's lithe body and she had returned the favour. Finally, exhausted, they'd tumbled into his bed and Tommy had pulled the dishevelled bedclothes over them before, entwined together, they'd fallen asleep.

Somewhere over Canning Town way a bomb hit its target and the noise boomed around the room. Jo shifted and, setting his senses on fire, her fingers feathered across his chest as she turned onto her back.

She sighed and although her eyes remained closed a contented smile lifted the corners of her lips. Tommy smiled too. Wasn't this what he'd dreamed of since he'd met Jo? Well, yes and no.

Obviously, with blood pumping through his veins, her every movement and touch fired him with passion, but he'd really imagined their first night together being after a day of vows and family celebrations.

His gaze ran over her peaceful face then shifted down to where the sheet skimmed the top of her bare breasts. He was tempted to tug the sheet down a little with his foot but resisted the urge. She was on duty at seven so would have to leave his bed soon enough but just for now, he wanted to savour the feel of her skin against his, nestled into him, before the world and the war laid their demands on them both again.

An orange flash from an explosion close by burst across the room and Jo opened her eyes.

She smiled. 'Hello.'

'Hello yourself,' he replied.

She gazed up at him for a moment. 'What time is it?'

'About four.' His gaze ran over her face. 'Are you . . .?'

'Fine. In fact,' holding his gaze, Jo threw the sheet back and sat up, 'I've never felt better.'

Tommy's eyes travelled over her for a moment then he sat up and gathered her into his arms. Jo's mouth closed over his in a long hard kiss and, as his arms tightened around her, she pushed him back onto the bed. Rolling onto him, she straddled his right leg and placed her hands on the pillow either side of his head. She raised herself up and gazed down at him, her breasts resting on his chest, firing his passion in an instant.

He smiled up at her. 'You're so . . . so . . .'

'Shameless?'

'I was going to say beautiful.' He raised an eyebrow and cupped her right breast, rubbing the nipple with his thumb. 'And a little bit shameless, too.'

Jo's eyes smouldered for a moment then she kissed him and rested her head on his chest, idly tracing her fingers along the muscles of his arms and shoulder.

The Mudchute ack-ack guns sent a ribbon of shells into the sky as she lay in his arms, breathing out and breathing in.

'Jo,' he said, as St Anne's Church clock chimed out the half-hour.

She raised her head and looked at him.

'About, Lou.'

313

She smiled. 'It doesn't matter. Not now.'

'It does to me, especially now,' he replied. 'Jo. I swear I never slept with her.'

Jo's gaze ran over his face for a second or two then she smiled. 'I believe you.'

'And believe me, too, when I say I love you.'

Jo gave him a quirky smile. 'I'd have to, wouldn't I, after the way you were shouting it last night.'

Tommy grinned. 'I got carried away and I'd like to point out, you weren't exactly quiet yourself.'

'I was taken by surprise by . . . you know.' She gave him a sideward look.

'Good,' said Tommy, feeling a vigorous surge through his body again. 'And I'd like to continue to surprise you as Mrs Tommy Sweete for the rest of my life.'

'Would you now?' she asked.

'Yes, I would.'

A smile tugged at the corner of Jo's mouth. 'Is that a proposal?'

'It is.'

'Then I accept.'

Feeling like the King of the World, Tommy started to draw her closer but she braced her hands against his chest. 'But you'll have to speak to my dad.'

'I will,' he replied, as the memory of Jo's bear of a father at the boxing club flashed through his mind.

Smiling down at him, Jo's hands slid up his chest and around his neck.

Tommy gazed at her for a moment then hooking his legs around hers he rolled her onto her back. 'And I'd also like to point out to the future Mrs Thomas Sweete, that the night's not over yet.'

Resting back into the chair, Mattie put her feet on the box containing Post 7's spare gas masks. It was the last Friday in November and the clock high above the door to the infant school's hall showed it was just past six in the morning. She was sitting in the recreation area of Post 7, which they'd kitted out as best they could with old lounge furniture and a rug. Opposite her was the small bookcase containing both fiction and non-fiction, chess sets and packs of cards. At her elbow was an old kitchen table strewn with magazines and periodicals that people had brought in.

The all-clear had sounded a while ago; a thick blanket of fog had spread its way up the Thames, covering the whole of London, which meant they'd had a reasonably quiet night. Flying blind, the last couple of waves of German bombers had dropped their munitions and returned to their bases at four. No others had come so the locals, knowing the nightly rigmarole was over, had started packing up their belongings in the Tilbury shelter as soon as the pea-souper appeared. This meant that Mattie finished her duties just after five when she'd strolled back to Post 7 for a well-earned cuppa.

Well, when she said stroll that should really be waddle as over the last couple of weeks she'd really 'blossomed', as her mother put it. 'Blown up like a barrage balloon' would have been a more accurate description, so it was just as well she was giving up her warden job at Post 7 in a week.

Truthfully, she should have given it up at the beginning of November rather than December but being busy helped keep her mind from dwelling on Daniel. Except it didn't, of course, because Daniel was her last thought as she collapsed into an exhausted sleep and her first thought when her eyes opened, especially as the latest postcard from his chief was long overdue.

Pushing the ever-present fear in her chest aside, Mattie reached over to the table and picked up a pair of scissors and a newspaper that she started cutting into strips.

'Mrs McCarthy.'

She looked around to find George Granger, the controller from HQ at St George's Town Hall, standing behind her. A year ago, he'd been the council's senior clerk responsible for the roads, housing and schools, and now he was the senior Civil Defence officer charged with defending them.

'Mr Granger,' she said, setting her task aside and swinging her feet off the box. 'Nice to see you.'

'And you, Mrs McCarthy,' he replied.

Grabbing the arms of the chair, Mattie shifted forward but he raised his hand. 'No, you stay put.' He glanced at the strips of newspaper. 'I'm a bit surprised you still have windows that need paper strips pasted on them.'

'No, they're not for the windows, they're paper chains for Post 7's Christmas party,' said Mattie. 'The children around here have had a rough time of it so some of us have donated our sugar rations and we're putting on a spread for them a week before Christmas. Mr Potter wasn't too keen but me and a couple of the girls talked him around.'

Mr Granger's rounded features grew serious. As always, he was dressed in a navy military-style jacket with a wide white stripe on the left upper arm that denoted his Civil Defence rank.

Pulling a chair over so it was next to Mattie, he sat down. 'It's your chief warden that's brought me down here at this time. I'm afraid, Mrs McCarthy, Cyril's been found under a collapsed building in Dock Street.'

'My goodness,' said Mattie, shocked at the news. 'Does his wife know?'

Mr Granger nodded. 'I sent someone around when I heard.'

Mattie frowned. 'I wonder what he was doing there.'

'What do you mean?' asked Mr Granger.

'Not that it matters, I suppose,' Mattie replied, 'but he was on Turner Street patrol last night and Dock Street is at least a mile away.'

'Giving a hand, probably,' Mr Granger replied. 'He was discovered by Leman Street heavy crew about an hour ago and they sent a messenger to Central.'

'Poor old Cyril,' said Mattie.

'Indeed,' said Mr Granger. 'But it leaves us on a bit of a sticky wicket, which I'm hoping you might be able to help us out with. I know you're supposed to be leaving next week but would you consider staying on for an extra week until we can sort out his replacement? Truthfully, it ought to be you as you know as much as anyone about the running of the post but . . .'

'I'd like to help,' said Mattie, 'but the Tilbury Shelter is—'

'I wouldn't expect you to do warden duties,' Mr Granger cut in. 'Please. You can sit with your feet up and give orders – all night, if you like.'

'Fat chance,' laughed Mattie.

He gave half a smile. 'I only ask that you oversee things here for a week, two at the most. That's all.'

Placing her hand on the pinned-together waistband of her uniform trousers, Mattie gave a wry smile. 'I suppose there is a war on.'

'That's the spirit,' he said, looking visibly relieved.

'But only until the second week in December,' said Mattie,

as the baby inside her shifted position under her fingers. 'Because I'm planning to have this baby in the East London Lying-in Hospital, Mr Granger, not while I'm on duty in Post 7.'

As they turned the corner of Schoolhouse Lane, in sight of Post 7, Tommy drew Jo into the shadow of the corner shop's doorway and gathered her into his arms.

'Just one more,' he murmured, his lips closing over hers again.

Winding her arms around his neck, Jo closed her eyes and let the magic of his kiss wash over her once more.

The all-clear had gone at five , just after she and Tommy had made love for the third time, and so they'd dozed in each other's arms until the first streaks of red morning light were visible over the Blackwall oil refinery an hour ago. It was now just after six thirty and although she'd had no more than three hours' sleep all night she didn't feel at all tired. Quite the opposite, in fact, as it was all she could do to stop herself skipping down the darkened street whooping and laughing.

After a long blissful moment in Tommy's embrace, Jo tore her lips free.

'I have to go,' she said.

'Do you?' he replied, planting feathery kisses across her cheek.

'You know I do,' Jo replied.

He pressed his lips on hers briefly. 'I don't know anything except I love you.'

'And I love you,' Jo replied. 'But if I don't go now I'll get a dressing-down from Cyril Potter and—'

Tommy's mouth stopped her words as he held her to him. Jo curled into him and gave herself over to the pleasure of his embrace again but hearing hoof beats accompanied by the chink of milk bottles in their crates, Jo broke free.

'I'll see you later,' she said.

'What time?'

'As soon as I clock off,' she replied.

'Won't your family be expecting you for tea?' he asked.

'I'll tell them I'll be late,' Jo replied. 'Then I'll head off home when you go on duty. I should be at your place by five as long as the sirens don't go off.'

'Well, let's hope this fog lingers for a few days,' he replied.

'Yes, we might even get a full night's sleep if it does,' Jo said.

His hand clasped her bottom and held her against him. 'Or something.'

Excitement shot through Jo as images of the night before flashed through her mind.

'Oh, Jo,' Tommy murmured as his arms tightened around her again.

He lowered his head to capture her mouth again but reluctantly Jo placed her hands on his chest.

'Tommy . . .'

He pressed his lips onto hers for a moment again and then released her from his embrace. 'Until later.'

Holding his hands until her arms could stretch no more, her gaze ran over him for one last time then she turned and hurried across the road.

Stopping by the Post's entrance she turned and waved. Tommy waved back and then walked away.

Jo waited until he'd disappeared into the fog then walked through the double gates and into the yard.

319

The mobile ambulances were both still out, as were Blue and White heavy rescue teams' lorries, but unusually there was a police car parked amongst the handful of fire, decontamination and ambulance vehicles in the playground.

Adjusting her bag across her shoulder and hoping no one would be able to tell by the smile she couldn't keep from her face that she'd been cavorting about naked in Tommy's bed for the past twelve hours, she pushed open the door and strolled in.

As ever, after a busy night, her sister Mattie was up on the stage, her rounded stomach protruding between her unbuttoned warden's jacket. However, instead of updating the incident board as she usually did at the end of the shift, she was sitting alongside a young police officer who appeared to be making notes as she spoke. There were three or four other officers dotted about the place, talking to members of the various ARP squads.

Seeing Gillian over by the serving hatch, Jo wandered over.

'Morning, Jo,' yawned her friend, as she stopped in front of her.

'Morning, Gill,' she said, handing over a tuppence and picking up a mug of tea. 'What are the police doing here?'

'Cyril Potter copped it last night,' said Gillian.

'How?'

'The usual way,' Gill replied. 'He was in the wrong place at the wrong time. They found him buried under the rubble in Dock Street.'

'Poor old Cyril,' said Jo, crossing herself. 'He and his wife lived opposite us in Mafeking Terrace for years.'

'Yeah, poor old sod,' echoed her friend. 'Mr Granger came down to break the news—'

A two-tone whistle shrieked between them as Reggie Sweete strutted into the hall like a returning hero with the men of Blue heavy who were pratting about behind him. Making a cuppa signal to the WVS women making the tea, he swaggered around, slapping backs and shadow boxing a couple of cronies. He spotted an officer talking to one of the fire auxiliaries and spoke to one of his card-playing partners standing close by.

His expression went from puzzled to shocked and then sad as he heard what had happened. He quickly imparted the news to the rest of his team who all looked equally shocked.

'Bloody hypocrite,' murmured Gillian, as Reggie hugged one of the WVS women who looked a little red-eyed. 'He didn't have a good word to say about Mr Potter while he was alive and now he's acting as if he's lost an old pal.'

The police officer put his notebook away and took his leave of Mattie. As the officer left the stage, Reggie bounded up the steps at the side and took his place.

'You're right there,' said Jo, watching Reggie deep in conversation with Mattie. 'But I wonder why he's talking to my sister.'

'I'll tell you why,' said Gillian with a harsh laugh. 'Cos Mr Granger put her in temporary charge and Reggie Sweete always knows what side his bread is buttered.'

Chapter Twenty-Two

WITH HIS FEET resting on the pile of unpaid bills on his desk, Reggie flicked through a couple of pages of his magazine until he reached the centre fold of *Stripperama* and turned it side-on. Thinking that was an unfortunate place to have a staple, he flicked his ash-laden cigarette on the floor.

It was the first Tuesday in December and, as the Admiral didn't open for another hour, he'd decided to while away the time until it did catching up on some paperwork.

It was also five days since pinching Upington & Sons' safe and he was feeling pretty good, mainly because for the first time since the incident with Potter he hadn't woken up in a cold sweat imagining he had a hemp rope tightening around his throat. And it was hardly surprising, given that the police were already sniffing around when he'd arrived back at Post 7 that morning. However, the officer taking the statements, a wet-behind-the-ears auxiliary, was clearly going through the motions as his superiors had already decided that old Cyril had died when the building collapsed.

So now, with the engineering company's safe delivered to Vic Bostock's boys and the hundred quid for his troubles securely stashed away in his hidey-hole at the back of the fire grate, he was feeling pretty chipper and once he'd off loaded the silver he was sure things would settle down again.

He frowned.

He had thought two-finger Ivor would take it off his hands without a murmur but the old Yid who lived in Spitalfields had been done for receiving stolen goods and was doing time in Holloway. Whitechapel's other main fence, Mick Flannigan, wasn't available either, on account of his missis finding out that he had another wife plus three kids in Fulham, causing him to have to lay low for a bit. This meant he'd have to seek out a dealer on someone else's patch, which would cost him money because he'd be in no position to haggle or call in favours.

Stubbing his cigarette out in the overloaded ashtray, Reggie flipped the page and was just admiring the imaginative use of feather dusters by the French maids in the feature when the door burst open and Inspector Tovey and his lapdog Flowers strolled in, with Fred and Jimmy, who'd been mooching about in the yard, close on their heels.

'Sorry,' said Jimmy, as he followed them in. 'I said you were busy but—'

'Don't worry,' said Reggie, tossing the magazine on the table. 'I've always got time for a chat with my old friends Inspector Tovey and Sergeant Flowers.' Swinging his legs off the desk he leaned back in his chair. Weaving his fingers together, he smiled at the two policemen. 'Now, what can I do for you two gentlemen?'

'Know anything about silver, Reggie?' asked Flowers.

Reggie forced a puzzled expression onto his face. 'You dig it out of the ground and it's shiny.'

'To be more specific,' said Tovey, his beady eyes boring into him, 'silver trophies that were nicked along with Upington & Sons' safe during the air raid last Thursday night.'

'Sorry,' Reggie said, looking blankly at the two officers. 'Not a thing. Although I'm surprised you're concerning yourself with trinkets when a safe stuffed with wages has gone, too.'

'How do you know about the wages?' snapped Flowers, glowering at him.

'Cos no thief worth his salt would have swiped the bugger if it hadn't been,' his senior officer said. 'Ain't that right, Reggie?'

'If you say so,' he replied, smiling across the desk at him.

Tovey chewed the inside of his mouth for a moment then spoke again. 'Do you know what I think, Reggie?'

'No, Inspector Tovey,' Reggie replied.

'I think that safe was half-inched by some local villains for someone like Billy Hill, Wally Thompson or Vic Bostock,' the inspector said. 'And that the safe's been cleaned out and is sitting at the bottom of some canal by now. But I think that when this local tea leaf spotted all that silver, just there for the taking, he got greedy.'

Out of the corner of his eyes, Reggie saw Jimmy and Fred exchange worried looks but Reggie's innocent expression didn't waver.

Planting his chubby hands on top of Reggie's girly magazine, Inspector Tovey loomed over him. 'So, I'm thinking those wages are long gone but when I find who has that silver I'll have enough evidence to have them for both jobs and then I can get them banged up for a least a fifteen-year stretch. Which would make someone who was, say, your age, Reggie, close on forty-four when he got out.'

An image of himself stooped and grey, tottering out of the front of Parkhurst Prison in 1955, flashed though Reggie's mind.

Tovey fixed him with a steely gaze. 'Are you sure you

know nothing about Upington's safe or missing silverware, Reggie?'

'Sorry, Inspector,' said Reggie.

'Well then, you don't mind if I get the boys to give the place the once-over, do you?' said Tovey.

'Of course not, Inspector,' said Reggie, straining his ingenuous expression to its limit. 'Be my guest.'

An hour and ten po-faced, hairy-policemen emptying every barrel, box and sack into a heap in the middle of the yard later, Reggie was again facing Inspector Tovey across his desk.

'As I told you, Inspector,' he said, puffing a satisfying stream of cigarette smoke towards the tobacco-stained rafters, 'I don't know nuffink about no silver.'

An angry flush spread across Tovey's heavy jowls.

'You might think you're off the hook, Sweete,' he said, jabbing his finger at Reggie, 'but there's another file on my desk that's caught my eye recently.'

'And what one is that, Inspector,' said Reggie, jollily. 'The one looking into Hitler's missing bollock?'

'No.' An unnervingly pleasant smile lifted the inspector's thin lips. 'The one on Cyril Potter, the ARP warden in charge of Post 7 where you and your motley crew of villains are stationed. He was found under a building not three streets away from the robbery when he was supposed to be patrolling two miles away.'

Somehow, despite the prickling sensation between his shoulder blades, Reggie managed to maintain the impassive expression on his face.

'Poor old bugger, copping it like that as he was doing his civic duty,' he said, hoping only he could hear the wavering in his voice. 'We sent his missis a bunch of flowers, didn't we, lads?'

Fred and Jimmy nodded obediently.

Frustration flickered briefly across the inspector's face and then he spun on his heels and strode out, rattling the glass in the door as he slammed it behind him.

Jimmy opened his mouth to speak but Reggie held up his hand.

Swinging his feet off the table again he stood up and crossed to the window just in time to see Tovey and Flowers disappear through the yard gates.

'Reggie, we were lucky this time but if Tovey finds the silver and puts two and two together,' said Fred, 'well, then we're looking at a long stretch. And I can't do time, not with my boy the way he is—'

'Will you fucking shut up about your poxy boy and let me think?' cut in Reggie.

Fred gave him a resentful look but clamped his mouth shut.

'Especially if he finds . . .'

Jimmy lowered his eyes.

'Finds what?' Reggie asked through gritted teeth.

'Potter's goggles,' mumbled Jimmy, not raising his eyes.

Reggie racked his fingers through his hair. 'I thought I told you to pick them up.'

'I did but they must have fallen from my pocket somewhere,' said Jimmy. 'Don't worry. If the cops find them they wouldn't know they're old Potter's. Unless . . .' He raised his eyes to the ceiling where the silver was concealed behind a false panel.

Panic flashed across Fred's face. 'We've got to get rid of it, Reggie. Dump it in the river even—'

'I ain't dumping seventy nickers' worth of silver in no bleeding river,' snapped Reggie.

'Well, we can't leave it where it is,' said Jimmy.

Gnawing on his thumb, Reggie didn't answer for a moment then he glanced at the Windmill Girls calendar hanging from a nail hammered into the wall.

'It's the fourth tomorrow, isn't it?' he said, as his eyes skimmed along the top row of the fresh month.

'Yeah,' said Fred. 'Three weeks to Christmas.'

Reggie grinned. 'And Santa's just given me an early present, cos I've thought of the perfect place to hide our loot.'

In the mute light of the moon hovering over the gin bottling plant in Three Colts Lane, Jo gripped Tommy's shoulders and, letting out a long ecstatic breath, let her head fall forward. Her unbound hair cascaded over his bare chest as his hands held her hips firm for a second or two longer then relaxed. Lowering herself onto him, Jo rested her head in the now familiar spot between his neck and shoulder and tucked her body into his.

'I love you,' Tommy whispered, smoothing a damp lock from her forehead and planting a kiss in its place.

Jo smiled, knowing he did.

Enjoying the feel of his hair-roughened skin against hers she glanced at the alarm clock beside the bed and seeing it was only just six, she closed her eyes.

It had been a clear night so the German bombers, who hadn't been able to pinpoint their targets for the past week because of the dense London fog, had been making up for lost time. The warning had gone off almost as soon as the blackout came into force and she and Tommy along with the rest of Post 7 had been hard at it all night until just after half past four when the all-clear sounded.

As both Jo's mobile dressing station and Green heavy squad had been on duty for twelve hours straight, Mattie sent them and two of the axillary ambulances home as soon as their day crews reported for duty.

They'd arrived at Tommy's flat some twenty minutes later and fallen into bed and each other's arms immediately.

'I can hear your heart,' Jo said, idly running her fingers through Tommy's chest hair.

'I'm glad about that,' he replied.

Kissing the nearest bit of him, Jo rolled to one side. Resting her elbow on the pillow and her head on her hand, she looked down at him for a second then kissed his cheek.

Although he didn't open his eyes, a little smile lifted the corner of his mouth and he gave her a squeeze.

'Are you sure you don't want me to come with you today?' she asked.

'Positive,' said Tommy.

'But it's your mum,' said Jo.

Turning, he opened his eyes.

'See, Jo, when you say the word "Mum" you think of someone who kissed it all better when you scraped your knee, gave you bread and jam when you burst in from school starving and sat up nights nursing you when you had a fever and,' he gave her that quirky smile of his, 'a clip around the ear when you were cheeky.'

'Not to mention the odd smack across the back of the legs,' added Jo.

Tommy laughed and then a sad expression crept into his eyes. 'But those things aren't what springs to mind when I think of my mum, in fact I don't even associate the word "mum" with the woman I'm saying goodbye to later.'

'Oh, Tommy,' said Jo, her heart aching for him.

He smiled.

'It's all right, honest it is.' He gave her another little squeeze. 'And after today I can put all that behind me so we can start planning our future. And the first thing I'm going to do is speak to your father. I thought I might catch him at the Catholic Club Sunday lunchtime.'

'When he's got a couple of pints of Guinness inside him,' laughed Jo.

'Precisely,' said Tommy. 'I doubt he'll be pleased to hear one of the Sweete brothers is intent on marrying his youngest daughter but I'm hoping I can talk him around, especially when I tell him . . .'

He paused.

'You're going to sign on,' she said quietly.

'I have to,' he replied.

She forced a smile. 'When?'

'Monday, after I've spoken to your dad. I don't suppose I'll go until the New Year.' He grinned. 'If I make a good impression on your father, he might even invite me for Christmas dinner.'

Jo reached up and lightly ran her finger along the bristly line of his square jaw.

'I do love you, Tommy,' she said, snuggling a little closer.

They gazed at each other for a long moment then Tommy stretched across and grabbed the open packet of French letters lying beside the clock.

'Good,' he said, rolling back and taking her with him. 'I've got one left and as I'm not seeing you for two days—'

'We might as well make use of it now,' laughed Jo, slipping her arms around his neck.

*

Taking another Benson & Hedges from the crumpled pack lying on his desk, Inspector Leonard Tovey clamped it between his lips and lit it from the spent one before stubbing the butt out in the overflowing ashtray.

He scanned the file sitting in front of him and, drawing in a lungful of nicotine, turned to the next statement.

The glass in the half-glazed door rattled as Eric, his sergeant, strolled in carrying two mugs.

'You still fretting over that ARP warden's case, Gov?' said Flowers, closing the door with his foot and shutting out the noise from the raucous Arbour Square's CID office.

'I am,' Leonard replied, as Eric placed his steaming cup of mid-morning coffee in front of him. 'Especially now I've got the coroner's report back. It says he was killed by a blow to the head.'

'I could have told you that,' said Eric, the seat alongside the desk creaking as he sat on it. 'After all, it was me who had to lift that bloody lump of concrete off his bonce.'

'But according to this,' Leonard tapped the top sheet of paper, 'the mark on the back of his head shows it was a blow from a long thin metal implement that killed him not the block of rubble that crushed his forehead.'

'Perhaps he fell backwards first,' said Eric, 'and then got caught in the blast.'

'Possibly,' Leonard agreed. 'But then how is it that he was seen by the fire crew from Bow Common alive and well a full hour after the cardboard factory where he was found was hit. And what was he doing there anyway; it's two miles off his patch?'

The detective sergeant took a noisy slurp of coffee. 'Perhaps he went to help someone.'

'Again, that's possible,' Leonard said. 'And I might go along with the idea but, according to everyone we interviewed at Post 7, this Potter was a bloody stickler for the rules and was forever tearing people off a strip for being off their post, so it's out of character for him to stray from his patch. I might go along with it if there had been someone trapped in the factory but there weren't. Plus, it seems that our illustrious chief ARP warden went to meet his maker on the self-same night someone waltzed off with Upington and Sons' safe and swiped the company's trophies from their factory in East Smithfield – a factory very much on Mr Potter's patch.'

'Coincidence?' asked Eric, scratching his head and dislodging a limp tendril of Brylcreemed hair in the process.

Leonard blew a stream of smoke towards the bare light fitting dangling above. 'You know my thoughts on coincidence, don't you, Eric?'

'There ain't no such thing?' the sergeant replied.

'Correct,' said Leonard. 'And certainly not when the Sweete brothers and their band of jokers are nearby.' He took another drag on his cigarette then stubbed it out. 'If only we could find the silverware.'

Picking up his coffee, Leonard took a swig then screwed up his face. Thumping it back on the desk he pulled out his bottom drawer and extracted half a bottle of whisky and two glasses. Pouring a generous measure in each he slid one towards his constable.

'Well, we've searched Reggie's yard twice and the Sweetes' gaff,' said Eric, taking up his glass. 'We even took the floorboards up but nothing.'

'Pity.' He poured himself another drink. 'I tell you, Eric, after twenty years of chasing tea leaves and conmen, I know in my water that those Sweete boys are connected to Potter's death.'

'Murder, don't you mean?' corrected the sergeant.

'You'd have a job sneaking that one by the judge,' Leonard said, pressing the cork back in. 'But they're bang to rights for manslaughter.'

He reached for his packet of cigarettes but finding it empty, tossed it in the bin.

'All we have to do,' said Eric, offering him one of his Senior Service, 'is find the silver.'

'We do,' said Leonard, holding the match to his fresh cigarette. 'So where on God's earth have they hidden it?'

Shaking out the flame, he clamped his cigarette between his teeth, and weaving his fingers across his considerable stomach, leaned back in the chair.

He studied the peeling paint on the opposite wall for a moment then jumped up. Striding across the small office, he tore open the door and looked across the heads of the detectives hunched over their desks. He spotted the elderly police officer tucked in the corner, surrounded by maps and mugshots pinned to a cork board.

'Oh, Chalky?'

PC White, the station's collator and font of all knowledge regarding H Division's criminal underworld, looked around.

'The Sweete boys,' Leonard bellowed. 'Where does that old drunk mother of theirs live?'

Tommy tied a knot in the threadbare sheet which contained the last of his mother's clothes and tossed it on the box containing her half a dozen pairs of scruffy, downtrodden shoes.

His mother's mid-morning funeral the day before at the City of London Cemetery had been brief, with no flowers other than a small bunch of winter pansies he'd paid a vendor at the crematory gates an extortionate amount for. He was glad, as the half a dozen blooms sitting on her coffin brightened the otherwise bleak chapel.

Surprisingly, he hadn't been the only person sitting in the pews as Dolly Walker from the pie and mash shop plus a couple of his mother's old friends who obviously remembered her in better times had also attended.

Having received the handful of mourners' condolences and thanked them in turn for taking the trouble to come, he'd walked the half-mile to Manor Park Station and caught the train back to Stratford. As the tram lines were down he'd then walked the further mile and a half to get back to the flat in Limehouse. He'd collapsed into the crumpled sheets that still had the comforting smell of Jo wrapped in them and only woken when the siren went off five hours later. After another twelve hours of the Luftwaffe raining down death on them while he and Green Squad had propped up tottering walls and shovelled rubble, the all-clear had gone at five and Tommy had stumbled back into the same dishevelled bed he'd got out of fourteen hours before.

He'd finally awoken and switched on the wireless just as *Melody Hour* started at one o'clock and, after shaving and a strip wash, he'd spent the past two hours clearing out his mother's few possessions, which were now bundled up for the rag man.

Of course, he still had to tackle the rest of her room. There was the pile of boxes in the corner and god only knew what lurked under the bed but at least he'd made a start.

He glanced at his watch.

Although he wasn't on duty until seven, Jo was off at six so he wanted to get to Post 7 early to make sure he saw her.

Each time he saw her all he wanted to do was take her in his arms, but for now they had to pretend they just happened to be having a cup of tea at the same time. Hopefully, once he'd spoken to her father and gained his permission to walk out with Jo, they could drop the charade.

Going into the bedroom he took his uniform jacket out of the wardrobe and hung it over the door. Hooking his thumbs in his braces, he was just about to slip them off to change into his work boiler suit when someone started hammering on the front door.

'All right, all right,' he shouted, striding back into the hall. 'I can hear you.'

Grabbing the handle, he opened the front door to find Inspector Tovey, Sergeant Flowers and three uniformed officers filling his doorway.

'Inspector Tovey,' he said. 'To what do I owe this pleasure?'

'Last week, while Hitler's buggers were flying above, some little toerags,' the inspector gave him a bald-eyed glare, 'or should I say *gang* of little toerags, decided to break into an engineering firm in East Smithfield and make off with something they shouldn't have. Know anything about it, Sweete?'

'Not a thing, Inspector,' Tommy replied.

'All right then, let's do it by the book. I have here a warrant to search these premises.' He waved a sheet of paper in Tommy's face. 'I have reason to believe that stolen items —'

'You're having a joke, aren't you, Inspector?' laughed Tommy.

'In you go, lads,' barked Tovey. 'Search the front room. Tear the place apart if you have to but they're here somewhere and I want 'em found.'

Barging past Tommy, the three constables marched into the flat and headed for the lounge. Tommy hurried after them and got there just in time to see them rip out the sideboard drawers and spill their contents on the carpet. Tovey and his sidekick followed him in and all three watched as the three constables upended furniture, flung cushions about and spread his mother's clothes, which he'd spent all afternoon sorting into neat piles, all over the floor.

Ten minutes later, having demolished that room, one officer marched into the kitchen while the other two turned their attention to the rest of the flat.

'What precisely are you looking for, Inspector?' asked Tommy, as the sound of crockery shattering started in the kitchen.

'The silver stolen from Upington and Sons' trophy cabinet last Thursday,' Tovey replied.

'Well, you're wasting your time,' said Tommy, 'because you won't find it here.'

'Guv!' shouted one of the police officers.

Tovey's thin lips lifted in a self-satisfied smile.

'Coming,' he shouted back, his sharp eyes fixed on Tommy.

With his heart pounding in his chest, Tommy followed the inspector out of the room while Flowers brought up the rear. As they walked into his mother's room, something akin to an icy hand gripped Tommy's chest.

'They were under the old girl's bed,' said the officer, as Tommy stared incredulously at the pile of shiny tankards, cups, trophies and plates sitting on his mother's washed-out patchwork counterpane.

'Wasting our time, are we, Sweete?' sniggered Flowers.

Tommy opened his mouth to speak but the full horror of what was happening stopped his words.

The inspector took hold of Tommy's arm.

'Thomas James Sweete,' he said, his voice booming around Tommy's head, 'I am arresting you for the burglary that took place at Upington and Sons during the night of the twenty-eighth November and for the murder of Mr Cyril Potter—'

'No!'

Ripping his arm free of Tovey's grip he sprang forward but three pairs of hands grabbed him and cold metal snapped around his wrists.

'You're not obliged to say anything,' continued the inspector as Tommy struggled against his handcuffs, 'but anything you do say will be taken down and may be used in evidence—'

'Thursday the twenty-eighth?' said Tommy.

'Yes,' said Tovey. 'Why?'

'Nothing,' said Tommy, as the image of him and Jo entwined together that first night flashed through his mind.

'Right, get him in the back of the hurry-up waggon,' said the inspector. 'Then take him down the station and throw him in the cell with his low-life brother and the rest of the crew.' He grinned. 'Perhaps this time we will be able to throw away the key.'

Chapter Twenty-Three

'OI, DOLLY-DAYDREAM, DO you want a bun?' said Joan who was standing next to Jo in the tea queue.

'No, just tea for me,' said Jo, dragging her eyes from the hall doorway and wondering why Tommy hadn't arrived yet for his early shift.

'So, who is he?' asked Joan as they shifted forward.

'I don't know what you're talking about,' said Jo, trying not to look around at the door again.

'Pull the other one it's got bells on,' Joan scoffed. 'You've been walking around like a tit in a trance for days, it must be some fella.'

'I can't say,' said Jo.

Joan looked shocked. 'He's not married, is he?'

'No, he's blooming well not,' Jo laughed. 'Well, not yet, anyhow and—'

Wally Riley, the second-in-command on Red heavy rescue team, barged into the queue in front of them to join two of his mates.

'Hey, you'll never guess,' he said to those gathered around him. 'The cops have arrested the whole of Blue Squad.'

The chattering stopped in an instant as everyone turned their attention to Wally.

'Straight up,' he continued. 'Granger from the Town Hall rang Mrs McCarthy a few moments ago to tell her.'

'What, all of them?' asked one of the WVS women manning the tea bar.

Wally nodded. 'Yes, both Sweete brothers plus that bunch of villains they hang around with.'

'What they been nicked for?' asked the man next to him.

'The Upington and Sons' job two weeks back,' Wally replied.

There were mutterings of 'about time' and 'bloody thieving scum' around them.

'And that's not all.' A smirk spread across his long face. 'They've been done for old Potter's murder, too.'

The floor seemed to tilt and rush towards Jo for a moment or two before it returned to its usual position under her feet.

'I suppose that means we'll be working short,' grumbled someone behind her.

Wally grinned. 'Yeah, but at least we won't swing.'

There was a ripple of laughter with the odd 'serves 'em right' and 'got what they deserved' thrown in.

'You all right, Jo?' asked Joan from what seemed like a long way away.

Forcing her mind to work, Jo looked around.

'Yes,' she replied. 'Yes, I'm fine. Shocked, that's all.'

'I know, it's terrible,' said Gillian. 'But I'm surprised they nabbed Tommy Sweete too, because Green team were working down East India Dock Road the night Potter was killed so surely he could have got Mick to tell the cops.'

The blood in Jo's veins turned to ice and her head swam again.

She grabbed Joan's arm.

'I've got to go somewhere,' she said. 'Can you cover for me until I get back?'

Her friend glanced at the clock. 'We're taking over from A team in half an hour.'

'I know, but it's only around the corner,' said Jo. 'And I promise I'll be back.'

Joan raised an eyebrow.

'All right,' she said. 'But if the warning goes off you'd better scoot back here on the double or—'

'Thanks.'

Gripping her bag, Jo dodged between the milling crowd and was just about at the other end of the hall when a familiar voice called her name.

Taking a deep breath, she turned to see her sister waddling towards her.

'Wait a moment, Jo,' Mattie said, coming to a breathless stop in front of her. 'I'm sure you've . . . heard that—'

'Blue Squad have been arrested?' said Jo.

'Yes,' said Mattie, putting a hand on her heaving chest. 'And I just . . . want . . . to say—'

'That you were right about Tommy Sweete,' cut in Jo. 'And perhaps now I'll realise that you telling Mum about catching us together was for my own good.'

Mattie glared at her. 'No . . . I was actually . . . going to say—'

'Mrs McCarthy!'

Mattie turned around and looked across the hall at the warden standing on the stage next to the desk holding the red telephone receiver aloft.

'It's Mr Granger,' he called.

Mattie shouted something back but Jo didn't hear her sister's reply because the doors were already swinging shut behind her as she dashed from the hall.

*

After a half-mile dash through the blacked-out streets, Jo ran up the few steps into Arbour Square police station. Grasping the long handle on the door, she yanked it open.

Although the temperature outside was close to freezing, in the inner sanctum of Stepney's main police station the atmosphere was cloying and smelt of bodies and fried food. If it hadn't been for the telephones on the desks and the tinny sound of the police car radios crackling, what with the blackout shutters in place and the low wattage light bulbs, you could be forgiven for thinking you'd slipped back in time to when the police station was built seventy years before.

The public counter was some six feet long and flanked on both sides by a wall, behind which the low hum of male voices could be heard.

At the far end of the room, half-hidden by a frosted-glass screen, were a couple of young constables chatting to an older colleague who was pointing at a map of the area, while a policewoman sitting at the desk next to a filing cabinet was bashing away on an antiquated typewriter.

None of them looked over as she stood waiting to be attended to, so Jo hammered her palm on the bell.

A beefy-looking policeman with three chevrons and a crown stitched to the upper arms of his uniform appeared from around the corner.

Red-faced with an impressive set of sandy-coloured mutton-chops, he gave Jo the once-over.

'Yes?' he asked, opening the leather-bound station register on the desk and taking the pen from the inkwell.

'Um . . . I believe you've got Tommy Sweete in your cells for some burglary two weeks ago,' said Jo.

'What of it?'

'Well, he didn't do it,' said Jo. 'Steal from Upington's warehouse or kill Warden Potter, that is.'

'How do you know?'

'Because he was with me,' said Jo, in a small voice.

'And who are you?'

'Miss Brogan,' said Jo. 'Miss Josephine Brogan.'

The officer's moustache waggled from side to side as he chewed his lips for a moment then he jabbed his pen back where it came from.

'Hanson!' he barked.

A fresh-faced young officer with a prominent Adam's apple and shaving rash stepped out from behind the partition.

'Yes, Sergeant Mills.'

'This is Miss Josephine Brogan and she says Tommy Sweete couldn't have been screwing the Upington warehouse or bonking the ARP warden on the head cos he was with her,' said the sergeant.

'Is that so?' said the constable.

'Yes,' said Jo. 'We were at his mother's flat.'

'All night?'

'Yes, Sergeant,' said Jo firmly.

'Doing what?' asked the constable.

Jo felt her cheeks glow hot.

Mills sneered. 'What do you think?'

The constable's eyes slid over her. 'Lucky bugger.'

Squaring her shoulders, Jo held the two officers' lewd stares. 'So now Tommy's got an alibi you can let him go, can't you?'

Scorn flickered in the sergeant's eyes. 'Constable Hanson, could you tell this young lady how many of the Sweete brothers' dollies we've had in here wasting our time so far?'

'Four, I believe,' said the constable. 'All giving it that the Sweete boys were with them.'

'But Tommy *was* with me.' Jo gripped the edge of the counter. 'He was. I swear it.'

Placing his spade-like hands on the mahogany surface, Sergeant Mills loomed over her. 'If that's the case, you won't mind standing up in court on Monday when he comes up before the Beak.'

'But couldn't I make a statement now?' said Jo, as the thought of telling a crowded court that Tommy was innocent because he'd been in bed with her flashed through her mind.

'You could,' said the desk sergeant, 'but we've got better things to do. Reggie's got one of those shysters from Glasson and Webb to represent him and his brother so why don't you trot along and tell them? Now, if there's nothing else, I'd thank you to sling your hook.'

Slamming the station ledger shut, he and Constable Hanson disappeared back from whence they came, leaving Jo standing at the counter.

Chapter Twenty-Four

WITH HIS BACK wedged against the cold white wall tiles behind him, Tommy sat with feet on the wooden bench, his arm across his knees, staring at the small oblong window high above his head.

Judging by the light seeping into the cell between the tightly packed bars and the noise of steel-tipped boots marching back and forth along the concrete corridor outside, he guessed it must be just after nine on Monday. Two whole nightmare days since Tovey's men had dragged out the hoard of stolen silver from under his mother's bed.

The spyhole snapped open for a second then snapped shut again. Tommy looked up as the key jangled in the lock and the cross bolts shifted, then the door creaked open.

Two blank-faced prison officers marched in dragging Reggie, with a fresh black eye and blood crusted around his nose, between them.

Tommy swung his legs off the bench and stood up.

'You two are up next so don't get too comfortable,' one of them said, shoving Reggie in.

He stumbled but regained his balance and swung around, lunging at them as they slammed the door in his face.

'Bloody brave, aren't you, two against one,' Reggie yelled, kicking the metal with the sole of his boot. 'Ain't got the balls to face me man to man, have you, poxy scum?'

He kicked the door again. Pulling down the front of his suit jacket, he turned. 'I wondered if you'd be here.'

'Of course I'm bloody well here,' shouted Tommy, springing forward and grabbing his brother's lapels. 'Where else would I be after you—'

'All right, all right,' barked Reggie, trying to break free from Tommy's grip. 'Keep your ruddy hair on and your fucking voice down.'

Tommy shot a glance towards the grey-painted iron door. Giving his brother a final shake, he threw him from him.

Reggie shot him a belligerent look which Tommy returned, balling his fists as he battled the urge to smash both into his brother's face.

'I've spent the whole bloody weekend banged up in a cell under Arbour Square nick because of you,' Tommy snarled, under his breath.

'You were ruddy lucky, weren't you?' Reggie replied in the same low tone. 'Tovey threw me into one of those cesspits under Wapping nick for two days.'

'Good,' spat Tommy. 'I hope it gives you piles.'

A pair of size-nine hobnail boots marched along the concrete passageway outside the cell and the two brothers studied the door until the footsteps passed their cell.

Sending Reggie a hateful look, Tommy threw himself down on the bench and resumed his former position. Reggie paced back and forth a couple of times then took up a similar spot at the other end of the wooden seat.

They sat in silence for a moment and then Tommy looked across at his brother. 'So, what are you going to do?'

'Plead not guilty, of course,' Reggie replied.

'I meant about me,' said Tommy.

Reggie looked baffled. 'What about you?'

Tommy looked incredulously at his brother. 'I wasn't there.'

'Neiver was I,' said Reggie, studying a point just above Tommy's head.

'In case you haven't heard,' Tommy ground out, 'along with burglary, we're both up on a murder charge, which is a capital offence.'

'They'll never make it stick,' said Reggie, dismissing his words with a wave. 'It'll be involuntary manslaughter at most.'

'That's still twenty yea—'

'Hang on a minute,' said Reggie, shifting his attention back onto Tommy. 'Why didn't that Paddy on Green heavy tell Tovey you were with him?'

Tommy frowned. 'Because I wasn't on duty that night.'

'Where were you?'

'At the flat.'

'By yourself?'

Tommy didn't answer.

'Oh, now I get it,' laughed Reggie.

'I can't drag her into this,' said Tommy, 'which is why I'm asking you, as my brother, to come clean and tell the rozzers I've got nothing to do with any of this.'

Reggie held his gaze for a long moment then shook his head.

'Sorry, Tommy boy, you better get your bird to give you an alibi or . . .' He shrugged. 'You know the rules.'

Tommy stared at him for a moment then, springing to his feet, he grabbed Reggie by his jacket.

Dragging his brother off the bench, Tommy smashed him against the wall. Reggie broke free of his grip and swung a punch but Tommy ducked. Circling around, Reggie tucked in his head and charged at Tommy in an attempt to wind him but his younger brother twisted at the last moment and Reggie crashed into the wall.

Clenching his right fist, Tommy punched Reggie's jaw, sending him reeling back. Stepping between Reggie's flailing arms, Tommy grasped the front of his jacket again and pinned him against the wall. Reggie struggled but Tommy leaned his weight into him and held him firm. Catching his breath, he thrust his face into his brother's until he could smell the blood oozing from his brother's busted lip.

'If I go down for this, Reggie,' Tommy said, staring eyeball to eyeball with Reggie, 'then I swear I'll—'

The jangle of the key turning in the lock and the bolts sliding back cut off Tommy's voice. The cell door creaked open. Without relinquishing his grip on his brother, Tommy looked round to see the doorway filled with the same bovine-looking court officers who'd thrown Reggie in the cell earlier.

The one on the right, who had a couple of medal ribbons from the last war pinned on his chest, grinned.

'Ah, bruverly luv!' he said. 'Ain't it touching?'

With the metal from the handcuffs biting into his wrists and fury still raging through him, Tommy was bundled through the prisoners' door and into the crowded courtroom ten minutes later.

The officer behind him poked him with his baton and Tommy trudged up the three steps into the dock to join Jimmy, who was already there.

'Where's Fred?' he muttered as Tommy shuffled along next to him.

The police officer jabbed Jimmy in the side. 'Button it.'

Thames Magistrates' Court had been built at the same time as the police station it was attached to and, as such, had the same solid red-brick exterior. However, unlike its counterpart, the court did its best to emulate a middling country house. Although the holding cells were sparse and cold, the main courtroom, with its high-ceilinged, oak-panelled interior, had more than a touch of the upper crust about it.

Police officers milled about in the sectioned-off area in front of the magistrate's bench, while the local press and friends and family of the accused were squashed into the public gallery. This small space could comfortably accommodate twenty or so people but today it was jammed packed with something close to double that number as word had got around that the Sweete brothers were standing in the dock accused of murder.

As the clock above the public-gallery door was now showing eleven o'clock, magistrate Sir Randolph Ewing JP, who had already been dispensing summary justice to the miscreants of East London for two hours, called for order. If his sour expression, under full bonnet and horsehair wig, was anything to go by, it had not been a good morning so far.

Ewing had been the resident magistrate at Thames Court for as long as Tommy could remember. His unwavering view on those he cast his judicial eye over was that they were the un-reformable scum of the earth and he sentenced accordingly.

'All right, Officer, I know the way,' said Reggie, as he bowled up the steps to the dock.

A murmur went around the public gallery as people nudged each other and pointed across. A couple of women who Tommy vaguely recognised as being members of his brother's scattered harem waved and blew kisses.

Barging past Tommy, Reggie took centre stage in the enclosure, acknowledging their tributes with a jaunty smile and a wink.

Of course, that was part of the 'rules', too. Showing bravado and contempt for those who put you in the dock was expected, but Tommy wasn't impressed.

The magistrate finished scribbling on the papers in front of him and handed them to the clerk.

He peered over his glasses at the court. 'Next.'

Tommy turned his attention back to the man sitting behind the bench.

A clerk in a black gown and with ink on his fingers shuffled the papers on the desk in front of him and rose to his feet.

'The crown versus Thomas James Sweete, Reginald Raymond Sweete and James William Rudd, Your Worship,' he said in a ponderous plummy voice. 'For one count of murder and two counts of burglary in that on the night of the twenty-eighth of November last the accused did break in and steal a safe containing £2,362 and 17s of company wages and commemorative silver estimated to be between £300 and £350 from Upington and Sons. They are further charged that during the course of said burglary they did murder a Mr Cyril Robert Potter, senior air raid warden at Civil Defence Post 7.'

The magistrate gazed around at the handful of lawyers sitting at the benches in front of him as they waited for their clients to appear before him. 'Is there representation?'

A sallow-faced individual wearing a tired-looking suit stood up. 'Yes, Your Worship, Glasson and Webb will be representing the defendants and ask for bail for all three defendants on the grounds that they are local men and of good character.'

There was an outbreak of laughter in the public gallery and murmurs of 'he's having a joke' and 'who's he trying to kid'. Reggie grinned but Tommy remained stony faced.

The public-gallery door opened to the side of Tommy and there was a small commotion as people shuffled around to accommodate the late-comer.

The magistrate shifted his gaze to Inspector Tovey. 'Any objections?'

The policeman sprang to his feet. 'Yes, Your Worship. Due to the serious nature of the crime, the police strongly object to bail.'

'I should think so, too,' said Sir Randolph, casting a contemptuous eye over the three men in the dock. 'Bail denied. The defendants will remain—'

'No,' shouted a voice from the gallery. 'Tommy Sweete wasn't there.'

Tommy turned around to see Jo, looking a picture as always in her AAS uniform, hanging over the rail of the raised area to his left.

'Quiet, miss!' snapped the clerk of the court, giving her a sharp look.

Jo ignored him.

'He wasn't there, Your Worship, I swear he wasn't,' she continued, her voice amplified by the domed arch above and the absolute hush. 'Because he was with me that night.'

'You dog,' laughed Reggie.

Tommy shot his brother a ferocious look.

There was a gasp in the gallery as the locals squashed alongside Jo started whispering behind their hands.

'Silence!' yelled the magistrate. 'Or I will clear the court.'

'But it's true.' Jo crossed herself. 'I'll swear he was.'

Fixing his beady eyes on Jo, Sir Randolph's mouth pulled into a tight line.

'You, young lady,' he jabbed his finger at her, 'will have a chance to give any evidence you have when the defendants stand trial at the Old Bailey but until then if I hear another word from you, you'll be facing thirty days in prison for contempt of court. Do you hear?'

Although Jo's eyes flashed angrily at the man behind the bench, she pressed her lips together and gave a small nod.

With love brimming in her eyes she looked at Tommy and the space between them vanished.

His gaze ran over the softness of her cheek, the sparkle of her eyes and the full curve of her mouth so as to imbed the image of her into his brain to sustain him in the long months ahead.

'Good,' barked Sir Randolph, his brusque tone destroying the fragile moment. 'Now if there's nothing else. I commit—'

'Actually, Your Worship,' interrupted the inspector, 'there is another matter which I have to bring to the attention of the court.'

'And what is that, pray?' asked the magistrate crossly.

'We received new evidence last night which means the police are reluctantly withdrawing all charges against Mr Thomas Sweete.' Inspector Tovey forced the words out between clenched teeth.

Sir Randolph's considerable eyebrows rose.

'Are you sure, Inspector? After all, you have both Sweete brothers in the dock on a capital charge,' he said, sounding quite buoyed up at the prospect of seeing the two men swing.

'I am, sir.' Inspector Tovey shot Tommy a mocking look. 'And believe me, I wouldn't unless I had to but Mr Fredrick

Paul Willis, who participated in the events that night, has given a written statement and will testify under oath that Tommy Sweete was not with his brother at any time during that night nor had any knowledge of the silver that was found in his abode.'

Fear replaced bluster on Reggie's face.

Jimmy leaned towards Tommy.

'What's he on about?' he asked, under his breath.

'Fred's turned King's evidence,' Tommy replied, suppressing the urge to jump over the edge of the dock and do cartwheels around the court.

'Well, I suppose in that case we will have to accept your submission and release Thomas Sweete,' said the magistrate.

Tommy thrust his manacled hands towards the policeman standing behind him in the dock and grudgingly the officer unlocked the cuffs.

Rubbing his wrists, he looked at his brother.

'Fortunately for me, not everyone abides by the rules,' he said.

Reggie grinned. 'Well, let's hope your luck holds when 'er father catches up with you.'

As the closing bars of *Music in Your Home* played out the programme at a quarter to twelve, Mattie placed the last newspaper-wrapped parcel into the fruit box on the floor bedside her.

'How many's that?' asked her grandmother, who was sitting opposite her.

'Two dozen,' said Mattie. 'Twelve for the boys and twelve for the girls.'

She and Queenie were sitting in the family parlour warming themselves by the fire, enjoying a cup of tea and a quiet hour before her father came home for his midday meal. That was simmering on the stove in the kitchen with the family smalls, which Queenie had washed that morning, hanging them on the dryer above.

Mattie had finally handed all her warden equipment to the new senior warden and was looking forward to enjoying the last three or four weeks at home before the baby arrived. To be truthful, what she was really enjoying was having her gran fuss over her and, given the fact she'd carried on at Post 7 two extra weeks because poor Cyril died, she deserved it. Of course, the drawback of having time on her hands was that she had more opportunity to worry. Worry as to why she'd not received a postcard from Aunt Fanny now for almost three months, which is why she had volunteered to set up the Christmas tree and help the WVS to make the food for the spread for the Post 7 children's Christmas party later that afternoon.

'Will that be enough?' asked Queenie, cutting across her troubled thoughts.

'It should be,' said Mattie, glancing at the presents. 'But Brenda's done another dozen, just in case.' She sighed. 'It's not much. Just socks and mittens for the small children and scarfs and balaclavas for the older ones and a penny chocolate bar.'

'I'm sure the young 'uns' eyes will fair light up when they open them,' said Queenie.

'I hope so,' said Mattie. 'Because we've been unravelling old jumpers and knitting for months and those without their own children at the post have been donating their Christmas sweet ration.'

'It's a bit different from last year,' said Gran.

Mattie laughed. 'Yes, Mum did go a bit mad.'

'A bit,' said Queenie. 'I'd say your mother must have taken leave of her senses and bought everything in the market as there wasn't space to put the gravy jug on the table.'

'Poor Mum,' said Mattie. 'She's beside herself worrying that if the butcher can't get her an ox heart, she'll only have half a dozen lamb chops and potatoes for Christmas dinner. Still, at least Charlie will be home so no matter what—'

Mattie gasped and clutched her expanded waistline.

'Pain?' asked her grandmother.

Mattie nodded.

'Has it gone?'

'Yes, just about.' Mattie shifted in her chair. 'But I've had back ache all morning and I feel like I'm sitting on this poor child's head.'

Her grandmother cast her eyes over her. 'I thought you'd dropped a bit.' Rising from her chair she tottered over and placed her hand on Mattie's tightly swollen stomach.

'I'd say the sweet babe will be with us before too long,' she said, as her fingers feathered over her bump.

Mattie looked puzzled. 'Sister Sullivan at Munroe House said I had weeks yet.'

Queenie's eyes twinkled. 'Did she now?'

Running her gnarled finger over Mattie's cheek, she kissed her briefly on the forehead and then returned to her chair. However, before she got her rear back on the seat there was a knock at the door.

Mattie swung her feet off the footstool and went to stand up but her grandmother raised her hand.

'You stay right where you are, my girl,' she said, heading towards the door.

Mattie smiled. Resting her head back, she closed her eyes. The baby moved again and her hands automatically closed around her bulge, imagining the small hands and feet contained within. Would it be a boy or a girl? Would it have Daniel's hazel eyes or her brown ones? Perhaps its hair would be wavy like hers instead of—

'Mattie, sweetheart,' her Gran said softly.

She opened her eyes.

It took a moment for Mattie to recognise the man in the long raincoat, with a club tie at his throat and holding a fedora in his hand, but then her heart leapt in her throat.

'Brigadier,' she said, as she looked across her family's cramped back parlour at Francis Lennox, her husband's commanding officer at MI5.

'Hello, my dear,' he said, turning the hat in his hands around as he spoke. 'How are you?'

'Well, I'm . . . I'm very well,' she managed to force out over the lump clogging her throat.

'I'm pleased to hear it,' he replied.

'And this is my gran,' Mattie added.

'Mrs Brogan.' He inclined his head towards Queenie. 'We met at the wedding.'

'And a grand day it was, too,' said Queenie. 'Can I get you some tea, Mr Lennox?'

'Thank you, no, Mrs Brogan,' said Francis, still fiddling with his hat. 'I have to get back to Whitehall.'

'Then I'll leave you to talk to Mattie,' said Queenie.

Francis raised his hand. 'Perhaps if you wouldn't mind staying, Mrs Brogan.'

He gave Queenie a sorrowful look.

Mattie's heart thumped and the baby wriggled around in response.

Taking one of the upright chairs from the table, he pulled it close to Mattie and sat down. He took Mattie's hands and a cheerless smile lifted his sandy moustache.

'There's no easy way to tell you this, my dear,' he said. 'I can't tell you where Daniel was posted but you know he was somewhere in Northern France working with the French resistance.'

Unable to speak, Mattie nodded.

'Up until three months ago we were in contact with him on a regular basis,' he continued. 'But twelve weeks ago, the radio line from him went dead. Often when the enemy get too close the operators have to shift their location so we weren't too bothered for a week or two but after a month we started making enquiries of other operatives in the area. It took a few weeks but we heard three weeks ago that the resistance group he was linked too had been infiltrated by collaborators. However, as sometimes things are misreported we contacted another unit in an adjacent location to Daniel's and asked them to investigate.' His rough hands held hers firmly. 'I'm afraid, Mattie, we had a radio message back from them today confirming that Daniel's cell had been captured. I'm afraid I can't tell you what's happened to Daniel with any certainty but it's not looking good.'

Her gran put an arm tight around Mattie's shoulders. 'So you're saying Daniel's a German prisoner?'

Francis looked wretchedly at Mattie.

'No, Gran,' she said, 'he would have been treated as a spy and—'

The word 'shot' wedged itself in her throat.

With the baby inside swirling around in protest at her hammering heart, Mattie stared dumbly at him.

'Daniel was a very brave man,' the commander continued.

'And he was someone I admired greatly and although it won't take away your grief, my dear, I hope you might draw some comfort from knowing that he saved countless lives.'

Mattie didn't reply.

Queenie cleared her throat.

'Well, thank you for coming to tell us,' she said, her gnarled fingers gripping Mattie's hand firmly. 'And I hope you won't mind seeing yourself out.'

'Not at all.' He stood up. 'The secretary of defence will be in touch in due course, regarding your husband's pay and effects.'

'Thank you,' Mattie whispered.

Francis's gaze flickered down to her heavily pregnant stomach and then back to her face.

'I'm so sorry,' he said softly with the glint of moisture in his eyes.

He turned his hat in his hand a couple more times then put it on and walked out of the house.

Mattie sat perfectly still for a moment, watching the particles of dust playing in the up draught from the fire and listening to the tick of the clock as it counted away the seconds to the half-hour but as it chimed twelve thirty she turned and gazed up at her gran.

'Ten days we were married, Gran,' she whispered.

With her thin lips pressed together, Queenie nodded.

'Just ten short—' She covered her face with her hands and as Queenie's scrawny arms closed around her, Mattie sobbed into grandmother's frail chest.

'Well,' said Tommy, 'I suppose the die is cast.'

Jo forced a smile. 'Well and truly.'

It was just before midday and she and Tommy were sitting on the long bench in Arbour Square police station's reception awaiting the return of his property. It was some thirty minutes since Tommy had been released in Thames Magistrate Court. Yesterday's drunks had been turfed out of the cells earlier and the pubs had only just opened so the public area was quiet. Jo was extremely grateful for this small mercy as she'd attracted quite enough attention already that morning.

'I'm so sorry, Jo,' he said.

Jo gave him a puzzled look. 'For what?'

'For getting you involved in this mess,' he said.

'It's not your fault,' she replied. 'I was the one who decided to announce to the world we'd spent the night together.'

'What will your father say?' he asked.

'I don't know,' said Jo.

Actually, she did, and the rest of her family, but she was trying not to think about it.

'And I'm sorry about Reggie,' she added.

Raking his fingers through his hair, Tommy sighed. 'So am I. Sorry the gormless idiot was too stupid to listen to me and now he's facing . . .'

Tommy pressed his lips together and fixed his eyes on the royal crest above the door in front of them.

Stretching up, Jo kissed him on the cheek.

'I love you,' she whispered.

He gave her that quirky smile of his.

The metal and glass doors of the police station burst open with such force that they crashed against the walls on either side. Jo jumped and looked around to see her father filling the doorway.

Dressed in his rough working clothes with his leather

cap backwards on his head and his hobnail boots crushed with mud and dirt, he'd clearly heard of the morning's events while out on his rounds. He spotted Jo with Tommy and his expression went from furious to murderous in an instant.

Tommy rose to his feet and, with her heart beating wildly in her chest, so did Jo as the two men she loved most in the world squared up to each other.

'Didn't I warn you?' Jerimiah yelled, jabbing his finger at Tommy. 'Didn't I warn you straight, boy, to stay away from my daughter?'

'You don't understand, Mr Brogan,' said Tommy.

'Understand,' bellowed her father, his massive hand balled into tight fists. 'I think I understand clear and plain what you've been up to, Tommy Sweete. As does every gossip and old wife from the Aldgate Pump to Bow Bridge.'

He stepped forward but Jo blocked his path.

'Don't, Dad,' she said. 'It's not Tommy's fault.'

'Move aside, Jo,' her father said. 'Cos I'm going to teach that bastard beside you a lesson he'll take to the grave.'

He tried to walk past her but Jo planted her hands on his chest. 'No, you're not, Dad.'

Her father's eyes, full of hurt and disappointment, held hers for a moment then, sweeping her aside, he strode across the mottled grey lobby tiles and grabbed the front of Tommy's jacket. Holding him firm, Jerimiah drew back to headbutt Tommy but, jamming his arms up between Jerimiah's, Tommy broke free.

'Help!' screamed Jo, stepping between them.

'I'll not fight you, Mr Brogan,' Tommy said, sidestepping out of reach. 'Because I'm going to marry Jo and—'

'Marry, are you?' yelled Jerimiah, raising his fist. 'You'll be fortunate to have your balls attached to your body when I'm done with you, let alone—'

'Someone help!' Jo screamed, shoving her father back.

Two thickset policemen rushed through from the front office just as Jerimiah was about to spring at Tommy again. They grabbed him and pinned him against the wall.

'Oi, Paddy, pack it in,' yelled one of the officers.

Glaring at Tommy, Jerimiah thrashed about for a second or two more then the fury faded a little from his eyes and he stopped struggling.

'That's better,' said the other officer as they let go of Jo's father. 'Now I suggest you take your daughter home and deal with her there or you'll be up in front of the magistrate yourself for causing an affray.'

Jo's father shook himself like a wet dog then straightened his coat. 'Thank you, Officer, I most surely will.'

Letting go of the breath she was holding, Jo looked at Tommy and their eyes met for a second before her father grabbed her arm. He dragged her towards the door but after a couple of steps he stopped and turned back.

Watching him warily, the officers braced themselves for another onslaught.

'Sorry, lads, me hat's escaped me,' he said, pointing to his leather headgear lying on the floor.

The policemen relaxed again but as Jo's father picked up his cap with his left hand, he stepped forward and, with a sickening crunch, smashed his right fist square onto Tommy's nose.

Jo screamed and sprang towards him but her father caught her arm and propelled her through the front doors of the police station.

Chapter Twenty-Five

HAVING TO DO a little half-step every fourth or fifth stride, Jo, with her father still hauling her along, turned into Mafeking Terrace some twenty minutes later. As it was now just after twelve thirty there was only a handful of women milling around the street; however, by the time they turned down the alleyway there were three times that number to witness Jo's walk of shame.

With her arm aching from his grip, Jo glanced up at her father's stony face as he kicked open the side gate and strode in to the yard. Without pausing, he marched up to the back door, pushed it open and continued through the kitchen into the parlour.

Mattie was sitting in the fireside chair with Queenie perched on the footstool in front of her, holding her hands. Both looked around as Jerimiah and Jo burst into the room.

'What in the name of all that's holy has happened?' asked Queenie.

'You tell her,' her father bellowed, shoving Jo into the centre of the room. 'Tell your gran and your sister what you were so proud to announce to the world and his wife this morning in court.'

Squaring her shoulders, Jo raised her head and looked at the two women. 'That me and Tommy Sweete were together the night Upington's was broken into and Mr Potter was killed.'

Mattie looked stunned.

'Now why in heaven's name did you do that, girl?' asked Queenie.

'Because if I hadn't he'd have been sent to prison for something he didn't do,' Jo replied.

'Well, son, you can't be riled at the girl for speaking the truth, can you now?' said Queenie.

'It's not her honesty I'm querying, Mother,' said Jerimiah between tight lips. 'It's the truth itself – that Jo got herself tangled up with Tommy Sweete – that has raised my fury.'

'I'm not tangled up with Tommy,' Jo shouted at her father. 'I'm in love with him and he loves me and we're going to get married.'

Her father gave a mirthless laugh. 'The Sweetes don't marry women, they just use them. The Lord himself only knows how many kids without a name Reggie Sweete has, sure wasn't their father the same? Went through women like a knife through butter did Harry Sweete and his boys are no different.'

'Reggie might be like that but Tommy's different,' said Jo. 'He's decent and honest—'

'Is he?' Her father cut in. 'I suppose that's why he persuaded you to open your legs—'

'You're a fine one to talk,' Jo yelled. 'You must be daft in the head if you think any of us believes that Charlie was a six-month baby. And if you must know Tommy was actually going to speak to you at the Catholic Club yesterday but—'

'He got arrested for burglary and murder instead,' said her father.

'Which he had no part of,' Jo replied. 'Can't you get it into your head that Tommy's not like his brother?'

'He's done time like Reggie,' said her father.

'He was sent to borstal,' said Jo. 'And, of course, you've never seen the inside of a police cell, have you, Dad?'

A flush spread up her father's face.

'Me and your mother have worked our fingers to the bone so we could afford for you to go to grammar school,' he said, jabbing his finger at her. 'But instead of using your education to make something of yourself you get mixed up with one of the Sweetes.'

'For the Love of God,' shouted Jo. 'He's not "one of the Sweetes", he's Tommy. Who's honest and hard-working, kind and funny, brilliantly clever and the man I lov—'

'And it wasn't just me and your mum who worked so you could go get an education, but Charlie, Cathy and Mattie, too.' He pointed at her sister, who sat stony-faced in the chair.

'About Mattie,' said Queenie, glancing at her grand-daughter. 'If the both of you would hush up for a second—'

'Your sister,' continued her father, still glaring at Jo, 'had to do her school certificate at night classes after working in a clothing sweatshop all day because we couldn't afford to send her to Coburn Girls—'

'Let's talk about Mattie, shall we?' said Jo, watching her father's hard expression. 'You keep going on about the Sweetes this and the Sweetes that and how Tommy's a villain and crook like his brother but what about her husband?'

She pointed at Mattie and the colour drained from her sister's face.

Queenie grabbed Jo, her fingers biting into her bicep. 'That's enough.'

Jo snatched back her arm and rounded on her father. 'I don't hear you telling Mattie how she's thrown her life away by getting herself in the family way by a bloody Nazi.'

Mattie let out a little cry and covered her mouth with her hands.

'Who told you such a thing?' demanded Jerimiah as he stood rooted to the spot.

'Cathy,' Jo replied, looking defiantly back at him. 'She told me that it was Mattie's never-seen never-heard-from husband who got Stan put away and so it's as clear as the nose on your face that the reason no one mentions him is because he's in prison too. I suppose that's why his aunt has to write or perhaps he can't because he's got his just deserts on the gallows.'

Her father and gran stared at her in horror.

There was a moment of utter stillness then, with tears shimmering in her eyes, Mattie hauled herself up from the chair.

'They'll be setting up for the party soon so I'd better get these around to the Post,' she said, grabbing the cardboard box full of newspaper parcels from the floor.

Knocking into the arm of the chair and nearly stumbling over the pouffe, she hurried from the room.

'Mattie!' Queenie shouted, dashing after her granddaughter but the back door slammed before she'd got halfway across the room.

The old woman stood there for a moment, then she turned and smiled sweetly at Jo.

'I suppose you're proud of yourself,' she said, in a soft lilting voice. 'I mean, for working out all that Nazi stuff about your sister and her husband.'

'I just put two and two together,' Jo replied.

Quick as lightning, Queenie's right hand swiped Jo around the head.

'Ow!'

'Now that one was for arguing with your father like a gob of shite and this one' – she whacked Jo again – 'is for upsetting your poor sister who's had enough worry on her mind to last her a hundred lifetimes.'

'Now, Ma,' said Jerimiah, trying to pull his mother off. 'Don't get yourself all riled up, you know what the doc said about your blood pressure.'

'Feck me blood pressure and feck the doctor,' Queenie replied.

Ripping the coral rosary hanging from the statue of the Virgin Mary that stood on their mantelshelf, and making the figurine shake precariously in the process, she thrust it in Jo's face.

'This,' she said, her face screwed up like a gargoyle, 'was my great-grandma's. Her pa brought it all the way back from Rome where the Pope himself blessed it. Now I want you to swear that you'll repeat nothing of what we'll be telling you.'

'I swear,' said Jo, rubbing her head.

'Kiss it!'

Jo did, feeling the beads smooth against her lips.

'Right, me girl,' said Queenie, her furious expression abating slightly. 'Now you know the Almighty is looking down on you and will judge you wanting if you breathe a word. You remember Father McCree?'

'The priest who came to help Father Mahon last year and then joined the army?' said Jo, thinking about the tall athletic young man who sent female parishioners' hearts a-fluttering.

'Well, he wasn't a priest. He was an agent from MI5 sent here to track down Nazi spies,' her father said. 'The Hitler-loving snake he was after was that Christopher Joliffe, that smarmy bank manager chap Mattie was knocking about with for a time. Cathy's Stan was part of the gang, organised by Joliffe, to land SS commanders in London Dock. They were caught red-handed by Father McCree with Mattie's help and she had to give evidence at their trial.'

'But I still don't understand about Mattie's husband?' said Jo.

'Father McCree's real name is Daniel McCarthy,' said her father.

Jo's eyes widened with surprise.

'Your sister's husband, the father of her child, was working undercover with the resistance in occupied France.' Queenie gave them both an exasperated look. 'I say *was*, because not half an hour before you two burst in here like a couple of warring banshees, Daniel's commanding officer came and broke the news to poor Mattie that her husband of six months is missing, presumed dead.' Her sharp black eyes fixed on Jo.

Ice seemed to replace the blood in Jo's veins. Dumbly her mouth opened and closed a couple of times then she found her words.

'I have to go to Mattie,' she called behind her as she raced out of the back door after her sister.

With a stitch slicing through her left side and remorse ripping at her heart, Jo dashed the half a mile to Post 7 in five minutes flat and burst through the ARP depot's main door and into a festive scene.

With the melodic sound of 'Blue Moon' from the old EKO radio on the window sill filling the room, a dozen or so of Jo's fellow ARP colleagues were up ladders transforming the stark interior of the Victorian school into a fairyland grotto ready for the children's Christmas party later that afternoon. Jo, like many of the women in the post, had spent weeks gluing colourful strips from women's magazines into paper chains and these, along with Chinese lanterns made from painted greaseproof paper, were draped in scallops across the hall and lit from behind with the Auxiliary Fire Service's blue, red and yellow warning lamps. Someone had even managed to get a small Christmas tree from somewhere and this, too, had been decorated with homemade baubles.

Everyone looked around as Jo staggered to a halt by the rack of stirrup pumps. She looked over the sea of faces staring at her.

'My sister,' she gasped, holding her ribs as she caught her breath. 'Where's my sister?'

The ARP warden for the St Paul's Church area, who was standing at the top of a ladder as he pinned up some balloons, looked around.

'She was here,' he said, casting his gaze over the heads of those in the hall.

'I think she's taken the kids' presents down into the boiler room so the children won't see them when they arrive,' said one of the WVS women who was attaching cotton loops to bows made from yellow cellophane.

Taking a deep breath and ignoring the pain in her side, Jo ran between the child-size trestle tables and stacked chairs towards the stairs leading to the basement.

Grasping the ball at the top of the banister, Jo swung around the top and clattered down the flight of stairs.

The space below the school housed the old Edwardian boiler and all the school equipment, like PE benches, teachers' desks and easels. It was also where the ARP stored their spare equipment such as lamps, shovels and ropes. Casting her eyes across the jumble of equipment, Jo spotted her sister over by a box of spare gas masks. As she stepped off the last step, Mattie looked around.

In the dim light from the couple of light bulbs illuminating the space her sister looked red-eyed and drawn, anguish etched deep in her face. As the full enormity of Mattie's situation hit Jo between the eyes, remorse and shame cut through her.

'Mattie, I'm sorry,' shouted Jo, dodging around a stack of infant chairs, desperate to get to her sister. 'I'm so sorry. I should never have said what I did. It's my fault I'm just a horrible—'

A boom overhead sent the lights jiggling and then a burst of dust-filled air pulsed through the cellar, lifting Jo off her feet and throwing her against one of the upright pillars as a box of bean bags burst open beside her.

In the intermittent beam from the now solitary light bulb swinging above, Jo saw that the stairs she'd just run down were clogged with shattered bricks and crumbled mortar. The cast-iron boiler had crumpled like a plasticine model under a slab of concrete from the floor above and the pillar opposite the one Jo had landed against had buckled, crushing an old bookcase beneath it.

Coughing, Jo pushed herself upright and looked over to where her heavily pregnant sister had been standing just seconds before. The pale beam of light scanned over the debris in the basement once more then the bulb popped and Jo was plunged into darkness.

'Mattie!' she screamed.

Other than the pitter-patter of grit falling there was utter silence.

'Mattie, for the Love of Mary, answer me!' she yelled again, her eyes searching the pitch blackness around her.

'Jo,' her sister murmured from somewhere to Jo's right.

Utter relief swept over her. 'Stay where you are, Matt, I'm coming.'

Closing her eyes, Jo tried to visualise the layout of the room then, stretching her hands in front of her and sliding her feet along, she groped her way forward.

'Matt,' she said as she bumped into a box of something blocking her path.

'Over here.'

Jo turned in the direction of her sister's voice and edged her way over. Skirting around what felt like a pile of floor mats she inched her way forward until her toe nudged something soft.

'Jo.' Mattie's hand closed around Jo's ankle.

'It's all right, Mattie, I'm here,' said Jo, crouching down beside her sister who was lying on the floor. 'Are you hurt? Can you feel your fingers and toe—'

'Jo.' Mattie's hands gripped her upper arm painfully. 'My waters have gone.'

Chapter Twenty-Six

WITH HIS NOSE still throbbing from Jerimiah's fist, Tommy turned into Mafeking Terrace forty minutes after Jo had been dragged out of the police station by her father.

Although the desk sergeant was all for booting him through the front door too, one of the auxiliary women police officers persuaded him to let her patch Tommy up before sending him on his way.

Having held a cold flannel on his nose for twenty minutes and then cleaning away most of the blood, Tommy had strolled out of the station ten minutes ago.

To be honest, although his battered face would probably disagree, he couldn't altogether blame Jerimiah for his actions. He only knew the big-boned Irishman in passing but he knew enough to know that Jerimiah wasn't a man you'd tangle with lightly. Although he had a reputation for honesty, Jerimiah Brogan had an explosive temper, which meant he was no stranger to the inside of a police cell himself. However, given that his youngest daughter had announced to the world she'd given herself out of wedlock to one of the notorious Sweete boys, it would have been more of a surprise if her father hadn't tried to pummel him into a greasy mark on the floor. To be honest, if he'd been in Jerimiah's place he'd probably have done the same.

However, while he was happy enough to let her father win this round, he was determined to be the one standing at the final bell, which was why he was now about to stick his head back in the lion's den.

The woman scrubbing dust from her front window with a newspaper spotted him as he turned into the street. She went to the next door along and knocked. Another woman's head poked out of a neighbouring front door and when she saw who it was, she also hurried across to knock on a front window. A door behind him opened and someone across the road lifted up their bedroom window and looked out. By the time he'd reached Jo's door at the other end of the street, he had a small crowd bringing up the rear and a street full of spectators hanging out of their upper windows. Stopping in front of the Brogans' shamrock-green door, Tommy pulled the front of his crumpled jacket down and grasping the knocker, struck it twice on the stud.

There was a pause and then Jerimiah opened the door.

His bristled jaw tightened and his eyes flashed angrily as he saw who it was standing on his threshold.

Squaring his shoulders, Tommy looked his prospective father-in-law in the eye. 'Good afternoon, Mr Brogan. I would like to speak with Jo.'

Jerimiah smiled. 'Would you now?'

'Yes, I would,' Tommy replied.

'Who is it?' shouted a woman's voice.

'No one you need to concern yourself with, Ida,' Jo's father called over his shoulder.

Jo's mother's round face appeared at the corner of the door. Her lips pulled together in a tight bud and her red-rimmed eyes narrowed as she spotted him.

'Oh, it's you.'

'Good afternoon, Mrs Brogan,' said Tommy. 'I've come to speak to Jo.'

'Well, you can't because, thanks to you, she and Mattie have had a blazing row and she's gone down to Post 7 to make up,' said Ida. 'So you can push off. Because I'll not have you make more trouble for this family.'

'Perhaps, if I could come in and discuss—'

'Discussion you're after having, is it, boy?' Jerimiah said, rolling up his sleeves. 'Then I'm happy to oblige you.'

He stepped out of the door but as his foot touched the pavement, Ida caught his arm.

'Let me go, woman,' growled Jerimiah, glaring at Tommy. 'So I can teach this toerag a lesson he'll never forget.'

'Not in the street, Jerry.' She cast a look at their audience. 'What will the neighbours say?'

'Whatever they have a mind to,' Jerimiah bellowed, yanking his arm free from his wife's grip.

He lunged at Tommy.

'No,' screamed Ida, causing a couple of dogs sniffing around in the gutter to prick up their ears.

Tommy sidestepped and Jerimiah's fist swept past his right cheek.

A cheer went up from the gathered crowd, which set the dogs barking and jumping around. Jo's father was just about to lash out again when his mother, Queenie, shot out of the door and leapt between them, her spindly legs spread wide and her work-worn hands up ready to repulse her gigantic son.

Jerimiah loomed over his elf-like mother. 'Stand aside, Mother.'

'I will not,' she replied, matching her son's belligerent stance. 'Not until you stop lashing at the poor fella and—'

Jo's father shifted his weight onto his right foot but as his mother moved to block him he sidestepped her and lunged at Tommy.

There was a cheer from the spectators and a couple of wolf-whistles, which set the dogs yelping again as they dashed amongst the crowd.

Anticipating the blow, Tommy stepped back and caught Jerimiah's fist as it passed him then, pivoting on the balls of his feet, he twisted the older man's arm up his back.

Ida screamed as Tommy spun around and clasped his free arm across Jerimiah's shoulders.

'I had hoped,' Tommy shouted, as he held his future father-in-law in an armlock, 'that we could have had this conversation over a pint, but no matter. I would like to ask you, Mr Brogan, if I have your permission to marry your daughter Jo.' Jerimiah started to struggle again so Tommy shoved his arm further up his back. 'But I have to tell you that whether you say yay or nay, the day after she turns twenty-one we're getting—'

'Mum! Dad!'

Tommy looked around to see Jo's younger brother Billy racing towards them.

'A UXB just flattened Shadwell School,' he yelled, skidding to a stop in front of them. 'People are saying that Mattie and Jo were in there when it went off but no one's seen 'em since.'

'I've found a torch, Matt,' said Jo, flicking it on and shining the pale beam on her sister.

Jo let out a breath she didn't know she was holding when she saw that her dust-encrusted sister had landed on a pile of cardboard boxes, which had cushioned her fall.

Mattie had managed to prop herself against one of the cast-iron pillars. To her right was a vaulting horse, which had plywood stage scenery laying against it. Above her, although most of the plaster had fallen from the ceiling, the Victorian support beam looked sturdy enough, as did the wall to her left with the coal-hole door in it.

Jo crouched down next to her sister but as she did Mattie pressed her lips hard together and, cradling her stomach, started to breathe heavily. Propping the torch on a nearby box, Jo took her sister's hand until she finally relaxed.

'Are you all right?' asked Jo.

Mattie let out a long breath and nodded.

'Good,' said Jo. 'Are you hurt anywhere else?'

'My right foot,' said Mattie.

Kneeling down, Jo moved her fingers down her sister's shin bone. Gripping her leg just above her ankle with one hand and her foot with the other, she moved it slightly.

Mattie winced and gripped Jo's arm.

Jo lowered it back on the floor.

'Is it broken?' asked Mattie.

Jo shook her head. 'But I think you've torn every ligament in your ankle.'

Her sister screwed up her face again and Jo took her hand, feeling her bones cracking as Mattie clung to her. After a long moment, she rested her head back. A tear escaped and rolled down her cheek and her chin started to wobble.

'I can't lose Daniel's baby,' she whispered. 'I just can't.'

Jo gripped Mattie's upper arms and she opened her eyes.

'Now you listen to me, Mattie,' she said, holding her sister's gaze. 'You, me and your baby are going to get out of this, do you hear?'

Although another tear tracked down the dirt on her face, Mattie nodded.

'I know all the chaps on the heavy crews will be up there now, digging like fury to get us out,' continued Jo in the same robust tone. 'But until they do we'll just have to make the best of it and keep our chins up. Yes?'

Mattie nodded and brushed away her tears, leaving streaks across her cheeks.

She forced a laugh. 'I bet they had to fetch Wilf and Pete from Red crew out of the Bunch of Grapes as usual.'

'I bet they did,' laughed Jo. 'And that Doris Bigly is already brewing a cuppa for everyone.'

Mattie nodded. 'And women are in labour for hours before the baby's delivered.'

'Days, more like,' agreed Jo. 'Isn't Mum forever telling us how she was three days birthing Charlie? So don't worry, we'll be out of here long before that baby of yours puts in an appea—'

Mattie gasped and clutched her bump again. Jo put her arm around her shoulders and held her until the contraction dissipated and she relaxed back.

Her terrified eyes fixed on Jo. 'But what if it doesn't wait and—'

'Don't worry,' said Jo, trying not to sound as terrified as she felt. 'I've covered the theory of delivering a baby in first-aid classes so between us we'll deliver Master or Miss McCarthy while those up top are shifting the rubble. We're going to do our bit too,' stretching across, Jo dragged a rounders bat out from under a box, 'by letting them know we're here. I'm going to make us both comfortable on a couple of those,' she said, pointing the torch at a pile of rubberised floor mats that had spilled out of a box.

Retracing her steps across the rubble, Jo pulled out two mats from the pile and dragged them across to the wall. Having laid them as flat as she could, she got behind her sister and, tucking her hands under Mattie's arms, helped her shuffle across and onto the spongy surface.

'There, that's better. Now, let me snuggle down beside you,' Jo said, tucking herself in alongside her sister, 'before I turn off the torch.'

Panic flashed across Mattie's face. 'Do you have to?'

'Yes, to save the battery,' said Jo, smoothing a dusty lock of her sister's hair from her forehead. 'If your baby should decide to be born before the heavy crew reach us, I'll need to be able to see what I'm doing.'

Mattie's terrified eyes held hers for a moment then she forced a smile.

Jo pressed the switch and plunged them into total darkness.

Silently in the blinding darkness, images of the women and children huddled in the basement in Poplar started to play over in Jo's mind but she cut them short.

Carefully putting the torch in her pocket, she felt her sister tense as another contraction started to build. Jo held her hand.

'I'm so sorry, Mattie,' she whispered, when it subsided, 'for saying all those hateful things.'

'I know, Jo,' Mattie replied. 'And I never told Mum about you and Tommy. She had you evacuated with Billy so that you could look after him because Aunt Pearl threatened to take him back if she didn't.'

Feeling tears spring into her own eyes, Jo hugged her beloved elder sister tight. 'I love you.'

'I love you, too.' Mattie's body tensed again as another contraction began to build. 'Jo, I'm scared.'

'So was I when Gladys Williams started picking on me in the playground,' said Jo, struggling to master her own terror. 'Do you remember how you came over and gave her what for?'

Chapter Twenty-Seven

THROWING A LUMP of what had been the side wall of Shadwell School behind him, Tommy wiped the dirt from his eyes with the back of his gloved hand. Although the winter sun had almost gone from the sky and the December night chill was already putting a thin sheen of ice over shallow puddles, Tommy had sweat running down his face.

That's because he, along with the heavy rescue crews from Post 9, the neighbouring depot in the Royal Docks, had been looking for survivors in what was left of the old Victorian school for the past four hours. They weren't alone: in addition to the Civil Defence teams, people from the neighbouring streets were out in force, offering what help they could.

It was now close to four in the afternoon and the blackout would be starting in twenty minutes so soon they'd be digging in the dark.

Stretching to ease the muscles of his back, Tommy glanced across at Jerimiah, some ten foot away from him, who was working a crowbar under a huge lump of bricks and mortar.

Jo's father had arrived at the scene of the blast just a step or two behind Tommy and they had laboured side by side all afternoon, both of them locked in the hell of their imaginations.

Satisfied the crowbar was in place, Jerimiah crouched down and wedged his shoulder under the iron rod. Frowning, he leaned his weight onto it but after a moment or two of grunting, he let it go.

Muttering, he stomped around in a small circle then jammed his shoulder back under.

Stepping over a clump of brickwork, Tommy went over to him.

'Let me give you a hand,' he said, tucking his shoulder in behind Jo's father.

Jerimiah grunted by way of reply and then heaved again.

Taking the strain, Tommy followed suit and the massive clump of rubble rolled down, crashing into the pile they'd already shifted.

Balancing the heavy metal shaft lightly in his right hand, Jo's father looked across at him.

'Can you give us a hand shifting that bugger?' Tommy said, indicating a six-foot-high section of a broken pillar resting on a pile of crumpled bricks.

Jerimiah's massive hand flexed around the crowbar a couple of times then he gave a curt nod. Turning his back on Jo's father, and the metal pole in his hand, Tommy nimbly stepped across the rubble to the shattered square column, which was still clad in green tiles.

Tommy stood back while Jerimiah jammed the crowbar beneath the base and then they heaved in unison, sending the block tumbling down to join the lump they'd previously shifted.

As the street light went out, signalling the start of the blackout, Tommy turned and faced Jerimiah again.

'Mr Brogan, I—'

'We've found another one,' shouted Brian Oldham, one of Post 9's heavy rescue leaders, for the fourteenth time since they started digging. 'It's a woman.'

With his heart beating widely in his chest and with Jo's father just a step behind, Tommy leapt across the rubble towards the gap that had once been the school hall's tall mock Gothic window.

They arrived just as two light rescue bearers brought out a stretcher. The rescue crews stood with their caps off in respectful silence as the dust-covered body passed between them. Tommy, with Jo's father just a pace behind, followed them over to the row of shrouded figures lying on the pavement.

Placing the stretcher down the two bearers gently lifted the body onto a shroud spread out ready.

Tommy gazed down and relief flooded through him.

'Do you know who it is, mate?' asked Brian, coming to join them as the shroud was wound around the body.

'Doris Bigly,' said Tommy, looking down at the matron, whose green WVS uniform was hardly distinguishable under the layer of brick dust. 'Nice woman. Always giving out tea.'

Jerimiah stood in silence for a moment then, covering his eyes with his hands, he stumbled off across the rubble and around the corner of the building, out of sight.

Ida and her mother-in-law Queenie had been standing amongst the small crowd of waiting relatives.

'Is it one of the girls?' she sobbed, hurrying over with Queenie in tow.

'No, Mrs Brogan,' said Tommy, as she came to a halt beside him.

'Praise be,' she said, as she and Queenie crossed themselves rigorously a couple of times. 'When I saw Jerry run off like that I thought . . .' She placed her hand on her heaving chest. She glanced over to where he'd disappeared. 'Perhaps I ought to go and see if he's all right?'

'It's too dangerous,' said Tommy. 'I'll go.'

Leaving Jo's mother and gran talking to the rescuers, Tommy stepped over a mangled window frame and, placing his feet carefully in the failing light, headed off after Jerimiah.

He found him standing next to the largely intact west wall, staring up at the evening stars sparkling in the crisp winter night.

Although he stood with his shoulders straight, in the last rays of light his expression was one of utter desolation.

'I've been sick with fear every time they find a body,' said Tommy. 'So God only knows how you feel.'

Jo's father stood resolute and straight for a moment or two more then his face crumpled.

'Please, Mother of God, not both of them,' he murmured.

With his arms dangling loose at his side, Tommy stared helplessly at Jerimiah as his own grief held the breath in his lungs. And then he heard it.

A faint tapping.

Tommy grabbed Jerimiah's upper arm. 'Mr Brogan, listen.'

Jerimiah looked up. 'Where's it coming from?'

'Below us, I think,' said Tommy, looking down at the roof slates and broken bricks under their feet. 'There it is again.'

They stood stock still and listened to a muffled two taps followed by three taps then two again.

'What's under here?'

'The school's basement,' Tommy replied.

Hope flashed across the older man's face. 'Could Jo and Mattie be down there?'

'They could,' Tommy replied, as his spirits soared.

380

'How do we get down there?' asked Jerimiah.

'By the stairs at the back of the hall,' Tommy replied. 'But they're filled with rubble from the floor above.'

'Well, then we'd better get shifting it,' said Jerimiah, walking past him.

'Wait!' Tommy shifted the debris with his boot. 'The coal hole should be around here somewhere and as long as the door's not blocked on the other side—'

The droning wail of the air raid siren cut between them.

'We need to clear this lot,' shouted Tommy, pointing at the wreckage from the roof under their feet. 'And locate the cover.'

'You stay there and keep listening,' Jerimiah bellowed back. 'And I'll get us a couple of shovels.'

Tommy nodded but as Jo's father turned away, Queenie appeared around the corner of the building. Clambering over the uneven blocks of brickwork like a spindly elf, she stopped in front of her son.

'What are you doing here, Ma?' Jerimiah bawled, towering over her.

'Dancing an Irish jig, what do you think?' she yelled back.

'But there's an air raid on.'

Queenie rolled her eyes. 'Sure, don't you think I know that, you great eejit? Now stop wasting time and tell me what you're doing.'

'We think there's someone trapped in the basement and as Jo and Mattie haven't been found yet it's possible it's them,' Tommy hollered. 'So Mr Brogan is getting a couple of shovels so we can find the entrance to the school's coal bunker.'

'Fetch me one, too,' said Queenie, as the ack-ack guns on Barking Creek peppered the sky with shells to greet the oncoming enemy aircraft. 'And you, Tommy-me-lad, put your back into it and find that fecking hatch.'

'How're you doing, Mattie?' asked Jo, as her sister's grip on her hand relaxed a little.

The ground shook as another bomb found its target and Jo shielded her sister with her body as the grit dislodged by the blast pitter-pattered down on them.

'Fine, fine,' Mattie panted. 'But there's hardly a space between.'

Resting her head back against the vaulting horse where Jo had propped her, Mattie closed her eyes.

Although it was difficult to gauge time lying in the pitch black, Jo reckoned that as the blackout would have come into force at three twenty and the first wave of bombers usually arrived an hour or so later, it was close to five in the evening, maybe a little later.

She was starving hungry and her mouth felt like the bottom of Prince Albert's cage, but she wasn't worried by either because approximately ten minutes ago her sister had got the urge to push.

'Jo,' Mattie gasped, groping for her hand in the dark.

'It's all right, sweetheart, I'm here. Now, Mattie, when the next one starts tuck in your chin and push,' said Jo, her eyes fixed on the bulging area between her sister's legs in the mellow light.

When it was clear Mattie's baby wasn't going to wait for the heavy rescue teams to arrive, Jo had arranged her sister's skirt in a fan beneath her to keep her rear away from the brick dust and then spread her sister's knickers over that and tucked them under her bottom. She'd also ripped her handkerchief into strips and tucked them into the front of her brassiere, ready to tie off the cord.

Gripping behind her thighs, Mattie lowered her head as another contraction took hold.

'Come on, Mattie,' shouted Jo, the ground shaking as a cluster of bombs fell close by. 'Push that baby out.'

Mattie strained for a long moment then her head fell back.

'I can't,' she sobbed, sweat dripping from her nose despite the icy chill of the basement. 'I just can't.'

'Don't be daft, Mattie,' said Jo, sounding uncannily like her gran. 'Of course you can. Just a few more pushes.'

Mattie's lips pulled into a hard line and fixing her eyes on Jo, she tucked in her chin and pushed.

'I can feel it moving down,' she gasped, as her face flushed with the effort.

'Keep pushing!' Jo shouted, praying to every saint in Heaven that a small foot wouldn't suddenly pop out.

Mattie drew in a noisy breath then, planting her feet wide, she hunched forward and did as Jo urged her.

A circle of damp dark hair the size of a digestive biscuit appeared, protruding through her sister's stretched vulva as the contraction ebbed away.

'Can you see anything?' gasped Mattie.

'That your baby's got dark hair,' Jo replied.

A small smile lifted the corners of Mattie's mouth.

'Just like Daniel's,' she whispered.

A lump formed in Jo's throat.

'Come on, Matt,' she said softly, wiping a damp lock of hair from her sister's forehead. 'A couple more pushes and you can hold your baby.'

Mattie gave a sharp nod as the next contraction gripped her. The digestive-sized patch of damp curls expanded into a saucer-sized one before the pain waned.

Crouched between her sister's knees, Jo stripped off her coat and jumper.

'Right, Matt,' she said, 'the next one should have this baby born.'

Mattie's lips pulled into a determined line and then, as the primal urge to push swept through her, she bore down again.

Taking off her shirt, Jo slung it over her shoulder then with the icy atmosphere of the cellar raising goosebumps, she cupped her hand beneath her sister's rear.

'Push!' shouted Jo.

Mattie did.

A small head with a mass of curly black hair popped out and then rotated towards her.

'The head's out now, try not to push while I check for the cord,' said Jo, trying to conjure up the images of her first-aid textbook.

Breathing heavily, Mattie let her head rest back onto the vaulting horse while Jo's fingers felt under the child's chin.

'I can't feel a cord so it seems all right,' said Jo. 'So push.'

Her face screwed up tight with the effort, Mattie pushed again.

A gush of blood-streaked water shot out, wetting the floor beneath Jo's knees, and the baby slithered into her waiting hands.

Whipping her still-warm blouse from her shoulder, Jo wrapped it round the birth-smeared infant.

A bomb crashing somewhere close by shook the walls.

Jo tucked the infant into her as a shower of grit fell onto them.

'Is my baby all right?' sobbed Mattie, raising herself up in an effort to see.

The baby answered for itself by giving a loud cry and mother and auntie burst into tears. Taking her knitted jumper from inside her coat, Jo wrapped the baby again.

'Say hello to your new daughter, Mattie,' she said, laying the baby into her sister's outstretched arms.

'Hello, sweetheart,' whispered Mattie as she gazed lovingly down at her daughter's screwed-up face.

Taking two strips of handkerchief, Jo rummaged under the baby's improvised covering and tied off the cord in two places before tucking the jumper around the baby again.

'What are you going to call her?' asked Jo.

'Alicia,' said Mattie. 'After Daniel's mother . . .' Tears welled up in her sister's eyes.

Jo gathered her sister into her arms.

'Daniel would have been very proud of you,' she said, kissing Mattie's moist forehead.

In the dim light from the torch, Mattie gave her a brave little smile.

Another bomb, which felt as if it had landed beside them, rocked the cellar and the ground beneath them. The torch rolled off the box Jo had placed it on and smashed, plunging them into darkness again.

Mattie screamed as Jo groped around on the floor.

'It's all right, I've found it,' said Jo, grasping the Bakelite cylinder.

She flicked the switch but nothing happened.

'Jo?'

'It's broken,' said Jo, feeling tears spring into her own eyes. 'But don't you worry, Mattie. The heavy rescue should be with us any moment now.' Searching around her, Jo located her coat and, fumbling in the dark, she covered mother and baby with it. 'So, you just sit tight and keep you and Alicia warm.'

Dressed only in her trousers and brassiere, Jo rubbed her bare arms to warm them then grasping the rounders bat she crawled across the floor to the wall and struck the water pipes, using the two-three-two rhythm again.

Jo waited as the sound echoed up the lead pipes.

Nothing.

Just as it had been nothing for the last however many hours. Nothing as it might be for ever.

Collapsing against the wall, Jo closed her eyes as images of her family flashed in a jumbled sequence through her mind. Her father kissing a grazed knee better; her mother sponging her when she had mumps; her, Mattie and Cathy snuggled for warmth together in the old brass bed while rain lashed the window, and the look of pride on her gran's face when she came home from school with the prize for being top of the class. Her thoughts moved on to Tommy, and her heart ached as her mind and body remembered the little white fan lines at the corners of his eyes, the square bluntness of his chin, the scratch of his morning bristles on her bare shoulder, the sweetness of his mouth covering hers and the exquisite bliss of their bodies moving as one.

Tears pressed at the back of her eyes as despair started to engulf her. Alicia gave a couple of little cries and then in the dark Mattie started humming 'Too-Ra-Loo-Ra-Loo-Ral', the song her mother had rocked her to sleep with for as long as Jo could remember. The soft refrain that meant home, family and love.

In the dark, Jo's face took on a determined look. Grabbing the bat again she thumped on the pipes so hard the vibration juddered up her arm.

Again, the noise rattled up the old water pipes but before it faded there was a dull corresponding two-three-two wooden thud somewhere to the left of her.

Keeping hold of the bat, Jo scrambled to her feet and searched along the wall with her fingertips until she came to the wooden door of the coal hole. She banged on the door and got an immediate answering knock at the top of the frame.

'Jo?' Mattie called from the darkness.

'It's all right, Matt, someone's coming,' Jo shouted back. 'They're coming down the coal hole.'

Frantically, she searched around until she found the handle and then yanked it open six or seven inches.

Another explosion shook the wall and there was squeaking and rattling as nuggets of coal bounced across the floor.

Kicking them aside, Jo wedged her face into the gap.

'We're down here!' she screamed.

A beam of light from above blinded her vision. Shading her eyes, Jo looked up to see Tommy's face, looking sideways down at her from the top of a stack of coal.

He grinned, his teeth showing in stark whiteness against his coal-dust covered face.

'Over here, Mr Brogan,' he shouted, his eyes not leaving her face. 'We've found them.'

Chapter Twenty-Eight

'SHE'S SO BEAUTIFUL,' said Jo, gazing at her five-day-old niece, Alicia, resting across her mother's knee as she buttoned up her nightdress.

It was the last Saturday before Christmas and Jo was sitting at her sister's bedside in Marie Celeste Ward in the London Hospital. Mattie was in the third bed down on the right of the long Nightingale maternity ward.

Jo had been the first one through the door when ward visiting time started at three thirty and had spent the last twenty minutes admiring the latest edition to the Brogan family, marvelling at how much the baby had changed since she'd seen her the day before and again from the day before that. She had been in every day since the Poplar's light rescue stretcher bearers had carried Mattie, clutching tight to Alicia, out of Shadwell School's cellar.

'Isn't she?' Mattie replied, cradling her in her arms and pressing her lips on her daughter's downy head. 'And so like her father.'

Closing her hand over her sister's, Jo gave it a gentle squeeze. 'It must be so hard.'

Mattie gave her a brave little smile and kissed the baby's head again. 'Not as hard as it would be without this little sweetheart.'

Feeling a lump forming in her throat, Jo squeezed her sister's hand again.

Mattie looked up and she and Jo exchanged a tender look.

Neither of them had mentioned the argument at the house because it was already forgotten.

Alicia gave a windy little smile and farted.

'But she sounds like you in bed,' said Jo.

'Like you, you mean,' Mattie laughed.

'When are they going to let you out?' Jo asked.

'Monday,' said Mattie. 'And I can't wait to get home.'

'I bet,' said Jo. 'Mum's put all the baby clothes on the dryer to air them and Dad's shifted the beds around so you're in Charlie's old room with Alicia. Francesca's moved into the front room with me.'

'Where's Charlie going to sleep when he comes home?' asked Mattie.

'He'll have to bed down in the parlour, I suppose,' Jo replied. 'Anyway, he's only got a forty-eight-hour pass over Christmas so it's only for a couple of nights.'

'Is Mum still fretting about feeding up?' asked Mattie.

'What do you think?' said Jo. 'Every day she brings home whatever's on sale in Watney Street, but I'm not sure pilchards and semolina are any substitute for beef or chicken.'

Alicia hiccupped and a dribble of milk escaped down her chin.

'Do they know how many people were killed at Post 7 yet?' asked Mattie, wiping it away with a muslin.

'Fifteen,' said Jo, remembering the faces of her colleagues who were now lying at peace in the City of London cemetery. 'Including three of the WVS women who were setting up the spread for the party,' said Jo.

She and Mattie crossed themselves.

'I just keep thinking thank God that UXB didn't get off an hour later or there would have been children in the building too,' Jo added. 'Your mate Brenda had a narrow escape. She was using the girls' bogs in the playground so other than a few cuts and bruises she walked away unscathed. Once all the funerals are over we're being transferred to other posts. I've been allocated to Post 11 in Bow but some have been sent as far afield as Fulham.'

'Where's Tommy being sent?' asked Mattie.

'To Holborn,' Jo replied. 'But it's only to help out for a couple of weeks. I went with him to sign up two days ago and he's waiting to hear where he should report.'

'Has Dad said anything yet?' asked Mattie.

Jo shook her head. 'Although he's no longer banned Tommy from the house.'

'After listening to Mum and Gran telling me every time they visit what a hero "that lovely lad Tommy is" I don't think he'd dare,' said Mattie.

Jo smiled. 'Not with Mum and Gran treating Tommy like a returning hero every time he appears.'

'Well, he was a hero,' said Mattie softly. 'Just like you were a heroine, Jo.'

Feeling her cheeks grow warm, Jo waved her sister's words away. 'Don't be daft.'

'No, honestly,' said Mattie. 'I don't think me or Alicia would be here now if you hadn't been with us.'

They exchanged another fond look.

'Perhaps Dad will let you and Tommy get engaged at least before he leaves for the army,' said Mattie, shifting her daughter across to the other arm.

'It doesn't matter if he does or he doesn't,' said Jo, 'because even if we have to wait, me and Tommy will be getting married the day after I'm twenty-one.'

'Let's hope it doesn't come to that,' said Mattie. 'And if you want my advice, I'd say just keep badgering at Dad until he gives his consent because,' gazing down at her daughter, tears welled in Mattie's eyes, 'you have to grab happiness while you can, Jo.'

The lump reformed itself in Jo's throat as her eyes grew moist too.

'Mattie,' a male voice said softy.

Jo looked around and although it took her a moment or two to work out who the gaunt, dishevelled-looking man at the end of the bed was, her sister knew in an instant.

'Daniel!' she cried.

Mattie's husband crossed the floor in two strides and took her in his arms.

'Oh, Daniel,' Mattie sobbed, clinging to him with their baby in her free arm.

Feeling her heart ache with happiness for her sister, Jo stood up.

'I'll just leave you two to . . . to . . .'

Mattie continued to sob while Daniel held her and their new daughter.

With tears streaming down her face and the biggest smile on her face, Jo tiptoed away between the rows of beds towards the double doors at the far end of the ward.

Chapter Twenty-Nine

'SO,' SAID REGGIE, flicking his roll-up towards the brown Bakelite ashtray on the bench in front of him. 'You and that Brogan girl will be getting spliced then.'

'Yes, we will,' said Tommy.

'I suppose if things had turned out different I could have walked you down the aisle or summin, Tommy boy, but as you can see,' he raised his handcuffed hands, 'I'm going to be out of circulation for a while.'

It was two days before Christmas and just after midday. Tommy was sitting in the visitors' room in Wandsworth Prison along with a dozen or so other relatives and a handful of po-faced prison wardens. He was on one side of the mesh window in his allocated cubicle and Reggie on the other. They were about halfway through their pre-booked thirty-minute visit and had so far established that Reggie's cell was like a fridge, the food like pig swill and that none of the prison guards knew their fathers.

'Well, at least with you banged up in here when we're wed there's a chance we can get through the whole day without a punch-up,' Tommy replied, his breath showing in little puffs in the freezing air as he spoke.

'I wouldn't bank on it.' Reggie pulled a face. 'Your Paddy's rellies will probably just fight amongst themselves. And besides, it wouldn't be a proper wedding if someone on the bride's side didn't swing a punch at one of the groom's lot. Have you set a date?'

'Not yet,' said Tommy. 'But I hope it won't be long now I'm firmly in the family's good books.'

He told his brother about Jo's and Mattie's rescue.

'Blimey, they were lucky,' Reggie said when he'd finished.

'They were,' said Tommy. 'But the rest who were inside the school weren't.'

Flicking the ash off his cigarette again, Reggie gave him a considered look. 'I heard Ugly and Squeaky copped it.'

Tommy nodded.

'Poor sods,' said Reggie. 'How many were there all together?'

'Fifteen,' said Tommy. 'The last one was laid to rest on Friday.'

'I suppose we ought to be thankful none of the kiddies for the party were in there,' said Reggie.

'That's what everyone said. The other ARP depots chipped in and the children had their party on Wednesday at the Memorial Hall,' said Tommy.

The prison guard on his brother's side of the divide strolled past, tapping his baton lightly in his hand as he eyed the inmates under his supervision.

'I suppose you've signed up,' said Reggie, pulling a fresh roll-up from behind his ear.

'I have,' said Tommy. 'And I got a letter yesterday telling me to report the first Monday in January.'

'You'll look the dog's doodahs in uniform, you will,' Reggie said. 'But take my advice and find yourself a cushy number in stores or something. And keep your bloody head down. I don't want you coming home in a box.'

Tommy smiled. 'Don't worry, I know how to look after myself.'

One of the visitors at the far end of the room started

shouting and the prison guard standing behind Reggie hurried off to sort out the commotion.

'Do you know when you're getting transferred to Wakefield?' asked Tommy.

'Tomorrow,' Reggie replied. 'Just in time for Christmas. I hope Santa knows so he can deliver my presents.'

Tommy laughed. 'It won't matter, Reggie, because you'll be on his naughty list, for sure.'

Reggie chuckled then his expression became serious.

'Some bloody Christmas I'm going to have banged up in here?' he said, as the woman in the next cubicle started crying. 'With just a poxy date at the Bailey to look forward to.'

'At least they've dropped the murder charge against you and Jimmy,' said Tommy, blowing on his hands and rubbing them together.

'I suppose so,' Reggie replied glumly. 'I'll still go down for a twenty-five-year stretch for manslaughter.'

Keys jangled and a heavy metal door slammed, the noise reverberating around the stark tiled room.

'Time!' bellowed a warden, his hobnail boots echoing on the concrete floor as he marched behind the row of visitors.

Reggie took a long drag from his cigarette and looked Tommy over.

'Well, here we are then, Tommy boy,' his brother said, his heavy features lifting in a sad smile. 'You on the right side of the fence and me on the wrong.'

'But we're still the Sweete brothers,' said Tommy.

'But not like those three musketeer whatsits any more,' said Reggie, with just a trace of bitterness.

'No, not any more,' said Tommy, as a tinge of sadness crept over him. 'But I want you to know, Reggie, I'll always be grateful for what you've done for me.'

Reggie shrugged. 'Yeah, well, I'm your brother, ain't I?' Pinching out his cigarette he stowed it behind his ear and stood up. 'I suppose this is it for a while.'

A lump formed in Tommy's throat. 'I'll write and tell you what I'm up to.'

Reggie nodded.

'It was good of you to come, Tommy,' he said. 'Especially after all that business of me keeping schtum about Upington's, you might have—'

'Don't be daft,' said Tommy. 'Like you said. I'm your brother.'

They looked through the mesh grille at each other for a long moment then Reggie smiled.

'Mind how you go, little bruv,' he said. Shoving his hands in his trouser pockets, he joined the line of prisoners being marched back to their cells.

Tommy stared after him until the metal door slammed into place then, with a heavy heart, he made his way out of the room with the other visitors.

Images of him and Reggie as snotty-nosed urchins dashing barefooted over the cobbled streets flashed through his mind as he trudged between the battle-grey prison walls and past bolted iron doors.

He was almost the last one to exit through the prison's main gates and back into the bitingly cold outside world. The winter sun hadn't managed to penetrate the thick clouds so it was more like sunset than midday.

Turning his collar up against the icy air, Tommy was just about to head off across the common to catch a bus back to the city when someone called his name.

He turned to see Jo, in her AAS uniform, standing amongst a group of soldiers and ARP workers next to the WVS mobile canteen on the other side of the road.

'Tommy,' she shouted again, waving furiously at him.

He waved back and then hurried over to her.

Her cheeks were pinched and red with cold but her smile and eyes were warm.

'Jo,' he said, taking her into his arms.

Resting her hands on his chest she smiled up at him. 'I thought I'd come and meet you.'

She should have been on duty and he had no idea why she wasn't but in an instant the weight that had been pressing down on him since he'd watched the prison door close behind Reggie lifted. Captured in the love shining in Jo Brogan's eyes, Tommy smiled down at her, then pressing his lips onto hers, he embraced his future.

Chapter Thirty

TAKING A CHUNK of coal from the scuttle beside the fire, Tommy threw it on the other half a dozen lumps that were smoking in the grate. Straightening up, he placed a sheet of newspaper over the fire to draw it further. He held it there for a moment or two and then, satisfied that the fire was alight, he screwed it up and threw it on the flames.

Leaving the blaze to warm the room, Tommy went to the kitchen just as the steam from the kettle on the stove started to rattle the whistle as it came to the boil. Taking it from the range, Tommy poured it onto the Camp coffee he'd spooned into a mug then stirred in the last of that morning's milk.

It was now almost four o'clock and over three hours since he'd walked out of Wandsworth prison and into Jo's arms.

She'd swapped a shift on the MDS to meet him and he loved her for her thoughtfulness. They'd had a dinner in the British Restaurant in Blackfriars Road then caught the bus to Liverpool Street and walked, hand in hand, down to St Katherine's ambulance station where Jo was on duty that evening. Having kissed her goodbye, Tommy had jumped on the tram that ran along Commercial Road to St Anne's Church and then headed for his mother's flat to get ready for his own night shift in Gray's Inn Road depot, which started at eight.

With his mug in his hand, Tommy walked back into the lounge but as he placed his coffee on the table next to his armchair, there was a knock on the door.

'It's open,' he shouted, thinking it was Vera from two doors down bringing back his washing.

Going over to his jacket hanging on the back of a chair, Tommy took out the *Evening News* from the pocket and turned to see Jerimiah Brogan standing in the doorway.

Wearing a sheepskin coat over his Home Guard uniform, and with his piercing eyes fixed on Tommy, Jo's father looked like a grizzly bear contemplating its next meal.

'Good evening, Mr Brogan,' he said. 'How are you?'

'Fine enough,' said Jo's father.

'And Mattie?' said Tommy. 'Jo tells me she and the baby are doing well and that her husband's home.'

Chewing the inside of his mouth, Jerimiah stepped into the room, his thick hair scraping the top of the frame as he passed under it.

'The kettle's just boiled,' continued Tommy, dropping his evening paper on the chair. 'Can I make you a cuppa?' He glanced at the bottle of Scotch on the sideboard. 'Or perhaps something stronger?'

Jo's father scrutinised him for another long, uncomfortable moment then spoke.

'I'm sure you'll agree with me that the prospect of losing someone you love more than life itself has a way of focusing a man's mind on what's important and what's not.'

'It certainly does,' said Tommy, as the searing pain at the thought of losing Jo gripped his chest again.

'Do you know what people around here call me?' asked Jerimiah.

Tommy did but he wasn't about to repeat it.

'A tinker,' Jerimiah said, answering his own question. 'And that's when they're thinking kindly of me. The rest of the time I'm a thief.'

'Of course, you know they say much the same about me,' said Tommy. 'In fact, you did yourself when you dropped in to see me at the boxing club.'

'So I did,' said Jerimiah. 'But in the light of recent events I got to thinking that if people are wrong about me, then it stands to reason they may well be wrong about you, too.'

'I can assure you, Mr Brogan, they are,' Tommy replied, matching the other man's powerful stare.

'So Jo tells me,' said Jerimiah. 'In fact, over the last week Jo has told me a lot about you.'

'All of it good, I hope,' said Tommy.

Jerimiah raised an eyebrow. 'For the most part, although I've an inclination she's a mite biased on that score. I believe when you came around last week you had something you wanted to say to me but in the furore and commotion that followed you didn't get around to it so I thought I might give you the chance now.'

A grin threatened to break out but Tommy held it back.

'Yes, there is something I wanted to say to you, Mr Brogan,' he said. 'I love your daughter Jo and would ask that you give your permission for me to marry her.'

Jerimiah regarded him levelly. 'You may, but she's only just out of school so you can get engaged now but you'll not have my blessing to marry until she's twenty.'

Tommy let out a long breath he didn't know he was holding. 'Thank you, Mr Brogan.'

He thrust out his hand and Jerimiah took it.

'And I promise you,' he continued, shaking it vigorously, 'I will love and take care of her for the rest of my life.'

'You'd better.' A hint of a smile lifted the corners of the older man's mouth. 'Or you'll have her gran after you, lad, that's for sure.'

Tommy laughed.

'And now I suppose as you're family,' said Jerimiah, letting go of his hand, 'there are certain duties you'll have to undertake.'

'Indeed,' said Tommy, putting on a serious expression. 'I'm not much of a church goer but I want you to know I'm willing to take instruction at St Bridget's and St Brendan's.'

'I'm sure her mother and mine will be pleased you are but I was thinking of something a little closer to a man's heart: food,' said Jerimiah. 'Although between the soaring prices and rationing, God himself only knows what we'll have laid before us, I'd like you to join us for Christmas dinner.'

'Thank you,' said Tommy. 'That's very kind of you.'

'And if you'd care to join me and the family's menfolk beforehand at the bar in the Catholic Club at midday that would be grand, too,' Jerimiah went on.

'I'll be there,' Tommy said.

'Mind you are, son,' said Jerimiah. 'Because you're in the frame for the first round.'

Tommy grinned. 'My pleasure. And thank you again, Mr Brogan. I'm very grateful.'

Jo's father regarded him thoughtfully for a moment then he offered his hand.

'It's Jerry,' he said as Tommy took it. 'And tis I who am grateful to you, Mr Sweete.'

By the time Francesca, wrapped up in a woolly scarf, hat and gloves against the chilly evening air, turned into Mafeking Terrace at two thirty on Christmas Eve, the houses in the street already had their curtains closed ready for the blackout. Mrs Frazer who was the fabric and haberdashery supervisor at Boardman's department store where Francesca worked had told them the store would be closing at one thirty as it usually did on Christmas Eve. So, after cashing up her till and making sure the stock was tidy before she left, Francesca and her fellow shop assistants walked out of the staff entrance into the freezing winter afternoon three-quarters of an hour later.

The stalls along Stratford Market were selling off the last of their wares as the shops on the Broadway were already putting up their shutters in readiness for the two-day Christmas holiday. Unlike last year, when shoppers had been out in force spending lavishly on festive foods like dates and Newberry jellied fruits so they could have a blow-out Christmas before rationing was introduced, things had been much quieter. All luxury items such as bath salts and men's cologne had vanished from the shelves and even simple tin toys were in short supply as manufacturers switched from making children's fripperies to building fighter planes.

The staff at Boardman's had done their best to bring a bit of festive cheer to their customers by decorating the store with paper chains and having a Father Christmas in residence, but this seemed doubly artificial given that many of the children sitting on his knee would be hanging up their stockings in corrugated Anderson shelters in the back garden or next to their allocated bunk in overcrowded public refuges.

However, Francesca wouldn't be singing 'Silent Night' deep underground while bombs exploded above because, like everyone else in the Auxiliary Fire Service, she would be reporting for duty as usual. Christmas or not, the Luftwaffe were sure to pay a visit, as they had done nightly for the past four months.

Francesca had volunteered to do the night shifts all over Christmas so that members of the Axillary Fire Service with young children could be at home on those special nights. So instead of attending midnight Mass as she usually did on Christmas Eve, Francesca would either be huddled around the brazier at Bow Road fire station or dousing an incendiary bomb. She didn't mind. In fact, she wanted to be busy as it stopped her dwelling on the fact that her father and brother were still interned as enemy aliens in a camp somewhere.

The Aliens' Department at the Home Office had assured her that their case would be heard before Christmas but although the first thing she did each day when she got back from work was to look in the post, there had been no news.

However, the one bright spot in what was an otherwise bleak Christmas was that Charlie would be there. As his forty-eight-hour pass had started at midday and as it was only a forty-minute journey on the tram from Hackney Marshes where he was billeted, he should be sitting with his feet up by the fire when she got home.

Watching where she stepped on the uneven pavement and with her heart fluttering, Francesca walked down the narrow alley at the side of the Brogans' house. She crossed the back yard, already shimmering with frost, and entered via the rear door as family and friends did.

'Only me,' she called, as she plonked her shopping basket on the table and shrugged off her coat.

'We're in here,' called Ida from the other room. 'There's tea in the pot if you want a cup.'

Shoving her hat and gloves in the pocket, Francesca hooked her coat on a free nail on the back of the door and looped her scarf over it.

As always, the kitchen was warm, snug and homely, particularly tonight with the appetising smell of tomorrow's dinner roasting on a low light in the oven and half a dozen pots of peeled and chopped vegetables soaking in salt water ready for tomorrow on gas rings above.

After pouring herself a cuppa, and with her heart pounding in her chest, Francesca walked through to the parlour but instead of Charlie sitting by the fireside with his feet up and the family crowded around him, there was only Mattie and her mother in the room.

'Hello, luv,' said Ida, giving her a motherly smile. 'Had a good day?'

'Busy,' said Francesca. 'Where is everyone?'

'Dad's at the yard bedding Samson down for the night, Jo doesn't finish duty until six and Daniel went to meet some bods at Whitehall at lunchtime but should be home anytime now,' said Mattie, who was sitting opposite her mother by the fire.

'And Billy's upstairs sulking because I wouldn't let him open his present from Pearl,' Ida added, nodding at the enormous box wrapped in Father Christmas paper under the artificial tree.

'And Charlie, is he home?' Francesca asked in as casual a tone as her pent-up emotion would allow.

Ida's mouth pulled into a tight bud.

'He was but just to drop his kitbag off before muttering about having to see *that* floozy about something.' She rolled her eyes. 'Perhaps someone's told him what that so-called fiancée of his has been up to while he's been serving King and Country.'

'I hope so,' said Mattie, giving Francesca a sympathetic look.

So did Francesca.

The front door rattled as the postman shoved the last afternoon post for two days through the door.

'I'll get it,' she said.

Placing her drink on one of the cork coasters on the sideboard, Francesca went through to the hallway. There were a handful of Christmas cards and a couple of dull, oblong envelopes containing bills, but it was the large buff-coloured one with a crown and the Home Office insignia stamped across the top that grabbed Francesca's attention.

With trembling hands, she picked it up. Taking a deep breath, she slipped her finger under the flap and tore it open.

With the letter visibly shaking as she held it and the blood rushing through her ears, Francesca drew out the single sheet and unfolded it.

The words danced on the page as she scanned down the brief couple of paragraphs.

She read it again then burst back into the parlour.

'They're being released,' she cried, holding the letter aloft. 'Dad and Giovanni are coming home.'

'When?' asked Mattie.

'It doesn't say,' said Francesca. 'Just that the appeal board found in their favour and. . .' She peered at the letter again but the words danced in front of her eyes. 'And . . .'

'It's all right, Fran,' said her friend.

Standing up, Mattie came over and put her arm around her. 'Take a deep breath.'

Francesca nodded and did as she was bid.

'It says,' continued Francesca after a moment, 'I'll get further details in a day or two. There's a telephone number I can ring tomorrow if I want to speak to them on Christmas Day.'

'Oh, Fran,' said Mattie, taking her in her arms.

As the cloud of sorrow that had surrounded her for six months evaporated, Francesca closed her eyes and hugged her friend back.

Alicia gave a little cry and Mattie released her to check on her daughter who had been sleeping in the pram in the corner.

'Oh, luv, I'm so happy for you,' said Ida, taking her handkerchief from her sleeve and dabbing her eyes. 'But if you ask me, they shouldn't have been locked up in the first place.'

Although she had tears in her eyes, Francesca laughed. 'It's a pity you're not in charge of the Aliens' Department.'

'You're right there, luv,' agreed Ida. 'In fact, if the blooming bods in the government put women in charge of ministries we'd get more done.'

Mattie laughed. 'Well, they couldn't do any worse. I bagsy the Ministry of Home Security to sort out the poor old ARP's equipment problem.'

'Well, I'll take the Ministry of Food,' said Ida. 'I'd bang that lot of idiot heads together to knock some sense into them.'

Francesca laughed. 'I bet you would.'

'What about you, Fran?' asked Mattie, lifting Alicia from her pram. 'What do you want to sort out?'

Still laughing, Francesca shrugged. 'I hadn't thought. Perhaps I could shake up the so-called Ministry of Information so it actually tells us what's happening.'

Mattie and her mother laughed and Francesca joined in, as merriment bubbled up inside.

'Blimey, it sounds like everyone's been sitting on feathers.'

Francesca turned to see Charlie, his dark hair tousled in the winter breeze and his lovely blue-grey eyes sparkling with amusement, standing in the kitchen doorway.

'Oh, Charlie,' she said, her heart aching at the sight of him in his uniform. 'I didn't—'

Her words dried up as Stella's sharp, over-powdered face appeared just behind him.

'Francesca's just heard that her dad and brother are being released,' said Mattie, stepping forward to stand beside her.

'That's great news,' said Charlie, smiling down at her.

Francesca smiled as their eyes met for a second then Stella's harsh voice sliced between them.

'We've got a bit of good news, too,' she said, winding her arm possessively through Charlie's. 'Haven't we, darling?'

He took a breath. 'Mum, Stella and me are—'

'Getting married,' she cut in, smirking at Francesca.

Fran felt a rush of dizziness as the Brogans' colourful rug beneath her feet rose up to meet her.

'But I thought your dad said you had to wait until you were twenty-one, Stella,' said Ida, the colour gone from her cheeks.

'He did,' said Stella. 'But . . .'

She looked up at Charlie.

Desolation flitted across his face for a split second but then he patted her hand and smiled. 'He's changed his mind because, you see, Stella's in the family way.'

Chapter Thirty-One

'WHERE ARE THOSE blasted men?' Jo's mother said, wrapping the tea towel around her hands and opening the oven door. 'They'd better be home soon or they'll be having burnt meat and cold potatoes for their Christmas dinner.'

The last of the one o'clock pips had just sounded out from the wireless in the parlour and Jo and her mother were in the kitchen and had been since they'd got back from church two hours before. They weren't alone as Mattie was also bustling in and out to make sure everything was ready for the family's Christmas dinner. Queenie had gone to fetch some extra bread for sandwiches later and Billy had been sent upstairs to play to keep him from getting under everyone's feet. As Mrs Wheeler didn't want to join the family Christmas, Cathy had said she would spend the day at home with her mother-in-law and Peter. Ida had tried to persuade her otherwise but with no luck. Of course, the real reason she wasn't coming was because she refused to sit down for Christmas dinner with Daniel, whom she blamed for sending Stan to prison. As Gran said, only the Blessed Virgin herself knew how that conflict could be resolved.

After Mass, the men had continued celebrating the Lord's birth in the Catholic Club, a short walk from the church door, leaving the womenfolk to prepare the family feast. And it was, despite the rationing and shortages, a feast.

The butcher had made good his promise and after queuing for almost an hour, Ida had borne home a massive ox heart in triumph, which had only just fitted into the roasting pan. It had taken the breadcrumbs from a whole loaf, a box of sage and two chopped onions that Queenie had 'found' on her travels to stuff the thing.

As Ida had only ever cooked an ox's tail before she'd erred on the side of caution and had put the meat in the oven on a low light the night before. This seemed to have done the trick because when she'd tested it an hour ago the carving knife had slipped in with ease.

This, along with two cabbages, four pounds of carrots and ten pounds of potatoes, would be what the Brogan family would be sitting down to enjoy. There was also Christmas pudding, which Ida had been saving ration coupons since September to make. In addition to the food Jo's mother had hunted and gathered for the occasion, they'd had an unexpected delivery of a Christmas cake from Daniel's commanding officer and that, complete with its Fortnum & Mason packaging, sat in pride of place on the sideboard in the other room, ready for when they had a cup of tea and listened to the King's speech later.

'I'm sure they're on their way now,' said Jo.

She wanted the men of the family to come home too and not because the Christmas dinner would be ruined if they didn't but because Tommy would be with them.

She hadn't seen him since yesterday morning when he'd turned up unexpectedly as she finished a night shift, dirty and exhausted, to tell her about her father's visit and their conversation.

So, standing in the yard of St Katherine's ambulance station, she and Tommy, both wearing their ARP uniforms and bleary eyed with weariness, with hardly two ha'pennies to rub together, had officially become engaged to be married.

'Give us the serving plate, Jo,' said her mother. Grasping the roasting tray from the bottom of the oven, Ida heaved it out.

Dragging her mind away from Tommy, Jo took the oval carving platter from the rack above the hob and placed it beside the roasting tin then helped her mother lift the huge lump of meat out of the pan and onto the plate.

'Right now, get those potatoes into the fat and back in the oven to brown,' Ida said, throwing a clean tea towel over the meat to let it rest.

The parlour door opened and Billy, dressed in his school uniform, popped his head around the corner. 'How long till dinner?'

'Dinner's ready now,' said Ida, furiously stirring the gravy. 'It's your father who's keeping us from it.'

'Can I go and fetch him?' he asked.

'No, you can't,' said his mother. 'I'm not having you getting all dirty on Christmas Day so you'll have to wait like the rest of us.'

'But I'm starving,' wailed Billy.

'There's a bit of bread pudding in the larder that'll keep you going,' said Jo as she drained the water from the boiled potatoes.

Sliding them into the pan that the heart had been cooked in, the fat sizzled as it merged with the water.

'Ta, sis,' Billy said, barging past her to get to the pantry door.

Perching on the stool in the corner, he stuffed the bread pudding in mouth.

'Can I open Aunt Pearl's present then instead?' Billy asked, spraying crumbs as he spoke.

'You know we always open them after lunch,' said his

mother as she drained the cabbage water into the gravy pan.

'Pleeeeease,' begged Billy, giving her a doe-eyed pleading look.

'Oh, let him, Mum,' said Jo, sliding the tin of potatoes back in the oven. 'It'll keep him out of the way until we serve the dinner.'

Ida sighed. 'All right then—'

Billy jumped off the stool.

'But do it upstairs,' she shouted after him as he disappeared into the parlour.

The back door opened and Francesca walked in.

'Sorry I've been so long,' she said, shaking off her overcoat and hooking it on the back of the door.

'That's all right, love,' said Ida, taking the lid off the carrots and giving them a poke. 'Did you get through?'

'Yes, eventually,' said Francesca. 'Giovanni says he and Dad have been given a travel pass for next Monday so they'll be back for the New Year.'

'Pity they couldn't get home for Christmas,' said Jo.

'I know,' said Francesca. 'But at least it'll give me a chance to see if I can find us a place to rent.'

'Well, I hope you've got a bit put by,' said Ida. 'With all the families who've been bombed out looking for lodgings, the rents have gone through the roof.'

'Dad's got some savings we can use until we get back on our feet,' said Francesca. 'I thought I might see if there's something going near to where Mattie and Daniel have rented by St Dunstan's Church.'

'What about me?' said Mattie, strolling in to the kitchen.

Francesca told Mattie about her family's plans.

'That would be nice, to have you as neighbours,' said Mattie, taking the serving bowls from the dresser cupboard and setting them out ready for the vegetables.

A sad look flitted across Ida's face. 'The house is going to feel very empty when you and Mattie go.'

'I know,' said Francesca. 'And I can't say enough how grateful I am to you for putting me up like this.'

Ida waved her words away. 'Don't be silly. I'm sure your family would have done the same for our Mattie.'

'And at least you and Mr Brogan can have your bedroom to yourselves once you move Billy back into his own room,' Francesca added.

Ida forced a smile. 'I suppose it has been a bit of a squash.'

'A bit!' Jo rolled her eyes. 'It's been like musical beds with Mattie and Daniel taking over the front room, me and poor Francesca have been squashed like peas in a pod in the back room.'

Mattie and Francesca laughed.

There was room for her at Tommy's flat but Jo knew it was more than her life's worth to suggest she stay there. Of course, that didn't mean she didn't but that was something best kept to herself.

'Well, at least none of us have had to sleep on the sofa, like poor Charlie,' said Francesca, with a notable trace of tenderness in her voice as she spoke his name.

'If I'd known he was going to kip the night at Stella's, I wouldn't have bothered making him up a bed,' said Ida.

'Oh,' said Francesca. 'I thought he was just home late.'

'So did I,' said Ida, 'until I opened the door to get the milk in this morning and saw him strolling down the road.'

Pain flitted across Francesca's face and Mattie gave her love-lorn friend a sympathetic look.

The back door opened again and Queenie entered carrying two loaves wrapped in paper.

'About time too,' said Ida, her face red from the steam.

'You'd have been nagging at me if I bought stale bread so I waited for the second batch,' said Queenie, placing them in the stoneware bin on the dresser. 'Aren't the men back yet?'

'No,' snapped Ida, 'and if they don't get their skates on I'll—'

'Hello, where are all me sweet darlings,' boomed Jerimiah's voice through the house from the front door.

Ida's lips pulled together. 'I'll give 'im "sweet darling".'

Turning the gas off under the carrots, she marched through to the parlour with the rest of the women just behind her.

Jerimiah, dressed in his best suit with a colourful striped waistcoat beneath and a neckerchief tied in a flamboyant knot around his throat, stood in the middle of the room with Charlie in his khaki battle jacket to his right and Daniel in a suit and tie on the other side, but it was Tommy, smartly dressed in a navy suit with a Windsor knot at his throat, standing to the right of the group that Jo's eyes fixed on.

Her heart sang at the sight of him and when his dark eyes, full of love, rested on her, it was all Jo could do not to throw herself in his arms.

Of course, she'd have trouble getting to him because apart from the artificial Christmas tree tucked into one chimney alcove and Alicia's Silver Cross pram in the other, the rest of the room was taken over by the table, laid ready for Christmas lunch. To ensure everyone in the family could sit down for dinner at the same time, Jo's father had brought a door from the yard. One end of the door rested on their drop-leaf table while the other end was supported by trestle legs. Covered with two white sheets, which would serve as a tablecloth, it filled the room, which is why two of the armchairs had been moved into Queenie's room and covered with newspapers to prevent Prince Albert decorating them.

'There she is, lads,' said Jerimiah, giving his wife an exaggeratedly adoring look. 'Sure, isn't she a sight to warm any man's heart?'

Jo and Mattie exchanged amused looks but their mother's stony expression remained as Billy sneaked in behind the men, carrying an Airfix box under his arm.

'Don't you try that old blarney on me, Jerimiah Brogan,' Ida said, glaring at him. 'Didn't I tell you I wanted you home by twelve?'

'I don't recall you saying such a thing, my dear,' he replied, swaying slightly and looking innocently at her.

'I'm not surprised,' said Ida, crossing her arms tightly across her substantial bosom. 'You can barely remember your own name after a couple of Guinness.'

Queenie rolled her eyes. 'For the love of God, isn't a man entitled to have the odd drink from time to time?'

'And Dad's only had a couple, Ma,' said Charlie, with a barely suppressed smile.

Daniel laughed.

'See, Ida, he's only had a couple,' said Queenie. 'Isn't that right, Tommy?'

'It is, Mrs B,' said Tommy, placing his hand on his heart earnestly. 'Just a couple of pints and,' he winked, 'maybe the same again of whisky chasers.'

Queenie's mouth dropped open for a second and then she grinned. 'Mercy to Heaven, if I didn't have to fetch the ladder, I'd be boxing your ears for such cheek, Tommy Sweete.'

Everyone laughed and Jo knew God was in his Heaven.

'Well, now you are home you'd better sit yourself down while we dish up,' said Ida.

413

Jo turned to follow her mother into the kitchen but Tommy caught her hand. 'I think I've lost something.'

Ida gave them a fond look. 'Go on then, I dare say we can manage.'

Leaving Mattie and Francesca to help her mother, Jo let Tommy lead her into the dark hall where the coat rack stood.

'So what have you lost?'

'This,' he said, drawing her into his arms and closing his mouth over hers.

Moulding herself into him, Jo wound her arms around his neck and kissed him back. His splayed hand spread up her back and held the back of her head while the other grasped her bottom and anchored her into him. Excitement shot through Jo as images of them entwined together flashed in her mind. After several pulse-racing moments he lifted his head.

'I love you,' he said, his eyes dark in the dim light.

She smiled. 'I know.'

Stretching up, she hugged him around the neck and pressed her lips on his. Backing her into the coats hanging on the wall, his mouth opened and worked hungrily on hers.

The door handle rattled and a beam of light cut between them.

Blinking, they looked around to see Mattie standing in the doorway.

'It's all right, Mum, they've found it,' she said, with an amused look on her face.

With her cheeks on fire, Jo walked back into the parlour with Tommy half a pace behind.

Everyone was already sitting around the table with plates in front of them and grins on their faces. Her father was in his usual place at the head of the table, ready to carve the cooked ox heart set before him.

'We've left you a space,' he said, pointing to the two chairs at the corner of the table with the ten-inch bladed knife. 'You're a bit squashed but I'm sure you won't mind.'

'No, we'll be fine,' said Tommy, holding the chair out for Jo to sit down before taking his seat beside her.

The family bowed their heads as Jerimiah thanked the Almighty for food and family before slicing up the meat.

'So, lad,' said Queenie, her black eyes twinkling with devilment as they fixed on Tommy, 'what was of such importance that you were needing Jo's assistance to seek it out?'

'Now, Gran,' laughed Mattie, as her mother placed a loaded plate of meat and veg in front of her, 'don't make Jo blush again.'

'Well,' said Tommy, reaching into the inside pocket of his jacket, 'seeing as how you ask, it was this.'

He held up two letters. 'I found them on the mat when I got home yesterday morning. This one,' he held up an official-looking manila one, 'is from the army telling me to report to a Depot in Buckingham instead of Colchester but this letter . . .' He paused while he removed the single sheet of typed paper and shook it out. 'This one says, "Dear Mr Sweete, I am happy to inform you that your recent entry for the *Telegraph* word and number competition has come third and therefore we are delighted to enclose a postal order to the value of fifty pounds—"'

'Fifty pounds!' gasped Ida.

'Yes, Mrs B,' Tommy replied, as Jo's heart raced ten to the dozen in her chest. 'Fifty pounds, which I took straight around to the Mutual and Friendship Savings Bank. I'm hoping it will be enough to buy me and Jo a house.' He took Jo's hand and smiled at her. 'Of course, I'm going to take a small amount out first to buy a ring.'

'Fifty pounds for doing some puzzles,' said Ida, looking a little baffled at the thought.

'Well, they weren't easy, I can tell you,' said Tommy. 'But I've always had a bit of a head for numbers and a friend suggested I give it a try.'

Alicia, who'd been sleeping happily, started to niggle. Standing up, Daniel went over and lifted her out of her pram.

'Did it say whereabouts in Buckingham you are to report?' he asked, giving Tommy a nonchalant look as he cradled his new daughter in his arm.

Reaching out, Tommy took his plate from his future mother-in-law. 'Some place called Bletchley. Do you know it?'

Daniel shook his head.

'Not really,' he said, busying himself with Alicia's blanket.

'Well, son, congratulations,' said Jerimiah, laying the knife aside and sitting down. 'Now eat up and good health.'

Everyone started tucking into their dinner.

'Jo tells me you've both got a day off tomorrow,' said Mattie, spearing a roast potato. 'Are you planning to do anything?'

'I hadn't thought,' Tommy replied. He turned to Jo. 'Any ideas, sweetheart?'

Jo smiled. Slipping her hand under the tablecloth, she gently squeezed the top of his thigh. 'I'm sure we'll think of something.'

Chapter Thirty-Two

ALTHOUGH THE ICY January winds nipped at her ears and nose, enfolded in Tommy's Crombie overcoat and with her head resting on his chest and his arms around her, Jo had never felt warmer.

'What's the time?' she asked, breathing in the familiar smell of his aftershave.

'Ten to,' he replied, his voice reverberating in the cocoon of his embrace.

Jo snuggled closer. 'Ages yet.'

His lips pressed onto her forehead and his arms tightened around her.

It wasn't, of course, as the third-class ticket he had in his pocket was for the eleven-five to Northampton. But then, whether it was fifteen minutes, fifteen days or fifteen years it would still be too soon to say goodbye.

They were standing together on platform ten under the steel expanse of Euston Station while the engineers made their final preparations to the train Tommy would be departing on in just a few short moments. They weren't alone as around them stood dozens of other couples, the men with small suitcases and the women in their Sunday best, many holding on to small children with one hand and clutching handkerchiefs to their noses with the other.

It was the first Monday of the New Year, and the old Victorian station was awash with khaki as soldiers who, like Charlie, had wangled a Christmas pass were getting ready to return to their barracks. Mingled amongst the khaki was the odd dash of air-force blue as aircraft personnel and pilots who'd also been on leave headed back to their bases at Biggleswade, Cardington or High Wycombe.

Unlike Tommy who was wearing civilian clothes, Jo was dressed in her AAS uniform. She was also wearing Mattie's navy ARP overcoat, which her sister now no longer needed. To be honest, Jo was barely out of uniform these days as after the brief respite over the three days of Christmas, the Luftwaffe had returned with vengeance. St Katharine Dock had been pounded and Aldgate Art Gallery had suffered a direct hit, with another bomb narrowly missing old St Mary's Church on Whitechapel High Street.

A driver and a fireman, both wearing dungarees, loose-fitting jackets and caps with LMS badges on the front, strolled along the platform to the front of the burgundy-liveried London, Midlands and Scotland Railway locomotive and climbed up onto the foot plate.

'The eleven-five to Northampton is departing in five minutes,' the fireman called, swinging his lamp as he walked past Jo and Tommy. 'Calling at Watford Junction, Hemel Hempstead, Leighton Buzzard, Bletchley and all stations to . . .'

Around them, men gathered up their suitcases while women started quietly sobbing as they held babies up to be kissed.

'It's time, Jo,' Tommy said softly, as the clatter of doors opening against the carriages echoed around the vast space.

Although tears pinched the corners of her eyes, Jo looked up and forced a smile.

His brown eyes grew soft as they moved slowly over her face. 'I'll write as soon as I can.'

'I know,' she replied, in a tight voice.

A child further down the platform started shouting 'Daddy, Daddy' and a couple of others took up the cry.

A sad smile lifted Tommy's well-formed lips.

'Two years isn't so long, sweetheart, and then we can be married,' he said softly, moving a stray curl from her forehead.

'It'll be here before we know it,' said Jo, giving him her brightest smile and trying to sound convinced.

'And at least we're properly engaged now,' he said.

Jo twiddled her left hand so the solitary diamond on her third finger sparkled in the light. 'We certainly are.'

'I'm glad you like it,' said Tommy.

'I don't like it, Tommy, I love it,' said Jo. 'But you shouldn't have spent so much.'

'You're worth every penny and besides,' he grinned, 'I only entered the competition so I could buy you diamonds.'

The guard blew his whistle again, causing mothers to cling to their fresh-faced sons and wives and sweethearts to hang on to their lovers' necks.

Keeping his eyes on her face and his arm still around her, Tommy bent down and picked up his brown suitcase.

They stood for a moment then he took her hand and they walked a few yards to one of the open carriage doors. While people jostled and chatted around them as they boarded the train, Jo and Tommy stood with their gaze locked, in a wordless bubble of love and longing, until the station master's warning whistle broke the spell.

Dropping his case on the damp concrete of the platform, Tommy's arms shot around Jo, gathering her into his strong embrace. Jo's arms wound around his body, feeling the hard muscles of his back under her fingertips.

Lowering his head, his mouth closed over Jo's in an achingly deep kiss which sent shivers of desire and loneliness through her.

Jo matched his kiss, moulding herself into him as she clung to him. Then the station master's final whistle cut between them.

Tommy released her. Snatching up his case, he jumped onto the train just as the funnel belched smoke and soot into the air.

Slamming the door behind him, he pulled down the window and leaned out.

Jo raised her hand and Tommy caught it.

'I love you,' he said, as the wheels squeaked against the track and the carriage shuddered forward.

'I love you too,' said Jo, looking up at Tommy through shimmering tears.

Jo walked and then trotted alongside the train as it picked up speed.

Staring at each other, they held hands until Jo could run no faster and their fingers slipped apart.

Slowing to a halt, Jo's tear-filled eyes fixed on Tommy, hanging out of the window looking back at her, until the train turned at the end of the platform and disappeared in a billow of steam on its northerly journey.

He was gone: Tommy was gone.

Although she was surrounded by dozens of women and children an eerie stillness blanked them out as they stood united in the void left by their men's departure. The hissing steam and tinny megaphone announcement echoing in the cavernous space added to the dreamlike feeling of the moment, then suddenly the all-too-familiar sound of an air raid siren brought everyone back to the present.

Women screamed and dragged their children behind them as they dashed back down the platform towards public shelters, while guards herded passengers to safety.

In truth, two years seemed like an eternity but with the Luftwaffe raining death and destruction down on them nightly and Hitler's army poised to cross the Channel, it wasn't as if she didn't have other things to think about while she waited for Tommy's return.

With a last look down the track, Jo adjusted her bag across her then turned and headed off to do her bit to win the war.

Ida's Christmas recipes

Christmas 1940 was arguably the worst Christmas of the entire war. A great number of merchant ships bringing vital food across the Atlantic were lost all through 1940, and the American Lend-Lease scheme, which saw the arrival of spam, dried eggs and milk, was still a year away. The ration for fats had been cut in June 1940 and the meat ration was cut in December, although the tea and sugar rations were increased for a week at Christmas. Jo's mother, Ida, would have had her work cut out trying to prepare a Christmas feast for the Brogan family.

The Brogans had the advantage of being able to pool their rations but even so, Ida would have been saving as much as she could from the family's sugar ration as early as August. She would also have been bottling and preserving any autumn fruit, such as blackberries and apples if she was lucky enough to get hold of them, plus buying anything tinned that might be edible.

With everything in short supply and a large family sitting down to Christmas dinner, Ida was very fortunate to get an ox heart from her butcher as a substitute for turkey. Ox hearts fell under the offal grouping, which was never subject to rationing. As a child of parents who survived the war-time, I regularly had pigs' hearts for my evening meal – called tea in those days – and I have adapted the method my mum used to prepare and cook them for Ida's Christmas dinner. Enjoy.

Ox Heart

Preparing your ox heart

- Remove all the hard fat from around the top of the heart, then cut away the large blood vessel as near to the muscle as possible and discard.
- Soak the heart in cold, salted water to help remove all the blood clots from the upper chambers – use your fingers – then slice down through the lower chambers with a sharp knife and spread open.
- Clean out any remaining blood clots and cut out any large heart strings, then rinse again in cold water.
- Using a clean cloth, pat it dry.
- Set aside and make the stuffing.

The stuffing

170g (6oz) oatmeal
285ml (½ pint) water
2 large onions (or 1 leek can be used instead), chopped
225g (8oz) breadcrumbs, from stale bread
handful of dried sage
60g (2oz) lard or dripping
salt and pepper

- In a pan, boil the oatmeal in the water for 30 minutes.
- Combine the chopped onions with the breadcrumbs.
- Mix the oatmeal with the onions and breadcrumbs, and add salt, pepper and a handful of dried sage.
- Fill the empty heart cavities with the stuffing mixture and then fold the two sides of the heart together.
- Taking a large-eyed darning needle and some button thread, stitch the edges of the heart muscle securely.

- Melt the lard or dripping in a roasting tin and place the heart in the middle.
- Place on the centre rack of a moderate oven (160°C/ Gas 3) for 20 minutes per 450g (1lb) of heart.
- Check halfway through the cooking time and add enough peeled and halved potatoes to fill the area around the heart.
- Put back in the oven and continue until the cooking time has finished. Baste the potatoes and return the roasting tin to the oven for a further 30 minutes.
- Remove tin from the oven when completely cooked then carve and serve with vegetables.

Having served up the main meal Ida would have presented her family with a traditional Christmas pudding.

In peace-time, Ida would have made this before she went hop-picking at the end of August. However, with dried fruit being in short supply all through 1940 she would have bought what she could on the market each week, until she had enough to make her pudding. Sometimes, however, as you will see from the recipe below, which was given to me by a 90-year-old recently, you had to improvise.

War-time Christmas Pudding with no eggs

300g (10oz) national plain flour
300g (10oz) sugar
300g (10oz) dried mixed fruit
300g (10oz) grated carrot
300g (10oz) grated potato
150g (5oz) suet
2 tbsp black molasses or golden syrup
1 tsp mixed spice

1 tsp bicarbonate of soda, dissolved in 2 tbs hot milk.

NB: if golden syrup is used then the dark pudding is made by adding 1 tsp gravy powder.

(People sometimes substituted liquid paraffin for the fat in a recipe, which was not ideal if your lavatory was situated at the far end of the back yard.)

- Mix all the ingredients together and pour into a well-greased pudding bowl.
- Cover the top with greaseproof paper and secure with string.
- Boil or steam for 4 hours.

Lastly, when everyone had eaten their fill and turned on the wireless for the King's Christmas broadcast, Ida would have made everyone a nice cup of tea and a slice of Christmas cake decorated with candied fruits, as icing sugar was practically unobtainable during the war.

This is a recipe for a war-time boiled cake which my Aunt Martha gave me when I got married. I've used it for years as my Christmas cake.

Christmas Cake

110g (4oz) brown sugar
225g (8oz) butter or margarine
285ml (½ pint) milk
450g (1lb) mixed dried fruit
3 eggs, beaten
340g (12oz) self-raising flour
1 tsp baking powder
2 tsp mixed spice

- Place the sugar, margarine, milk and dried fruit into a large saucepan and bring to the boil. Simmer for 10 minutes then leave to cool off the heat for 30–40 minutes.
- Stir in the beaten eggs, then fold in the flour, baking powder and mixed spice. Mix well before pouring into a greased and floured 20cm (8-inch) baking tin.
- Place in a pre-heated oven at 160°C (Gas 3) and cook for 2 hours, then test with a knife. If it comes out clean, then the cake is ready to be removed from the oven. If not, bake for a further 20 minutes and test again.
- When cooked through, leave to cool in the tin before turning it out.

This is a lovely moist fruit cake which will keep for ages in an airtight container. It can be decorated with icing or left plain and can even be served as a pudding with custard.

I hope you enjoyed a little glimpse into the Brogans' 1940 Christmas Day food. If you would like to try them, be warned: I suspect today you'd have to order your ox heart specially.

Acknowledgements

As always, I would like to mention a few books, authors and people to whom I am particularly indebted.

In order to set my characters' thoughts and worldview authentically in the opening years of WWII, I dug deep into *Wartime Britain 1939-1945* (Gardiner), *The East End at War* (Taylor & Lloyd) and *London's East End Survivors* (Bissell). As Jo and Tommy's stories are set during the first months of the Blitz, I also drew on *London Was Ours* (Bell), *The Blitz* (Gardiner) and *The Blitz* (Madden).

I delved into *Wartime Women: A Mass-Observation Anthology* (Sheridan), *Millions Like Us* (Nicholson), *Women at the Ready* (Malcolmson) and *Voices from the Home Front: Personal Experiences of Wartime Britain 1939-1945* (Goodall). In addition, *Living Through the Blitz* (Harrisson) helped me to understand the various bomb shelters available and the rules within them.

I went back to *Put that Light Out!: Britain's Civil Defence Services at War 1939-1945* (Brown) and the illustrated guide *The British Home Front 1939-45* (Braley) to ensure I had the right feel to Post 7, where Jo and Tommy were stationed. As much of the area in the story was destroyed during the war, I used *The London County Council Bomb Damage Maps* (Ward) for the locations.

I also drew on *The Wartime House* (Brown & Harris), *A Wartime Christmas* (Brown) and *Ration Book Diet* (Brown, Harris & Jackson) to underpin Jo's mother's daily struggle to feed a family during rationing and shortages.

For Reggie's criminal activities I used *The Secret History of the Blitz* (Levine), as well as *Doing the Business* (Hobbs), which, although examining East London's underworld a decade after WWII, perfectly sets out the hierarchy and unwritten criminal code that was developed during those dark days.

However, my greatest research find for Jo and Tommy's story was *The Forgotten Service* (Raby), the diary of May Greenup, an ambulance driver during the Blitz. This not only enabled me to dress Jo in the correct uniform, but also to use many of the anecdotes and rules applied to driving in the blackout. The second was *Heavy Rescue Squad Work on the Isle of Dogs* (Regan-Atherton). This was the diary of Bill Regan who worked on the Heavy Rescue squad and was written throughout the war.

Again, I've sprinkled my Fullerton family wartime stories and anecdotes throughout *A Ration Book Christmas* and used several post-war photographic books including *Memories of Wapping 1900-1960: 'Couldn't Afford the Eels'* (Leigh) and *The Wartime Scrapbook* (Opie).

I would also like to thank a few more people. Firstly, my very own Hero-at-Home, Kelvin, for his unwavering support, and my three daughters, Janet, Fiona and Amy, for not minding too much that they have a distracted mother whose mind is often in another time and place. I'd also like to thank the members of Facebook group *Stepney and Wapping living in 60s early 70s*, who this time helped me get the location of the Tilbury Shelter correct and shared their families' wartime experience.

Once again my lovely agent Laura Longrigg, whose encouragement and incisive editorial mind helped me to see the wood for the trees. Lastly, but by no means least, a big thank you to the wonderful team at Atlantic Books and to my equally lovely editors Sara O'Keeffe and Susannah Hamilton, who once more turned my 400+ page manuscript into a beautiful book.